MORE THAN FRIENDS

Riley nodded knowingly. "Your mother thinks we're an item. And so did half the people in your backyard today."

Kellie leaned against the kitchen counter in embarrassment. "Did someone say something to you?"

"No, I could tell by the looks I kept getting."

"I kept telling everybody we're only friends."

He shook his head and looked into her eyes. "People are just so single-minded. They want to believe that just because I'm a man and you're a woman . . ."

God, she bet he was a good kisser.

She shook her head violently. "Just because you're available and I'm available . . ."

His gaze hadn't moved from hers. It was so intense. It didn't look like a *just friendly* gaze either.

They were all alone here. It would be so easy.

His eyes darkened. His gaze dipped to her lips. "Kellie . . ."

His voice was a bare rasp, yet it worked on her like a caress.

When Riley bent forward and touched his lips to hers, lightly at first in a quick, glancing kiss, she shut her eyes against the shock of heat that shot through her. *Just a kiss,* she vowed to herself. That was all she was allowing. But she got the feeling that Riley could go on doing this for quite a while. . . .

BOOK YOUR PLACE ON OUR WEBSITE AND MAKE THE READING CONNECTION!

We've created a customized website just for our very special readers, where you can get the inside scoop on everything that's going on with Zebra, Pinnacle and Kensington books.

When you come online, you'll have the exciting opportunity to:

- View covers of upcoming books
- Read sample chapters
- Learn about our future publishing schedule (listed by publication month *and author*)
- Find out when your favorite authors will be visiting a city near you
- Search for and order backlist books from our online catalog
- Check out author bios and background information
- Send e-mail to your favorite authors
- Meet the Kensington staff online
- Join us in weekly chats with authors, readers and other guests
- Get writing guidelines
- AND MUCH MORE!

Visit our website at
http://www.zebrabooks.com

HUSBAND MATERIAL

Liz Ireland

ZEBRA BOOKS
KENSINGTON PUBLISHING CORP.
http://www.zebrabooks.com

I must express my gratitude to two incredible people for helping me with this one. First, Meg Ruley, who got the book on its feet by finding it a wonderful home. And also my sister, Julia Bass, who got me on my feet when I would rather have had a nervous breakdown. Thanks!

Chapter One

It began with a telephone ringing.

Kellie was just surveying her latest bit of handiwork with a critical eye. Among other services, her nascent business, Copycat, copied photos onto T-shirts, and this one, a portrait of Einstein on a tie-dyed shirt ordered by an SMU grad student, was quite good, if she did say so herself. Against a psychedelic swirled backdrop, the old scientist chortled at her with an open-mouthed grin. She was grinning back at him when she snatched up the receiver.

Her smile immediately disappeared when she heard who was on the other end of the line.

"Mrs. Sumners? This is Dana Cooper, at All Day All Play?"

Even if the young woman hadn't identified herself, the upward inflection her voice took at the end of every sentence would have been a dead giveaway. Though starting up the business had already squeezed every last dime out of her measly funds, Kellie had managed to enroll her two children, Trevor and Tina, in a day camp that several of their friends attended. This was the kids' first summer after the divorce and their lives at home still had that hollowed-out, something's-missing feeling. She wanted them to have the luxury of a day camp, even if half the time the luxury seemed to go unappreciated. Dana was one of the college-age counselors at the camp who helped keep the twenty-odd children in line as they tackled everything from rock climbing to baking bread. A call from her could only mean one thing—trouble with a capital T, and that stood for Trevor.

It also stood for Tina, but the only time Kellie had received a call about her daughter was when Tina had wanted to check out too many library books at once.

It also stood for Tylenol, and Kellie had the sneaking suspicion she was going to be in need of one soon. Her brow pinched into a worried-mom frown. "Is one of the kids sick?" Last year Trevor had swallowed ten live grasshoppers on a dare, with predictably unpleasant results.

Dana cleared her throat. "N-not exactly. Actually, Mrs. Sumners, we'd like it if you could come down in person? And maybe pick up Trevor?"

Kellie spied her coffee mug sitting on the counter next to the cash register. Despite the fact that the liquid inside it was cold and the creamer had congealed into an oil-slick film at the coffee surface, she reached over nervously and took a swig. "Okay, Dana, I'm caffeinated now. You can give it to me straight."

"Well . . . Mr. Tildon—the camp administrator?—wants to talk to you about Trevor's, um, gambling."

"*Trevor's* gambling?"

Kellie nearly lost it. Her ex-husband, Rick, was a compulsive gambler. In fact, due to one of his bad days at the track, she wasn't sure where money for Trevor's Little League uniform or Kellie's summer piano lessons—things both she and Rick had promised the kids—would be coming from. But that was Trevor's father. Not Trevor.

"He won a week's worth of snack money out of ten of the other kids," Dana said.

"But how?"

"I think it was playing mumbly peg? I don't know where he got hold of the knife. . . ."

"I'm on my way." Kellie slammed down the phone, trying to hold back a shriek of frustration. *Gambling? Knives?* She turned to Alejandro, who was as yet her only employee. "Looks like I'm needed at camp."

Alejandro glanced up from the paper he was perusing during his break and smiled at her. Even in his nerdy store uniform of khaki pants and a red T-shirt with the silhouetted black cat logo, he was a real lady-killer. At least among the eighteen-to-twenty-two set. He was Ricky Martin with a ponytail. But to Kellie he was merely a lifesaver. She'd hired him because he'd seemed eager, was a student and needed the job, and more important yet, he'd actually had experience working in a copy store. Some days hiring him seemed to be one of the few decisions in her life she didn't regret.

"Trevor in trouble?" he asked.

"You don't sound surprised."

"When I was ten years old, my parents were getting calls about me every day. I grew out of it."

"When?" she asked, desperate for concrete evidence that this torment would end. She had so little experience with boys. Growing up, there had been just her and her little sister. But in their wildest dreams she and Rita couldn't have even imagined half the stunts Trevor was able to not only envision but successfully execute. *Knives!* "And please don't tell me it was last year, because I don't think I can handle a decade of Trevor the Terrible."

"Okay, I won't."

Ominous silence stretched between her and Alejandro till they both started laughing. "Actually, it was *three* years ago," he told her. "And I bet Trevor will snap out of it sooner. He's got a smart mom." He nodded toward their one customer, a well-dressed man attempting to make copies at one of the Xerox machines. "Don't worry, Kellie, I can hold down the fort."

God bless him. In less than twenty seconds he'd managed to soothe her fears as a both parent and a proprietress. Even if he was just schmoozing her, he was worth his weight in gold. "Thanks, Alejandro."

"No problema." He tapped on the newspaper. "And if it makes you feel any better, your horoscope says today is your lucky day."

Kellie grunted. Horoscopes! "That just goes to show what a crock astrology is!"

Alejandro grinned. "Day's not over yet."

Even though she considered herself a die-hard realist, something about that optimistic grin was infectious. *Soon as I can, I'm giving that boy a raise,* she swore to herself as she retrieved her purse from the tiny office in back. As a fledgling business, Copycat was still in the red, but in a few months things would pick up. The store was nestled in an old strip mall in a thriving business district, strategically close to a nearby community college. Once the fall semester started and word got around, she expected she would even have to take on more help.

"Back in a flash—I hope," she said, waving over her shoulder at Alejandro.

As she passed their lone customer, the copier emitted a sick sound. *Paper jam,* she thought immediately, stopping in her tracks. A belching noise issued from the machine and she frowned. *Okay, maybe not a paper jam.* She turned to the machine just as it began to give off a stunning light display. Every possible indicator was flashing or glowing, and yellow and blue colored paper was shooting out one side.

The man who was overseeing this catastrophe dove to

retrieve the paper, but in turning nearly knocked Kellie off her feet.

"Excuse me!" He reached out his hands and held her shoulders to steady her.

Which wasn't a bad idea. Looking into his eyes, which were a breathtaking shade of blue, almost glacier blue, Kellie felt her balance falter. She was certain she was staring at the best-looking man in the world, or at least in Dallas. She had to stifle a girlish giggle. But honestly, did jaws really come like that, squared off and perfectly shaved, or was there some cosmetic procedure rich men had done routinely now, the way women had nose jobs? Jaw chisels and waxes, maybe. He also had blond hair, immaculately cut, and an incredibly sexy dimple in his cheek. And he was tall, so tall that she had to crane her neck a little to stare at him—although *ogling* probably better described what she was doing.

But she so rarely came into close contact with his type—blond, tanned, blue-eyed, obviously wealthy—she couldn't help gawking at him. Just his suit probably cost more than two months of her rent. His haircut was a week's grocery bill. And his tan had to be the product of at least three spring vacations to exotic places she could only dream of. Of course, since the last experience she could remotely call a vacation was a fitful night spent in a pup tent at a KOA campsite, slapping at mosquitoes and trying to referee her two kids, her standards for luxury travel couldn't be considered exacting.

Her customer didn't look as if he'd ever suffered anything so plebeian as a mosquito bite. His blood was probably too rich for them.

After her divorce, Kellie had mostly given up thinking of the opposite sex in terms other than the nuisance factor, but as those baby blues twinkled down at her, she felt a definite flutter of arousal. She might be staring, but he wasn't exactly ignoring her, either. In fact, he looked as if he'd been struck by the same bolt from the blue that zapped her. His hands were frozen on her shoulders, and his eyes were giving her a once-over that made her blush even though she knew there was nothing for him to see besides a short woman, on the mousy side, wearing the same unflattering but functional outfit that Alejandro had on.

Staring at her? Yeah, right. Maybe what was surprising her most was that despite his good looks and obvious wealth, the man appeared to have a complete lack of that which she usually associated with his physical type: arrogance. In fact, he seemed completely absorbed in *her* predicament.

"Are you all right?" he asked, his rich voice reverberating with just a pleasant hint of a Texas drawl.

"Oh—" She quickly took stock. There was nothing at all wrong with her. Except, of course, for the fact that she didn't seem able to move.

Or breathe.

"Yes, of course," she managed to gasp out. Was she crazy? Her pulse was dancing way faster than necessary for such a light collision.

"Didn't bump you too hard, did I?"

"No, no." She dragged her gaze away from him and nodded toward the machine, which was still behaving like a leftover prop from *Poltergeist*. "Is there something wrong . . . ?"

The tanned, manicured hands let go of her, and he turned and let out a breath of exasperation. "Yes, but I'm afraid it's *me*. I've got technology-itis. Machines hate me." He grinned at her, and for a moment the light from the florescent overhead lamps actually seemed to glint off of his Pepsodent-white teeth.

As her son the hoodlum would have said, *wow*.

If Alejandro was a lady-killer, this guy could only be labeled a lady annihilator. With all the force of his smile radiating toward her like heat from the world's most powerful sunlamp, she felt herself grinning back idiotically. "They're supposed to be foolproof now, but they still give us trouble." She began opening doors, unjamming paper, checking levers. Anything to get her attention away from Mr. GQ-cover. But she could sense him watching her and felt her fingers shake giddily as she put the machine to rights again.

"Maybe you would rather have us do this for you," she suggested. "It costs only a little more. . . ."

"Oh, the cost is no problem." He shrugged self-effacingly. "I just thought that since I had a little time . . . See, I wanted to throw a birthday party for my secretary. I made up this flyer to pass around the office, but since Doreen's usually the one who does the copying . . ."

Translation: The man had never made a photocopy.

Kellie looked up at him, her lips parted in fresh wonder. Incredible! To him, a support-staff dependent, Xerox machines were probably as exotic as the space shuttle was to most people: they could recognize it when they saw it, but wouldn't have the slightest idea how to make it go *vroom*.

Since she was momentarily incapable of speech, he anxiously brushed a hand through his hair. "Look, I'm very sorry for screwing up your machine. I'll pay for it, of course."

She gaped at him in disbelief. In amazement. Was he serious?

He was.

Where did this guy come from, the planet of misfit millionaires? "You do pay for it—in the cost of the copies. I work machine glitches into the cost of doing business."

"This is your place?"

She nodded.

"And you don't think I killed it?"

"Believe me, it would take more than a few copies to do

this behemoth in—like maybe a buzz saw and a wrecking ball.''

He smiled appreciatively. "You sure know how to make a customer feel better." He picked up his original flyer. "I'll just take this up to the front . . ."

She watched him to make sure he didn't wreak havoc on his short walk to the counter.

Oh, who was she kidding? She stared after him because he was one guy it was difficult to peel her gaze away from. He moved with the grace of a jock, in long, sure strides. Was he a jock? With that tan she'd peg him for a tennis player, or . . .

She shook her head in disgust. As if any of this should matter to her. While Golden Boy left his flyer with Alejandro, she scribbled an ''Out of Order'' sign for the machine, then hurried out to her car. Time to get back to reality. Her budding juvenile delinquent awaited.

It was the kind of June day that felt as if it would melt sneakers to the pavement. The car's interior was so hot, Kellie let the door stand open for a moment before braving actually getting in. Her air-conditioning had conked out in 1996. Despite the lack of amenities, however, her old compact always sputtered to life at the turn of the key— one of the few things in her life Kellie could always count on. With a dented fender and faded red paint that usually bore messages like ''wash me'' fingered in something that looked suspiciously like her son's handwriting, the vehicle wouldn't win any beauty contests, but it was as constant as Jim Carrey's box office receipts. During the past year, with the upheavals of her divorce and getting her business started, she had thanked providence more times than she could count for not having to pay out for expensive car repairs.

If only her ex-husband had been a little more like her Toyota, she thought as she eased herself into the ovenlike interior. Instead, Rick had been undependable, unfaithful, and constantly needed bailing out of debt. Which wasn't so easy since Kellie had mostly held catch-as-catch-can clerical jobs when the kids were younger. Paying for the privilege of divorcing Rick had seemed a bargain, even though she had shouldered all the legal fees and all the heartache. By the time the papers were signed, he had already found himself a steady girlfriend and flitted off to Las Vegas without much more than a fare-thee-well. And the worst, most inexplicable part of it all was that even though Kellie had tried for years to keep the marriage together and had only reluctantly accepted the fact that Rick was never going to be a good father or husband, when the end finally came, she somehow felt as if *she* were the failure.

After all, before they were married, they'd had good times. Rick had been funny—a little irresponsible, always, but back when they were teenagers that hadn't seemed so terrible. In fact, to her it was refreshing. He was so different from her! He didn't angst over grades or what people said about him. He just wanted to float along, he'd said. A person could always find work. The main thing was to have fun.

But fun hadn't lasted long once they'd had a baby and rent payments and then another baby. Money might not be able to buy happiness, she'd discovered, but a lack of it could certainly bring its share of misery. There was a two-year period at the end of their marriage when she and Rick had barely spoken to each other, much less laughed together.

Suddenly awash in gloomy thoughts as well as sweat from the incidental sauna her car was treating her to, she sighed and inched out of her parking space. As she cast a perfunctory last-minute glance to both sides, her heart stopped. Speeding straight at her from the passenger side was a black BMW with tinted windows, looking like doom on wheels. Brakes squealed as Kellie instinctively braced herself for the impact, which came in the blink of an eye. She was thrown sideways into her door, her head hitting the window as she heard the tearing of metal and crashing of glass. She looked over and saw that both side windows had cracked into a million pieces and collapsed into the car's interior. Thousands of shards of sparkling glass twinkled up at her like icy confetti. She lifted a hand to where her head had bumped against her own window. It didn't hurt too much, but there would probably be a large bump there by evening.

She groaned, remembering suddenly that it wasn't even noon yet and already she'd endured a wreck and her son's being ejected from day camp. *Lucky day?* Whoever was writing the horoscope these days for the *Dallas Morning News* needed to be reported to the Better Business Bureau.

"Miss! Miss, are you hurt?"

Before she could look up or even reply, her door was thrown open and two strong arms hoisted her out of her seat. As if she were in a subplot on *ER*, she felt herself being rushed from the accident and laid out on the pavement. Her body rested against the steamy cement, though her head was cradled against something soft.

"Can you hear me?"

Kellie, blinking, opened her eyes and found herself again staring up into those glacier-blue eyes. "*You?*" she whispered.

It was the inept guy from the copy store. Didn't it just figure that a man who didn't even know how to run a Xerox machine would drive a car that cost twice what she would ever make in a year before taxes?

His face contorted in anguish. He looked as though he'd just killed somebody, which made Kellie anxious. Maybe she was worse off than she thought. "I'm so sorry," he said. "Are you all right? Should I call an ambulance?"

If she didn't say something fast, Mr. Moneybags looked as if he might start performing CPR whether she needed it or not. "I'm fine, I'm fine," she mumbled, lifting her head. The moment she did, however, she felt woozy and dropped back down. She tilted her head and saw that it was cushioned by the man's jacket. The most intimate she would ever be with Armani.

"You don't look well at all. I'll call 911."

"No!" She couldn't afford to be hurt right now—she couldn't spare the time. She couldn't afford a prescription drug co-payment, either. Besides, she was all right. She knew she was. At least well enough to go pick up her racketeering ten-year-old. "I just need to get up and drink some water."

In a flash, the man was gone. He dashed into Copycat just as Alejandro came running out. "Kellie, are you all right?" Her coworker knelt down beside her.

Again she nodded. The faint smell of expensive men's cologne still clung to the man's jacket. A rich, comforting smell. Suddenly she felt as if she could have curled up on the sidewalk and taken a nap.

Alejandro clucked his tongue. "Well, you better rest for a minute then, 'cause you certainly won't feel so hot when you get a load of your car."

She shot up to sitting. Then she moaned.

Squashed. One whole side of her Toyota was bashed in like a can crumpled for the recycle heap. The two passenger windows were shattered, as well as the front windshield, which hadn't collapsed yet but had a spiderweb of cracks emanating from one side. One dented passenger door was thrown open, and from the mangled appearance of things, it didn't look like it would be closing again any time soon. The whole body of the car was thrown out of alignment.

Alejandro shook his head in wonder. "I heard the crash, but I never dreamed it was you. Thank God you weren't going very fast."

She hadn't been *going* at all, in fact. Only *she* would have an accident standing absolutely still!

"My poor car."

So much for the one thing in her life she could depend on.

Damn, damn, damn.

Riley found the water cooler in the small back room, filled two paper cups, and dashed back through the copy shop, cursing himself. Why had he been going so fast? Why hadn't he seen her? Why did he have to hit *her?*

One answer seemed to work for all three—he had been thinking about *her.* The compact woman with the brown eyes. There was something about her, something he'd felt the moment he'd bumped into her at that copying machine. . . . What troubles was she attempting to camouflage with her wisecracking swagger? What weighty problems was she carrying on those surprisingly strong, sturdy, narrow shoulders?

It made him edgy to feel such a strong reaction to a woman—especially a beautiful woman with brown eyes that seemed to physically tug at him. The rest of her wasn't half bad, either. She had a great figure—well-toned arms and full breasts and hips that flared sexily from where her boxy T-shirt tucked into her practical khaki trousers. She was a little on the short side, but he bet her legs were shapely. . . .

Damn.

He'd spent three years immune to disturbing reactions like that. So he'd run from the copy store, unthinking, and managed to crash right into the one person he most wanted to avoid.

Riley sprinted back outside with his Dixie cups, trying to keep all the water from sloshing to the pavement. When he saw the woman sitting up and staring at her shell of

a car, he felt her pain viscerally. She was eyeing that pile
of metal as if it were her best friend.

Her terminally ill best friend.

More slowly, Riley approached the woman. Her assistant glared at him in shaming accusation. Riley felt about
two inches tall. How did he even begin to apologize for
something like this? How could he make it better?

"I'm sorry," was what he settled on, holding out the
cups for the woman.

She took a cone-shaped container and swigged down
its contents without even glancing at him. "You know,"
she mused to no one in particular, "I think I loved that
car even more than my ex-husband."

It seemed an odd thing to say, but Riley found himself
greedily gleaning useful information from her words. *Ex-*
husband? Against his better judgment, he glanced down
at her hand and duly noted her bare ring finger.

Stop it! a voice in his head warned. But he seemed
hopeless to stop himself from gazing at her, wondering
about her. He tried to concentrate on the woman's problem, not the woman herself. He couldn't imagine loving
a mere car more than a person, but then, he could buy a
new car every week if he wanted to, while that Toyota
looked as if it had been with her for a while. . . .

Guilt settled over him like a shroud. "I'm sorry," he
repeated. He couldn't say it enough. "The accident was
completely my fault. Naturally I will compensate you for
any damages."

She swung toward him, an eyebrow arched. "You
sound awfully eager."

"Like I said, it was my fault. Completely." He
frowned. She still wasn't standing up. "Are you sure
you're all right?"

She nodded; then, taking a breath, she pushed herself up
to standing. "Perfectly sure," she said, weaving a little.

He reached out a hand to steady her. She stiffened and he—*he*—nearly jumped out of his skin!

White. A flash of bridal white nearly blinded him so that for a dizzying moment time seemed to stop. He was sure she was frowning at him, and yet in his mind he saw her smile—a radiant, gloriously happy smile, full of hope and promise and love—directed at him and him alone. And then he saw a hand reach out to her—his hand? someone else's?—and clasp her smaller one. Where once that hand had been bare, the ring finger now boasted a chunky diamond solitaire and a band of gold.

It was only short flash of a vision, but it was enough for him to understand.

It was enough to knock the wind clear out of him.

He'd had an odd, edgy feeling ever since he'd entered her store—and especially since he'd run into her at the copy machine. It wasn't just that he was physically attracted to her, either, though God knew he was. That was inexplicable in itself. Pretty she certainly was, but nothing spectacular. He wouldn't have called her a knock-out. Yet she had those eyes . . . eyes that seem to understand trouble yet also projected strength. She appeared so self-contained, so in charge, and yet . . .

And yet he'd felt that strange tug. That edge. So he'd tried to get away from that store as fast as humanly possible. Tried to run. And in so doing he'd almost flattened her with his car. And now here he was with those dark eyes fastened on him again, looking curious and . . . vulnerable.

That vulnerability, combined with the mental flash he'd received, seemed to seal Riley's fate. This woman, whoever she was, was someone he needed to avoid like the plague.

Breaking eye contact, trying to shake himself out of whatever funk he was in, he fished into his pockets for a business card. On the back of it he scrawled his insurance information. "This is my insurance carrier," he said, pointing to the words he'd just written. "There won't be any problems about the whole matter, I assure you."

She blinked at the proffered card, but didn't take it. "We'd better call the police. We'll need their report for the claim."

"I accept all responsibility," he said, in one big hurry to get the hell out of there.

The woman frowned at him. "You can't just wait ten minutes?"

If he stared into those brown eyes of hers for another ten seconds, never mind ten minutes, he just might be lost forever. "I'm sorry—I'm sort of in a rush."

"Aren't we all!" She laughed humorlessly. "But some of us don't have any means of getting where we're going."

Guilt washed over him again. Guilt and regret. Why the hell hadn't he watched where he was going? She was just a working woman, struggling along, and he'd bumbled into her life like the proverbial bull in the china shop. Didn't that prove he was the last thing she needed in her life?

More importantly, she was the last thing he needed in his.

He dug into his back pocket and yanked out his wallet. He pulled out two hundred dollar bills, all the cash he had on him, and thrust them into her hands along with the card she still seemed reluctant to take. "This should cover the cost of a rental car until you can contact the insurance company. If you need any more, please contact me at the business address on my card. My secretary will help you in any way she can. Now if you'll excuse me . . ." He started to turn away.

"Wait!" She jabbed the money back at him. "I can't take this."

He held up his hands, suddenly recalling a phrase from his youth. "No backs."

"But that's ridiculous. I can't—"

"Think nothing of it. The accident was my fault—I owe you that money, and much more. So that's that." He smiled, praying that this would be the last time he would ever have to see her doleful, funny, beautiful face. "I hope your day gets better."

"It can't get much worse," she allowed matter-of-factly. "But I really do think you should stay. It would make it much simpler to sort through if we have problems later. . . ."

That beckoning look she had . . . there was something about it. He felt another fierce tug come right from the center of his being and, in spite of it, began backing away. Toward his car, toward escape. His BMW, naturally, had suffered only an infinitesimal dent.

"There won't be any problems," he repeated.

"But how can you know? What if—"

"If you have any troubles at all, just call my office, Ms. . . . ?"

"Sumners," she supplied. "Kellie Sumners."

He practically winced. That was way more information than he wanted to know. He should never have asked. *The woman whose car he'd hit*—that would have been enough. Doreen, his secretary, could have discovered the particulars of Kellie Sumners's life and dealt with her. But now that he had a name, he was sure not to forget it. Kellie Sumners.

Kellie Sumners. There. That was the last time he would even allow himself to think it.

He turned and practically sprinted the rest of his way to his car. He opened the door, sank into the driver's seat and peeled out of the parking lot as if he were trying to escape a fate worse than death. When really it was just plain fate he was trying to escape.

Fate in the compact, enticing form of Kellie Sumners, the woman he was almost certainly going to marry.

Chapter Two

"That was weird." As the roar of the fleeing BMW faded into the distance, Kellie finally flicked a sidewise glance at Alejandro for confirmation. "Didn't that guy seem weird to you?"

"Definitely weird—and nervous," Alejandro agreed. "He probably thinks you're going to sue him. Those rich types are always paranoid. If he really was rich."

"He certainly looked it—and smelled it, too. That wasn't Old Spice he was wearing." She glanced down at his card. *Riley C. Lombard*, it read. *The Lombard Group*. "A fellow business owner!" she cracked. "Somehow I doubt we're playing in the same league." She tapped the card. "I wonder what that C stands for. Probably Cornelius or Corning or something old-money sounding."

"You'd better just hope it doesn't stand for crook," Alejandro said.

"His two hundred dollars look real enough."

"Yeah, but it's gonna take a lot more than two hundred dollars to fix your Toyota."

Her gaze lit on her car and she felt her heart constrict.

Was this the end? Had the crazy rich guy dealt her car its deathblow?

Kellie had worked herself up into a state by the time the police arrived. Her car had been murdered and the assailant had flown the coop. Why had she let him get away? She felt comforted by the chubby cop who stepped out of his blue-and-white and goggled in amazement at her poor Toyota. She felt in desperate need of some official sympathy.

She gave her side of the story and the information about Riley C. Lombard—dwelling, perhaps, an extra long time on Riley and the fact that he seemed to be of the privileged class. She wanted the cop to officially document her status as the true victim. She also wanted it duly noted that Riley Lombard was a villain who'd left the scene of the accident before the cops arrived, when he obviously could have afforded to stick around.

The policeman nodded. "Lombard, huh? I've heard of that guy."

Oh, great. His picture was probably all over the police station. For the first time this morning, Kellie felt real despair. "You have?"

"Sure, seen 'im in the papers. You know, society page."

The policeman, who had a pot belly that hung lazily over his busy cop belt, didn't look the type to peruse much beyond the sports section. "*You* read the society pages?"

His eyes widened. "Yeah, do you mind?"

"No, but . . ." She supposed one never could tell.

He huffed at her. "You think I'm some kind of jerk who just reads the sports section?"

"No, but—"

"Think I'm just a donut-eating cop? Some black-coffee-consuming working class grunt?"

Kellie's face reddened. "I never meant to imply . . ."

He cut her off. "Look, I can see that you're stressed, ma'am, but that's no reason to give me your guff. All I said was that I'd seen the fellow before. I keep my eyes open. That's what I'm paid to do. Maybe it was an article about a breaking ground on a new building or something. Give me a break!"

"I'm sorry, I—"

He ripped a copy off the pad he'd been writing on and handed it to her. "This is an accident report for your insurance. I'll contact Mr. Lombard myself. Have a nice day."

"Too late," she murmured. Then she prayed he hadn't heard her. She didn't want to set him off again.

"Does it seem to you that everyone is on the edge of sanity today?" she asked Alejandro as she went back inside.

He laughed. "Say, speaking of insanity, shouldn't you call your sister?"

She frowned. Rita? "What for? I've got to wait for the tow truck."

"Yeah, but after that you'll need a ride. Remember day camp? Trevor, your son?"

She groaned. "Why did that jerk have to crash into me today of all days? If I ever talk to him again, I'll give him a piece of my mind."

Alejandro laughed. "That's one thing you'll never have to worry about. The way that fellow peeled out of here, you'll never see him again."

"Good!" She grumbled as she picked up the phone to call her little sister to come pick her up. "I hope you're right. As long as I get my car fixed, I don't care if I never set eyes on the guy again."

Work was impossible. All afternoon Riley was still too out of sorts from his collision with Kellie Sumners to care whether trading was heavy or light, whether the Dow was up or down. He felt restless, as if he were about to explode out of his desk chair at the slightest provocation. But of course there was nothing to provoke him. He had a whole flock of employees who absorbed all his headaches for him.

So he dragged through the rest of the afternoon, trying to work but mostly thinking about Kellie and engineering paper clip structures on his desk. He wished there were *something* he could do for her.

When he arrived home that evening, his butler swung open the door and glared at him. Nathaniel's impatient stance stopped just short of tapping his toe and pointing at his watch. "You're *late* for *dinner*."

Riley let out a baleful sigh. It was going to be one of those nights. Doreen might keep his troubles at bay at work, but his home life wasn't quite so smooth. "It's not even six-thirty yet."

His house was really a rather modest mansion by Dallas standards. The old gray stone estate along Turtle Creek was large without being egregiously expansive or ostentatious, and the household could still be wrestled into order with minimal help. Riley had bought the place on impulse three years ago, back when he was desperate to flee the site of his old life. Now sometimes he questioned the wisdom of his choice. The stone was dark; the rooms were drafty. The mustard-yellow velvet drapes—artifacts from the twenties, surely—were depressingly moldy looking. If he'd gone out of his way to choose a gloomy place to retreat, he couldn't have picked better.

Granted, he'd done little to improve the Dracula's-castle ambiance. In fact, he'd barely unpacked. Most of the rooms still stood so sparsely furnished that they echoed. There were no pictures on the elaborate marble mantel, few paintings decorating the walls. Just a jumble of furniture from the old place, a rug here or there, and of course the two servants who had loyally followed him from his old house to this one. Mostly out of loyalty not to him, but to Joanne.

Long-suffering Nathaniel was one. Fayard, the six-foot-tall Dominican cook with a Mike Tyson temper, the lungs of Caruso, and free access to any number of sharp implements was the other. They both prided themselves on standing by Riley, even if in so doing they suffered personally. Somewhere in the past, Nathaniel and Fayard had been a couple. Riley could vaguely remember Joanne gossiping about them—giving him long-winded details about spats and breakups and kitchen reconciliations, to which he'd only half listened. Back in the happy days, Nathaniel and Fayard had seemed minor players in Riley's life. Now that they were front and center, he'd wished he'd paid more attention to Joanne's gossip. Their relationship had turned from sour to poisonous somewhere along the way. Sometimes Riley felt as if he'd walked in on the last act of a Greek tragedy.

"It's *lobster* night," Nathaniel reminded him, taking his briefcase and shooing him toward the dining room. Nathaniel was wraith-thin, but hours in the gym had made his physique wiry and strong. His pale blond hair was always neatly trimmed and his clothes impeccably pressed. One raised-brow look could make Riley feel as if he'd turned into Ralph Kramden. "Fayard's in a perfect snit now, and that crustacean is going to be as tough as tire rubber."

"All right, Nathaniel—it's nothing to fuss about."

"Fine." Nathaniel sighed, straining for patience. "If the lobster stinks, blame Fayard, not me."

"I'm sure it will be perfectly delicious." Which was a bald-faced lie. He didn't even like lobster. In fact, his blue-collar taste buds made him by nature particularly unequipped to appreciate Fayard's culinary prowess. But that was something he tried not to let on. He didn't want to hurt Fayard's feelings. Even though he, Nathaniel, and Fayard had been rattling around uneasily in this half empty place on Turtle Creek for three years now, he feared making the slightest misstep that might cause either of them to leave. He was afraid of losing the last remnants of the life he'd once so rashly tried to escape.

Though occasionally he did allow himself to wish Joanne had hired a calm, elderly couple way back when. Or an efficient pair of spinster sisters.

"Delicious? *Rubbery* lobster?" The butler shuddered as he waited for Riley to proceed into the dining room. Nathaniel had been contemptuous of Riley's taste ever since he caught sight of his employer toting home an Arby's bag on Fayard's night off two years ago.

Once Riley was seated, Nathaniel brought out a water pitcher to fill his glass and hovered over him worriedly. "Rough day at work?"

Riley tried not to laugh. When, exactly, was the last time he'd had a rough day at work? He didn't waste energy worrying about money anymore. Of course, it was easy not to when he had so much of it, but he'd also learned the hard way that money wasn't everything.

He doubted Kellie Sumners thought that way. She'd looked at that crumpled car of hers with the desperation of a woman who didn't have the means to replace it. He would have done anything, paid any price, to rid himself of the memory of Kellie Sumners's pinched, worried expression as she'd looked out at her wrecked Toyota. Maybe if he didn't have this guilt on his conscience he wouldn't think of her at all. . . .

Or at least so much.

Maybe he could forget that vision of white.

His phone rang and he snatched his Nokia out of his pocket, eager for any kind of distraction.

It was his best friend, Jay Howard, but Riley could barely concentrate on what he was saying. Something about a woman, which wasn't surprising, since Jay was always having woman trouble. But woman trouble just reminded Riley of her. Of Kellie Sumners. He shouldn't allow that name to even enter his mind; yet he couldn't help thinking that he needed to make amends to her in some way. He kept remembering the wounded expression on her face as she stared at that crumpled, ancient car of hers. . . .

Over the phone, Jay's voice rattled on. "And so I told Nancy, I said, 'But we've only known each other for two weeks. How can you be so sure we're not meant for each other?' *That's* when she told me that she was a lesbian. And I said, 'Since when?' And she said, 'Since *two weeks ago!*' Two weeks, Riley. Don't you think that's a little bit of a coincidence?" Silence crackled over the phone. "Riley?"

Riley snapped to, unsure of what he'd heard. Something about lesbians. "I'm sorry, what was the question?"

"I said, can you believe that?"

"No . . ."

"So do you think I should call her again? I mean, maybe her condition's only temporary."

Riley sighed. Trying to wrestle with his own turmoil and Jay's complicated love life over the phone was more than he could handle right now. "Jay, you want to meet somewhere?"

"I still have heartburn from that last place you dragged me to," Jay said.

Riley's friends never could seem to understand his preference for greasy spoons. "Don't worry, no restaurants. Meet me in thirty minutes at that Toyota dealership off the LBJ Freeway."

"Huh?"

"The Toyota dealership. I'll explain when we get there."

But how could he explain when he wasn't quite sure

himself what he was doing? Riley pushed away from the table and stood, feeling as if he were running on autopilot.

"I told you, you wouldn't eat it," Nathaniel said, startling him out of his thoughts. He nodded at the plate that Riley had barely touched.

Riley tossed his napkin onto the table. "Apologize to Fayard for me. Tell him I had to go out again unexpectedly."

"But you just got here!" Nathaniel crossed his arms as if to say, *Oh, sure, leave* me *to do your dirty work!* "You're sneaking out for a grilled cheese again, aren't you?"

Riley shook his head. "No, I swear I'm not." Then he cocked his head, curious. Nathaniel might have the temper of a diva, but he did have impeccable taste. "If someone were trying to apologize to you, Nathaniel, for say—well, some offense—which would you rather receive—a Toyota, or maybe just the cash for one?"

"You've got to be kidding!" Nathaniel thrummed fingers on his arms. "A Toyota? As far as I'm concerned, you should either have a Lexus delivered to my door or don't even bother."

A Lexus. He hadn't thought of that. Riley nodded slowly, smiled, then looked at his watch. He needed to hurry to meet Jay. "Thanks, Nathaniel."

The butler gasped and lifted his knuckles to his lips. "Wait . . . is this for real?"

"I'll be back later." Riley turned on his heel and walked back out the way he'd come in.

"Oh—leather interior!" Nathaniel called after him. "Don't forget the leather!"

Riley had first met Jay Howard when they were freshmen at the University of Texas. A tall, gangly son of one of the wealthiest men in Texas, who could have coasted through life on just the fumes from his daddy's oil wells, Jay was nevertheless eager to be liked and accepted. In those days Riley, who was a business major on a track scholarship, thought that Jay was the nicest guy he'd ever met. The nicest—and the unluckiest with women. And the intervening fifteen years had barely changed Jay, except physically. He was even thinner now, with shoulders that seemed to stoop a little more with each passing year and every additional romantic disappointment. Gravity had worked on his face a little, too, so that his cheeks sagged and his big blue eyes bulged in their sockets. He bore a striking likeness, in fact, to Don Knotts, a resemblance that he accepted with good nature. Once Riley had even seen him sign an autograph.

It always puzzled him that he'd never found a girlfriend for Jay. Riley prided himself on his ability to know when two people would be good together—but Jay defied all his matchmaking skills. For a man so eager for matrimony, he had absolutely no luck dating.

"What are we doing here?" Jay asked as they stood in the lot crowded with shiny new vehicles. His hands were buried deep in the pockets of his much-worn jeans, and a Helmut Lang shirt hung on him as casually as an old rag. There was a warm breeze blowing, causing the colorful pennants to flap noisily above them.

"Buying a car."

"What for? Something happen to one of yours?"

"It's not for me."

Kellie's car, which was an ancient model, didn't really have an equivalent in the modern world, Riley soon discovered. But it had obviously been purchased for practicality; to him that translated into an SUV. Something multipurpose would probably be useful to her in her business as well, in case she needed a vehicle for deliveries.

"What's it for then?" Jay asked.

Riley shrugged. "A woman I met today."

Jay's eyes bugged. "Son of a gun! I never thought of *that.*" For a moment he stood with his mouth agape, contemplating the vehicle they were staring at, a mammoth green off-road vehicle, which of course would probably never see action more rigorous than the on-ramp to Central Expressway. "You think if I got one of these for Nancy . . . ?"

Riley shook his head. "Maybe Nancy is best forgotten."

Jay gave the SUV's new steel-belted radial tire a gentle, frustrated kick with the toe of his loafer. "But I *like* her."

Riley's heart went out to Jay. The man sincerely wanted to get married . . . and had been trying to for years. Of course sometimes he didn't pick wife candidates very wisely. "Last month you liked that other woman . . . What was her name?"

"Tiffany."

"What happened to her?"

"The Marines transferred her to Sierra Leone."

Riley frowned. "That's tough luck."

"That's *my* luck." He sighed in resignation, then tried to put a positive spin on his latest disappointment. "But you know, I don't think I was really cut out to be an army spouse. All that moving around can be a real strain on a relationship."

"You'll find someone," Riley assured him.

"Oh, I know." Jay rarely stayed down for long, no matter what the setbacks. "In fact, I've already hit upon a great new strategy."

"What?"

"Book clubs."

Riley blinked. "Book clubs?"

"Sure. Women love them—you know, Oprah and all that. I've joined three. In fact, I need to scoot soon to make it to my classic fiction group. We're reading *The Charterhouse of Parma.*''

Riley's nose wrinkled. "Couldn't you find a bunch of women who read something a little more entertaining?''

"Oh, sure. Have you ever heard of Bertrice Small?''

Riley shook his head.

"Well, one of my groups is doing her. She's pretty good. And then my third group is a little more into nonfiction. Thought I'd try for a variety. Right now they're doing a Joseph Campbell discussion. That's philosophy.''

"Thanks for the translation.''

"I figure even if I don't find the love of my life, I'm going to learn a lot, especially from this Bertrice Small woman. She's a real eye-opener! Riley, we thought we'd heard it all back in our days in the Fiji house, but let me tell you. Did you know—''

"Uh-oh.''

A dealership salesman had honed in on them and was bearing down like a spider with a moth in its web. Riley and Jay both stiffened in response. Riley had been so gung-ho to come out here, he'd forgotten that he would have to reckon with a car salesman.

The salesman, who seemed to be ninety percent teeth and hair, introduced himself as Mike and offered to let Riley take the SUV for a spin. In fact, he was already tossing a set of keys in the air. "Four-wheel drive. Anti-lock brakes. Six-disk CD changer and surround-sound speakers. You gotta experience it to believe it, Riley.''

They were already on first-name basis.

Riley smiled politely. "I'm just window shopping.''

Mike, not to be discouraged, kept on smiling. "Well, let me ask you this, Riley, what price range are you lookin' at?''

"No range. Just whatever it costs.''

Mike's brows soared. "Well . . .'' You could almost see the dollar signs in his eyes.

"It's not for me anyway," Riley explained. "It's a gift."

"Oh, for your wife."

"No, for another woman."

"Oh, well . . ." The unctuous smile turned into an uncomfortable grimace.

Riley laughed, realizing how his statement had sounded. Like Kellie was some slightly scarlet woman he had hidden away on a back street. "I mean, it's for a woman I just met. I don't know her at all, really."

Mike squinted at him in confusion.

"I still don't quite get this, Riley," Jay said. "It's not like you at all! Lately you've gone out of your way to avoid female attention . . . and now this. What's the deal?"

Riley still didn't feel able to explain. He'd never told Jay about what some would call his gift of insight. His friend would think he'd gone off the deep end.

Jay pressed on. "Is this vehicle for some woman you're trying to impress?"

"No, I'd say it's more of an apology, really."

His friend nodded, considering. "You know, I don't want to lead you astray here, bud, but if I were apologizing to a woman, I don't think I would go the Toyota route." He turned to Mike. "Would you?"

The man, who had been listening to them attentively, had to cast about his befuddled brain for his sales pitch. "Well, now, as for value and dependability . . ."

Jay nodded. "Value, sure, but let me ask you this. If you were a woman, Mike, wouldn't you rather have a Cadillac?"

Mike looked from Jay to Riley, then back to Jay again. This was turning into a real conundrum. "Nathaniel suggested a Lexus," Riley said. But of course Jay would say Cadillac. The Howards, he often liked to point out, were Cadillac people from way back. In fact, his prized possession was his grandfather's 1953 Cadillac convertible.

Mike glanced at Riley. "Who's Nathaniel?"

"His butler," Jay explained. Then he turned back to Riley. "What does Nathaniel know about the fairer sex? I still say a woman would want a Cadillac. Right, Mike?"

Mike actually appeared to try to puzzle it out; then his face went suddenly red and he tossed up his hands. "Oh, sure! A Cadillac and a diamond ring would just about make my day!" He spun on his heel and beat a hasty retreat. "Screwballs!"

Jay stared after the man, offended. "What's the matter with him?"

"I think we hurt his feelings by mentioning other cars."

"He sure got snippy about it. Did you hear what he called us?"

"Screwballs. He's probably right."

"That's nuts!" Jay said. "You come all the way out here to hand the guy a huge sum of money and he insults you. Just flat-out insults you. I tell you, Riley, I just don't know what this world is coming to. You can't buy a car; I can't find love. Sometimes it seems like the world just doesn't appreciate multimillionaires anymore. We're being taken for granted."

Riley took one look at the woebegone expression on his friend's face and couldn't help laughing. "Poor us."

The next morning was the usual rush to get herself and the kids ready. Or, more accurately, Kellie rushed and her children watched her. This was probably how it would always be, she thought with wry acceptance. Over the years Trevor and Tina would watch her slow descent into madness as she dashed about from fridge to dryer to work to grocery store, until finally they would be older than she was now and come one day to have their weary mother hauled off to the old folks' home. Or the lunatic asylum.

She plopped a brown paper lunch bag in front of Trevor and fixed him with her sternest mother stare. ''I don't want to hear another word from your counselor about knives.''

''It was just a butter knife,'' he said defensively.

''*Any* knife,'' she warned him. ''And if I receive one more word about your financial shenanigans, you'll spend the rest of your summer standing by a copier handing out paperclips. Understand?''

Trevor squinted his blue eyes at her, his face looking squarer because his sandy brown hair was newly buzzed off for summer. His jaw set tightly, just the way Rick's had so often when he finally had to face up to the consequences of his dumb actions. She didn't like the reminder of her ex-husband, or the example he'd set for their son.

''No gambling or swindling. Not even sandwich swapping,'' she said. ''Got it?''

Trevor rummaged through his sack, wrinkling his nose in distaste as he pulled out its contents. ''A bologna sandwich and a banana doesn't give me much to work with anyway, Mom,'' he said, completely without remorse.

How on earth had she spawned such a nervy kid?

Tina, her nine-year-old daughter, looked up from her library copy of *Little Women* and tensed in dread at her brother's sandwich. His lunches were always a harbinger of what was in store for her, and she, too, apparently found the offerings sub-standard. ''Margaret's mother uses black bread,'' she announced. Margaret Thurston was Tina's best friend, one of the richest girls in her grade-school class. ''She also uses Swiss cheese, not the cheap processed kind.''

Her words came out just as Kellie was in the middle of peeling the cellophane off a slice of orange cheese product. Wincing, she quickly slapped it on a slab of generic wheat bread, as if to hide the evidence of her slipshod motherhood.

Ever since the divorce, Tina's big bespectacled eyes were always watching her closely for flaws—which seemed to multiply daily. Or maybe Kellie just felt more pressure when it came to Tina, who was as exceptionally bright as Trevor was exceptionally troublesome. She made straight As, had skipped second grade, and could play Chopin preludes on the piano. When she looked at her daughter, Kellie's heart swelled with equal measures of pride and guilt. Tina was a gifted little girl who deserved to have the world at her feet. Instead, Kellie scrounged to make enough to keep her in piano lessons and eyeglasses. And as for the piano Tina so craved, that was like wishing for the moon. Tina practiced Beethoven sonatinas on a second-hand electric keyboard, while her friend Margaret Thurston pounded out "Old Dog Blue" on a Steinway.

"Margaret Thurston's a dweezil brain," Trevor said, plowing into a bowl of Cheerios.

Tina pursed her lips at him and disappeared behind her book.

"You shouldn't say things like that about people, Trevor," Kellie told him, although privately her thoughts were taking a much different turn from the parent-speak she was parroting. Like how there must be something terribly wrong with her when her opinion so closely agreed with her smart-aleck son's. "Margaret's very nice."

He laughed and swung his legs energetically beneath the table. "Her mother dresses her like a Madame Alexander doll. She's a geek and a dork."

"You shouldn't say—" Kellie stopped in mid-sentence, realizing that she sounded like a broken record. She could spend all day telling Trevor what he shouldn't do—shouldn't talk with his mouth full, shouldn't drop her sewing machine from the roof, shouldn't call people dweebs and geeks, shouldn't swindle his schoolmates or play with knives. The most important things he shouldn't do seemed lost on him for all the noise she made lecturing him about absolutely everything.

While Tina made her heart swell with maternal pride, Trevor steeled her heart in maternal determination. She would keep him from becoming a carbon copy of his ne'er-do-well father if it killed her. Which it just might. But she wasn't going down without a fight.

"You look nice today," she told him, trying to inject some positive reinforcement into his morning.

He scowled and shoveled in some more cereal. Speaking with his mouth full so that he was only semi-intelligible, with milk sprinkles spewing from his lips, he replied, "I combed my hair."

Tina shivered in revulsion. "You should comb your hair every day, Trevor."

Before a fight could erupt, Kellie ran a hand over her son's short bristles and said, "Maybe we should just run the Dustbuster over it every morning."

Trevor, who had the ability, rare in a ten-year-old, to laugh in spite of himself, howled at the joke while Tina eyed both of them sternly. "In the book I just read, the girl combed her hair a hundred strokes, morning and night. She had beautiful hair."

"That's fiction, dufus," Trevor barked at her. "Nobody would do that in real life!"

Tina blinked. "I would."

Kellie stopped to take a sip of coffee and grinned. She'd thought her daughter's hair had looked particularly shiny lately.

"You can't do things just because people do them in books," Trevor lectured her. "That's stupid."

Tina narrowed her eyes and stuck her chin out stubbornly. "It is not. If I had my way, I'd live in a book. Like this one," she said, holding up *Little Women* prominently. "Meg and Jo and Beth and Amy are poor, but they live next door to a boy with a rich grandfather, so they get to go to parties and have good food, and the old grandfather even gives Beth a piano."

Kellie, feeling as if her heart had just turned into a lump of lead, put Tina's lunch in front of her and made a solemn vow to herself to buy Swiss cheese and fancy bread next time she was at the supermarket. "If you two are finished with breakfast, rinse your dishes and get your stuff ready."

With his usual excess of energy, Trevor sprang from the table and ran to the sink with his cereal bowl, slopping milk on the floor. "You can't live in a book," he grumbled as a parting shot to Tina, then dashed off to get something from his room.

Kellie grabbed a sponge and mopped up behind him.

Tina, methodical and conscientious beyond any parent's wildest dreams, rinsed her bowl and spoon and stacked them in the appropriate spaces in the dishwasher. Then she washed her hands, dried them on the towel hanging on a cabinet doorknob, and went off to her closet of a room—no doubt to give her hair another hundred strokes before being forced from the house.

Kellie wondered momentarily if Trevor weren't the slightest bit correct in trying to instill some realism in his sister. Except weren't their lives real enough already? Ever since her accident yesterday, Kellie had engaged in some heavy escapism herself, dreaming of rich, handsome Riley P. Lombard, who had a secretary to deal with all the difficulties in life. *There won't be problems,* he'd assured her, and probably, in his life, there weren't. Was there anything in life a few million bucks couldn't make better?

She grinned in idle contemplation. Riley Lombard, who

thought nothing of doffing a five-hundred-dollar jacket and using it as an impromptu emergency blanket. She had calmed down considerably after she'd phoned her insurance company and picked up her rental car. Maybe it was fortuitous that a thoughtless rich guy had hit her, she'd decided. His insurance *was* good. And what the heck—looking at the guy had given her a few thrills.

Still, she'd tried not to call up his good looks—sort of Paul Newman from his *Hustler* period, only in a coat and tie. But despite her valiant efforts, those clear blue eyes of his had made star appearances in her dreams last night. Which was weird in itself. Most of her dreams this past year had been nightmares—of the sheriff-arriving-with-eviction-notice variety. Spending a night subconsciously unpeeling the designer layers off a tycoon was luxury indeed.

It was also dangerous. Waking up to her real life this morning had been decidedly more difficult. Not only was there no Paul Newman-modern millionaire hybrid in her life, there was the complete absence of all the fringe benefits that would have come with such a creature. If only she had a secretary who could perform her more unpleasant mommy duties—like explaining to Trevor for the thousandth time why he could not have a Sony Playstation. Or shutting off the Itty Bitty Book Light Tina hid under her covers till all hours every night. And cleaning up when Kellie felt too bone tired to handle laundry and dirty floors and dishes at the end of the day.

If only she had a man like Riley, whose blue eyes would twinkle at her every morning when she rolled over in bed. . . .

She gave herself a mental slap.

She'd had a husband, and he hadn't solved any problems. Instead, he'd created several fresh headaches per day, hocked half her furniture, and put her through enough mental anguish that, most of the time, she didn't care if she never went out with another man as long as she lived. Romance was a charade. And love . . . well, the last time she'd felt that emotion, she'd decided to marry a man who considered Adam Sandler movies intellectual stimulation. Riley Lombard was good-looking, heart-stoppingly so, but she hadn't struggled for a year just so she could hand all her hard-won independence on a silver platter to the first man with a handsome face who smashed into her car.

Not that he was asking her to, of course. And if she thought Riley had been the least bit flirtatious toward her, she was living in a richer fantasy world than Tina was.

Trevor streaked through the kitchen, hitting the screen door running and letting it slap shut behind him.

She hoisted her coffee cup for a last slurp and quickly shifted her focus back to Topic A: Riley of the dreamy blue eyes and sculpted bod and big bank account. No, he wasn't beating down her door. In fact, she remembered now with a puzzled frown, the man had behaved as if he couldn't get away from her fast enough. The rich, nervous type, as Alejandro had said. He'd probably been paranoid that she was going to chew him out or threaten to sic her lawyer on him.

As if she could afford one!

A few seconds later, Trevor was back from the driveway, looking surprisingly subdued. "Mom, I think you better take a look outside. There's something really weird out here. . . ."

Glad for the distraction, Kellie bit back a smile as she rinsed her mug. Trevor did this to her sometimes. He would fabricate some preposterous story and repeat it until Kellie finally gave it some credence, then howl with glee that she was so gullible.

"Don't tell me," Kellie said, playing along. "An elephant?"

"No, it's a—"

"A helicopter?"

He scowled, as if her patronizing tone were completely uncalled for. But that was always part of the game, too. "No, it's a Lexus SUV, fully loaded."

Ha! He was getting cagier in his old age, making the fantasy more realistic. Or it would have been realistic if a Lexus weren't as out of the bounds of their budget as sunken marble tubs and weekend flings in Tahiti. "What color?" she asked, playing along.

"Red."

Of course. Red was Trevor's favorite color.

"The sticker says Venetian pearl red."

Kellie slowly turned to him. *Venetian pearl red?* Where had Trevor picked up a phrase like that? She couldn't wait to hear what other responses he'd dreamed up. "What color's the upholstery?"

"It doesn't have a color," he responded quickly. "I mean, it's brown, like leather. In fact, I think it *is* leather." He came forward and handed her an envelope. "And I found this on the doorstep."

Eyeing it warily, Kellie opened the envelope, fully expecting a bug to crawl out. Instead, two keys spilled to the floor. She shrieked.

"Jeez, Mom, what is it?"

"Keys!" She picked them up and stared in wonder at her son. He'd been telling *the truth?*

"I bet they're to the Lexus," he said excitedly. "Let's go try them out!"

Kellie stumbled outside behind her son and gaped in stupefaction at the Venetian-pearl-red Lexus SUV parked behind the white Chevy rental car she'd picked up yesterday afternoon.

"Come look inside!" Trevor hopped up and down to peek in the driver-side window.

She pulled a piece of paper out of the envelope the

keys had come from. In tidy block print, someone had
penned a quick note on the car dealership stationary.

> *Dear Ms. Sumners: Please accept this vehicle as a
> token of my remorse for having ruined your day,
> and possibly your car. It's the least I can do, and
> it will provide you with an alternative means of
> transportation if your Toyota ever gets out of the
> shop. Sincerely, Riley C. Lombard.*

Kellie read the short letter five times through, her
astonishment growing with each perusal. *This* was what
the man considered "the least he could do?" A Lexus?
What would the most have been?

It seemed doubly strange that a man who couldn't be
convinced to wait for the cops to arrive at the scene of
an accident would take the trouble to go pick out an
automobile as an apology. Or maybe he'd just com-
manded his secretary to do it.

"Did Dad send it?" Trevor asked.

On a normal day, the absurd question might have made
her laugh. But this appeared to be shaping up into another
abnormal day, courtesy of Riley Lombard. Did the man
regard her as some sort of pathetic charity case?

Or maybe this was the modern millionaire's way of
hitting on women.

She turned resolutely and marched inside to grab her
purse and yell for Tina, who was dawdling as usual,
reluctant to give up her books and keyboard for a day of
mandatory fun. Although Tina had begged Kellie to send
them to the same camp Margaret Thurston attended, she'd
wearied of the place the moment she discovered she was
going to spend her summer the way she spent the rest of
the year—being pestered by annoying boys. "Tina, don't
be late!"

Kellie went back out and circled the new vehicle once in reluctant admiration.

"C'mon, Mom," Trevor said impatiently, "let's take our new wheels for a spin!"

She rummaged through her purse, hunting for the business card that Riley had given her yesterday. "That is not *ours,*" she said. "And no, your father didn't send it. It's from . . ." *A kook,* she thought as she searched for a suitable lie. "Well, the insurance company sent it over by mistake. I'm taking it back this morning."

"Can we drive it to camp, just this once?" Trevor's voice was a youthful whine.

"Yes, but only because I have to take it back." Then Riley P. Lombard could pony up more money for cab fare so she could pick up her rental at the house and get to work.

Tina trudged out the screen door and nearly dropped her Power Puff Girl book bag in surprise when she caught sight of the shiny new vehicle in their driveway. "What's *that?*" she asked, skipping forward. She saw Kellie opening the driver's door, and her face burst into a joyous grin. "Is it ours, is it really?"

In that moment, Kellie would have gladly strangled Riley Lombard. Her kids probably thought they had finally been freed from the curse of the rattletrap Toyota that she loved and clung to so desperately. Now another of their dreams would have to be shattered.

She tried to put a positive spin on the bad news. "It is for about twenty minutes, so get in, be careful not to get anything dirty, and enjoy the ride."

She unlocked the doors and was nearly knocked out by the scent of genuine leather. She stepped up and sank into the driver's seat, which felt more comfortable than most of the chairs in her house. Gentle light spilled in from the tinted moon roof. And when she turned the key in the ignition, the motor leapt effortlessly, almost soundlessly, to life and quickly settled into a quiet purr. Classical music issued from the state-of-the-art speaker system.

"Mahler, cool," Tina whispered from the back seat.

Riding shotgun, Trevor popped open the glove compartment and pulled out the owner's manual. "Cool— it's got a six-CD changer, Mom!" He began fiddling with the knobs for the climate control system. Perfectly chilled air immediately flowed noiselessly from vents—at her feet, on the dash, in the back seat. Kellie sighed, luxuriating in all that recycled oxygen. Air-conditioning in a car. It had been a while. . . .

For a dangerous moment, she actually considered accepting it. *Why not?* a little devil on her shoulder asked. *The man can obviously afford it. . . . He did wreck your car. . . .*

"Mom?" Trevor asked. "Mom, are you okay?"

Kellie swiped reflexively at her shoulder, then pretended to be adjusting the shoulder belt. She was *not* Riley Lombard's charity case. Besides, the last thing she needed now was to be indebted to some Lexus-spewing lunatic.

But when she swung onto the road, the little devil was back on her shoulder. Kellie felt as if she were at the helm of a parade float, trumpeting their good fortune to their neighbors. For once, Tina and Trevor weren't bickering. Her own nerves were calm, too, and maybe not by accident, she decided to glide her children to camp via an alternative route that happened to take them right past Margaret Thurston's house.

Chapter Three

"I've found the woman I'm going to marry," Jay announced.

"Congratulations." Riley had to work hard not to allow doubt to creep into his voice. Only last night Jay had been talking about Nancy. Could he have possibly have found *the one* in—Riley glanced at his watch—less than twelve hours? "What's the lucky girl's name?"

"Luanne."

"Are you sure she's the one?"

"How could I be wrong about something this important?"

He'd been wrong about fifty times before, but Riley didn't feel he should be reminding his friend of this over the phone. "I'm sorry. I guess I'm just a little surprised. Last night . . ."

"But last night I hadn't met Luanne. Didn't I tell you these book clubs are a bachelor's dream?"

Apparently. He laughed. "Why don't we go out for lunch soon and celebrate? You could bring Luanne along."

"Oh, no, I couldn't do that."

"Why not? I'd like to meet this woman who's swept you off your feet."

"Well, I haven't actually spoken to her yet."

Riley tapped his pencil against his desk calendar. "Then how can you tell that she's the one?"

"Believe me, I can tell. She's beautiful and smart. She's the most intelligent woman in my book club. She can talk circles around anybody . . . at least about Stendhal."

"Yeah, but do you really want a wife who yaks forever about *The Charterhouse of Parma?*"

There was a crackling silence at the other end of the phone. Finally, Jay said in a wounded tone, "I don't think sarcasm's called for, Riley, I really don't."

Riley had to remind himself that, although every foray into romance ended in disaster, Jay approached each new shaky relationship with a woman with wholehearted sincerity. "I'm sorry."

"What's gotten into you lately?" Jay asked him. "You seemed moody last night, too. Is it this woman?"

"No," Riley said quickly, lying.

"Or is it . . ." There was another silence. Then an apologetic sigh. "Bud, forgive me."

"For what?"

"Sometimes I get so carried away by my happiness, I forget all that you've been through."

Riley felt himself tense. "That's okay."

"Maybe it's time you got back into the swing of things," Jay suggested gingerly.

Riley was so panicked by the mere idea of "getting back into the swing," that he almost didn't hear the fracas coming from the lobby. Doreen, his extremely efficient administrative assistant, was adept at keeping hotheads at bay, but this time it sounded as if she was having a little trouble. He frowned.

"Riley?"

Riley yanked his attention back to Jay. "I don't know if I'm ready just yet, Jay." Or if he ever would be.

"Just the same, if you ever change your mind, I think I'm onto something with these book clubs. Take the nonfiction group, for instance—"

There was shouting now coming from the outer office, and a thump on the door.

"—it's a little more boring, I'd say, but there are still some nice women—"

The next moment, Kellie Sumners burst through the oak double doors leading in from Doreen's desk. She was wearing the same getup as yesterday, a red T-shirt with a cat logo above the breast pocket tucked into a pair of khakis.

Riley rocketed to his feet as Doreen tumbled after Kellie.

"I need to talk to you!" Kellie exclaimed.

"What's *that?*" Jay yelled into his ear.

"I'll call you right back, Jay," Riley said, hanging up.

"I'm so sorry!" Doreen said to Riley, her hands flurrying in front of her. Tall, and seemingly taller because her big red hair was coifed and sprayed to a peak some four inches above her actual scalp, Doreen was rarely bested by anyone. "I told her you *never* see anyone without an appointment. I've buzzed Security."

"Security?" Kellie asked in amazement, directing her question to Riley, not Doreen. Her lips turned up in a wry smirk. "Don't worry. I left my Uzi at home."

Riley chuckled uneasily. "It's all right, Doreen, you can call off the bloodhounds." Though, looking at the rather thunderous expression on Kellie's face, he gave the question of his security a second thought. What could she be so upset about?

He didn't have long to find out. As soon as Doreen marched out on her four-inch heels, Kellie dangled a set of keys in front of him accusingly.

He barely spared them a glance. He was too busy staring at Kellie. No sad eyes today—instead, they sparked with anger that went perfectly with the bright pink splotches in her cheeks. He realized suddenly that she hadn't been out of his mind for longer than five minutes at a stretch since he'd bumped into her yesterday.

"Just what did you think you were doing?" she demanded.

"When?"

"Don't play innocent with me," she huffed. "When you left a Lexus sitting in my drive, that's when!"

He tilted his head. "Apologizing?"

"Some apology!"

He clucked his tongue regretfully. "You would rather have a Cadillac, wouldn't you?"

She looked at him as if he were insane. "What? No. I only meant—"

"And technically, *I* didn't leave it," he interrupted calmly. "I paid a man from the dealership to drive it over." Riley gestured to the chair across from his desk. "Will you have a seat?"

She tapped her foot. "I'd rather stand."

"Some coffee?"

"No."

"Masseur?"

Her pink lips pursed unhappily. His efforts to soothe her obviously weren't working. "I won't be staying. I just wanted—" She stopped suddenly, then blinked. "Masseur?"

He nodded to the phone. "He runs the employee weight room on the thirteenth floor. I can call him if you like."

"No." She dropped the keys onto his desk. "I just wanted you to know that was a terrible, crazy thing to do."

Crazy he could see a case for. But terrible? "Pardon

me, but I wrecked your ancient car. Why was offering you something new such a terrible thing?''

She tossed her hands in the air as if he had just proven himself a few bricks shy of a load. "Because I can't accept it!"

He laughed. "Oh, well, if that's all, I can assure you—"

"*All?*" She collapsed into the previously spurned chair. "Do you have any idea what it's like to turn down something like that? A Lexus?"

He shrugged. "It functions the same as any other vehicle."

She gave him a disbelieving stare. "You don't get it, do you?"

"Frankly, no."

"Would you tell a homeless man that a suite at the Ritz is the same as a cot at the Salvation Army? That a meal at a five-star restaurant is the same as a Quarter Pounder? Do you realize that I just wasted fifteen minutes of a workday doing nothing but sitting in an idling, air-conditioned, soft leather cocoon, listening to Mahler and dreaming of *not* coming up here and giving you those keys?"

"Well, then, why—"

"Do you have any idea what it meant to my kids to step outside and see a shiny new vehicle in their driveway? Can you imagine how I feel having to take it away from them?"

"Well, then, why don't—"

Wait a minute. Riley shook his head. *Kids?*

He felt as if someone had just punched him in the gut, and he lowered himself into his chair again. "I didn't know you had children."

She frowned. "Why would you?"

No reason in the world, but now that he did know, his trepidation about Kellie Sumners increased tenfold. What was he thinking, sending her a car? Of course she wouldn't accept it! Of course she would come in person to return the keys! Of course he would have to see her again.

Maybe *that* was what he'd been thinking of, he thought, almost drowning in her brown eyes. Except that wasn't it at all. He'd really been trying to make amends. . . .

"What's the matter?" Kellie asked him.

"Nothing," he said, dismissing thoughts of kids and Kellie's eyes and his own subconscious motivations from his mind. "Actually, the solution to the problem isn't so difficult."

She tilted her head skeptically. "What do you suggest I do?"

He smiled. "Keep it."

She looked as if she might shoot out of her seat and start ranting again. "I can't do that!"

"Why not?" Riley gestured around the lavish office. It was paneled in walnut and furnished with American primitive antiques. Two Remingtons graced the walls. "It wouldn't hurt me if you did, I assure you. I make money for a living, mountains of it. It just keeps rolling in. The cost of a little automobile is practically nothing to me. It's no big deal."

"No big deal!" she sputtered. "No big deal to *you*, maybe."

"That's my point," he said logically. "You need a vehicle, I have enough money to give you one, and I *want* to give you one. It's simple."

She flopped against the seatback, looking exhausted. "It's clear you've never been hard up with children to raise."

Riley froze. "What makes you say that?"

"Because you would know that even if I had money enough to have a car like that, I couldn't have one."

"You couldn't?"

"No! Because even if I had that much money, I would

need it for more pressing things, like piano lessons for my daughter, and Little League baseball uniforms, and advertising for Copycat ... and that's not even mentioning mortgage payments, rent, and other nice amenities like food. Do you understand?''

Riley felt every bit as low as she wanted him to feel, and then some. She was saying that he was out of touch, pampered. ''I'm beginning to.''

Kellie Sumners had a complicated life. Didn't she say she was divorced? She was a single mom with two children, for heaven's sake; he must seem like a pest to her.

What had he been thinking?

Well, he knew. He'd been thinking of Kellie's eyes. He'd been thinking about that feeling he'd had, that flash of foresight that had threatened him almost as much as it had intrigued him. He wasn't like Jay, who absolutely yearned for marriage and family. It had taken Riley years to get used to being alone; now he wanted nothing more than to be left to rattle around in his house. If he ever got lonely, there were Nathaniel and Fayard to drive him crazy. That was enough for him.

So he supposed he'd been trying to toss money Kellie's way in hopes that he could ward off fate—appease the gods, as it were. He'd hoped that if he paid his debt to her, that would take care of the future, of the responsibility he felt for bumping into her. He'd thought, if the woman had any sense, she would count her blessings, take the vehicle, and that would be the end of the matter.

He should have known that nothing was that easy. Kellie appeared to have more scruples than sense.

''All right,'' he said, thinking the matter through. ''You don't want the car ...''

''I *want* it,'' Kellie corrected him matter-of-factly. ''I can't accept it.''

He nodded, shook his head, and steepled his fingers.

She had thrown him completely off balance. "Of course. I understand that."

"It's going to be very hard for the kids to get used to the Toyota again now," she said mournfully.

"How old are they?"

Stupid! This was more information he didn't need. Didn't want.

She smiled. "Tina's just nine, and Trevor's almost eleven."

He listened with a polite smile. When he looked down, however, his hands were in tense fists on the arms of his chair. Surely, surely, there had to be some way to trick fate into letting them go their separate ways. "Listen, I understand not wanting the Lexus," he conceded. "But isn't there something I can do . . . ?"

She hugged her oversized purse in her lap and leaned forward. "There is," she said, raising his hopes. "I would appreciate it if you'd give me enough money so I can call a cab and get home to pick up the loaner car I got last night."

His heart sank. Too easy. That would never assuage his conscience, or the fates. In a second, though, he brightened. "I can do better!" He reached for the phone.

Kellie began shaking her head and flapping her hands in front of her. "I don't want better, I just want—"

Riley spoke into his intercom. "Doreen, could you have Peter bring the limo around for Kellie Sumners, please?"

The hand flapping halted abruptly, and Kellie's face went slack. "Limo?"

"It's the company's car." Riley leaned back again, satisfied. Perfect! Kellie would go away pleased, and he could go about forgetting her.

Instantly, Doreen poked her red head through the door. With only the briefest of frowns flicked at Kellie, she announced, "The car's on its way, Riley, but don't forget you have that ten o'clock appointment downtown. Should I tell Peter to call a cab for you?''

Riley didn't have to look directly at Kellie to see the hand waving had started again. He sighed. He should have known nothing involving Kellie Sumners would be simple. "No, I'll drop Kellie off on the way." He would have taken his own car, but of course he'd taken it to the dealership this morning to have the dent repaired.

Ten minutes later, Peter was holding the door for them as they climbed into the limousine. Riley smiled warmly at the driver, who was an older man with red hair mixed with gray beneath his cap. "How's Barbara?" Riley asked him.

"Better now. She's walking again."

"Good!"

Kellie looked at Riley, clearly puzzled as they settled into the backseat. "His wife?"

Riley nodded. "She just had hip surgery."

She tilted her head. "You know his wife?"

"Oh, sure. I introduced them years ago. She was the dental hygienist at my dentist's office."

She sent him an odd look, then was distracted by her surroundings. In the next moments she couldn't stop testing or touching everything she saw. Vents were opened, the bar pulled out; CNBC appeared on a television screen. Riley laughed. He'd forgotten the car even had a TV.

Kellie looked at him, her eyes wide as she ran her hand across the control panel on the door. "I'm sorry. I'm behaving just like Trevor."

Trevor, he remembered, was her son. He leaned forward nervously. "Can I offer you a drink? Juice?"

"Do we have time?" Kellie looked much more eager to sample the beverages here than she had in his office.

"I think so." Riley popped open a can of apple juice, divided it between two glass goblets, and handed one to her.

"Cheers," she said, clinking her glass to his. He

smiled. "So what are you," she asked him, "an oil baron? A sheik?"

Riley almost spit up his juice. "Why do you ask?"

She gestured her crystal goblet around the roomy interior. "This doesn't exactly point to a wage-slave existence. I can only guess the Lombard Group traffics in gold doubloons or rock stars or something."

Riley tilted his head. "Close. It's an investment firm."

"So you're lucky in the stock market and in matchmaking."

He smiled. "You could say I know a good merger when I see one. I started out on my own, but business has been good in the past decade or so. There are now offices in Hong Kong and New York."

"And here," she said.

"Yes, this is where I started. I grew up here and . . ." He looked out at the city for a moment as they inched down Central Expressway. He knew Dallas like the back of his hand. Sometimes it seemed every street and building could spur a million memories. Not all of them good. Some of them terrible. And even though it would make more sense to be in New York, where the biggest office was, he couldn't leave here, couldn't force himself away from the place where he'd found love and success and heartbreak in equal measure. So he'd managed to formulate an existence that shut out all the things he couldn't bear. He had a gated house on a street he'd never walked down on foot, an office in an impersonal new glass building, and a host of people like Doreen, Peter, and Nathaniel to keep reality at bay.

He cast a sidelong glance at Kellie. Somehow, surely accidentally, she had battled her way through his line of defenses. How had she managed it?

He should never, never make his own copies.

She sighed, luxuriating in her buttery leather seat. "Must be nice."

He couldn't deny that. But still, with surprising frequency, he missed his other life with a fierceness that made him feel hollow with longing. That life had been messier, more loaded with the conflict of having to deal with loved ones. It was also vastly more fulfilling.

Kellie shot forward. "Hey! This is my street!" Her mouth opened in wonder as they swung through a neighborhood of modest square-looking houses. It was a post-war neighborhood, well kept but a little bit lonely during the day. Not a lot of housewives here. Kellie arched her brows at him. "How did your chauffeur know where I lived?"

"Doreen must have told him," Riley said. "She takes care of all of those things."

"But how . . ." Kellie's words died abruptly and she shrugged, laughing helplessly. "Never mind. Maybe it's better just to think rich people have magic at their fingertips that we mere middle-class mortals don't have."

When the car stopped at the appropriate house, Riley kept his gaze focused on Kellie. Maybe this would be the last time he saw her, he considered with equal parts hope and dread. Maybe now that he'd spoken to her, offered her a gift that she'd refused, and given her her first limo ride, that would be the end of it. He felt a little better already.

She handed him her half-drunk glass of juice. "Thanks a lot for the ride—and for the Lexus. You understand, don't you?"

He nodded, businesslike. "Of course."

She stared at him with those liquid brown eyes, and a rush of longing hit him like a tidal wave as their gazes locked and held. He would have given anything, paid any amount of money, to have been able to look away. But he couldn't. He felt as if the moment were stuck in time, and as those two stains of pink made a reappearance in Kellie's cheeks, he felt his own temperature rise a few degrees. Even though she'd opened all the air vents, he was suffocating.

"Well . . ." she said after an eternity. "Bye."

He nodded, and looked away. *Thank heavens*.

Except that the first thing his gaze caught was her house. A cute one-story brick house with a gravel driveway leading up to a carport. The front porch, shaded by a sprawling oak, had little pots of geraniums and impatiens stacked proudly on it, and an ivy wreath hung on the red-painted front door directly above the welcome mat. But in spite of Kellie's best efforts, signs of a messy life spilled forth—a single rollerblade next to a flowerpot, a basketball in the grass. Riley felt an itch to go pick the latter up, not to put it away, but to dribble, something he hadn't done in ages. Around the house's windows, tidy red shutters opened proudly on their hinges, like outstretched arms, beckoning him.

Riley swallowed, waiting for Kellie to let herself into her comfortable little home, where she was raising her family all by herself. Her two kids, Trevor and . . . what was the little girl's name?

He opened the bar again and reached into the drawer where he kept the Tagamet. His stomach was churning, and clenched tighter than a fist.

Finally, Kellie unlocked the door and waved them on, and the limo moved again, gliding past other little houses much like Kellie's. But they weren't all embedded in his brain the way hers now was. He flipped open his briefcase, turned on his Palm Pilot, and swallowed twice the normal dose of antacid tablets. He tried to forget, tried to think about business. The Nasdaq was up fifty points . . . bonds were holding strong. . . .

But his heart wasn't in it.

Oh, what was the use? Unhappily, he began typing words into his memo keeper. *Piano lessons, Little League uniforms, advertising . . .*

Chapter Four

Kellie never dreamed the day would dawn that she would again want to kiss her ex-husband, but as she showed Trevor the letter from U-Buy-All Uniforms and saw the look of joy mixed with relief on his face, she felt an undeniable wave of affection toward Rick. Somehow, her recalcitrant ex had come through with a fifty-dollar gift certificate to the store. They could go pick up Trevor's uniform just in the nick of time for the first big game Saturday.

"I wonder if Dad'll give me that Ken Griffey glove I asked him for, for my birthday," Trevor said, obviously seeing this gesture from his father as a good omen for future loot. "You think he'll remember?"

Kellie picked up the phone. "I'm about to call him right now, so you can drop another of your subtle hints." Trevor had been talking about that glove nonstop since spring. He hadn't wanted anything this badly since being sucked into the Power Ranger craze at the tender age of four. And he hadn't even mentioned the Sony Playstation in weeks.

Her foot performed an elaborate but private jig beneath

the counter as she listened to the line ringing on the other end. She didn't know exactly how it had happened, but all of a sudden the house seemed at peace—if not downright jubilant. Down the hall, Tina was playing an arrangement of "Ode to Joy" for the twentieth time this evening on her keyboard. Strange that Tina should be in such a good mood when today she'd had her last piano lesson for the summer with Miss Tibson. Kellie had hoped to come through with money for the summer, but that didn't appear to be possible. Most kids would be over the moon to be freed from formal piano lessons for the summer, though of course most kids didn't include Tina, the girl who never had to be told to practice. But as long as she was bucking up and practicing anyway, maybe things would all work out for the best. Perhaps, Kellie thought optimistically, Tina and Trevor might someday even look back upon this year as a real milestone in their lives. A time when they were tested but survived to become stronger and more self-sufficient.

Now who was full of Louisa May Alcott optimism?

" 'Lo?"

"Rick!" Kellie cried into the phone, all the gratefulness she felt gushing into her tone. "It's me, Kellie!"

He met her exuberant greeting with a long-suffering sigh. "What is it now?"

"I just had to call you, of course."

Trevor hopped up and down in front of her. "Can I talk to him now, Mom? Please? Please?"

Curses crackled over the line from Rick. "Kellie, for God's sake, will another two weeks kill you? Will it? Are you tellin' me you guys are starvin' out there or something?"

Her foot stopped dancing. "Starving?" She looked at the scattered remains of their egg salad and tomato soup dinner and frowned. What was he talking about? "Of course we're not starving. I was just calling to—"

"To nag me," he snapped. "Like you always do."

Trevor kept hopping and yelling "Pleeeaaase!" in supplication as Kellie tried to fathom Rick's surliness. After getting the letter, she'd expected him to be in as good a mood as she was.

"For Pete's sake, Kellie," Rick lectured, "are you always going to be calling me the minute I'm late? This is what caused all the trouble between us in the first place."

She couldn't let that bizarre claim pass. She turned away from her jumping, pleading child and said in a low voice, "Really? I thought what caused all the problems was your gambling and philandering."

He sighed. "There you go again, being all critical. Is this how it's gonna be now forever?"

She stared more closely at the gift certificate. For a moment she thought she'd dreamed the whole thing, but no, there it was. Fifty dollars in black and white. "Okay, Rick, so you didn't . . . ?"

"No, I didn't mail the child support yet, but I'm gonna. I had some bad luck over the weekend, but Starr promised to lend me the money once the club pays her."

Starr? Club? Kellie frowned. "Who's Starr?"

There was a pause. "Oh, uh, she's this woman I'm seeing—she's kind of a waitress. Not that it's any of your business!"

Kellie wound the phone cord tightly around her fingers. She didn't want to know about Starr. "So I guess you wouldn't know about this money from U-Buy-All Uniforms, would you?"

Trevor, still hopping, managed to yell into the mouthpiece. "Hi, Dad!"

Rick hesitated. "Uniforms? Huh?" Suddenly, it was as if he'd never heard of uniforms, Little League, or even baseball. "Have you gone crazy, Kellie?"

"That's a distinct possibility. Oh, well . . ."

"C'mon, Mom, let me talk to him," Trevor whined. "You always hog the phone talking about boring stuff."

Still confused, she mumbled, "Trevor wants to talk to you," into the phone, unwound her hand from the cord, and wandered away to pick at her half-eaten sandwich. If Rick hadn't sent it, how had a gift certificate to a uniform store suddenly arrived in the mail?

"Are you still coming back for my birthday?" Trevor asked his father. He listened impatiently and then broke in. "But you've just got to, Dad! You've been away forever, and we're having a big party and everything! And you're gonna get me that Ken Griffey glove, remember?"

No, it wasn't Rick, Kellie decided. She must have been deranged to think that he would be thoughtful enough to come up with such a surprise. She hoped there wasn't some anonymous donor—probably one of the other parents on the team—helping them out. That would be too mortifying. After all, she wasn't a pauper. She would have scrounged up fifty dollars somehow.

"Tina, Dad's on the phone!" Trevor's piercing yell probably could be heard all the way to Nevada without the aid of AT&T. "She's *practicing,*" he told his father in disgust. "She practices all the time. She's not normal."

The music abruptly stopped, and Tina practically toe-danced out of her room. Brother and sister wrestled with the phone for a moment before Trevor finally relented and let Tina speak to Rick.

"Hi, Daddy." Tina paused a moment while her father spoke to her, squinting in intense concentration as if the act of listening were an extra challenge when her ear was to a phone. Finally she broke in impatiently on whatever her father was saying. "Guess what? Miss Tibson's giving me lessons for free all summer long."

Kellie froze in surprise as Tina squinted again.

"Uh-huh. She said it was because I was such a good

pupil. She said she'd give her three best pupils their own recital next year, and I'm going to be one of them!''

When Trevor and Tina had signed off and hung up the phone, Kellie was still so stunned by what Tina had said that she barely managed to flag down her daughter as she skipped back down the hall toward her keyboard. ''Tina, Miss Tibson's giving you lessons for *free?*''

''Uh-huh.''

Kellie lurched for the phone again.

''You don't have to call her, Mom. Naturally I already thanked her on behalf of the entire Sumners family.'' Tina turned and hopped back to her room, back to Beethoven.

When Kellie reached her, Kay Tibson was adamant about giving Tina free lessons. ''I insist,'' she said. ''She's my best pupil.''

As kind as the woman was being, as appealing as the offer was, it just wasn't fair to Miss Tibson. Kellie's financial worries shouldn't become someone else's. ''But you can't give away your time for free,'' Kellie argued. ''It's just not good business sense.''

Kay laughed. ''If I had business sense, I wouldn't have majored in music in college.''

Kellie frowned. ''But there must be something I can do for you.''

''No, absolutely not.''

''My copy store would be happy to print whatever fliers you use for your lessons—for rounding up business, or recitals, or whatever . . .''

''I don't really need anything like that,'' she replied.

Kellie felt frustrated. ''What else can I offer you? Office supplies? Baked goods? My first-born child?''

Trevor looked up at her, alarmed.

''Oh . . . I was afraid you were going to make a big deal out of this,'' Kay said.

''But it *is* a big deal,'' Kellie replied. ''It's one of the nicest thing anyone's ever done for us.''

"Oh . . . gee."

"I don't know how I'll ever be able to thank you enough. If you could know what this means to Tina."

There was a heartfelt sigh at the other end of the phone. "Gosh, now you're making me feel guilty. See, this wasn't actually my doing."

Kellie shot a glance at the letter from the uniform company. "What do you mean?" But already she had a strong premonition of what Kay Tibson was going to say.

"Actually, Tina has a benefactor, but please don't ask me who it is because I'm pledged to absolute secrecy." Kay paused, then confessed, "I think it's sort of sweet. It's like what happened in that movie."

"Movie?" Kelly repeated.

"You know, that old Fred Astaire musical. *Daddy Long Legs.*"

"Oh, right." Kellie shifted and put a hand on her hip. With the possible exception of disaster epics and horror films, she wasn't accustomed to relating her own life to the silver screen. "This particular benefactor-spider wouldn't happened to be named Riley Lombard, would he?"

Kay tittered nervously. "My lips are sealed. I can't say a word more."

Not that she had to. Kellie hung up the phone and stumbled into the living room, where a rerun of Trevor's favorite show, *The Simpsons,* was about to come on.

She perched on one of their uncomfortable chairs. The living room had been the hardest hit, furniture-wise, from Rick's heavy gambling period. The couch, coffee table, end tables, lamps, and their one comfortable easy chair and ottoman had all been sold off, leaving them with only the two ancient unmatched chairs she and the kids had found at a garage sale. Kellie's mother had offered to buy a couch for them, but Kellie couldn't possibly take more from her mom. Linelle Taylor had lent Kellie some start-up money for her business and had generously helped when Kellie's sister, Rita, was going to nursing school. Even now Rita was still at home, living off her mother's hospitality while she paid off student loans and waited for her boyfriend of five years, Wendell, to pop the question. And given the fact that Wendell was the king of foot draggers, Kellie feared Rita would be living with their mother till both mother and daughter were old and gray.

As the credits popped up on the screen, Kellie drummed her fingers and considered Linelle some more. Could it be her own mother who was actually behind all this largesse, not Riley? Of course, Miss Tibson had chuckled nervously when she said Riley's name, but maybe that was only because Kellie had been so far off the mark.

She leapt out of her chair, rushed to the phone, and speed-dialed her mother, who answered on the first ring.

"Kellie! What's wrong?"

Her mother always assumed something was wrong, probably because there usually was. "Nothing, Mom. Everything's great—and I'll bet you know why!"

"Oh, honey!" her mother said joyfully. "You found somebody! I've been praying you would—I think it's wonderful!"

Kellie frowned. "Uh, actually, I'm not dating anybody."

There was a pregnant pause. "Oh . . . well don't tell me Rick's come back. After you let him go like you did, I didn't expect—"

"Mom! This has nothing to do with Rick or any man." Was she being purposefully obtuse? "I'm going to give you one hint. Listen carefully." She hummed a few bars of "Take Me out to the Ballgame" and waited for a reaction. All she got was a line silent with confusion.

"Kellie, you haven't been hitting the bottle, have you?"

"No, I—"

"I wouldn't be judgmental if you were, God knows."

"Mom, I just—"

"You're overworked and stressed. And I'll admit that after your father passed on, I would indulge in a little nightcap."

"Mom, I just wanted to—"

"Nothing to be ashamed of!"

Kellie slumped in defeat. Not only had she not unmasked her mother as the secret benefactor, she had somehow convinced her mother that she was a closet alcoholic. "I'd better go, Mom—*The Simpsons* is on."

Linelle *tsk*ed at her. "I really do think you would do better to get out once in a while rather than watching TV with the kids all the time. You'd know I'd love to baby-sit."

Meaning she loved to keep the kids up till all hours playing board games. Or as Trevor called them, *boring* games. "I'll foist them off on you soon, Mom, I promise."

"All right, hon. Bye now."

Kellie returned to her chair and stared unseeingly at the TV screen. During the commercial break, Trevor glanced over at her. "What's the matter, Mom? You look all freaked out."

That was putting it mildly. For the past week, Kellie had thought she'd done a pretty good job of banishing Riley Lombard from her thoughts. Since his limo had dropped her off at the house, she hadn't heard another peep from him. In fact, she'd put the whole Lexus incident from her mind, and now Riley was just a vaguely disarming memory. In odd moments, she'd remember how good-looking he was—and how completely beyond her reach. The truth was, they might reside in the same city, but considering his wealth and the circles he must run in, he might as well have been worlds away.

She'd been certain she'd heard the last of him. But who else could have done these things if it wasn't Rick and it wasn't her mother? She just didn't know many people with cash to spare.

She was still staring at the television in muzzy confusion when suddenly the Copycat logo appeared, accompanied by a little rumba beat. Both Kellie and Trevor leaned forward, as if magnetized, and then jumped when the little cat came to life and started dancing around the screen. As they blinked in astonishment, a narrator announced all the great deals to be had at Copycat, including personalized calendars and half-off copies for orders over a thousand. At the end of the segment, a picture of the building itself flashed on the screen, and the little cat danced up to it and flashed a show-stopping grin.

Trevor fell back in his chair, so blown away that he didn't even care when Bart Simpson came on screen again. "Whoa! That was so wicked!" he cried, which Kellie translated as meaning that he actually liked the commercial. "Awesome! Did you do that yourself?" he asked, disbelief loud and clear in his tone.

She could hardly speak, she was still so flabbergasted. "No, I didn't. I don't know who—"

But that was a lie. She *did* know who—but she was still having a hard time wrapping her mind around that fact. A commercial was an elaborate way to pay her back for wrecking her car. But why else would he be doing all these things for them?

Trevor grinned. "I know!"

She looked up at him. "You do?"

"Dad! It's been Dad doing all this neat stuff for us."

"You heard me talking to your father, Trevor. He didn't know anything about all this."

"He just doesn't want us to know 'cause he's out in Nevada and can't be with us. But he's doing it because he doesn't want us to forget him."

If there was ever a course in wishful thinking, her son would get an A-plus. "I'm not sure about that . . ."

His brows knit together accusingly. "You never want to think anything good about Dad!"

She sent him a level stare. "Come on, be fair. Do I ever criticize Rick?"

"No," he grumbled, "but you're never really nice to him, either. If you were really nice to him, maybe he'd come back. I bet he could get construction work in Dallas just as easy as he can in Nevada."

Kellie doubted construction work was the real reason Rick had moved across the country after the divorce. Las Vegas—and girls named Starr who were sort of waitresses—was probably a bigger draw than employment.

She jumped off her chair and marched back to the kitchen. Having an argument with her son over Rick made her all the more angry at Riley Lombard. Why did he keep butting into her life? *What was his deal?* She felt torn between slavish gratitude and indignant anger, but right now anger was winning out. What did he see her as, one of the hundred neediest cases? She'd worked damned hard over the past year to make sure she and her family wouldn't be dependent on anyone.

She flopped open the massive Dallas phone directory and let her fingers do the walking through the Ls. Riley was there, but only his name was listed. No phone number, no street address. Naturally.

Donald Trump probably never listed his number, either.

She dropped down onto a kitchen stool and buried her head in her hands. She didn't know what she was going to say to Riley about all of this anyway. He certainly couldn't take back a commercial that had just aired all over the city, and yanking lessons and uniforms away from Tina and Trevor at this point would be tantamount to torturing them. So what in heaven's name was she going to do?

The commercial brought in a blizzard of orders for Copycat. In fact, they had more business in a few hours than they'd received in the weeks since they'd been open. What was most promising, though, was that their biggest uptick in trade came from people wanting a high volume of copies made (high enough that they didn't want to tie up their own Xerox machines). Potential return customers. Kellie and Alejandro took in all the orders greedily, but by noon it was beginning to dawn on them that they had a major problem on their hands. The store now had so many rush orders that they would have difficulty filling them all in time. Someone had to be available to help the walk-in trade. All this new business would be counter-productive if their first-time customers went away disgruntled.

"I could call one of my girlfriends," Alejandro offered. Kellie raised an eyebrow at him, and he shrugged sheepishly. "Well, she's *really* my girlfriend. The rest are just friend friends."

"I see. They're on hold."

He grinned. "Sort of."

Kellie debated the wisdom of having Alejandro working with his girlfriend. Wouldn't all that young love be distracting? But clearly, they needed aid. Quickly.

She was just about to give His Studliness the go-ahead to start contacting his harem when a thin young woman, aged twenty, tops, in a wisp of a dress, came through the door. Kellie could practically hear Alejandro panting as the girl swished her long, fine red hair over her shoulder, squared her shoulders so that her breasts pushed a little more tightly against her top, and made her way to the counter. "I'm Lana," she announced.

Lana, she pronounced it. As in Turner.

Kellie didn't want to be impolite, but the girl seemed a little unbalanced. She acted as if Kellie should know her. "Is there something we can do for you?"

"I'm the temp," she explained.

Of course this made nothing clearer. Kellie and Alejandro exchanged befuddled glances.

"Temp?" Kellie asked Lana. "I didn't send for a temp."

The girl bit her lower lip uncomfortably. "I've been paid to work here for the next week."

This time Kellie didn't have to wrack her brain to figure out who had arranged this windfall. "This is the limit!" she exclaimed to no one in particular. Nevertheless, poor Lana recoiled as if Kellie had walloped her. "I'm sorry, Lana," she said, "this has nothing to do with you. It's someone else I have a bone to pick with. Do you know your way around a Xerox machine?"

She nodded. "Oh, sure! I can make copies, file, and type like a house afire!"

Kellie crossed her arms. She certainly looked like a girl who could set a house afire.

"Incredible!" Alejandro proclaimed enthusiastically. But his gaze, which was locked on her calves, said that he was interested more in her measurements than in her words per minute.

Wonderful, Kellie thought. Her calm, orderly workplace was being turned into *The Young and the Restless.*

She cleared her throat to catch Alejandro's attention. Not an easy task. When he finally, reluctantly, swung his gaze her way, she said, "I might be gone a while, but when I get back, you can take an extra long lunch break. I for one am taking a punch-Riley-Lombard-in-the-nose break."

Alejandro laughed, apparently snapping out of his

erotic funk. Then he warned, "Don't be too hard on the
guy. Remember, we both have loans to pay off."

His practical words knocked some, but by no means
all, of the wind out of her sails as she charged out the
door.

This time, Riley was ready for her. "I deny everything," he stated flatly as Kellie barreled into his office
spewing accusations, while Doreen again chased after
her.

Riley told a red-faced, apologetic Doreen that everything was all right and that she could go.

Kellie stood rigid in front of his desk. "I bet you've
never even heard of U-Buy-All Uniforms."

"Nope."

"Or Kay Tibson?"

Riley crossed his arms. "That name doesn't ring a
bell."

Kellie looked hot. "I don't believe you. Besides, the
piano teacher practically fainted when I said your name,
so I almost have proof."

"Ah," he said, wagging a finger at her sagely.
"*Almost.*"

"And I suppose you never watch *The Simpsons*,
either."

This one caught Riley by surprise. "What are you
talking about?"

She crossed her arms. "I'm talking about the ad that
ran last night, during *The Simpsons* and God knows when
else, for Copycat."

Riley smiled. He was glad to know that had worked
out so well. He'd hired the best agency in town to take
care of the thirty-second spot, and had approved the little
cartoon himself at the beginning of the week. He'd had
no idea they'd be able to get them on local television

that quickly, however, so he was delighted with her news. "Did you like the ad?"

"It was great!" she yelled. "My business has already surpassed my five-year plan. I'm going to have to hire on new people. Which reminds me, you've probably never seen a redheaded siren named Lana the temp, either."

Riley shook his head, holding back a laugh.

"It's not funny! My business now feels like hormone heaven." She let out a little howl of frustration and sank into a chair. "Look, I know that somehow this is all my fault . . ."

"*Your* fault?" he asked.

Kellie looked chagrined. "Yes, well, if you have to know, I *wanted* all this to happen. The day after I met you—after the accident—and you told me about who you were and how much money you had, and about your secretary who did everything for you, I stood in my kitchen and wished for just this sort of thing. I wondered what it would be like to have someone to take care of problems for me."

"Well then?"

Her dark eyes glittered. "So now I know how it feels and I've had enough! It's driving me crazy. Doesn't this genie have an off button?"

"Why would you want to pull the plug on something that's helping you?" he asked, genuinely curious. He couldn't imagine, for instance, doing without Doreen. Or Nathaniel. If someone switched off Nathaniel, he would be lost.

"Because ever since my divorce I've been on my own. It's been the crappiest, most exhausting, exhilarating year of my life, but at least I've learned to do everything for myself and for my kids alone. It gives me pleasure to be independent, and I want my kids to see that through hard work, good things happen. But over time, not immediately. You can't just wish upon a star like in fairy tales."

"But you did, and apparently it worked."

She fixed her beautiful eyes on him entreatingly. "Listen, I appreciate all you've done for me, I really do. I can't give any of it back because ... well, because it's done now, and Trevor and Tina are so excited by their good fortune that I can't find it in my heart to take anything from them. And the ad was a wonderful, incredible thing for anyone to do."

"Good." Riley was pleased. Everything had worked out just as he'd wanted it to—except that Kellie was sitting in his office chair again.

"But honestly, Riley," she said, "I've had car accidents before. Do you know what usually happens?" She didn't wait for him to answer. "The two parties exchange insurance information."

"We did that," he said.

"Yes, and that would have been fine. Plenty. Enough. You don't have to feel guilt, or remorse, or obligation. I'm forgiving you, do you understand? Here and now, I formally absolve you of any more responsibility toward me and mine." To emphasize her words, she made a semi-official hand gesture that looked as if it might have originated from a high jungle priest in an old Tarzan movie.

"You've done some incredibly wonderful things for us," she finished, "but now I assure you that my kids and my business will thrive without you. Once Lana finishes out her week, I assume that will be it. Done. *Finito.*"

Riley wanted to assure her it was. He wanted to, but he couldn't. Because after all she had said, she never mentioned whether *she* would thrive. And how, given the information he had, was he going to be able to go day to day for the rest of his life not knowing how she was, or what she was up to?

He sat down again, trying to think it all through.

"Is something wrong?" she asked.

"Well . . ." He wasn't sure if he could even begin to tell her the truth. She was such a practical, two-feet-on-the-ground type.

Suddenly, her hand clapped across her mouth and she looked at him through wide, luminous dark eyes. "Omigod! I think I know what this is all about!"

"You *do?*"

"About you . . . and me." She swallowed, and her eyes were as round as saucers. "Isn't it?"

He straightened, startled. "Yes, it is."

She frowned, then stumbled on. "Maybe I should have guessed at something when you sent the Lexus. And I did, for a moment, but I dismissed it. It was such a strange gift—not at all like the normal flowers or chocolates . . ."

Flowers? Chocolates?

She squinted, as if trying to puzzle through her memories for more clues. "Your note, I must say, wasn't of a very personal nature, either—"

"Kellie, wait," he said, stopping her. "I don't know what you're talking about."

She blinked. "I-I just thought that maybe all of this was leading up to your, you know, asking me out. On a date." Dark eyes watched him doubtfully for a moment. "Am I right?"

Riley squirmed uncomfortably. "No."

"Oh!" Now she looked insulted.

"I should have been more upfront with you right from the very beginning," he said. He took a deep breath. "You see, I didn't want you to thank me."

"You didn't?"

"No. In fact I didn't really want to see you again."

She crossed her arms. "I see."

But obviously she didn't. How could she? He was screwing this up royally. "The truth is, I never counted on your pride, that you would have such a hard time accepting a little help, which I felt obliged to give you. Especially since I discovered you had children, which of course made the whole situation that much more complicated and difficult."

"Whoa, whoa, whoa! What have my kids got to do with anything?" She shook her head. "Are you saying this wasn't some elaborate way to ask me out—that in fact it was a way to try to pay me off and get rid of me?"

"No!" He sighed. "That is, I wouldn't say *get rid of you,* exactly."

She looked mortified.

"Not that I wouldn't *want* to ask you out on a date," he added quickly. "What man in his right mind wouldn't? It's just that I can't . . ."

She tilted forward. ". . . Can't?"

"I don't socialize much anymore."

She shot out of her chair. "Me, neither!" she exclaimed, pacing the carpet in front of him. "That's why this is all so upsetting to me!"

"But I—"

"I'm beyond all that," she proclaimed, interrupting him. Her pride was on overdrive. "I'm a mother of two kids, and I've got a business that's still in the diaper stage. I only mentioned dating at all because I was confused and thought that *you*—"

Riley felt so nervous watching her that he had to stand and cross around the desk. "I don't go out on dates."

"Me, neither."

"I haven't dated anyone in two years," he confessed.

"Eleven years, for me," she said, topping him. "That's when my ex-husband and I married."

"I tried once," he went on, "but it didn't work out."

She glanced up at him and finally stopped her pacing. "I couldn't even think of trying. Life is too hectic . . ."

He put his hands on her shoulders—her surprisingly delicate shoulders; he could feel her collarbones beneath her T-shirt. For a moment, he willed them both to calm down and take deep breaths. But it seemed, as he looked down into Kellie's dark eyes, that he himself had trouble taking in even a single, shallow breath. Maybe because this close up the air was thick with her perfume—jasmine, a sweet fragrance, so at odds with the bustling, all-business facade she presented to the world. And maybe because as much as he wanted to breathe, he wanted to bend down and kiss her. He could almost feel how warm and soft her lips would be against his.

But of course he didn't kiss her. He couldn't. "If you knew all that had happened to me, you would know why I can't ask you out, tempting as that might be." He dropped his hands from her arms. "If you knew how easily I've made all this money, you'd understand why I care nothing about giving it away, especially to you."

She tossed her hands in the air in frustration. "Why *especially* to me? You barely know me."

Only her confusion could have brought it out of him. This wasn't something he wanted the world to know. Even his closest friends didn't know, and when he'd told his mother years ago over Sunday dinner while he was visiting her in Florida, with her usual blunt honesty she had lovingly pronounced him peculiar and told him to pass the mashed potatoes.

"I can't ask you out because I know something about you and me," he said.

"Know something?" She tilted her head and looked at him doubtfully. "What could you possibly know?"

He gulped and answered, "That we're going to be married."

For a moment, she said nothing, but stared at him, her

wide brown eyes blinking as she absorbed his words. Then she looked worried, as if she feared any loud noises would set him off. Finally she laughed. ''Oh, we are? And how do you know this?''

Riley finally took that deep breath. Here went nothing . . . and everything.

''Because I'm psychic.''

Chapter Five

For a moment, Kellie could only stand, mouth agape, wordless, stunned.

Then, slowly, certain thoughts began to dawn on her. First, this man was far nuttier than she'd given him credit for—and she'd already been very liberal in her assessment of him as an oddball. She'd considered him plenty strange back when he was just giving her hundred-dollar bills and luxury vehicles. Now he had tipped the scales toward kookdom. She'd always assumed the age of eccentric millionaires was past, if indeed it had ever existed outside motion picture houses and the Broadway stage, but Riley Lombard apparently was bent on taking the musty old tradition out of mothballs and giving it a new-age twist.

Yet what shocked her most was that he had somehow decided to focus all his bizarre manic altruism on *her*. Kellie had always led the most normal life—well, at least she'd made all the normal mistakes. Dropped out of college after a semester. Married a good-looking louse. Had kids before she had sense. How had things suddenly turned so bizarre? Having run-ins with rich oddballs was not in her usual frame of reference. If anything, she'd assumed that if any notoriety were to come her way, it would be through her children. She could imagine Tina, for instance, winning the Van Cliburn piano competition, and herself, the proud mother, beaming behind her on the evening news. And Trevor . . . well, she could imagine him landing them all on Jerry Springer someday.

So maybe this was the oddest revelation of all. Maybe Trevor wasn't going to put them in the harsh glare of klieg lights and public shame. Maybe she was. The shout caption across the bottom of the screen could be, *My mother is a magnet for weirdos!*

Or at least one specific weirdo. Mr. I-Am-Your-Destiny.

"Kellie . . ."

Just as he stepped toward her, she stumbled backward, lifting her hands as if to create an invisible shield between them. Maybe if Mr. Wizard here believed in psychic phenomena, he would respect her mental boundaries.

And, in fact, her reaction did seem to stop him. He cocked his head, peering at her with a rueful smile. "You don't believe me."

She held back a shriek of near-hysterical laughter. "Believe you? I came closer to believing my son the morning he told me there was a Lexus parked in our drive!"

"And yet that *was* true."

Right. But there was a big difference between a car, which after all was a tangible, earthly, if overly expensive item, and the embrace of psychic mumbo jumbo. Psychic! The very idea would have made her double over with laughter if Riley hadn't been standing there looking downcast. "I'm sorry, Mr. Lombard—"

"Riley."

Nut. "I'm sorry, but I'm not a . . . believer. I don't buy

into the paranormal—witches, UFOs, psychics . . .any of it. In fact, I think it's all a scam.''

He folded his arms across his very handsome chest. ''I'm not trying to sell anything, Kellie.''

Now how could a man be so off-putting and strange and yet so attractive at the same time? Just the way he said her name sounded intimate. His deep drawl sent a little shiver through her. Or maybe that was part of his . . . whatever he was up to. ''I'm not sure what you're trying to do, frankly, except wig me out. I don't know what your little crystal ball of a brain has told you about me, but I assure you, it's false.''

''There's no crystal ball. It's just a flash I get some-times.''

''A flash? As in—poof!—we're going to be married?''

''Well . . . there were certain details.''

She crossed her arms. ''Such as?''

He cleared his throat, and suddenly a dead-serious expression came over his face. ''You were wearing white. Blinding white. A wedding dress. And your hand was held up, and a band of gold was being slipped onto your ring finger.''

''You were doing the slipping?''

''I assume so.''

Kellie hitched her purse on her shoulder and chewed this over. But it was ridiculous! The man had some sort of weird hallucination—it could have been heat stroke or something. ''How many times has this little flash— the one concerning you and me and the wedding—hit you?''

''Just once.''

''When?''

''The first time we met.''

She rolled her eyes. ''Great! I got a bonk on the head and *you* started seeing things! Are you sure the glare from the Xerox didn't affect your brain?''

"Believe me. I've had these flashes before. They're usually pretty reliable."

If looks could be trusted, he wasn't joking. In fact, he didn't appear very happy about this alleged gift of his at all. His brilliant blue eyes didn't have their usual sparkle, and the dull resignation in his expression told her that he saw his psychic powers as something less than a blessing.

"You mean, something you saw actually came to pass?"

He nodded. "Several things."

"Such as?"

"A car accident."

She frowned, still grasping for reason. "But there are a ton of car accidents in the world."

He sighed. "This was very specific. Horrifying, actually. I saw rain, and an eighteen-wheeler losing control. It jackknifed, then slid across the median into oncoming traffic."

His voice was very persuasive. She needed to be on guard. Because, actually, even accidents of the kind he described weren't all that rare, were they? Eighteen-wheelers hydroplaning and jackknifing? That probably happened a lot.

And yet his tone was so believable. Or maybe it was his surroundings that seemed to give him authority. She looked away, staring at his office. The old, battered furniture that looked as if it cost a mint and impressive art on the walls, carefully lit to let a viewer know it was the real thing. Of course he had all the latest computer equipment. One notebook screen on his desk appeared to be a virtual stock ticker, striped red and green and constantly blinking. The man had made a fortune in the stock market ... which was practically gambling ... and now he claimed he was a psychic?

She practically slapped her hand upside her head, suddenly getting it. "Oh, I see! Is this some kind of advertising? The broker who can see the future? You said you had a feel for mergers. When you're not imagining wedding ceremonies, are you getting mental feed on bonds and pork bellies?''

He didn't laugh. ''It hasn't hurt, I'll admit it. To you. But Kellie, this isn't something I advertise. I don't have an urge to start up an eight-hundred-number hotline. In fact, you're only one of two people I've ever told about my . . . problem.''

Some problem. A gift that made him rich!

But of course it hadn't. It couldn't have, because Kellie just did not believe in *the gift* or any of this nonsense. The man had simply had a lot of luck and was probably convinced now that he was special. Like Roman Emperors who thought the gods had blessed them, when really they were just born at the right time to the right people. She was surprised he wasn't trumpeting this news all over the land, though. There were enough gullible fools in the world to turn him into a millionaire.

Which, of course, he already was. . . .

''I'm the *only* person you've told?''

''Besides my mother.''

''And what did she say?''

The faintest of blushes appeared in his fabulously tanned cheeks. ''She told me I was full of hooey.''

At least his whole family wasn't crackers. ''Look, I'm not sure why you're telling me all this. Or why you even zeroed in on me in the first place.''

''The vision.''

''Oh, right.'' She winced. ''Well before you get carried away with your delusions of white lace and wedding bells, let me assure you that you're in no danger. I've been married. I have no burning desire to date again, much less marry again.'' *Especially to a man tuned into Martian command central,* she added silently.

''Me, neither,'' he said.

She raised a brow. "You were married before?"

He nodded.

She crossed her arms. "You mean there was a woman who was able to walk away from all this magic you possess?"

His expression remained implacable, and his voice betrayed no emotion. "My wife died."

If she could have, she would have sunk right through the plush carpeted floor. Her arms fell to her sides, noodle-limp, and her skin burned. She was probably glowing like a supernova. She looked around the room again—anything to avoid those harsh, blue eyes staring at her so stonily.

Why couldn't she keep her mouth shut? "I'm so sorry."

As if he couldn't stand to linger over the subject one minute longer than was necessary, he said quickly, "Like you, I have no desire to marry again. But perhaps for different reasons. We were very happy."

She tilted her head, trying a little harder to understand this man who so unexpectedly had barged into her life, handing out much needed gifts and then assuring her that he wanted nothing to do with her. Was he telling the truth? Could she trust him?

"It's not that I have anything against marriage," she attempted to explain. "It's just that women tend not to act rationally when it comes to men. Not that I have anything against *men*, mind you—I mean, I'm not—"

He smiled, a glint back in his eye again. "I didn't for a minute think you were."

"I'm babbling, right?" She sighed. "Frankly, this whole psychic business makes me uncomfortable."

"It makes me uncomfortable as well. That's the problem."

Her rational mind scrambled to make sense of all this, to put some reasonable label on what he'd seen that day he met her. "But maybe it wasn't you and me that you were thinking of. I mean, maybe you had a premonition of a wedding. It could have been anybody's. Your sister's, maybe."

"I don't have a sister."

"Oh." So much for that theory.

"But you're right," he said, helping her out at last. "Perhaps it had nothing whatever to do with you and me."

She frowned. He didn't sound at all convinced and now neither was she; her brain felt scrambled. What was going on here? Was just standing in the same room as this guy confounding her good sense?

His blue eyes glinted at her, and for a moment she half thought the man might not be psychic, but possessed of some mesmerizing powers. A love hypnotist. Because even she—sober, reasonable, realistic Kellie Sumners— felt a little weak in the knees and flustered when she was staring into those eyes of his. It was almost as if he had some sort of pull over her.

But that was crazy! Impossible!

She straightened to her full five-foot-two and planted her feet firmly on the carpet. "Listen. There's a simple test to tell if this is all nonsense, which of course I'm sure it is."

"And that is?"

"Leave me alone."

He smiled until that dimple of his made an appearance. "You think it's that simple?"

"Well, frankly, you've got to do a better job of it than you have been. No more gifts or tokens of your wish never to see me again."

"Just like that," he said.

She nodded. He made it sound as if it were going to be next to impossible, when really what could be easier? "Dallas is a huge city. We should be able to coexist here without bumping into each other, especially given the differences in our circumstances.''

"We should," he agreed. But still he made it sound doubtful. "If destiny isn't conspiring against us."

She jutted her chin stubbornly. "I don't believe in destiny."

He said nothing.

She looked at him suspiciously. "You don't think my plan will work, do you?"

"No."

"But think of it this way, just for the sake of argument. Had you ever seen me before two weeks ago?"

"No."

"And I had certainly never heard of you, while even the cop who filled out our traffic report seemed to know who you were. If destiny was so strong, wouldn't we have had some knowledge of each other before now?"

"Maybe, maybe not."

"That's a wishy-washy way of saying you don't know," Kellie shot back. "Because you can't know. Because there's no such thing as fate, and this vision you had was just a fluke, a trick of the Xerox machine. I remember that machine blinking like mad. The light . . . then the accident . . . the heat of the afternoon . . . it probably all just went to your brain."

"I hope you're right."

She looked at him distrustfully. She still wasn't certain whether to be relieved or offended when he assured her that their combined destiny was not his wish. This was all so screwy that she couldn't make heads or tails of any of it. "Anyway . . . you'll agree not to do anything more for me?"

"All right, if you insist."

"Shake on it?"

She held out her hand to seal the deal, and when he clasped his over hers, she felt suddenly quivery, as if there were a weird pulse traveling from his hand to hers. Heat pooled at the pit of her stomach, and when his gaze caught hers, her spine seemed to turn to Jell-O. Spooked, she tugged her hand free.

"That's that, then." Her voice croaked like a fifteen-year-old boy's.

"Okay. See you around."

"No, you won't!" she retorted, losing patience. "That's the whole point!"

"That's right. What should I say then? *Au revoir?*" A laugh escaped him. "No, definitely not." He lifted a finger, thinking, then smiled. "I've got it. Have a nice life."

She glowered at him. He definitely wasn't approaching their problem with the appropriate solemnity. "I guess that will do," she admitted at last. "Have a nice life yourself, Riley."

"At least you called me Riley. Now we're getting somewhere."

"No, now we're getting nowhere, because I'm leaving." She began backing out. "I won't see you again."

"Not if you're right, no."

But his tone, and the irresistible dimpled grin, left little doubt that he thought she was wrong.

"So . . . good-bye."

"Bye," he said.

When she finally backed against the colossal double doors that led out to his waiting room, she felt relieved. Turning, she pushed through them and sped toward the elevator as if she were running toward sanity.

But somehow, when she got back down to the lobby of the building, she couldn't bring herself to go straight back to work, where Lana would be a vivid reminder of Riley. Xerox machines were also a reminder of Riley. Heck, in her present state of mind it didn't take much. She was still too confused.

Her destiny? An incredibly handsome—yet obviously mentally unhinged—millionaire? It was just too ludicrous.

Her heart felt fluttery, unstable. She decided to call on the one person who was more mired in strange man problems than herself. What she needed was a good old-fashioned gabfest with her sister.

"I finally spoke to her."

"Who?"

Jay rolled his eyes. "Earth to Riley! I'm talking about Luanne, the love of my life. Remember?"

Riley pointed to his plate. "Would you like a rib?" After Kellie's departure, Riley had felt ravenous, so he was glad he'd agreed to meet Jay for lunch. He'd ordered the biggest heap of food available in order to sate the hunger burning in him.

Though, to be honest, he doubted the food would do it.

Jay made a face as he looked at the heaping pile of greasy meat. "No, thanks." Wiggie's Rib House was one of Riley's favorite haunts, but Jay usually opted for a cup of coffee and a Tums chewable. "I had my lunch at the soup kitchen."

The Wednesday soup kitchen was part of Jay's rigorous volunteer regime. No one could ever accuse his friend of being a heartless corporate villain. Jay had dedicated his life to turning his family's oil billions into good works. And to trying to find a wife, of course.

"Luanne's agreed to come to my nonfiction book club with me."

"Can't you think of better things to do with this woman than read?"

His friend pulled a disapproving grimace. "It's not just

reading, it's discussion. The exchange of ideas. I don't want a wife just as window decoration, you know.''

Riley took a swig of iced tea. ''That's broad-minded of you.''

Jay nodded, but then he slumped against the wooden bench, looking vaguely depressed. ''Also, I thought if I asked her to join another book group, she'd be more likely to accept than if I just asked her out for a date.''

''Why would you think that?''

''Because I asked her out for a drink and she told me she had to get home to catch the lottery numbers.''

''Maybe she was telling the truth.''

''They print them in the paper the next day, Riley.'' He let out a lovesick sigh. ''I don't get it. Why am I having such a hard time? I'm everything a woman could want, right?''

''Of course—including modest.''

''Okay, maybe I'm not Tom Cruise.''

No, he was Don Knotts. ''Looks aren't everything.''

''No kidding!'' Jay leaned forward and drummed his fingers in agitation. ''Get this. I read somewhere that Ernest Borgnine has been married five times. Five times!''

''Yeah, but he's Ernest Borgnine.''

Jay tossed up his hands. ''That's what I'm saying!''

''I mean it's not a fair comparison,'' Riley explained. ''He's got movie-star status working for him.'' He frowned thoughtfully before grabbing a rib. ''Plus, wasn't he married to Ethel Merman?''

''I don't know. Why?''

''Would *you* want to be married to Ethel Merman?''

''That's not the point,'' Jay said.

Riley laughed. ''I've lost track. What exactly is the point?''

''The point is, if Ernest Borgnine can convince five separate women to say 'I do,' why can't I manage to coerce one measly female to the altar? I've got brains, and as for money, heck, the stuff practically pours out of my pockets. That's what amazes me. Most men in my position would have to worry about women wanting to take advantage of them. But I haven't even been lucky enough to be the target of a sleazy gold digger yet.''

"Just wait," Riley said reassuringly. "It could still happen."

"Well, it had better happen quick. I'm thirty-six! My youth is fading."

"Maybe Luanne will turn out to be the one."

"I hope so." Jay let out a ragged, impatient breath. "If you could see her, Riley. She's beautiful."

"But you love her for her mind," Riley reminded him.

"Of course."

Riley chuckled. "You know, Jay, you're so good at seeing the best in people, maybe you should work on being a little more discerning."

"I am discerning," Jay said defensively.

"Critical, then."

"What's to criticize?"

"Take . . . what was her name? The one who borrowed your Cadillac convertible overnight that time?"

Jay crossed his arms. "Linda. You *always* bring her up! That was years ago."

"But you never would admit that it was mighty suspicious that after she returned the car you found a strange pair of Fruit-of-the-Loom boxers in the back seat."

"Linda *explained* that."

Riley guffawed into his napkin.

"She *could* have been dusting with them back there," Jay said. "That car was neat as a pin when she returned it."

"Yeah, except for the size thirty-six men's underwear, wedged in the backseat armrest."

"All right," Jay admitted. "Maybe I am apt to give a woman the benefit of the doubt. But that's all the more reason why I'm such good husband material. I'm very forgiving of people's little faults.''

"Like infidelity?"

"I just happen to see the good in people. Is that so bad? A person with my romantic luck needs all the options he can get. I bet I could make myself fall in love with the next woman who comes through that door." He waited. "There! Two women coming in. Both beautiful."

Curious, Riley was about to swing around when Jay stopped him by barking, "*Don't* turn around! They're coming this way."

"What do they look like?"

"One's sort of plump and cute with dark, curly hair—she's a nurse."

"You never could resist a woman in uniform," Riley pointed out.

As Jay followed the women's progress across the room—they were obviously coming closer—he dropped his voice and spoke almost without moving his lips, ventriloquist style. "The other's also in a uniform. Khaki pants and sexy little red top that shouldn't be sexy but it is because she's got this curvy figure . . ."

Oh, no. Riley couldn't help it; he began to swerve.

Jay hissed at him in alarm. "No, jeez, don't-don't-don't—"

Stare.

It was undoubtedly Jay's next word, and it was also undoubtedly what Riley was doing. Gaping, in fact. He knew he was, because Kellie was doing the exact same thing. She slammed to a halt right next to their table and regarded Riley as if he were a very unwelcome apparition. Her companion in the nurse outfit rammed into her back, and the cheery Wiggie's hostess was already galloping past in her hurry to seat the two new customers. But Kellie stood her ground. Gawking.

"*You!*" she bellowed.

Her gaze was a mix of anger and indignation—and just a hint, Riley realized, of wonder. Somewhere in the back of her mind a niggling doubt was being born. *Could he really be . . . ?* she was probably thinking. That possibility gave him satisfaction.

"I thought we had an agreement!" she said.

"We did." He shook his head. "I mean, we still do."

"Then what are you doing here?" She planted her hands on her hips. "Did you follow me?"

Riley shrugged innocently. "How could I? We've been sitting here for fifteen minutes. As you can see, I've already been served."

"You must have raced out of the office the minute I left so you could beat me here!"

"I had no way of knowing you would be here."

"Ha!" She tossed her head back. "You've probably got the pay phones around your office building bugged."

"It's lunch time," Riley pointed out. "I'm having my lunch. I had no idea you would be here." He smiled. "Honest."

"I don't believe it!"

Jay, trying to melt the hostility in the air, half rose and gestured gallantly to the vacant places at their booth. "You ladies want to join us?"

Kellie's eyes snapped with fire. "No!"

Jay recoiled.

For the first time, Riley looked behind Kellie and noticed her companion, the nurse who shared Kellie's height and coloring but wore more makeup and was a little chunkier looking in her boxy nurse dress. The woman cast him a rueful, apologetic glance.

She nudged Kellie. "Jeez, aren't you being . . . ?"

Kellie's shoulders squared as if she were just now readying for battle. "I consider this whole business suspect, Riley. I don't believe it for an instant!"

He lifted his hands innocently. "But here I am, and here you are . . . unless *you* followed *me?*"

Her eyes flew wide with alarm at the very idea. "I did not!"

"Well, then . . ."

As the possibility of a true psychic connection hung in the air between them, she backed up, turned, and began shooing the nurse back toward the door. "C'mon, Rita, we're getting out of here."

"But Kell—"

She lowered her voice to a sotto-voce growl. "I said *let's go.*"

The woman named Rita hopped backward in confusion. "But why? Who are those guys?"

Kellie swung around for one last glance, one last zinger. She raised her voice so the surrounding few tables could hear. "They're just *kooks,* is all!"

And then she herded her nurse companion quickly toward the door.

Riley turned back around, not even questioning the way his heart seemed to pound furiously. The more he saw Kellie, the more he was getting used to it.

Jay, however, was in quite an agitated state. His face was red, and he glanced nervously at the people around them who were pinning curious stares on them. "What was *that?*"

Riley tried hard to appear casual. "A woman I know."

"Did you hear what she called us?"

He nodded and took a swig of tea.

Jay's voice looped up about an octave. "Kooks!"

"She's a little high-strung."

"High-strung? She seemed positively paranoid!" Jay leaned forward. "What was she so upset about? She seemed to think your sitting there was a federal offense or something."

Riley smiled to himself. "She just couldn't believe her eyes, that's all."

"Why not?" Jay asked in exasperation. "Well, I guess that little encounter just shot both our theories."

"How?" Riley was still thinking that Kellie's appearance proved him right. Destiny was taking a hand. Which at best was a Pyrrhic victory for him.

Jay leaned back. *"That* was not a woman whose faults I could forgive. Or a woman I could fall in love with. The nurse, maybe. She was cute. Seemed nice, too."

"You didn't think Kellie Sumners was cute?"

"Kellie Sumners? Is that her name?" Jay asked. "I'll have to make a mental note of that."

"Why?"

"Because she's someone to be avoided at all costs, that's why! How did you meet her? And why did your mere presence set her off like a nuclear missile?"

"Oh, well, I ran into her car."

Jay gasped. "Oh, no!" His face drained of color, leaving him all bug-eyed astonishment. "Dear God. Please don't tell me *that creature* was the woman you were going to buy a Cadillac for!"

Riley shook his head. "I didn't buy her a Cadillac."

"Thank heavens!"

"I bought her a Lexus."

Poor Jay, who never said a bad word about anyone, looked as if he might keel over. "For that shrew? What could have possessed you?"

Riley shook his head, smiling to himself. "I wish I knew, Jay. I really wish I knew."

"Red light!" Rita shrieked in alarm.

Kellie slammed on the brakes, then fell back against her seat, sweating. That was a close one. What was it about Riley Lombard's effect on her that seemed to result in traffic accidents?

"What's the matter with you?" Rita asked. "You're driving like you're in a bumper car at the State Fair."

"I'm sorry." Kellie let out a long breath, trying to regain her composure. But it was difficult. What had Riley been doing there? Wiggic's, a barbecue dive near Rita's hospital, was a place she went to all the time. But it wasn't the sort of restaurant that would attract an entrepreneurial clientele.

"Who were those guys?" Rita asked. "And why did you go ballistic all of a sudden?"

"I didn't go ballistic."

"Kellie, you were screeching at the poor man."

Poor man? "Ha!" she said. "I might have been screeching, but that man is *not* poor. In fact, I'll bet he's one of the richest men in Dallas."

Rita's mouth dropped open reverentially. "Really?"

Kellie nodded. "His name is Riley Lombard, and for some reason he's developed this weird ... fixation on me."

"Oh! The man who hit your car?" Rita's eyes widened with interest. "You didn't tell me he was so hunky."

"Well, yes, he's good-looking and majorly strange. He keeps giving me things."

Her sister squinted at her. "Wait a second. Let me get this straight. A good-looking gazillionaire is lavishing gifts on you, and for this you're hunting him down and hollering at him in barbecue joints?"

"I did *not* hunt him down!" Kellie said, then realized that she was now hollering at her sister. The light turned green, and she proceeded through the intersection trying her best to put forward an attitude of calm. "If anything, *he* was the one who did the hunting."

"But Kellie, he was right. He was there first."

That was the tricky part. She tapped her fingers on the

steering wheel. "I don't know how he knew we would be there. ..."

One answer that came to mind was that he might have had one of those little flashes of his. *Poof! She's going to be eating barbecue!* But of course she didn't believe in those flashes, so that couldn't be the explanation.

Could it?

Oh, hell. He was making her as bug crazy as he was. She just didn't understand it, though. How could she have run into him so soon after swearing that she would never see him again? How?

"I don't get it," Kellie said. "There are all sorts of people in Dallas I try to avoid. People I wouldn't want to run into in restaurants. Old boyfriends. My ex-in-laws ..."

"And do you run into them?" Rita asked.

"No!" Kellie sighed. "So *why* would I run into Riley Lombard thirty minutes after we pledged to avoid each other forever?"

Rita blinked at her uncertainly. "Maybe you were both hungry?"

"Do you know how many barbecue joints there are in this town? Plus, he could afford to eat at four-star restaurants every meal of his life if he wanted to."

"Okay ..." Rita cast about for another explanation. "Maybe it's destiny?"

Kellie moaned.

"Coincidence," Rita corrected quickly, trying to simmer her down. "I'll bet that's what it was."

"Of course it was just a coincidence," Kellie said, attempting to convince herself. She tried to banish words like *fate* and *kismet* from her mind.

Rita sighed. "I wish Wendell was a millionaire."

Kellie should have known it wouldn't be long before the boy wonder of the slacker set entered the conversation. But for once she was actually glad to discuss her sister's quicksand love life. Anything to get her mind off Riley. "You'd be ahead if Wendell were simply employed."

"He *can't* work, Kellie. He's a student."

"He's a philosophy student, which means that he never will be employed."

"Once he gets his doctorate . . ." Rita's voice trailed off.

"Then he'll be Dr. Wendell, philosopher. Do you know how many job openings there are for philosophers? Even with four-percent national unemployment, three-and-a-half percent of those are probably people with degrees in philosophy."

"He's working on a book he says is sure to get published."

Kellie groaned. "He's been working on that book ever since you've known him. Are you even sure it exists as anything else but as an excuse for him not to work and to renege on dates?"

"Of course it exists," Rita said, offended. "I've even read a chapter. It's called *The Courage to Be Indigent.*"

Sometimes Kellie despaired of Rita's ever freeing herself from the saga of *Waiting for Wendell*. "This man will never be a millionaire, Rita."

"That's okay. Once I pay off my student loan, I can move out of Mom's and Wendell and I can get married."

"Has he ever spoken about getting married?"

"Well, no. He said he thinks we should go on just as we are."

"Rita, you're stagnant just as you are. All you two have is a standing date for him to come over and do laundry at Mom's house every Friday night."

Rita sighed. "But he's so cute, Kellie."

Kellie didn't see it. Wendell, who usually had a musty, unkempt smell about him, was gaunt and pale, with shoulder-length red hair he kept in a scrungy ponytail. In her view, he was twenty-five going on twelve.

"There are better-looking men in the world," she assured her sister.

"Oh, sure, maybe millionaires—"

"Not just millionaires," Kellie said, though she had to struggle like a sumo wrestler to get the mental image of Riley out of her head.

"Well then, who?"

Kellie shrugged. "What about the guy Riley was sitting with? He was nice-looking."

"Oh, Kellie!" Rita said with a gasp. "You've got to be kidding. You must think I'm a complete loser."

"Why?"

Rita squinted at her. "Didn't you get a look at that guy?"

"Well, not *too* good a look," she admitted. And of course, for the split second she was focused on him, she'd been screaming like a nut.

"He looked like Don Knotts!" Rita pouted in her seat. "Boy, you must think I should just take anything that comes down the pike. And I can see now that you must *really* hate Wendell."

"I don't hate Wendell," Kellie argued, "but forgive me, I'm your big sister. I don't like to see you wasting your life on some guy who's likely to flake out after you've waited a decade for him to grow up."

"At least I'm not turning into an embittered old woman of thirty-two!" Rita shot back. "Burying yourself in a print store only to come out to shriek at men in public because you're angry you chose the biggest jerk in the world to marry!"

Kellie screeched to a stop at the next intersection, sending them both bucking forward in their seats. For a moment, the two sisters sat red-faced and seething at each other. If it were twenty years earlier, she would have reached over and yanked a hank of Rita's hair until she screamed and ran to their mother. Now they were both grown up, supposedly, but they still needed a mediator.

My God, she thought in panic. *I'm thirty-two years old and I'm thinking like Trevor.* She forced herself to count to ten—an adult time-out.

"Kell?" Rita said meekly.

"What?" Kellie was only vaguely aware of the fact that people were honking behind her.

Rita smiled. "You stopped at a green light."

Kellie looked into Rita's face and saw the same flushed, rueful expression that she saw in her own face in the rearview mirror. Suddenly, she laughed, and Rita was laughing with her.

"I'm so sorry, Rita." She proceeded through the green light. "My only excuse is that I'm going insane. Riley Lombard is making me insane."

"I'm sure running into him was just a fluke," Rita repeated soothingly. "A coincidence."

Coincidence. Kellie clung to that word.

Chapter Six

She was just going to have to be more careful, Kellie decided.

In the weeks that followed her run-in with Riley at Wiggie's, she no longer blithely ran errands in her old helter-skelter way, racketing from work to day camp to grocery to home. Instead she plotted out her route in advance so she could avoid those places where she might, even on the slightest off chance, run into someone she wouldn't normally run into. It seemed a little silly, like playing Spy vs. Spy, but better to feel silly than to run into Riley again.

She even did some detective work. On Thursday, when she took Trevor and Tina for their weekly library visit—to a building, she noted with irritation, that was called the Lombard branch—she logged onto the public computer and did a search for Riley C. Lombard III. There was, for a man who didn't even list his number in the phone book, a staggering amount of information about him. She looked up articles on his business ("a phenomenal success story," according to *Fortune* magazine). She downloaded pictures of his office building, stats on his company's earnings, read an interview with that masseur he had told her about (in-house masseurs, apparently, were a hot new employee benefit in large companies). *D* magazine had published an entire puff piece on Riley years ago, detailing a "ratty jeans-to-riches" background. His father, who like her own had died when Riley was still in school, had been a plumber. Riley went to UT on a track scholarship. Then, after college, he'd moved to Dallas, quickly clawed his way up a few corporate ladders, then started his own company. After that, the article listed his achievements—his incredible good fortune in business, his beautiful Highland Park house, his beautiful wife and little girl . . .

Little girl? Riley hadn't mentioned her.

Kellie shamelessly pored over the two pictures of his wife. *Beautiful* fell woefully short of the mark. The Joanne Chamberlain Lombard in those pictures was drop-dead gorgeous. Tall and willowy, a natural blond, a former Miss Dallas. She exuded grace, confidence . . . exuberance. *She* didn't have ratty jeans in her background, but blood as blue as it ran in this state.

And Riley had said she was gone. Dead. That was so hard to believe—it made it all the more difficult for Kellie to drag herself away from the pictures. And the little girl, who was a blond, plump miniature of Joanne—where was she now?

Trevor found her sitting in a trance in front of her screen. "Can we go now, Mom?"

Kellie dragged her attention back to her son. "What?"

"I said, can we go now? It's so boring here. It's like being in school again. Why bother even having summers if we're just going to come to the library all the time?"

She looked across the cluster of microfiche machines and computers to where the old periodicals were kept. A newspaper, that's what she needed. "Why don't you go look through the videotapes for something we can watch?"

His thin shoulders sagged. "Oh, all right."

She barely noticed that as he walked away he squeaked his sneakers against the tile floors—a long-standing no-no. She was too preoccupied with the prospect of poring over those newspapers like a ghoulish Nancy Drew. This went beyond the bounds of finding out enough about Riley so that she could avoid him. This was about nothing other than avid curiosity.

There was no need to find out all this information about Riley's private life. If she had any shame, any at all, she would stop now, she scolded herself.

But of course she didn't stop.

It took some hunting to find Joanne Chamberlain Lombard's obituary, which was a lengthy one. The unsigned piece successfully managed to relay the shock of the community of losing someone so young, so beautiful, and so seemingly charmed. Kellie had a hard time just making herself read it. The picture, a Christmas shot of Joanne with her almost identical little girl in coordinated plaid dresses, seemed especially poignant. And then Kellie's eyes caught the second paragraph.

The Lombards' daughter, Abigail, was also killed in the accident.

The accident. Kellie frowned and scrolled down the microfiche page quickly, past Joanne's privileged youth of private schools and exotic travel. Past scholarly accomplishments and her Miss Dallas crown. Past her wedding and her brief, happy marriage. Past charitable deeds and committee memberships.

Several paragraphs from the end, Kellie found what she was looking for.

Mrs. Lombard was traveling southbound on I-35 to Austin with her daughter to visit her parents when a northbound tractor-trailor jacknifed. The truck fell on its side, crossed the median, and slid several hundred yards before hitting Mrs. Lombard's car. She and her daughter were killed on impact, according to police, who cited rainy conditions as the cause of the accident. Four others, including the driver of the truck, also died.

Kellie leaned back in her chair, numb with shock. It was exactly the accident Riley had described to her in his office. The one confirmed vision he'd mentioned.

A shiver ran through her. She felt spooked.

But how did Riley feel? How did a person cope when such a terrible thing happened? Kellie couldn't imagine losing two people she loved so abruptly, so violently. She scrolled back up to the picture, and tears welled in her eyes. It was almost more than she could comprehend.

Had Riley really foreseen this accident? Or had the vision come later ... a sort of hindsight belief that he could have done something, that he might have stopped the tragedy somehow. Either way, the man was probably living with a Mount Everest of sorrow built up inside him. She felt a fresh stab of shame for even broaching the subject of his wife with him, and especially in the callous, unthinking way she had.

Things he'd told her made sense now. About how he couldn't date. Looking at his late wife, blond and radiant and beaming on the microfiche screen, she could well understand why someone new would pale in comparison. The man was probably so weighted down with emotional baggage, it was a wonder he could still function.

Which was yet another reason why she still needed to keep looking over her shoulder. To be careful. She was *not* going to run into Riley again.

"C'mon, Mom, I'm going to be *laaaaaaaate!*"

This, from the girl who had to be pried out of her room

in the morning to get to school or camp on time. But
when it came to spending the night at Margaret Thurston's
house, Tina was Miss Punctuality. She stood in Kellie's
bedroom doorway, pink suitcase in hand, popping with
tension.

Kellie, who had just arrived home from work, could
have used ten minutes to wind down. Apparently she
wouldn't get even ten seconds. Marshaled by her daughter's ferocious impatience, she shoved her foot into a
sandal and stood, half hopping as she simultaneously
walked and settled her foot into the shoe. "I don't see what
the hurry is. Mrs. Thurston said any time before—"

"Margaret's mom always has *the best* cookies in the
afternoon," Tina said, as if this explained the rush. "Margaret's mom bakes the best oatmeal raisin cookies *ever*.
From scratch."

Kellie, whose idea of a homemade cookie had over the
years become the slice-and-bake variety expelled from
a refrigerated plastic tube, trundled after her daughter,
snatched up her purse, and began to root for her keys.
All the while, she had the image of pencil-thin Barbara
Thurston harvesting her own oats and drying her own
grapes on her patio.

During the drive to the Thurston house, Tina looked
pinched and nervous as she always did in the Toyota (it
was battered but back, much to the children's dismay and
Kellie's immense relief and secret delight). She let out a
feverish sigh. "Oh, I wish something would happen to
us!"

Kellie twisted to cast an anxious gaze at her. "Something? Like what?"

"Oh, I don't know! I keep wishing for *something*.
Don't you?"

She thought about this for a moment. To her, it seemed
the past year had been full of too much—a divorce,
opening her business and all the hassles that entailed.

Surprises were something she didn't particularly relish at this point. "The business is doing well. Maybe in a few weeks, when we begin extended hours, we'll have enough money to take you shopping for new school clothes."

"Oh, Mom—I'm not talking about shopping! I mean something big. Something wonderful!" She turned to her. "Like that morning when there was a new car in the driveway."

Uh-oh.

"Don't you remember what that felt like?" Tina asked her.

Kellie stiffened, pushing uncomfortably against the shoulder belt. *Did she remember?* She wasn't kidding herself. Not a day had gone by that she didn't think of the wonder of that moment when she'd sunk into that luxurious vehicle and wondered for a charmed, fleeting moment if she could accept such a gift. She'd never felt such a stab of temptation for pure material pleasure.

"I remember," she said, a little resentfully. "You *are* talking about shopping. Because if it's luxury you want, that has to be paid for. I've explained that to you. Riches just don't fall from the sky. You have to work and save and—"

Tina pursed her lips and sent her a gaze that was both crestfallen and defensive. "I was just talking about *wishing!*"

"I know, but . . ." Kellie stopped herself. Good heavens. When had she become such an expert wet blanket?

"Don't you ever just want something magic to happen?" Tina asked her. "Like what happens in books?"

"Sure," Kellie admitted. "Believe me, if a leprechaun knocked on my door with an offer of a pot of gold, I wouldn't kick him off my porch. I'm just trying to make sure you keep both feet on the ground, Tina. Life isn't a fairy tale."

Behind their spectacles, Tina's eyes rolled in dramatic frustration. "You mean you're just trying to make sure I know my life will be boring. You don't believe in magic or anything!"

It was true she didn't believe in magic any more than she believed in psychics, but she'd never been so taken to task for her realistic nature before. Yet here was her daughter, nine going on thirty, lecturing her.

Kellie turned onto the Thurstons' elm-lined street, along which all the houses boasted green, uncluttered, manicured yards. Visiting this picture-perfect world from her own messier domestic milieu was probably difficult for an impressionable girl like Tina. That inevitable frustration settled over Kellie. She constantly reminded her kids that life wasn't always fair, and that you simply had to do your best and not compare yourself to others. But did she accept that herself? Why should Margaret Thurston, with her homemade cookies and picture book Tudor house, be so much luckier than Tina, who made do with her claustrophobic little bedroom and Chips Ahoy?

She braked in the Thurston driveway and turned to Tina, who was unbuckling her seatbelt and reaching back for her little pink overnight bag at lightning speed, getting ready to dart out of the Toyota before anyone saw her actually sitting in it. Tina was reaching the independence phase much faster than Trevor had, Kellie realized with some sadness. "I want you to have every opportunity in the world to become what you want to be, Tina. You're smart and talented and I'm so proud of you."

Tina nodded impatiently, her hand on the door handle. Their magic argument had apparently been forgotten in anticipation of the pleasure of an evening *chez* Thurston. "Thanks, Mom. I'll call you tomorrow."

Kellie opened her door. "I'll take you to the door so I can have a word with Barbara."

"You don't need to." Tina bolted out of the car. "I'll tell her thank-you on your behalf."

"But—"

"*Mom* . . ."

Kellie got out of the car, but as she did, Barbara Thurston came breezing out of her house alongside Margaret, who ran across the yard to Tina and took her bag.

Barbara waved enthusiastically. "Hi, there!" She was a petite woman with ash-blond hair that looked as if it was carefully sculpted into place each morning—and wouldn't dare get out of line for the rest of the day. As always, she was perfectly dressed in a crisp white linen shirt that showed off tanned, perfectly toned arms and pink shorts short enough to exhibit shapely yet toothpick-thin legs. "What a cute top, Kellie! You always look so *comfy!*"

Kellie stopped awkwardly just as she was about to close her car door and looked down at her T-shirt. It was amazing how a compliment could sound so insulting. Part of the problem was that she wasn't accustomed to having shouted conversations across people's yards, but Barbara seemed perfectly happy yelling. She had one of those voices that made Kellie suspect cheerleading had featured prominently in her teen years.

"Thank you for having Tina over."

"We *love* having Tina!" Barbara boomed, clasping her hands together. *Give her a* T, Kellie thought ungraciously. "She's always *such* fun. I even baked her favorite oatmeal cookies in honor of her visit!"

As the girls disappeared inside, Tina sent Kellie a fleeting, offhand wave.

"Tina was just telling me about them."

Barbara hooted, delighted. "She's *so* nice! They're just plain oatmeal cookies with Irish oats, fresh ground cinnamon, and those *lovely* organic raisins they sell up at Fresh Choices! Don't you just love that place?"

Kellie smiled. Fresh Choices was a lavish new grocery store she hadn't had time—nor, she feared, the ready cash—to investigate. "I'll call before I pick up Tina tomorrow afternoon."

Barbara waved. "Don't bother, Kellie—I'll bring her home."

"Oh, that's too much bother—"

"It's no bother!" she echoed back. "And Tina just *loves* riding in our new Mercedes! She's so cute!"

Kellie sank back into her car and for a moment stared numbly at the heavily carved door that had just shut behind Barbara Thurston, who unfortunately was too loudly cordial for her to mentally vent her frustrations on. *Damn it.* The woman was just too nice to Tina to hate.

She pulled out of the drive and puttered slowly, uneasily, down the street, consumed by her own thoughts.

Maybe it was just her. All this frustration, this guilt, this petty jealousy was simply masking the fact that she was at loose ends. For the first time in what seemed like years, she had a night to herself. Trevor was at a sleepover with his Little League friend Joey in preparation for a big game Saturday morning, in which Salty's Burger House was hoping to slaughter Merrill Lynch (why did everything sound like class warfare to her these days?). She didn't know how she was going to spend this rare free night. She would have called Rita, but Friday was the night her sister usually reserved for laundry with Wendell. She was even tempted to go back to Copycat, but Alejandro and Lana, who was now a permanent employee, were both there. No doubt creating sparks as well as getting all their work done. What would there be for her to do—refill the staplers? Feel the flirty vibes? If she couldn't allow her two employees to handle a dead Friday night, she was bound to become a hopeless workaholic.

Besides, this was a luxury problem. More times than she could count during the past year, she had dreamed of having an entire child-free evening alone yawning ahead of her. Visions of long, uninterrupted bubble baths, adult meals of salmon and asparagus, and glugging down wine while lost in front of a real R-rated movie (a five-hanky romance, preferably with Harrison Ford or George Clooney, with tasteful nudity and a minimum number of explosions), had filled her idle thoughts as she'd done three people's laundry and cooked pots of bright orange macaroni-and-cheese and sat through the millionth viewing of the videotape of *The Little Princess* that her mother had given Tina for Christmas last year.

Now, for the life of her, she couldn't think of a thing to fill her time. The thought of watching a videotape, even to moon over George Clooney, made her sigh listlessly. It sounded so passive. A bubble bath? Trevor always forgot to clean up after his shower, so she'd have to scour the tub before she could run a bath. That seemed like too much of a hassle right now, and ultimately wouldn't she wonder if she weren't actually soaking in trace amounts of Comet cleanser?

To be honest, she dreaded going back to the empty, noiseless house. She drove slowly, idly, curving around unfamiliar streets and taking her time. Finally she struck a main traffic artery. Fresh Choices, the grocery store Barbara had been raving about, which sold things like fresh cinnamon, stood across the busy road.

Kellie stared at the brick building, intrigued. Now that she thought about it, she wasn't entirely certain what fresh cinnamon was. A root? A bark? A leaf? What did cinnamon look like in its raw state? Deciding to investigate, she crossed the street and wrestled the Toyota into an economy space at the farthest reaches of the crowded parking lot.

Inside the store, harried upscale marrieds winged items

into small carts and blared at unseen spouses via palm-sized cell phones; other, generally younger, folk strolled more slowly up and down the wide, gleaming aisles with wire baskets on their arms, self-consciously gathering jars of imported Greek peppers or tiny cans of pâté, always darting glances for fellow shoppers of the opposite sex. The grocery store as weekend yuppie cruise joint.

Try as she might to approach the place with a proletarian wariness, Kellie was seduced by the exotic nature of the goods she perused. Just the jams and jellies shelves were a wonder to her. There were oddly-shaped jars with fancy checkered cloths covering the lids, in flavors like guava-strawberry-kiwi and mint-mango-passion fruit. In the flour section, she found sacks of organic oat flour, rice flour, barley flour; even the plain old white flour was decked out in old-fashioned cloth bags that looked like plump pillows. Everything was just a shade more interesting, more *attractive* than her normal groceries—and sometimes the place just impressed her with sheer quantity. Thirty-five different types of citrus fruits, they boasted, and eight different pears, which were individually cradled in tissue paper, making them seem unspeakably precious.

But the real jaw-dropper was their cheese section, which was a tribute to upscale excess. It lined both sides of an entire aisle. The store had cheese from everywhere, great wheels of the stuff imported from Switzerland and the Netherlands and France. Italy's cheeses alone took up as much room as the entire dairy section at the Shop-Save. Kellie stood amazed, gaping at the gouda, when she remembered having a daughter who was choosy about her cheese. She'd vowed to buy Tina something better than Kraft when they could afford it. Well, business had been brisk. Copycat had had to extend its hours even before the school year started. They were going to be in the black for the first time this month, earlier than she'd dared hope. Maybe now was the time for a little culinary splurge. Tomorrow, Tina would be sandwiching in style.

She took her time, completely absorbed in her task. Eventually, after what seemed like hours, she settled on a baby Swiss, a generous block of which cost six dollars. An outrageous sum, it seemed to her, though a real bargain compared to some she'd looked at. You'd think cows in Europe were munching on gold-plated grass.

She reached for her cheese only to discover someone else grabbing the same cellophane-wrapped hunk. She glanced up in surprise; she hadn't even been aware of anyone standing next to her.

"Well, hello."

Riley Lombard was smiling at her, the lights practically glinting off those blue eyes of his. Kellie let out a gasp and relinquished the baby Swiss immediately. What was *he* doing here?

Was the man some kind of wacko stalker?

"I didn't follow you," he said, explaining.

Was he a mind reader, too?

She shook her head, reminding herself that he wasn't anything. Not a psychic, not a mind reader, just a man—albeit a stunningly handsome one. Nor was he a stalker. Riley struck her as many things—impossibly handsome, a disarming oddball millionaire, maybe even a Grade A loony—but he didn't seem dangerous.

Dangerously handsome, maybe. He'd obviously come from work because he was still wearing business attire—a gray-blue suit cut to look almost casual that she knew had to be foreign made and very expensive. And yet it was the casually sexy way that Riley carried himself that made his appearance so heart-stopping. He was just a man who had an effect on women. Or at least on her.

Maybe especially on her, a little voice in the back of her head said.

No!

This meeting was just a coincidence. Just an unfortunate coincidence. She hadn't been paying attention—she'd forgotten to watch where she was going.

How had she let that happen? How had she again wound up in the position of staring up into those blue eyes, her nerves jangling as they always seemed to around him? Only this time it was a little different, because now she knew more about Riley than she should have. She was aware of all the pain he'd been through, maybe was still struggling with, so that the sparkle in his blue eyes seemed more heartbreaking than it had before. How could a man who'd had such a horrible thing happen to him present such a pleasant face to the world? She hadn't suffered anything close to what he had, and she still was given to bouts of self-pity, of thinking that life wasn't fair.

She angsted about cheese, for heaven's sake.

"I'll go," she volunteered, grabbing at her as-yet-empty basket.

He laughed. "There's no need for that, Kellie." He looked down at the cheese. "Was this what you were reaching for?"

"You can have it."

He handed it over graciously. "I'm sure I can find another package here. It's not as if there's a limited supply."

She looked up into his face and leaned against the display case as she felt her knees going a little rubbery on her. Silly, really. She'd seen the man plenty of times—she should be used to the dazzling good looks. That bone structure that might have been sculpted by Michelangelo. That tanned skin that contrasted with the light coloring and tooth-paste commercial white teeth. That little dimple when he smiled that practically brought a gooey sigh to her lips every time.

Before, however, it had been easier for her to dismiss

him. He'd been an eccentric, a nuisance. Now . . . she was curious about him. Her heart went out to him for what he had been through. And for some perverse, crazy reason, she found herself liking him more.

"Well, thanks," she said, relenting under the dimple's influence. She was dying to flee, yet her feet felt glued to the shiny checkered tiles beneath her feet.

"How are things?" he asked, apparently likewise glued.

"Just fine." She added quickly, "Trevor and Tina are staying with friends tonight, so I . . ." Her voice petered out. *I'm at the grocery store.* What a life!

His smile broadened. "Me, too."

Her brows arched in surprise. She would have thought business tycoons never lacked for company. At the very least, she wouldn't have thought he'd have to stock his own larder.

"Cook's night out," he explained, following her train of thought with eerie accuracy. "I was going to attempt something simple. A sandwich, maybe."

A cook? Her mind struggled to comprehend that luxury. "Are you sure you know where the help hides the knives and forks—or are you the kind of employer who keeps a sharp eye on the silver?"

"I'm lax in all regards, I'm afraid," he replied good-naturedly. "I'm only as well acquainted with the kitchen as Fayard allows me to be."

Fayard, his cook. She shook her head in amazement. Even the name had a Cordon Bleu ring to it.

Still smiling, he looked down at her empty basket, then cast her a wary glance. "I've got an idea . . . we're both not getting far shopping. Why don't we pack it in and go for a bite together? My favorite coffee shop is right around here."

She began refusing even as her pulse picked up at the idea of sitting across from that face for the length of a meal. It was more appealing than the idea of a George Clooney video had been. "I couldn't."

He tilted his head. "Oh! I thought since you said you were all alone for the evening ..."

Big mouth! Why had she blurted that out? "I am, it's just—"

Blond brows arched. "Just?"

Was he being thick? "Don't you remember our agreement?" she reminded him. He was the one who made such a big protest about not wanting to see her, not wanting to get involved at all. "We weren't supposed to do this. I mean, I thought this was the very situation we were trying to avoid."

"I tried."

She rolled her eyes. "Please don't start. And let me apologize for that last time I saw you."

"There's no need."

"No need? Your friend must think I'm some kind of a lunatic!"

He laughed. "That's okay, he's sort of a lunatic himself."

"Still, I overreacted. I'm sure our meeting up last time . . . and this time . . . well, it's just a coincidence. I mean, Dallas isn't *that* big."

"Right. Just a few million people."

"Neighborhood by neighborhood, though," she argued, "it's not that big. It could happen to any two people."

He smiled at her patiently. "I've been wanting to talk to you anyway, Kellie. I think we need a pow-wow."

She didn't like the sound of that. Or maybe she liked it too much. "What for?"

"To figure some things out." He hastened to assure her, "This wouldn't be a date, or anything remotely romantic, I assure you. I don't have ulterior motives, and if it makes you feel better, we can take separate cars.

You can even pay for your own dinner, though naturally I'd prefer it if you'd let it be my treat.''

She opened her mouth to protest—which point, she wasn't quite sure—but he just kept on talking.

''Look, we're both obviously at loose ends tonight, and we have to eat, and I assure you there are some things we could hammer out.''

She was still about to protest, to decline, to nix the whole idea, but something weird he'd said stopped her. *Hammer out what things?* What was going on in that brain of his?

She tilted her gaze on him quizzically. ''What is this all about, Riley?''

''Come have dinner with me and I'll tell you.''

With that, they had a mini stare-down. Her curiosity was piqued by his maddeningly oblique answer. His lips slowly turned up in that now-familiar smile as he could see he was wearing her down. Finally, he was grinning ear to ear, and that dimple made another star appearance.

The dimple won out.

''A quick bite,'' she agreed at last.

She didn't want to be rude. Besides, what could it hurt?

Chapter Seven

"You really meant a coffee shop, didn't you?" Kellie asked as she settled into the red vinyl booth across from Riley. The backrest was patched in one torn spot with silver duct tape.

"What did you think I meant?"

"I was afraid—well, I just assumed—you meant one of those stuffy eateries that litter the neighborhoods around here. You know, for java snobs. Four dollars a cup."

He wrinkled his nose as he took up a gigantic plastic menu from behind the napkin dispenser against the wall. The menu was finger-smudged from a day's use. The most expensive beverage at Joe's Café was a milkshake for two dollars and fifty cents. Coffee was still a buck. "Nope, I meant a coffee shop. You don't mind, do you?"

"No. As a matter of fact, I'm relieved." She glanced down apologetically at her T-shirt. "I'm not exactly dressed to the nines."

He could have told her that the way her breasts filled out even a simple T-shirt was nothing to apologize for. But no doubt such a comment would send her running for the hills. She looked halfway ready to bolt already. But would she have been any more astonished by his train of thought than he was himself?

He cleared his throat and peeked over his menu to confide, "To tell you the truth, I have pretty dreadful taste in food. Give me a hamburger and fries, and I'm happy."

She grinned. "Does Fayard know?"

"It's not a very well-kept secret, I'm afraid. But he keeps challenging my blue-collar palate, and I keep sneaking off to places like this on his day off."

"Poor you."

He sighed dramatically as he scanned his culinary options, which he practically had memorized anyway. "We all have our crosses to bear."

They sat in silence until the waitress delivered coffee. "Hi there, Riley!"

He grinned back at the dark-haired woman. "Hi, Audrey. How are you?"

"Oh, just dandy. Nate bought a boat and we've been going out to the lake every weekend." She frowned. "Till now! I tell you, I'm a slave to this darn place."

She took their orders and left them with a promise to light a fire under the cook.

Kellie stared at Riley, puzzled. "You must like this place a lot."

He chuckled. "Audrey's married to my tree surgeon. Nate."

Her brows darted up. "Your *what?*"

"You know, he trims my trees every year."

"Oh." She frowned. "Wait . . . you introduced them?"

He nodded. "It's worked out well, I think."

"Apparently." Kellie eyed him skeptically.

After that she occupied herself with the cream pitcher and little packets of sweetener—she seemed to take exactly an envelope and a third of the pink stuff. She finally flicked an impatient gaze at Riley. "So you're saying that you set up your chauffeur *and* your tree surgeon with women they just happened to end up marrying?"

"Is that so bad?"

"No . . ."

"I just seem to have a knack for knowing what things go together."

He could tell what she was thinking. If he'd been right about those couples, then could the vision he had of himself and her have been wrong? He'd been wondering the same thing himself. He *had* to be wrong. He just wasn't ready for another relationship.

He smiled. Anything to get that dire look off her face. Anything to crack this tension between them. Back at the grocery store, he'd felt something different—as though she were thawing toward him a bit. "You should have been there the first time I tried honey dijon mustard."

She laughed. "Okay, Riley, what's this about?"

"What's what about?"

"You said you had a reason for wanting to have dinner together. What did you want to talk about?"

"You and me, of course."

She sputtered into her coffee cup. "You *are* a sneak!"

"Why?"

"You made it sound as if we were coming here to deal with some kind of, well, business. 'Hammer it out,' you said."

He'd never met a woman who was so defensive. That ex-husband must have done a real number on her to make her so prickly and tough. "Will you listen?"

She put her cup down, leaned back, and folded her arms.

"I just thought we should both admit the fact that it's not working," he said.

Her brown eyes opened wide. "What's not?"

"Avoidance."

She stared at him stonily.

"It isn't, Kellie."

"Why? Just because of a run-in or two?" She waved a hand in the air. "That's nothing."

"Right." He grinned. "Dallas is just a big city full of little neighborhoods."

"Well, how was I to know about your plebian food tastes? I didn't know you'd show up at Wiggie's, or—" She frowned, then tilted a curious glance at him, her forehead wrinkling adorably. "Say, if you're a junk-food guy, what were you doing in a place like Fresh Choices?"

He shrugged. "I honestly can't say. I was just driving by and felt . . . compelled . . . to go in."

She tapped her fingers against the waxy Formica. "Compelled? Please! I mean, if you're a man with no taste, wouldn't you have been *compelled* to reach for Velveeta slices instead of expensive baby Swiss?"

"Exactly," he said.

She stared at him, her lips slightly parted. Then, quickly, her mouth clamped shut and she rolled her eyes. "Oh, brother—listen to us!" she exclaimed, reversing herself. "Mulling over our cheese choices like gypsies reading tea leaves!"

"But you were the one who said . . ."

She practically hooted. "Destiny does *not* reveal itself in the cheese aisle."

"Maybe just this once it did."

"No," she insisted.

"Tell me," he asked her, "is that the grocery store you usually go to?"

"Actually, it was the first time I'd been there," she admitted. "But so what? I was just passing by. It was just a *coincidence*. Just like seeing you at Wiggie's was a coincidence. My sister and I meet there for lunch a lot.

It's near the hospital where she works.'' As he continued to stare at her, she reiterated, ''Coincidence.''

He sighed, then leaned back. He'd debated not telling her, but he didn't really see how he could refrain now. ''Hang on to your hat, because I've got news for you.''

Her brow beetled. ''What kind of news?''

''We've met other times, too.''

The puckers fell out of her forehead and she eyed him with waning tolerance. ''Oh, God! Are you some kind of Shirley MacLaine nut? Please don't start in on past lives or—''

He laughed, cutting her off. ''No, we didn't meet in past lives. I meant *recently.*'' He watched her closely. ''You haven't noticed, have you?''

She tossed her hands in frustration. ''Noticed what?''

''I nearly ran into you at the gas station yesterday, for one thing.''

''You did?''

He nodded. ''I saw your Toyota and ducked into the car wash so you wouldn't notice.''

She grappled with this information for a moment, then shrugged. ''Okay. Three times.''

''And last Saturday morning I saw your car parked along the street by a baseball diamond.''

''It's there every Saturday morning,'' she explained. ''My son has Little League. You *know* that. You bought his uniform, remember?''

He sighed. ''But I didn't know the park where his team played.'' He wished it were as simple as she wanted it to be, but it wasn't. ''Also, last Thursday night you were at the public library, sitting at a computer terminal.''

Finally, something he said seemed to have some impact. Her face went scarlet.

''Am I wrong?'' he asked.

''How did you know?''

"Because I was there—that is, I just saw you there briefly."

"*You* were at the library?" She sounded astounded by the very idea. "How long were you watching me?"

"Not long."

She absorbed this new information. "Okay. There has to be some rational explanation."

Was she ever going to believe him? "Not only that, but I also know that over the weekend you were at the Happy Burger drive-through, Spotlight Video, and the right lane on Preston Road."

She gazed at him for a good long while. Audrey delivered their food, and for a moment Kellie transferred her look of disbelief to her Caesar salad. She popped a crouton into her mouth and chewed it slowly, ruminating. Riley watched her closely, observing her argue the matter internally until she could come up with some sort of logical explanation.

Which was exactly what he had done. In the past week, as he kept spotting her everywhere, he'd considered their conundrum from every angle, and coincidence just didn't begin to cover it. There was something else going on between them. He didn't know what to call it, exactly. Kismet? Magnetism? He wasn't any happier about it than she was. It wasn't as if he'd wanted this to happen; he had tried to avoid her. He'd done his best.

"Okay," she said finally, pushing her plate forward, the food on it mostly untouched. "This is what I think. I think that, for whatever reason, our paths have probably always been crossing. I mean, how can we know they haven't? We could have been bumping into each other all the time, really. There might have been years when we were in the same place several times a week, only we didn't know it. But then one day, boom, you noticed me."

He nodded. "Maybe."

His small concession gave her momentum. "It's like when you suddenly notice a particularly spectacular tree you've never taken in before, but you know you've passed it every day on the way to work. Then you'll see it, really see it, every day and wonder how you could have missed it all those years."

"A tree," he said.

She gulped some coffee and nodded. "Sure. It happens all the time."

"The trouble with your theory is, the tree is immobile. It can't avoid running into anybody. Two people constantly in motion, however, with two very different lives . . ."

He let the conclusion dangle unspoken.

She picked at her paper placemat in frustration, then let out a burst of laughter. "Well, for heaven's sake, Riley, what do you want us to do now?"

"I was wondering if you had any ideas."

"Let's see. . . ." She cocked her head. "Maybe we should start getting a little more extreme. For instance, we could agree to leave our respective houses in opposing shifts."

Riley smiled, catching on. "I'll take six a.m. to two, and you can have afternoons and evenings."

"Right. Of course that might be a little inconvenient, workwise." Her own smile remained frozen in place for another beat; then just as quickly the curve of her lips collapsed into a frown. "Honestly, Riley, what else can we do?"

"How about this," he proposed. "Why don't we agree to be friends."

She gaped at him as if he'd lost it. "What kind of a solution is that?"

"Gauging from your reaction, a pretty terrible one."

She leaned toward him. "What do you mean by *friends*, exactly?"

"I suppose I mean *not* trying to avoid each other. And not freaking out when we do see each other. Maybe we could talk, have a cup of coffee. Just what we're doing now."

"But what about your visions? The white wedding thing?"

He smiled. "I thought you didn't believe in that."

"I don't," she insisted firmly, "but if you're going to have psychic moments, won't that get in the way of a friendship?"

"I don't see why," he said. "I've thought about this a lot, Kellie. In all the time I've seen you, I've only had that one little vision. Could be it was just a fluke."

She looked interested. "Or maybe you imagined me getting married to somebody else! Have you ever thought of that?"

He nodded. "Could be."

"Now *that's* intriguing."

He laughed. "You're great for my ego."

She blinked at him. "But you said you didn't *want* to get married, and—"

Her cheeks bloomed afresh.

"And what?"

"Well . . . we wouldn't be much of a match. I mean, I'm probably not your type. . . ."

As if Kellie wouldn't be any man's type. She must honestly have no conception of how cute she was, how her hair was so thick and shiny that a man's hands would just itch to touch it, how her eyes drew him into her every thought until he felt almost mesmerized, how her compact body seemed so perfectly proportioned. More times than he could count this past week he'd caught himself dreaming of what she might look like beneath her Copycat clothes. . . .

He pushed that last thought aside. "I thought you didn't want to date anyone."

Her shoulders squared off. "I don't!"

"Then why did your eyes light up when you considered the possibility of getting married to somebody *else?*"

"Just a natural curiosity, I guess. Like reading a fortune cookie that says you're going to meet a handsome stranger. You might not believe it, but the prospect in the abstract certainly has its appeal."

He nodded. "So you wouldn't mind getting married . . . someday."

She eyed him steadily. "Someday," she said cautiously, as if she were admitting to a taboo desire. "When it's more practical."

The answer surprised him. *"Practical?"*

"What's the matter with that?" she asked. "Last time I got married, I was eighteen and thought I was in love. Well, love lasted about six months and then the marriage limped along for another eleven years."

"That's a long time."

"I know. I had the kids to consider, though." She sighed. "And I guess deep down I just didn't want to admit to failure. Trouble was, the longer I stayed in the marriage, the more I thought I had invested in it. Every year that passed made it harder to contemplate jumping ship. Does that make sense?"

"I can understand wanting to keep your family together."

She uttered a faint laugh. "In the end my efforts didn't make much difference because Rick bailed."

"I'm sorry."

"Well, that's the long version of why I'm leery of love. If there's a next time, I want to marry for companionship. That's what lasts."

"You've really thought this through."

"After Rick left, it seems like that's what I would be thinking about as I drifted off to sleep at night. *Never again,* I'd think. And then I'd think, *unless* . . . I've got a list of characteristics a mile long that the next guy's going to have to possess. But I gotta tell you, it would take a helluva guy to come along and overcome all the unlesses I've got built up in my head.''

He looked across at her and pictured her lying in her bed, making up her list of prerequisites. Unfortunately, his imagination quickly skipped from what she was thinking to what she looked like, hair spilled out against the pillow. Did she wear nightgowns, he wondered, or was she the old T-shirt type?

''What about you, Riley?''

Her voice broke through to him and he felt a jolt. ''What do I think about love?''

She nodded and gulped down the rest of her coffee.

He stared ahead, feeling as if she were going out of focus again. Love was about the only thing he did care about. Maybe because he missed it so much. Because he knew he'd never again find anything like what he'd felt for Joanne.

''Riley?''

His shoulders hunched as he crossed his arms. He couldn't seem to force himself to straighten back up. ''Yes?''

''You've just given up?''

She made it sound like an active decision he'd made, when really he was just not thinking about it, mostly. He couldn't consider any kind of happy domesticity without feeling as if his insides were being put through a grinder. After the accident everyone, even people he loved and whose opinions he respected, had assured him that someday he would feel better. And he did, superficially. But there was no change in the certainty in his heart that there would never be another Joanne, another Abbie.

''It's just not a possibility for me.''

To his surprise, she nodded, and there was something

like understanding in her eyes. So understanding that he was almost taken aback.

It was the first time this had ever happened to him—the first time someone hadn't tried to present the case for "moving on," whatever that was supposed to mean. People could be very fervent about it. In the past years, he'd been pressed to go on dates, to take up a hobby, to turn more fervently to religion. He'd been given women's phone numbers, free golf lessons, and sometimes more cloying sympathy than he could handle. But Kellie wasn't pressing him to visit her church, or to date her sister, or to consider swing dancing.

Why not?

They sat in silence as long as they could handle it; then they both, as if responding to some unspoken cue, began to eat their dinners. Riley had ordered a cheeseburger and now he gulped it down in large bites he took far too long to chew. He didn't taste the burger. He was too interested in Kellie. Was it her divorce that somehow made her understand his reluctance to simply shed the past, or was it an innate empathy in her nature?

When they had finished eating, Kellie dabbed her paper napkin to her mouth. Her lipstick had worn off long ago, and now only vestiges of it appeared in the creases of her lips—thin veins of darker red amid the healthy pink blossom color. Kellie was one of those women who would look beautiful with her face freshly scrubbed, no makeup. Would she believe it if a man told her that?

Probably not.

She eyed him warily for a moment, obviously hesitant to speak. Then, quickly, she blurted out, "I'm having a cookout Sunday. Nothing fancy, very low pressure as social events go. Just a few friends . . . family."

Ah. So here it was. Maybe she wasn't so different after all.

"You don't have to come if you don't want to. In fact,

I'm sure you probably don't want to. I certainly wouldn't blame you if—''

"Of course I'll come." The words, out of his mouth before he could think twice, surprised him.

Her too, apparently. "You will?"

"Sure. It's nice of you to invite me."

She smiled. "Call it my first friendly gesture."

"This evening's been such a blast, I'm sure you must think I'm a whiz at conversation."

"This evening was an ice breaker, I guess," she said. "At any rate, maybe you're right. We've been silly about the whole thing. For heaven's sake, why should I be running from fate when I don't even believe in it?"

They went Dutch, as agreed upon before their arrival. Outside the restaurant, in the glare of the high street lights, as a welcome night breeze whipped around them, Kellie dug her hands into the pockets of her jean shorts and leaned back on the balls of her feet. "See you Sunday, then?"

"Yes."

"Around noon would be fine."

"Good."

They both hesitated. What now? If they were friends, did they shake hands? Wave good-bye?

Unwittingly, he found his gaze straying again to her lips. When he looked back up into her eyes, they had widened.

"Bye!" She pivoted abruptly and marched toward her car, the long-strapped handbag that was looped around her shoulder banging her hip as she walked.

He waited until she installed herself in the front seat, with the seatbelt securely buckled. When he heard the engine turn over and sputter to life, he headed for his own car.

Sunday. That was only two days away. And yet he was already impatient for it, already craving the pleasingly acrid smell of charcoal, the cloying taste of cold, sweet tea, the sight of Kellie bustling around a backyard he had never even seen yet could picture more clearly than his own. A low-pressure social event, she'd called it. Just friends. A little family, which he presumed meant that sister of hers, and . . .

The children.

He stopped in his tracks and groaned. How could he have forgotten?

The children would be there, too. Front and center. No doubt about it. He would have to watch them streaking across the yard, roughhousing together the way kids did at outdoor events. Most dreaded of all, he'd hear their laughter. It had been so long since he'd allowed himself to hear a little girl's laughter.

Suddenly, the enormity of the mistake he'd just made struck him like a two-by-four.

He walked heavily over to his car like a man just condemned to a life sentence. What was he going to do? Cancel? He *should* cancel. He should simply call her up. Just say, "I made a mistake. There's no way."

There wasn't, was there?

Hunched in his front seat, he remembered Abbie's laugh, heard it as clear as a bell. He flicked his eyes toward the rearview, half expecting to glimpse her in the backseat, chafing at being confined to the car seat. But of course she wasn't there, any more than Joanne was sitting in the seat next to him, chattering on forever the way she used to. The incessant talking—regardless of whether he was answering back—had grated on his nerves sometimes. Now he felt remorse for the irritation he had felt all those years ago. He'd been the luckiest man alive, and he hadn't appreciated it. Oh, he'd known he was happy, and fortunate. God, yes, he'd have to have been the world's biggest ingrate not to thank his lucky stars. The trouble was, he'd been so arrogant about time. He'd expected that good fortune to go on and on.

Instead, only he had gone on. And now he was sitting here contemplating visiting Kellie's house, meeting her children. . . .

He took a good look at his car, wondering why he suddenly felt so haunted. Neither his wife nor his daughter had even been in this car; it was new. This wasn't even the replacement car he'd bought when he was still woozy with grief as he went about seeing to practical matters—new house, new car, forget, forget, forget. That car had turned out to be a lemon. So he was two cars removed from his family. That was how long ago it had been. And in fact months had passed since he'd had a moment like this, when he'd just sit stunned at what he'd lost, wondering how the people who had been the very center of his life could not even exist anymore.

He'd thought he was stronger than this, but all it had taken was the right trigger. Just a promise to go to a simple backyard barbecue.

Just call her. Cancel.

But he knew he wouldn't be able to. Kellie wouldn't understand. How could she? She didn't know the first thing about him. And he'd never have the nerve to tell her. It had been three years and he couldn't talk about it. He couldn't even say Abbie's name aloud without feeling as if his whole body was trembling. As if he were simply going to fly apart.

So he couldn't tell her. And if he couldn't tell her, he would have to go to the barbecue.

A leaden lump of dread settled in his stomach.

At first Kellie considered not telling Trevor and Tina that Riley had been invited to the cookout, although she wasn't sure where the impulse for secrecy came from.

The kids didn't even know the man—she had no reason to suspect that they would look upon him any differently than any number of other people she had casually invited over at one time or another.

For that matter, why *should* she mention him? He would be just one guest among many. She'd invited Alejandro, too, and his girlfriend (one of them). Also Lana said she would be attending. Rita would be there, and maybe Wendell—it would be a miracle, but maybe. Neighbors would probably pop over. No big deal.

Then again, what if Trevor saw Riley at their front door, assumed he was interested in her in more than a friendly fashion, and then decided to make his displeasure known in ways that only a ten-year-old boy could dream up? Her mind sifted through the possible calamities. Last Christmas there had been the fiasco of Trevor's broken ant farm—but he'd sworn that was an accident. She'd even detected him crying a little as they had sucked up his insect friends with the vacuum cleaner. Of course, before that there had been a horrible incident involving an annoying baby-sitter and a pan of chicken spaghetti Trevor's grandmother had sent over. Kellie didn't have all the details about that evening, but from the look of white-lipped hysteria on the teenager's face when she'd come home, and the state of her hair and clothing, she'd later understood why it was impossible to find baby-sitters anymore. The word on Trevor and chicken spaghetti had obviously spread.

But those incidents were well in the past. Trevor was almost eleven now—not far from being a teenager. She had no reason to believe he would have any evil deeds up his sleeve for the picnic.

It was just a hunch.

And then she remembered that Riley, after all, had been very good to her children, even if it had only been part of some bizarre scheme to keep her out of his life or assuage his guilty conscience. . . . She still wasn't sure *what* Riley had intended with those extravagant gestures of his. But she did know that she would be mortified if he ended up being thanked for his pains by having a frog dropped down his shirt.

So she decided to very casually insert Riley's name into a conversation. This way she hoped the kids would pick up on the fact that Riley's appearance at the barbecue was no big deal—just big enough of a deal that Trevor should spare their guest the torture treatment that he had been occasionally known to inflict on people he felt any hostility toward.

She waited till the most opportune moment. Saturday night she let Trevor, still flush from victory on the baseball field, phone in a pizza order. Pizza was one of the rare foods both Tina and Trevor absolutely agreed on. They loved it. After renting a video and picking up their dinner, she waited until the kids were sated with lots of pepperoni and cheese and milk before springing her news on them.

"Oh! Guess who I ran into last night!"

Trevor, down to a crust, folded it into an accordion pleat and then stuffed the whole thing into his mouth. "Moo?" is how the question came out as he chewed, swallowed, and spoke all at once.

Tina was absorbed in gingerly trying to gnaw a dangling string of cheese.

"A . . . friend," Kellie began, not as breezily as she'd hoped. "His name's Riley and he might pop by tomorrow. You know, for the barbecue. I thought since we were having people over, why not one more? Right?"

Tina was still absorbed in her pizza—for a moment it looked as if she was going to have a mozzarella avalanche on her plate. Trevor, however, was not to be fooled. He gulped down his mouthful, all alertness. Kellie felt rather than saw those legs of his start swinging beneath him.

"Who is this guy?" he asked.

She raised her shoulders. "Just a friend. I barely know him."

"You invited a guy you barely know over to our house?" he asked with rising alarm.

"He's a nice man, Trevor. You'll like him. He—"

"*Why* will I like him?" Trevor asked.

"Because he's very nice, that's all."

"You mean I'm *supposed* to like him. Is that it?"

"Of course you're supposed to," Kellie said, trying to keep her voice upbeat. She was afraid she sounded like Mrs. Cleaver. "You're supposed to like everyone, unless they give you a specific reason not to."

Trevor definitely wasn't the Beaver. "Oh, brother!" he groaned.

Tina finally began to tune in. "What's his name?"

"Riley Lombard," Kellie said.

"That's a weird name," Trevor said. "Is this guy weird?"

You have no idea, Kellie wanted to say. Actually, she'd been dying to tell someone, anyone, about her run-ins with Riley, but Rita couldn't get over the fact that he was so rich, and Alejandro was just so grateful for the business the man had brought Copycat's way that anything Riley did would have been A-OK with him.

And of course she wasn't going to start telling Trevor about Riley's psychic proclivities.

"What does he look like?" Tina asked.

"You'll see tomorrow."

"I bet he's ugly," Trevor put in.

Kellie pursed her lips. "No, he's not. In fact, Rita thought he was very good-looking."

Trevor's voice cracked up an octave. "Aunt Rita? Mom, she's crazy! You're not taking her word for anything, are you?"

"I only said that she thought he was good-looking."

Trevor folded his arms and jutted out his chin. His

whole body seemed to be vibrating. "Mom, is this guy your boyfriend?"

Tina gasped delightedly. "Boyfriend?"

Kellie couldn't help it; she laughed. The idea was so absurd. It was easier to envision the man on the moon as her boyfriend than Riley Lombard. "No!" She tried to stop giggling as Trevor continued to glower at her. "You'll understand when you meet him. He's sort of eccentric. Not even sort of, actually. The man has so much money, he builds libraries in his spare time. You might as well ask me if I'm dating Ross Perot."

That last bit just seemed to confound Trevor all the more. "Ross *who?*" he asked, no doubt envisioning another troublesome suitor.

"Never mind. Believe me, it's not a possibility. But I do want you to be nice to him."

"Why?"

"Because he'll be our guest."

"So?"

Tina finally swung on her brother. She wasn't balking at the idea of a rich, good-looking man coming to the barbecue. "It's just common courtesy, Trevor!"

He pinched up his face, mimicking her. "Common courtesy? You sound like a kindergarten teacher!"

"Trevor . . ." Kellie warned, finally reaching the end of her patience. "Try to be civilized tomorrow, just for a few hours."

"But *why?*" he asked, his voice becoming a keening whine. "Why are you making such a big deal of this?"

"It's *not* a big deal," she insisted, though she knew from the brittle edge to her voice that she was making it sound as if Riley's being there would be an event. And that made her angry, because she knew she was losing control.

As if she'd ever had it!

"What's Dad going to say when he comes back and finds you with this other Riley guy?"

Oh, for heaven's sake. Did the double standard start as young as eleven? Surely Trevor had picked up on the fact that his father had been fooling around for years before he'd left their family. She only barely managed not to spill that information now.

"Who is this guy, Mom?" Trevor whined.

She slapped a hand on the table, harder than she'd intended. Then she blurted out, "He's the man who paid for your baseball uniform, that's who."

"He did not!" Trevor retorted. "Dad did!"

Kellie shook her head. "No, he didn't. Riley Lombard paid for it, Trevor. Also for Tina's lessons."

"He *did?*" Tina was enraptured by the idea of a benefactor.

"Yes, and also . . . well, some other things." Kellie didn't know how much detail she should go into, so she hurried on, "He's just a very nice man. A philanthropist, you might say."

Trevor scowled. "A what?"

"Philanthropist. That's what they call millionaires who give away lots of their money. So that's why I invited him, as a way of saying thanks." She suddenly feared she'd implied that they should make a point of thanking Riley, and she wasn't even certain Riley wanted them to know. "But you don't have to mention the things he did for us—just be nice to him. That's all I'm asking. Okay?"

Tina was beaming all over. "Oh, I'll be the nicest girl he's ever met! I'll even help you cook and clean tomorrow. Okay?"

"That would be great," Kellie said appreciatively. Then she looked over at Trevor. His face was the color of a Big Boy tomato. "Trevor? Have some more pizza."

"I'm not hungry!" he said, rubbing a greasy hand

across his cheek as he scraped his chair back and ran from the room.

Kellie sighed, but decided to wait a moment before going after him. Then she looked over at Tina, who was positively glowing, and felt a little hope begin to rekindle inside her. Maybe tomorrow wasn't going to be a total catastrophe, after all.

Chapter Eight

Tina woke Kellie by poking a finger repeatedly against her shoulder through the bedspread and whispering loudly, "Mom . . . Mom . . . Mooooother!"

Kellie pried open one eye, since she was unable to lift her head from the pillow to use the other one. She was still half asleep. There was only the faintest dawn breaking through the curtains by her bed—until the lamp on the bedside table was popped on, sending shock waves of light straight to her tired eyes. Kellie bleated in protest. "Ouch! What time—"

"It's late! You don't want to oversleep!"

When her bleary vision shifted and focused on Tina, she saw that her daughter had somehow squeezed herself into a dress she'd worn three years ago when she was the flower girl at a cousin's wedding. It was made from a yellow satiny material with a huge baby-blue sash around the waist, which now struck Tina right under her armpits. Kellie didn't know how she could breathe.

She bounced against the mattress impatiently. "Mother, get up! We'll never get everything done in time!"

"Tina, what are you doing in that outfit?"

"It's the best dress I have," Tina said, her face sweaty with the beginnings of panic.

"Is that my lipstick you're wearing?"

"I want to make an impression!"

She certainly would. Kellie didn't know exactly how a nine-year-old could make her appearance reminiscent of Bette Davis in *Whatever Happened to Baby Jane,* but Tina had pulled it off like a champ.

She pushed herself up to her elbows and tried to shake the cotton out of her brain. "Give me ten minutes," she pleaded. "I'll be out and make breakfast." Then they could work on getting Tina back to something approaching normal.

"I've already fixed breakfast!" Tina hollered as she ran toward the door. She stopped only long enough to give Kellie one last vocal nudge. "You're not going back to sleep, are you?"

As she crashed against the pillows, Kellie answered, "The thought never entered my mind."

"Good, 'cause we'll need all the time we can get!"

Tina had been a dervish at the toaster since five-thirty, so that when Kellie stumbled into the kitchen, she discovered three places neatly set with piles of toast on each plate, each piece bearing a blob of half-melted butter.

"Everything's all ready!" Tina gave a little hop. "Except for your coffee. I didn't know how to do that."

"That's okay." Kellie went about making it herself. "Where's Trevor?"

"Asleep." Tina tipped a frustrated expression toward Kellie. "He called me something really bad, Mom!"

Kellie sighed as she gave up measuring and simply tipped the Folgers can into the cone-shaped filter. It was too damn early for precision. "What?"

"I shouldn't say, 'cause it'll just make you mad," Tina said, lifting her chin. Any number of four-letter options that would have made her see red crossed Kellie's mind. Then Tina, unable to withstand the urge to tattle for one instant longer, blurted, "He called me a little idiot!"

That wasn't so bad, was Kellie's first thought. But of course it would be to Tina. "I hope you told him sticks and stones—"

"Naturally that's what I told him," Tina said, as if that were the only possible answer.

"Good."

"And he said, 'Oh, yeah, so why are you crying?' "

In other words, the drama had begun early. Kellie considered crawling back into bed, but there was no question of rest. Especially when Tina was behaving like Martha Stewart on crack.

She should never have said anything about Riley. What if the man didn't even show up?

Even the possibility of his ditching the barbecue caused a disappointed lump to take up residence in her throat. Preposterous, of course. Riley's coming over meant no more to her than ... well, than Alejandro's appearance would mean. They were just friends, he'd said.

Yeah, right. She'd been mooning over this friend's blue eyes all weekend. In idle moments she'd recall that moment when he revealed that he'd seen her in the library. But had he known that she was snooping on him? Reading his life's story?

And then when he'd told her that he could never think of getting married again ... it just about broke her heart. He'd seemed so stoic. She'd wanted him to open up about Joanne and his daughter, but of course he hadn't. Seeing the heartache in his eyes, knowing exactly why it was there and yet being unable to say anything, was torture. She'd had the urge to reach across the table and take his hand. But of course she hadn't. All she'd been able to do was issue the invitation to the barbecue.

Which he probably didn't even want to attend. Why would he?

She needed to think about something else. She looked down at Tina assessingly. "Don't you think that outfit's a little formal?"

Tina's eyes bulged behind her glasses. "Do I look stupid?"

"No, but it's just a barbecue. You might be . . . over-dressed. Maybe you should just wear your jean shorts."

"Shorts! Mom, I wear those to *camp!*"

"Most of the adults will be wearing jeans."

"But I want to make an impression!"

Nevertheless, after breakfast Kellie managed to per-suade Tina to change into some leggings and a T-shirt with a ladybug appliqué on it. She looked more normal, but still nervous.

"Shouldn't we start on the potato salad?" she asked while Kellie perused the paper. It was only eight o'clock.

Then, fifteen minutes later, Tina dashed into the living room wearing a more elaborate lavender shirt with an eyelet collar and announced that they didn't have nearly enough snack food.

"Rita's bringing onion dip," Kellie told her.

Tina's jaw dropped, and she was suddenly quivering with nerves. "But Mom! Last year Trevor ate Aunt Rita's dip and then vomited all over Missy Baker!"

"I'll advise him to go easy," Kellie promised. If she could corner him. He'd grabbed two pieces of cold toast off the breakfast table this morning and retreated to the backyard, sulking.

"Tell him he can't throw up on a philanthropist!" Tina yelled, then ran back into her room.

At nine, Kellie began the potato salad, and the sounds of activity in the kitchen brought Tina streaking out of her room. The Mary Janes were back on, and her hair was in pink rollers.

"Tina, *what* are you doing now?"

"I'm trying to fix my hair. I want it to look nice."

When Kellie explained that Tina would have to leave her hair in that type of roller overnight to see any results, it was as if she'd stuck a pin in her daughter. Tina sagged, crestfallen.

"Why don't I just braid your hair? That would look nice."

Tina wasn't convinced. "A French braid, maybe."

Kellie had never felt her kitchen was so small until she spent an hour tripping over Tina every time she turned around. The child was frantic that Kellie would leave something out of the potato salad recipe, or that there wouldn't be enough food, or that the presentation wouldn't be appealing. Finally Kellie resorted to sending her into the backyard to find Trevor while she went to her room to get dressed.

She pulled her jeans out of her dresser, then found herself staring at them in displeasure. Her gaze cut to a colorful sundress hanging in her closet—she hadn't worn that in ages, and it would certainly be cooler. . . .

Then she shook her head. She was acting like Tina! She was going to be flipping burgers in the backyard, not idly lounging. Still, she couldn't quite force herself into her jeans. She put on a pair of red shorts and a fitted ribbed black shirt over it, which went well with a pair of strappy black sandals. She had a chunky necklace Rita had given her, and she added it to the ensemble on a whim. Then she hit the makeup.

Never mind that she'd told her kids this was "no big deal." Never mind that for her last barbecue she'd worn boxer shorts and a bowling shirt. Her unconscious seemed to have taken over.

* * *

He was hanging upside down when little Miss Mozart found him. Trevor didn't bother holding back an annoyed sigh as his sister prissed across the grass toward him in her polished black shoes.

He wished she would calm down about this stupid barbecue. He didn't even know why they were having the dumb thing. You'd think there was something to celebrate, but there wasn't. He couldn't remember feeling so gloomy. Last year this time their Dad had just left . . . and nothing had gotten better since then.

Not that you could tell it from Tina. She didn't care about anything so long as she played on her stupid keyboard all the time and got her lessons and hung out with stinky Margaret. You'd never guess that their parents were divorced, the way she acted. She didn't mind all the change they'd been through at all because she was their mom's little pet. She didn't care about their dad. Nobody did, except for him.

Sometimes it seemed that he was the only one who even noticed their dad was missing.

The sun glinted off Tina's glasses as she poked them up her nose to look at him. "Trevor, what are you doing?"

"I'm not Trevor," he said said stubbornly. "I'm a bat."

"You're too old to play bat," she lectured him. She was always lecturing—she was even worse than his mother. How could a stupid nine-year-old girl manage to act so icky and old? It didn't make sense. It was like having a middle-aged little sister. Except that sometimes she could be such a dork; no adult could live to be thirty and be that weird.

"Mom said for you to come inside," she told him.

He mimicked her because it was the easiest way to get her goat. Sure enough, she balled her hands into fists at her side and tensed her mouth so that her lips disappeared. He laughed, then felt just the slightest bit guilty for laughing. He swung up to sitting on the tree branch. He'd been upside down for so long anyway that his head felt as if it was going to explode. As he took another good look at his sister right side up, he laughed again. Her hair was sticking out every which way. "What'd you do, Tina, stick your finger in a light socket?"

"Shut up. I'll bet *you* haven't even taken a bath."

"Why should I?"

"You heard what Mom said. Mr. Lombard's going to be here."

"So?"

"So you at least ought to wash your face."

"I don't want him here anyway."

"Trevor . . ."

"Well, what's the big deal?"

"I'm going to a lot of trouble to make an impression, Trevor, so don't you spoil it. I'm going to play something on my keyboard for him." Her brow crinkled up worriedly. "Or maybe I should just play something on the CD player so he won't think I'm bragging."

Trevor rolled his eyes. "Tina, this guy is just a jerk."

"He is not!" Tina shrieked. "He gave me my lessons."

"He doesn't even know you. Don't you understand what's going on?"

"All I know is, I've got to figure out what to play."

"Don't play anything!" Trevor shouted at her.

"I will if I want to!"

Trevor felt heat rush to his face. "He's going to think Mom told you to, dork! He's going to think she likes him!"

"Maybe she does."

"She can't!" Trevor howled. His head still felt about to explode, and it wasn't from hanging upside down anymore. "She can't. What about when Dad comes back?"

Now Tina's face was all red, too. "He's not coming back, Trevor."

"He is so. He's coming back for my birthday."

"But that's just for a few days."

"So? If everything goes right, he might stay for good."

His sister glared at him. She looked the way he felt—like something about to boil over. And then she did. She started yelling and crying so that he could just barely make out what she was saying. "He's *never* going to come back for good, Trevor! Can't you get that through your head? Daddy left us! He left us forever!"

He jumped down from the tree just as their mother came flying out the back door. The timing of it made him groan. Life was so unfair! Now it looked as if he'd been torturing his little sister. His mother always blamed him when they got into fights, even just yelling fights, and it was hardly ever his fault.

Tina flung herself at their mom. "It's true, isn't it?" she blubbered. "Daddy isn't ever going to come back here. Why shouldn't we be nice to other people now? Especially if they're nice to us!"

Their mom's face was white as she rubbed Tina's crazy hair and looked stingingly at Trevor. Of course. He always got in trouble when Tina went wacko.

"I didn't do anything, Mom," he said before she could accuse him of making Tina cry. "She just turned into psycho-girl for no reason."

"I did not!"

To his surprise, his mother didn't yell at him. Instead, she looked down at Tina. "Come on, Tina. Let's go inside and fix your hair."

But Tina shook her head furiously, then leapt away. "I don't care about that now!" she said. "I don't care about anything!" She turned and fled inside.

Trevor and his mom stared at each other for a moment in shock.

"I think you should tell her that she needs to try to be normal, Mom."

She let out a laugh that really wasn't a laugh. "Normal? What's that?"

It certainly wasn't his sister.

Suddenly, the wind shifted and Trevor got a whiff of perfume. Lots of it. And his mom *never* wore perfume that heavy. He glanced at her outfit and felt his heart sink. She was just in shorts, but they were the dressy kind of shorts. She looked way better than she usually did.

"*I'm* not dressing up," he warned her.

"That's okay. You look fine."

Fine? Didn't she notice that he hadn't bathed or washed his hair? She wasn't even yelling at him for wearing his same clothes from yesterday, and *that* usually drove her crazy. Now he knew something was up.

She swiped a hand across his head. "Don't worry about Tina. I'll try to calm her down."

She turned and walked back inside with a bounce in her step. Their mom hadn't *bounced* in . . . well, he couldn't remember when.

More change. He felt depressed just thinking about it. And it was all this Riley Lombard's fault.

All morning he waited for a flash of vision to hit him again, or a sign. An omen to tell him, firmly, *Beware the barbecue! Don't go!* Seeing that happy little family unit was just going to rip him apart inside, he knew it. He'd been avoiding this kind of situation, the kind that brought a sharp pain to his chest and made his head ache with misery and longing, for years. Years.

But the sign never came.

So at twelve-fifteen, Riley knocked on Kellie's front

door, which was swung open immediately by a boy with a scowl on his face. They surveyed each other warily.

"I guess you're the philodendron," the boy finally said.

Maybe being called a plant was the sign he'd been waiting for. His cue to leave. But his feet felt glued to the porch.

"I'm Riley Lombard. And you must be . . . Trevor?"

"Right." The boy moved aside with his head down to indicate Riley could come in. "Mom's out back." Trevor darted a look at him. "That's why you're here, right? To see my mom?"

"Oh, well . . ." Riley swallowed. "I wanted to meet you, too. I've heard you're quite a baseball player."

The boy's eyes narrowed on him suspiciously, which was the first time Riley noticed that the kid resembled Kellie at all. Trevor had different coloring from Kellie— short, spiky blondish hair and gray-blue eyes. But that look, that tilt of the head, and that skepticism—he knew *those* well enough!

"I play Little League. My daddy's going to get me a new glove for my birthday. Did Mom tell you about Dad?"

A deep uneasiness settled over Riley. "No, um . . . no."

"He's living in Las Vegas," Trevor said, in what sounded like a cross between an excuse and a boast. "Temporarily."

Temporarily? He'd assumed Kellie's ex-husband was out of the picture for good. Divorces were usually pretty permanent.

"He's a really neat guy," Trevor went on, "Dad is. Mom probably didn't mention him because it makes her sad. She still cries over him. A lot."

Riley felt himself edging toward the glass door that

looked as if it might lead outside. "I'm sure it's been a difficult time. . . ."

Trevor planted himself between Riley and escape. "Oh, sure. But Dad's coming back for my birthday. That's just in July. See, he promised me this glove I've wanted. And then he and Mom'll probably want to spend a whole lot of time together, on account of how they haven't seen each other in so long and they've got so much in common. Me, for instance. Oh, and my sister, too. They'll probably want to be together a lot because of us."

"I bet." He was beginning to wonder if he should feint left and then make a dash for the backyard, when suddenly a thunderclap of sound blared from a source unseen to him.

"Oh, no!" Trevor moaned and rolled his eyes.

Riley turned toward a hallway where a little girl appeared. She was wearing a green plaid dress and Mary Janes with lacy socks, and for a moment Riley felt a band of steel constricting his heart.

He shouldn't have been worried that she would remind him of Abbie. This girl wasn't golden-haired and laughing like his little girl. Instead, she had big eyes that looked even bigger behind her thick, black-framed glasses. She was pale and freckly, with a nose that was red around the nostrils, and her hair . . . well, something unfortunate seemed to have happened there. She looked like the kind of pale, bookish girl boys always made fun of in school. The kind who always darted up her hand when the teacher asked a question. In kid vernacular, a real cootie-carrier. In adult-speak, the school librarian's dream.

Yet there was that band, squeezing him, for no other reason than that she was standing there, nine years old. Just a little older than Abbie would have been.

"Are you Mr. Lombard?" she asked in a breathy voice.

He swallowed, and nodded. He tried to pretend he didn't want to turn and run right back out the front door.

Slowly, she walked toward him. She held her shoulders back and almost seemed to be marching in time to the Tchaikovsky that boomed from the hallway. Then, when she stopped in front of him, craning her head at an uncomfortable angle to look him in the eye, she crossed her arms and spoke to him in a direct, disconcertingly adult manner.

"We're not supposed to know how you did those things for us, Mr. Lombard, but we do."

His discomfort swelled. For some stupid reason, he hadn't considered the possibility that Kellie would have told them. But of course she would have. Kids asked questions. "Oh, well . . ."

"Mom told us we weren't supposed to thank you, but playing the piano means everything to me. I'd play you something now, but I don't want to brag about how good I am or anything. I'd rather play piano than read, and reading is just about the most important thing in the world, I think."

The librarian's dream, all right. His lips crooked up in a smile.

She took a deep breath. "So even though I'm not supposed to, would you mind if I said thank you?"

Maybe he should have told her that no thanks were necessary, because they weren't. And yet it seemed so cute that she was being so formal, so polite. How could he say no?

"I'd be delighted," he said.

Unfortunately, the minute he gave her permission to thank him, something went terribly, terribly wrong. Tina Sumners started trembling. Her face turned splotchy and red, and her eyes squeezed shut beneath the thick lenses of her glasses.

And then she flung herself at him. Not just in a hug, either. She leapt into his arms, weeping and proclaiming, "Thank you, thank you, thank you!" She clung to his neck like a barnacled alien space creature, and breathed in loud, wracking sobs between words. Looking at her while she was still on the ground, when she'd seemed to stand so awkwardly in the doorway, somber and comically wrong in her little-girl clothes, he never would have guessed how light she was. But when she flew into his arms, she felt wiry and small, and feather-light.

More strangely, he never would have guessed how light *he* would feel, holding Kellie Sumner's crying child. His head felt strangely clear, and that band around his chest let up. A happy, smiling little girl might have dragged him down. Tina, in her misery, gave him something to focus on.

Something to fix.

"Honey, I am so glad you're getting on with your life!"

Kellie regarded Linelle warily. She didn't like the joyous tone her mother was taking. Nor was she comfortable with the rapturous gaze her mother aimed at Riley, who was mixing in surprisingly well with the other guests in her backyard. But when it came to keeping tabs on Riley's whereabouts, Linelle had nothing on Kellie. Though she'd tried not to, Kellie had been alert to his every move, as if he had some sort of tracking device her hostess radar was following, like on a PBS nature show. She had heard Riley talking sports with Mr. Hubert from next door. He'd spent a long time discussing action movies with Alejandro and his girlfriend, Katie. And he had defused a possibly explosive situation by paying special attention to Lana, who had gawked at him as if he were a movie star (Alejandro *who?*). Riley had refereed a game of freeze tag with all the kids (except Trevor, who was in a tree and wouldn't come down) and listened to old Mrs.

Gibbon complain about her arthritis while he'd consumed three hot dogs.

The fact of the matter was, seeing him there in her backyard was doing strange things to her.

"I think it's wonderful the way you're moving on to a new chapter," her mother said approvingly.

Kellie took a breath for patience. She knew *just* where her mother's conversation was leading and made a stab to cut her off at the pass. "Could you possibly be talking about how well the store is doing?"

"The store!" her mother hissed. "Are you crazy? I'm talking about that man you brought with you!"

For man, substitute incredibly rare, precious jewel a woman would have to be blind or half witted or both to pass up, Kellie translated dutifully. Her mother seemed to have forgotten that Kellie was at her own house and hadn't brought anyone.

"Mom, I just invited him as a friendly gesture."

Linelle put her hands on her hips and fixed Kellie with a scolding stare. "For heaven's sake, Kellie, give yourself a little credit. He's here, isn't he?"

"Yes, but—"

"And for that matter, why aren't you over there talking to him? You'd think he was Tina's boyfriend, not yours."

It was true; Riley had mingled with everyone, but Tina had monopolized most of his time. "That's because he's *not* my boyfriend. He's just a friend, Mother."

Linelle, whose opinions had been cemented pre-Betty Friedan, blinked obtusely. "A what?"

Kellie laughed. *"Friend.* People you like to hang out with? You have them yourself," she reminded her. "You know, those people you play bingo with on Wednesday nights?"

Linelle remained stubbornly unconvinced. "Kellie honey, if you're wasting your time with that man playing bingo, you're more of a birdbrain than I ever imagined!"

Kellie's breath came out as a puff of exasperation. All her life she'd heard of people pressured and plagued by overly supportive parents. Parents who believed their children could do no wrong. People so deluded by parental devotion that they would follow their children to the gas chamber howling about how their little baby had been ill treated. Kellie envied that kind of loyalty. When it came to her private life, her mother always thought she was making disastrous, irreversible mistakes. She'd been wrong to marry Rick (well, Kellie did give Linelle credit for that opinion); then, eleven years later, she'd been wrong to divorce Rick (never mind that Rick was with another woman, in another state, and Kellie didn't have a whole lot of choice in the matter). Now there was something wrong with her because she was trying to be careful and not just plunge into dating again.

"Mother, I barely know him."

"Did you know he drives a BMW?" her mother asked, her eyes practically glittering. "High end."

"I should. His high end almost killed me."

The way her mother's pointy jaw flopped open indicated that Linelle thought that would be a fine way to go. "He must be very wealthy!"

Kellie nodded. "He's stinkin' rich. His name's Riley Lombard."

"Riley Lombard? The . . ." Linelle swallowed. "The man who donates so much for libraries and swimming pools? Lombard Park? *That* Riley Lombard?"

Kellie nodded. How come everyone knew about this guy except her?

"But I thought he'd be much older," Linelle whispered reverently. "Balder." It was as if it were all too much to wrap her mind around.

"Think Daddy Warbucks with Rogaine, Mom. It's a brave new world."

"I guess so!"

"But we're still just friends," Kellie said.

Linelle began to look sort of panicky. Her hand locked on Kellie's arm, and her voice lowered to a furious whisper that reminded Kellie too much of Tina. "Honey, I certainly don't want to tell you how to run your life, but do you think you're being wise?"

Kellie steeled herself for what she knew what was ahead. "What do you mean?" As if she didn't know!

"I mean . . . you might think of your children, Kellie. Now don't start fussing at me! I admit I'm old fashioned, but I don't think it's good for a boy to be raised by just one parent. I saw Diane Sawyer talking about children of divorce just last week, and she said—"

"It's not like I had a lot of choice in the matter, Mother."

"You need to go *on!* So you lost Rick—find yourself another husband."

Kellie laughed. "You act as if I'd just misplaced Rick, Mother. And it's not as if a husband is as easily replaced as a lost umbrella. There's a matter of personalities involved."

"Well, goodness, I know that!" her mother said in exasperation. "Haven't I been a widow all these years? Luckily, *my* children were practically grown before I lost my husband."

There she went again. The way Linelle talked about women losing their husbands, you'd think there was a lost-and-found department somewhere with unclaimed men waiting for their absent-minded wives to remember where they'd left them.

"At least give it some thought, Kellie! If you want friends, you can always join a club. Finding a good man is a lot harder. Finding a Riley Lombard . . ." She let the sentence dangle tantalizingly.

Kellie snorted with laughter. "It's easier than you

think. At least for me. My trouble is trying *not* to find him.''

Her mother threw up her hands in despair. "Oh, Kellie!"

By the time her mother was finally distracted by a neighbor, Kellie had that limp, wrung-out, inadequate feeling that only a conversation with a disapproving parent could leave a person with. And no sooner had her mother freed the spot next to her than it was filled again, this time by Rita.

"I thought that was the guy you couldn't stand," Rita told her, gazing admiringly across the back lawn to where Riley still sat next to Tina.

"Why would you think that?"

"Kellie, you chewed him out in public and then, as I recall, you nearly killed us both because you were so freaked out by the guy. Last time I heard, you were calling the man a weirdo and a psychotic."

Kellie lifted her shoulders. "Mm."

"He doesn't seem to be annoying you now," Rita pointed out with a meaningful grin.

"We're just friends."

But Rita didn't seem any more eager to accept that explanation than Linelle had been. "A friend? With *that?* Kellie, are you nuts? That guy's not somebody you have friendly thoughts about. That's lust city sitting over there on your red picnic bench."

Kellie glanced over at him listening patiently to Tina, and felt as though the tough ground beneath the Bermuda grass had gone mushy all of a sudden. It wasn't just because Rita had pointed out that he was a hottie. That salient fact had come through loud and clear from the moment she'd first clapped eyes on him. What struck her now was that he was looking very intently at something Tina was drawing on a napkin with a Bic ballpoint pen. He wasn't just slumming. He'd been talking to Tina now for over thirty minutes, she realized, and not just smiling patiently and waiting for her to leave. Tina was going to be impossible to live with after this. After a morning of despair, her prince had come and swept her off her feet, just like in a fairy tale.

As she watched them, Kellie felt as if she might be in jeopardy of being swept away, too; remembering her agreement to just be friends, however, she shook away the notion. She wasn't the kind of woman men swept off their feet, anyway.

She was distracted by Trevor, who was finally down from his tree but still standing next to it, picking at bark. He scowled at Riley, as though it were possible to put some kind of voodoo hex on the man.

"Just friends, huh?" Rita crossed her arms and sighed. "Too bad. If I weren't spoken for, I might go for him myself."

Kellie looked at her curiously. "Spoken for?"

Rita blushed like a schoolgirl—you'd never guess that she was twenty-eight and had been dating the same unresponsive slug for five years. "I probably shouldn't tell you this, but Wendell and I are probably going to get engaged this year."

"Get *engaged* this year?" Knowing Wendell, he'd insist on a interminable engagement. The guy was definitely on the slow track. "Has he asked you?"

"Wendell?" Rita asked. "Oh, no! I mean, not yet."

"Well then, how . . . ?"

"It's just a hunch I have," Rita confided. "For one thing, he told me he wanted me to meet his family sometime."

Kellie's jaw dropped. "His *family?* You mean you've been going out with the man for five years and you've never met his parents?"

"No! It's the strangest thing, isn't it? I thought he was an orphan."

Kellie shook her head, unable to resist playing disapproving older sister. "Don't you think that it's sort of strange that you've never met these people?"

"Well . . . not really," Rita answered. "After all, he's only met *you* a few times."

Kellie tossed her hands in frustration. "That's because the man's a hermit! It's not as if you don't invite him over here. Where is he today? Why didn't he come?"

"He said he needed to do his grocery shopping."

"Rita, that's no answer!" Kellie, who hadn't been offended by his absence before, felt offended now both as a sister and a hostess.

"Well, you know how shopping is. It can take time."

"Oh, sure. It can take an hour, tops. Which leaves, let's see . . . how many waking hours does Wendell have these days? Eight?"

"Kellie, would you quit bitching about him? I really do feel like introducing me to his parents is a step in the right direction. It seems sort of old-fashioned and romantic."

Romantic? Sunday dinner with Mother and Father Wendell? "I think you guys need couples counseling."

"I *know* it," Rita replied. "I've been trying to get Wendell into a therapist for at least a year, but he won't hear of it. Said he spent half his life on a psychiatrist's couch and it didn't do a damn bit of good."

Kellie stared at her sister in disbelief. "Half his life? You never told me this!"

"It's not his fault he's so messed up, Kellie. He says it's his parents' fault."

She nodded. "Right, the people it would be so old-fashioned and romantic to meet." She sighed. "And since when have you been trying to drag Wendell to couples counseling?"

"Oh, you know . . ." She turned pink. "Since we started having intimacy problems."

Kellie shuddered, wishing now that she'd never asked. Of course now that she *had* asked, she couldn't not know the whole story. "What kind of intimacy problems?"

"He won't. We don't . . ." Rita now resembled a fire engine with a spiral perm. "Well, we stopped all that a long time ago."

"Stopped all what?"

"You know . . ."

Kellie gaped at her sister's beet-red face as the meaning finally dawned on her. "Are you saying you're not having sex? Well, what's the point in getting married? You two are acting as if you already are!"

Rita laughed. "Oh, Kellie, you're such a card! Well, it's like Wendell says. Life isn't all fireworks."

"So you two have discussed this?"

"Well, sure."

"And you've been going on mutually agreed-upon, celibate laundry dates?"

Rita nodded. "Sometimes we go to restaurants. Wendell always says the best part of dating is going out to dinner anyway. You know how he likes good food. He says he still enjoys that."

Kellie sighed.

Rita's brows furrowed. "Do you think there's something wrong with that?"

"Look, I can't tell you how to live your life, but . . ."

"I mean, all relationships cool off, don't they?" Rita asked. "Isn't that what you're always telling me. 'Don't trust love,' you say."

"Yeah, but . . ."

At that moment, Kellie glanced over and happened to catch Riley's eye. He'd been staring at her. She could tell because he flinched just a fraction when she caught him watching—and yet he didn't look away. If nothing else, that brilliant gaze of his seemed to regroup and intensify, causing a heavy warmth to settle in the pit of her stomach. She sank down to sitting on a plastic lawn chair and forced herself to look intently down at her toenails sticking out from her black sandals. She took a long, bracing swig of iced tea.

"Kellie?"

"Huh?" she mumbled absently.

"I was just asking, don't you think all relationships cool off sooner or later?"

I know one that wouldn't.

Stop it!

She shook her head, trying to clear it.

"You don't?" Rita said, a little panicked. "So you think Wendell and I are weird?"

Kellie glanced up at her, trying to rejoin the conversation. "Wendell is definitely weird." At the same time she was ever so slowly craning her neck back toward that picnic bench where Tina was holding forth, Riley was grinning secretly at Kellie, and Trevor was walking right behind him carrying a huge Tupperware bowl of potato salad aloft on one wobbly palm like an inept head waiter. Trevor, too, was grinning secretly.

Something about the scene made her heart stop and her mind think about . . . chicken spaghetti! Panic shot through her, and she leapt to her feet with a muffled cry.

"Kellie, what is it?" Rita asked.

"Potato salad!" she shrieked.

Too late.

In the next moment, Riley's blond head was dripping new potatoes in creamy mustard sauce.

Chapter Nine

"I'm grounding him. Till doomsday."

She could hear Riley on the other side of the bathroom door, shaking out his hair. She'd insisted he rinse off there; she couldn't have him dripping potato salad all over that high-end BMW.

"It was just an accident, Kellie."

Kellie folded her arm across her chest. *How?* How could her own flesh and blood do this to her? And it wasn't just Trevor, though heaven knew she wasn't letting him off the hook. No indeed. As far as she was concerned, he'd be *on* the hook—skewered, you might say—till the day he left for college or the penitentiary, whichever came first. But to make matters worse, after Trevor's potato salad avalanche, Tina had fallen apart again, hysterical over having just been shamed. She had directed her anger at Trevor, but all her tears had fallen on Riley's already soggy shirt.

Kellie shouldn't have been surprised by Tina's outburst. After finding her kids fighting this morning, she was beginning to reassess some old assumptions. One, she'd always thought Tina was the mild-mannered, sweet one. But inside that Anne of Green Grables loving exterior was a powder keg of emotion. Two, she'd assumed that of her children, Tina was the one who was walking around with her head in the clouds. But now she was beginning to sense that Trevor harbored some unrealistic dreams himself about his father coming home. Probably running off Riley was part of a demented master plan to get his father back.

Earning Kellie's eternal gratitude, Rita had offered to whisk her niece and nephew away for a Sonic limeade in order to let Riley put himself to rights without worrying about being sabotaged again by Trevor or having his shirt used as a Kleenex by Tina. The rest of the company had cleared out pretty quickly after the so-called accident—herded, no doubt, by Linelle, who saw this as the perfect opportunity to leave her daughter and her new millionaire boyfriend alone.

But of course Kellie was almost as embarrassed as Tina had been; the mishap had been no more an accident than the Japanese raid on Pearl Harbor was. It was her son declaring war. She remembered Trevor's sly grin right before the tub of potato salad had tipped. She had lived through the moment in her mind a hundred times already, always wishing she'd been able to leap across the yard in a single miraculous Keri Strug-like vault and rescue Riley from Trevor's assault-by-sidedish.

"But your shirt . . ."

On the other side of the doorway, he chuckled. "Actually, I like this one better."

He stepped out of the bathroom in one of Rick's old T-shirts she had scrounged from the garbage bag in her closet—her rag bag, which was what she had dubbed the clothes Rick had left. The shirt was red and had the slogan *Coke is it!* emblazoned in diagonal white letters across the front. She'd seen Rick wear it a million times, of course, had seen him in it till she was sick of the sight of the thing, but now she greedily eyed its snug fit over Riley's muscled chest and arms. Nothing about his appearance reminded her of how the T-shirt used to flop over her ex-husband's wiry frame.

How could it be that a man who worked at a desk all day, who didn't even have to drive himself places if he didn't want to, could fill out a T-shirt so much better than a construction worker? Life really wasn't fair, she guessed.

Just this once, however, she felt she was actually benefiting from its inequities. Riley standing in front of her, his hair still damp, his skin glistening, was a blast of Ivory-clean adult male, something she hadn't been around in a while. Perhaps too long a while. He seemed to be one of those men whom fragrances clung to; she smelled her apple shampoo mixed with the shower soap. The scent of him worked on her senses, bringing to mind all the hundreds of lonely nights she'd spent in her double bed. Her double bed that was only a room away.

Suddenly, the hallway seemed to close in on her, making it seem tighter, more intimate. Too intimate. She stepped back, clamped her mouth closed, and forced a tight smile. "If you like the shirt, it's yours."

"No kidding?"

"Consider it a souvenir from your day in hell."

"I know you'll never believe this, but I had a good time."

He continued smiling at her, and she felt overly warm. Maybe she'd stayed out in the afternoon heat too long. Sunstroke was manifesting itself as lust. "Come to the kitchen. I'll fix you something to drink."

She turned and tried to walk calmly toward the kitchen, although in truth she felt as if she were skittering across the hardwoods. She was too aware of him walking behind her; she could almost feel his gaze watching her from behind.

Which wasn't her best angle, she thought with a frown.

There was still tea left in the ceramic pitcher, so she excavated some ice out of the solid bag in the freezer. Most of her glasses were in the dishwasher, but she scrounged two from the back of a cabinet and filled them with tea. When she handed one to Riley, his gaze was so intent on her that he didn't appear to notice that he was drinking from a *Lion King* glass with a cartoon wildebeest on it. He said thanks and downed his drink in one gulp, then set the glass aside on the counter.

He cleared his throat. "I'd call today a big success, wouldn't you?"

She laughed. "Which part? My daughter having Chernobylesque emotional meltdowns, or that potato salad bath you took?"

"I told you I had a good time." He seemed surprised to be saying so. "I had fun."

She still wasn't convinced. "This probably wasn't your normal gathering."

"That's why I liked it. It was relaxed. Easy."

"Easy?" Was she imagining things, or had he somehow inched closer to her without her noticing? "Dodging bowls of potato salad?"

"You can't imagine the things I'm usually stuck at."

"Right—all those charity fund-raisers." She remembered all the pictures she'd seen in those articles. "The Museum of Fine Arts, the Children's Hospital, the library. Black-tie ballet premieres . . ."

"How do you know about all that stuff?" He eyed her suspiciously.

And no wonder! She sounded as if she'd been snooping on him. Which of course she had—pawing shamelessly through every article she could find on him in the public library. Heat suffused her cheeks, and she took several more glugs of tea, which she proceeded to choke on.

He slapped her back. "Are you all right?"

The feel of his hand against her back nearly choked her more. She nodded through teary eyes and found her voice again. At least nearly gagging, while not winning her any awards for daintiness, had bought her time to think of an excuse. "Oh, you know ... they always feature society stuff on the local news."

"Mm." He sighed. "I don't mind socializing for worthy causes, but I wouldn't exactly call it relaxation. You know what I mean?"

"Too stuffy for you?"

"It's hard to get a good hot dog at an opera premiere."

She nodded. "The curse of bad taste."

When she looked up again, she knew he had inched toward her. The kitchen was closing in on her the way the hallway had, and that apple scent was stronger than ever. Unfortunately, she was standing in the corner of her cabinets, so there was nowhere she could back to. She tapped her fingernails anxiously against the Formica as her heart seemed to pound against her rib cage.

He looked down at her fingers. Then, in a move that seemed friendly yet was far too intimate, he covered her hand with his. "You've got great kids, Kellie."

She was flushed with confusion at the feel of his hand over hers; but then his statement was so surprising that she almost forgot they were touching. Almost. "I do?"

Sure, she might think so, but how could he?

He grinned. "They weren't what I expected."

"Oh!" She directed herself to pull her hand back, but it wasn't going anywhere. "It would be hard to expect Trevor. It would be like anticipating a Dallas blizzard. He's not something nature serves up very often."

She didn't know whether or not Riley heard her muttered "thank God." He was frowning thoughtfully into her eyes. Again she had the sensation of being mesmerized by that gaze of his, pinned in place like a bug on a board. If she didn't know better, she would have said she felt she was being . . . charmed.

Her legs felt as if they were going out on her once more, only this time there was no lawn chair to sink into. She locked her knees to keep herself upright. His gaze lowered to her lips and she wondered if even her locked knees would sustain her.

"I'm sorry I seemed to have chased everyone away."

"Oh . . ." She lifted her hands limply. "It wasn't your fault. It's just . . ."

He nodded knowingly. "It's just your mom thinks we're an item. And so did half the people in your backyard today."

She sank against the counter in embarrassment. "Did someone say something to you?"

"No, I could tell by the looks I kept getting." He did a dead-on imitation of the coy half smile, the arched brow, the questioning glint in the eye. But somehow Riley made it look sexy. Then he laughed. "Ridiculous, isn't it?"

She swallowed. "Ludicrous. I kept telling everybody we're only friends."

He shook his head and looked into her eyes. "People are just so single-minded. They want to believe that just because I'm a man and you're a woman. . . ."

God, she bet he was a good kisser.

She shook her head violently. "Just because you're available and I'm available . . ."

His gaze hadn't moved from hers. It was so intense. It didn't look like a *just friendly* gaze, either.

They were all alone here. It would be so easy.

He chuckled. "Aren't people . . . ?"

"Ludicrous?" she asked faintly.

His eyes darkened. His gaze dipped to her lips. "Kellie . . ."

His voice was a bare rasp, yet it worked on her like a

caress. Like someone's hand tracing her spine. It drew her closer to him, even though she knew she should probably turn and run. But she was too much of a coward for that. Too cowardly . . . and too curious.

When Riley bent forward and touched his lips to hers, lightly at first in a quick, glancing kiss, she shut her eyes against the shock of heat that shot through her. *Just a kiss*, she vowed to herself. That was all she was allowing. After all, she had been so good for so long—a year since the divorce and even longer before that since she and Rick had engaged in so much as a smooch. Didn't her lips deserve this little refresher course?

And her lips took to Riley like eager students. Riley's tentative kiss deepened, his mouth slanting against hers more forcefully. His tongue touched hers; then her arms got in on the action, curling around Riley's neck and tickling the short, soft hair of his nape.

Oh, yes, it was all coming back to her rather quickly, and this time it actually seemed better than she remembered. Riley was both surer and more giving than anyone she'd ever kissed before; Rick had always been a sort of perfunctory kisser, now that she thought about it. As though it was just a necessary step they needed to get through. But she got the feeling that Riley could go on doing this for quite a while.

Or maybe she just wanted him to. It seemed she'd been dreaming of this moment, of Riley kissing her, for years now. But that was impossible. She'd only known the man for three weeks.

Yet sometime in those three weeks, somewhere in the back of her mind, she'd speculated about how his chest would feel when she pressed up against him, where he would hold his hands, how warm his lips would be. She'd dreamed about him, daydreamed about him without realizing it; but now those illicit thoughts came back to her, and she only knew it because every time they shifted against each other, moving in a dance that was both familiar and completely new, she thought, *This is even better than I thought he would be. . . .*

She heard herself let out a sigh—of satisfaction, of impatience, of wanting more. And who knew how much more there would have been. She was so out of it, she was little more than a wet noodle in his arms. He might have hauled her up on the kitchen counter and had his way before she even thought to remember that they were "just friends," had not the sound of a car engine pulling up the drive shot a shiver of cold reality through her.

She froze. Riley froze.

When she looked up into his eyes, his pupils were dilated and the whites of his eyes wide with shock. He was staring at her as if he'd forgotten whom it was, exactly, that he was kissing. Which wasn't exactly flattering, now that her brain cells were regrouping enough to let her think the matter through.

She pushed against his chest and took a step back. "That's my sister with Trevor and Tina."

Riley did a flea-hop backward. "Kellie, I'm sorry."

Her neck and face felt as if they were on fire, and the last thing she needed right now was for her kids—not to mention Rita—to see her blushing. "No, please—"

Afterwards, she couldn't remember what she'd intended to say. *No, please, I wanted that kiss as much as you did?* Or, *No, please, we're both adults . . . it was bound to happen?* Or maybe she'd meant *No, please, could you just quickly sneak out the back door and never come back?*

Who knew? She never got the chance to finish because Riley cut her off. "That was a horrible mistake," he said. And then, when she just stood blinking at him in disbelief, he added, "I'd better go."

She didn't see him out. She doubted she could have kept up with him anyway, he streaked out of that kitchen so fast. The front door opened, and she heard murmured greetings and good-byes, then the heavy footsteps of her children tromping toward her through the living room. Her feet were still glued to the linoleum when they appeared.

Trevor stalked straight toward the fridge. She heard Tina head for her bedroom.

Rita was standing in front of Kellie, arms crossed, a tentative smile on her lips. "So . . . ?"

A horrible *mistake*. That was what he'd said. Not just your plain old garden variety mistake. A *horrible* mistake. And then, "I'd better go." Not, *I didn't mean for that to happen.* No *I'll call you later.* Just oops and farewell. She felt like the victim of a hit-and-run.

"Well . . . ?" Rita prodded.

Kellie wasn't sure what to say. Clearly, Rita wanted some savory gossip to take home. But Kellie felt distinctly unsavory at the moment. What was she supposed to tell her sister? That Riley was apparently less into intimacy than Wendell?

For once she was glad to have a Trevor problem to concentrate on. She caught her slippery son by the T-shirt collar as he was attempting to slink out of the kitchen with a can of Sprite. "Hold it!"

He yelped in surprise, all choir boy innocence. "What did I do?"

"You're grounded," she told him, glad she'd had the chance to rehearse this, since her tongue was having difficulty forming any words at all. "Till doomsday."

It was all wrong. He wasn't ready for this.

It was the kids who had thrown him, Riley kept telling himself. Not because he hadn't expected them. Of course he had. In the day leading up to the barbecue, he'd thought about little else. He'd sweated bullets over being around those kids.

Trouble was, in his head he'd gotten them all wrong. He'd kept imagining a smiling, happy family. A sitcom family straight out of the fifties. But Kellie's crew wasn't picture perfect; in fact, it was teeming with troubles. Unlike what he'd feared, it didn't remind him of the family he could never get back. Trevor and Tina didn't stir up feelings he couldn't deal with. Instead, he found them imminently *dealable*. They were kids with problems; he was used to fixing problems. Riley had felt drawn into all the churning drama.

But of course Kellie had thrown him, too. The intimacy of her kitchen, mixed with her fresh smell of charcoal and sunshine, had surprised him. He hadn't realized how much he'd wanted her, needed her, until she was in his arms, until he'd felt the warmth of her lips, tasted the sweet tea flavor of her kiss. Until just that moment, he hadn't realized how serious the situation between them really was.

Just friends? Who was he kidding?

He didn't have that many women friends. The closest woman friend he'd had was Joanne, in college. And look what happened.

The same thing that had happened with Kellie, in fact. . . .

He sank into an overstuffed chair in his library, wobbly and boneless feeling even hours after that kiss. He was still wearing the Coke T-shirt. He wanted to call Kellie, to rehash the whole thing and ask her what she was feeling, but of course he couldn't dare. He'd seen the look in her eyes when she pushed away from him. *I can't believe I just let that happen,* her gaze had said.

And he'd felt the same way. Only now he also felt guilty for having scuttled out of her kitchen so hurriedly.

But he doubted she would have wanted him to stay. Would she?

It wasn't right. He obviously wasn't ready. If he were ready, he wouldn't be feeling this panic, this confusion. As much as he wanted Kellie, he couldn't see himself starting over. It was too wearying, too dangerous. Yes, dangerous. When you cared for people, you had to consider all the things that could go wrong. And there were so many things that could—things you never dreamed of till they actually happened.

What was he going to do? He couldn't pretend he just didn't care about her—and now her family. He did. But he couldn't care too much. Why wasn't there some graceful halfway point beyond friendship and just short of romantic love where they could meet?

Nathaniel whispered into the room, then cleared his throat noisily. Riley never could understand why Nathaniel bothered to be so quiet when he clearly had no intention of being ignored.

The butler held out a crystal custard dish containing a perfect circle of blackberry sorbet, artistically decorated with a sprig of mint and an almond biscotti. "Fayard fixed this snack for you, though frankly I don't know why he bothered. The minute his back is turned, you betray him. That Dolce & Gabbana shirt you wore today had mustard stains all over it. *Yellow* mustard." He sniffed in distaste.

Riley chuckled. His insides might be in a knot, but at least his domestic staff was on an even keel. "Are you and Fayard getting along?" Last time he had checked in, there had been an incident with the coffee pot being hurled across the kitchen.

Nathaniel lifted his head and gave a long-suffering sigh. "I'm *trying* to be reasonable. But honestly, whoever said the course of true love never did run smooth was smart, smart, smart." He frowned at Riley's T-shirt. "I hate to tell you this, but corporate logos on casual wear are *so* not stylish."

"I wasn't trying to make a fashion statement. I had an accident."

Nathaniel rolled his eyes in renewed grief for Riley's recently destroyed garment. "Oh, your shirt! The garment *reeked* of potato salad. The Fannie Farmer kind," he said, his upper lip curling in distaste. "I ask you, is that any way to treat your dry-clean-onlies?"

Maybe he should send Nathaniel over to talk to Trevor. On the other hand, Trevor was probably being punished enough without having a caustic butler lecturing him about fine fabrics.

The thought gave Riley an idea, though. "What do you think about children, Nathaniel?"

Nathaniel looked for a moment as if he might drop his sorbet. "You know I love kids."

Of course. Nathaniel had been Abbie's first best friend, her baby-sitter while Joanne went shopping. Her favorite place had been in the kitchen with Fayard and Nathaniel.

Riley wondered if he shouldn't have brought up the subject. But now that he had, he just couldn't drop it. "I need some help. You're always good for advice."

"Yes, but you so rarely follow it." He put a hand on his hip. "What children are you talking about?"

"Just in general. For instance, were you a happy child?"

Nathaniel shifted uncomfortably. "What's your definition of happy?"

Riley leaned forward, interested. "What was your situation?"

Nathaniel looked distracted. "My father left us when I was eight."

"And did you miss having a man around the house?"

"Hm?" He snapped to and quipped, "Oh, no. Or at

least, I was too busy being fixated on my mother to notice."

Riley leaned back again, sighing.

"Are you thinking of adopting?" Nathaniel asked, cocking his head. His brow was pinched.

"No." He wasn't sure what he was thinking of. "Only ... what do you think it would take to make a child happy?"

"Oh, are you playing fairy godmother? Well, that's easy—just give them their heart's desire." He laughed. "It's a snap."

For a moment, it *did* seem like a snap. Their heart's desire. Having the notion put so succinctly crystallized the situation for Riley. Tina, who had performed for him on her keyboard, clearly yearned for an instrument worthy of her talents, like the one her friend had.

Like he had.

Riley thought of the antique upright grand gathering dust in his living room and felt a little ashamed. He didn't even play piano. Not even "Chopsticks." What was he doing with a Steinway?

Then he remembered ... Joanne. She'd wanted Abbie to learn to play and had intended to start her on lessons the day she turned five. She'd read in a book that five was the perfect age to begin serious musical training. A rush of memories came flooding back, unbidden, unwanted. Abbie pounding on the keys making an unbearable racket so that suddenly neither Joanne nor Riley was sure they could tolerate having the instrument in the house. How long would it take Abbie to become proficient enough that her practicing wouldn't drive them all bananas?

Well.

Nathaniel cleared his throat again, and Riley looked up through his fog of memory. "Yes?"

"Did you want this sorbet or should I take it back?"

"Oh . . ." He felt indecisive, even about dessert.

"I'll take it back," Nathaniel said with a sigh of resignation. "Don't think I don't know about those Snickers bars hidden in your desk."

"Thanks for reminding me."

When Nathaniel was gone, Riley leaned back, thinking again about Trevor and Tina. And Abbie. They were all swirling around his mind now. As was Kellie, and their kiss. No, he wasn't ready. This was just the sort of emotional miasma he'd been trying to avoid all these years. Why had he let this happen?

He remembered that vision. That flash of a smile, that blinding white. It had seemed so strong. But he wasn't ready. He had to have been wrong. Maybe his wires had gotten crossed.

Kellie certainly hadn't been smiling at him today before he scuttled out of her house. It was hard to know what she'd felt. But whatever it was, he felt the need to make amends.

Oh, are you playing fairy godmother? Well that's easy.

At least playing fairy godmother made a lot more sense than his misguided stab at being Don Juan.

The piano arrived on Wednesday.

The antique upright grand—a Steinway!—could barely fit through the front door, and for a moment Kellie had prayed that it *wouldn't* fit, that she would have a solid reason to break Tina's heart and send the instrument back. Because although the piano deliverers relayed no message with their surprise package, there wasn't a doubt in Kellie's mind who had sent it. She knew only one person in the world with the means to send such a gift.

But the piano did fit through the door, and of course Tina also knew who her benefactor was. She called Riley immediately and thanked his answering machine profusely every hour on the hour until Kellie finally sent her off to bed.

What was Riley up to? She sat up till midnight, staring at the piano that now devoured their living room. Was it really a present for Tina, or was there some other hidden meaning lurking there? It was a puzzle.

He was a puzzle. Maybe he thought she wasn't so horrible after all. Or maybe he liked Tina but still felt Kellie was horrible, which wasn't Tina's fault. Or maybe this was an indication that he was back in his send-gifts-to-push-people-away mode. But didn't he realize by now that she would have to thank him for this?

Or was that what he was waiting for . . . ?

It was maddening. She didn't understand his state of mind any better than she could make sense of the push-me-pull-me feelings churning inside herself. One minute she was angry, the next she was seeing things in proper perspective again: Riley was a nut, and she was a reasonable woman with too much going on in her life to worry about the whims of a fickle millionaire.

The next day Copycat did a brisk business in the morning, but settled down in the afternoon. During a lull, Kellie went to the back of the store and called Riley's work number.

His secretary answered in her usual crisp manner. It became even crisper when she realized the caller was the woman who had twice stormed the fortress she was supposed to protect and defend. "Mr. Lombard is not in."

"Oh. Could you give him my name and have him call me?"

"Mr. Lombard won't be in for quite some time, I'm afraid."

Kellie frowned. "I hope he's not sick."

"No, he's in Hong Kong."

When Kellie hung up the phone again, she felt numb.

All her efforts at trying to think like a reasonable adult and not a lovesick teenager went down the toilet. Hong Kong! And his secretary made it sound as if he intended to be there for an eon. Was that why he sent the piano over? She had a vision of him closing up his house, throwing sheets over all the furniture he couldn't bear to part with, drawing the shutters closed, and giving Fayard the year off.

Wouldn't a normal person have mentioned the fact that he was about to pack himself off to Hong Kong? Or maybe millionaires thought nothing of jetting themselves off to Asia for extended visits. Or maybe he thought he needed to put some distance between them. But did a mere kiss warrant a couple of continents' worth of distance?

And what was she supposed to do now? Wait for him to send a postcard so she could figure out where they stood?

She stumbled back out front to see Alejandro posting a new flyer up on the cork board at the front of the store. The board had flyers for people seeking roommates, trying to sell musical instruments, cars, or computers, and advertising various services such as lawn mowing or dog walking. It was a little messy, but Kellie felt the bulletin board gave the store more of a community feel.

"Get a load of this one," Alejandro said, pointing at the latest addition. "This crazy woman brought it by just now. A real character."

> *Love Problems? Money Dilemmas?*
> *Madame Mira Can See Into Your Future!*
> *Palm Readings. Tarot Cards. Low, Low Rates.*

The flyer had a drawing of a crystal ball and was fringed at the bottom with tear-offs bearing Madame Mira's phone number.

"Incredible!" Kellie stared at the sign, frowning. A

month ago, she probably would have yanked the flyer down and thrown it into the trash. Letting lawn-mowing services advertise was one thing; allowing a charlatan to use her store to drum up suckers was another matter entirely. Moreover, a month ago she would have spent at least ten minutes stewing over how gullible people were. She would have griped aloud about how working people could throw away their hard-earned money on nonsense. Utter nonsense.

And now?

Now the moment Alejandro's back was turned, Kellie ripped off Madame Mira's number and hid it in the pocket of her khakis.

Chapter Ten

"Oh ... I don't know about this."

Rita was frozen on the cracked steps leading up to a crumbling brick duplex in East Dallas. It was a part of town that had long been on its way to gentrification, only the gentry hadn't seemed to make it to this particular building yet. The roof was concave, with graying, weathered, warped shingles curling toward the sun. The yellow brick was so porous that Kellie was reminded again of the Swiss cheese she had failed to buy for Tina. An overgrown, half-dead althea bush camouflaged the windows, preventing a preview of what to expect inside, and a bare limb stuck out into the small, narrow porch as they approached. In the dirt driveway was an old Ford station wagon pasted over with faded bumper stickers. *Practice Random Acts of Kindness and Senseless Beauty,* one read. *My other car is a broomstick,* said another. And Kellie's personal favorite: *Expect a miracle!* Maybe that last one was intended for the potential driver of the old tank. The two flat tires gave the car, like the building next to it, a deflated look.

"This place doesn't look so hot." For some reason

Rita was uncharacteristically susceptible to the obvious today.

"Maybe the low overhead accounts for the 'low, low rates,' " Kellie answered.

"I think we should just go have lunch."

"Don't be silly," Kellie said, poking her sister up the last step. "Where would you expect a fortune-teller to work, a mansion in Highland Park?"

Her sister shook her head and clutched her purse to her chest in an old-ladyish way. "No, but . . . oh, I don't know about this."

"Do you want to find out if Wendell's stringing you along or not?" As if anyone needed a fortune-teller for that! Actually, Kellie had just wanted someone to come with her to Madame Mira's, so she'd called up her sister and convinced her that *she* needed to see a fortune-teller. Now, looking at the place, she was glad she'd brought Rita along. She could be the guinea pig.

She jabbed her finger against the doorbell, which set off a loud buzzing inside the building. The buzzing didn't stop, either, not even after Kellie pulled her finger away. A string of curses screamed inside now, along with the buzzing; the button Kellie had pressed was stuck. As the cursing became louder, and closer, she tried to work the button out with her fingernail, to no avail.

Rita stood next to her, worrying her lip. "I don't know, Kellie. This place doesn't have an aura of success."

"Aura!" Kellie muttered, still struggling with the damn button. "That's nutty!"

"You used to say fortune-tellers were nutty," Rita pointed out.

"Yeah, well . . ." Not having a rational explanation for her sudden change of heart, she bit her lip as she kept jiggling at the doorbell.

Then the door flew open, and she and Tina were met by even louder buzzing, a blast of blue smoke, and several cats shooting out the door. Tina let out an "Oh!" and Kellie looked up from the buzzer to see an older woman in polyester shorts and a striped tank top. She wore thick glasses with the round frames popular in the seventies. The woman was small, almost roundish, and she wielded a cigarette in one hand and a rubber mallet in the other.

"Let me at that dang thing!" she said in a raspy drawl, and when Kellie jumped back, poking her head on an althea branch, the old woman began pounding the door frame with her mallet.

"Dang thing gets stuck in the heat, ya know!"

The pounding worked, eventually, and the buzzing stopped. "Phew!" the woman said, then sucked on her Kool. "Think I'd be used to it by now, but it drives me crazy every time!" She opened her mouth and exhaled more smoke at them, along with a blast of gutteral laughter.

Kellie smiled and grabbed Rita, who was edging backward down the steps. "Are you Madame Mira?"

"Sure am, hon! C'mon up."

As they ascended a narrow staircase, the smoke grew thicker. Rita, still in her starched white nurse's uniform, coughed delicately, but Kellie elbowed her sharply. "Be polite!" she mouthed.

Kellie had expected a more gypsy-looking place; in fact, she was hoping for something comfortingly bohemian. Authentically scammy. Beads and scarves and throw pillows. But the large living area Madame Mira escorted them into was dominated by a Naugahyde couch, a new twenty-seven inch television, and a La-Z-Boy chair that was reclined even though no one was sitting it except a fat, long-haired calico cat. The coffee table and various end tables were bare of knickknacks or candles. Just a few overflowing ashtrays.

Madame Mira led them over to an old chrome dinette table. "Who's first?" she rasped, eyeing Kellie.

"Oh, it's just my sister who needs her fortune told . . ." Kellie jabbed Rita down into a chair.

Madame Mira lit another Kool, grabbed Rita's hand, then looked up at Kellie. "Sure you don't want me to tell your future?"

Kellie laughed. "Me? No, I don't think so!"

"Sure? I got a special discount for pairs. One fortune at full price, the second's half off."

"Hm . . ." Kellie made a show of looking hesitant, when really she wanted to knock Rita out of the chair. "Well, maybe. I'll think about it."

Madame Mira looked at her doubtfully, then turned her attention back to Rita's palm. The woman's eyes widened, and she exhaled a puff of smoke and shook her head. "Holy mackerel! I never seen anything like it!"

Kellie leapt forward. "Really? What is it?"

"Nothing!" Madame Mira explained.

"Nothing?" Rita and Kellie asked in unison.

"Absolutely nothing! Honey, your hand is *vague!*"

Rita's brow turned into a mass of worry lines. "What do you mean, vague?"

"I mean you've got a flat hand, hon."

"Flat?" Kellie asked, interested. "What's that mean?"

"It means no strong lines. No mounts. No nothing, frankly."

Rita sputtered. "B-but that's ridiculous! I must have *something.*"

"You're flat and square, hon," Madame Mira told her, giving her the bad news point-blank. She beckoned Kellie even closer as a witness. "Look at this. Like a pancake. Flat. Square-shaped, indicating a lack of imagination and initiative. Then what lines you do see are just these thin, veiny things going all which-a-way. Lines ambling off into a million different other lines. Hon, your future's a mess!"

Rita stared at her with rounded eyes. "Do you think I'll ever get married?"

The fortune-teller shrugged. "Who can tell?"

"But you must be able to predict something!" Rita said desperately.

Madame Mira squinted at Rita's flat, square palm again. "Maybe you'll marry eventually, but it won't be easy. In fact, you might get stuck with somebody you're not expecting. In fact, I'm sure of it."

Rita looked alarmed. "Not Wendell?"

"Who's Wendell?" Madame Mira asked.

"Never mind," Kellie said, practically booting Rita out of the chair. Madame Mira's predicting vague confusion for her sister seemed right on the money. In fact, it gave her confidence in the woman's skill that she hadn't expected. "I might as well take advantage of the half-off offer," she said brusquely. "As long as I'm here, I mean."

"Uh-huh." Madame Mira didn't look fooled, but she grabbed Kellie's hand and flipped it over. "Well, I'll be!"

Kellie hovered over her hand. *Dear God, don't let me be flat and square....* She was sure she was turning green from smoke inhalation, but she was too curious now to care. "What, what?"

"I ain't seen one of these in a coon's age!"

"What?"

"A perfect hand!" the woman rasped at her gleefully. "Girl, you got it made. Look at these strong mounts— Jupiter, Mercury, and Venus. Power, success, and love— all yours. I see money in your future."

"Uh-uh!" Rita exclaimed jealously, leaning over the table now, too.

"Plus she's got this lifeline that goes on forever. And lookee here—lots of kids, this says."

"Well, of course," Kellie said, clinging to her last shred of skepticism. "I have two children."

"Well get ready to have more, hon. See this? Children. Happiness and stability. And best of all—money. More of it than you'll know what to do with."

Kellie gasped.

So did Rita. "It's Riley!"

"Don't be silly," Kellie scoffed. Though of course she'd already leapt to the same conclusion. How many rich guys did she know?

Madame Mira winked at her. "I've a mind to take back my discount."

"Are you *sure* I'm vague?" Rita asked, inspecting her unfortunate hand more closely. "I mean, we're sisters. Seems like our hands would be somewhat similar. . . ."

"Hon, reading your hand is like trying to drive in a pea-soup fog." Madame Mira stood up and clapped Rita on the shoulder. "But don't worry. Didn't I say everything will work out eventually?"

"Well, sure. Eventually. But that could be when I'm eighty. And what about Wendell?"

"Who's Wendell?"

"We'd better get going." Kellie got to her feet and started rooting through her purse. She pulled out two twenties and handed them to Madame Mira. What was the correct etiquette when it came to tipping palm-readers? "Keep the change."

Madame Mira stuffed the bills into her shirt pocket. "Thanks, hon. And look after your sister when you're rich and she's wallowing in misery and indecisiveness, won't you?"

"Misery?" Rita moaned miserably.

Madame Mira winked at Kellie and lit up another Kool.

"Of course," Kellie said, leading Rita away.

Once she got back in the car, Kellie felt strangely deflated, even though Madame Mira had told her everything she could have hoped to hear. *But so what?* the waning voice of reason in her head told her. *So a crank tells you that Riley's your man.* Kellie probably could have gotten the same information from an eight-hundred number. And for a lot cheaper.

These people always predicted marriage, wealth, and happiness. That was how they made their money.

Of course, she hadn't predicted anything like that for poor Rita. . . .

But face it, Madame Mira hadn't told her things that she really wanted to know. Like what was *really* going on in Riley's head. Not to mention his heart. He could send her daughter all the pianos in the world, but she wasn't one step closer to understanding the man. She'd spilled her guts about her divorce and about what she'd thought about as she lay sleepless at night, but he'd never mentioned what he felt about being alone. He'd told her the name of his cook, but he'd never mentioned his wife or child by name. She just had to guess what he was thinking by looking into his eyes. And what did that tell her? His expression seemed to ping-pong between sadness and lust.

And of course, she couldn't even look him in the eye while he was in Hong Kong.

Next to her, Rita was still staring at her square, flat hand. "Why is it you always have all the luck?"

"Me?"

"Didn't you hear what Madame Mira said? You're going to have it all. Money. Love. More kids."

Kellie had to laugh at that. "Rita, I need more kids like a moose needs a hat rack."

"Of course *you* would say that! At least you've been married and have kids. You can afford to take it all for granted. You're not an old maid. You're not vague!"

"Oh, for heaven's sake."

"Plus you have your own business," Rita went on.

"Mother is always telling me that I should be more like you."

"Really? She's always telling *me* that I should have been sensible and studious like you, and not have married that good-for-nothing Rick. And then not have let that good-for-nothing Rick get away from me."

Her sister was inconsolable. "Oh, well ... but what about your future? You've got all the luck."

"Rita! Don't tell me you're taking all this hocus-pocus seriously. She's just a fortune-teller, and obviously not a very successful one. Look at the dump she lives in!"

For a moment Rita's mouth opened and closed in astonishment. She looked like a suffocating fish. "But you said ..."

"Oh, I know. I was curious. But really, it's just all a hoax, isn't it? What does she know? What could she possibly know?"

"Well, why did you drag me over here if you didn't believe in her?"

"Because ..." She couldn't bring herself to say it. Because she was beginning to wonder if Riley's mumbo jumbo about their being made for each other contained just the tiniest grain of truth. After all, there were all those run-ins they'd had. And then that kiss ... a kiss that felt like a lightning bolt to her system. And now Madame Mira seemed to confirm the fact that there was a mysterious millionaire in her future. Heaven knew those weren't growing on trees in her neighborhood. "Well, it was just an experiment. A lark."

Rita harrumphed resentfully. "Well, maybe you're right. If she thinks I won't end up with Wendell, she *can't* know what she's talking about."

Kellie shot her a dubious glance. "What makes you say that?"

"Because I'm sure Wendell's the one for me. It's destiny. I really feel it in my heart."

Lord, Kellie wished she could be that sure about something. Even if she was pretty certain her sister was dead wrong about that boyfriend of hers, at least Rita was one-hundred-percent deluded.

Riley usually went straight home after overseas flights, but not this time. After all this time away, what he most wanted to do was see what Kellie was up to. He'd been away a solid week, and he hoped that the fallout from the kiss was behind them.

He drove over to Copycat and found her stuffing boxes into her Toyota. When she saw who had pulled up next to her, a smile lit her face. But the smile had already disappeared when he popped out of his car.

"The prodigal returns," she quipped.

"I've been on a business trip."

"I know."

She must have called his office. "Did Tina get my present?"

Kellie laughed. "Are you kidding? Your answering machine's probably jammed with tearful thank-yous."

"So she liked it?"

Kellie eyed him in disbelief. "Riley. What's not to like? You sent my nine-year-old daughter what appears to be an antique Steinway. It was too much."

He felt a ripple of unease. "But you're going to let her keep it, aren't you?"

She dropped her purse on the hood and leaned against her car. "What kind of ogre would I be if I didn't? Not to mention, piano movers cost an arm and a leg."

"It was just sitting in my house unused."

"It's getting used now. Every waking hour, practically."

He laughed. "I figured it would."

She wasn't laughing with him, though. Instead, she

was staring at him in that disarming, straight-from-the-hip way she had. "Riley, you must be out of your mind. There's no way I can repay you for that piano."

"You don't have to," he insisted. "I just wanted Tina to have it. It was just a friendly gesture."

The word *friendly* launched Kellie's brow into a skeptical arch. "Friendly?"

He grinned. "And now I thought maybe you'd join me for a friendly lunch. I just got back from the airport and I could use some sustenance."

She shook her head. "I've got a delivery to make."

"I'll help you. Put that stuff in my back seat. It's bigger anyway."

She sighed. "I don't have time for lunch."

He frowned, catching her drift. "You're lying. You're just trying to put me off. Why?"

She pushed herself away from the car, hands on her hips. "This is confusing the hell out of me, Riley. No offense, but the last time I saw you, you were fleeing my house like I had the ebola virus. So I figured that was that. So much for Riley. And then you send my daughter a piano. And then, when I called to thank you, I discovered you weren't even in the country."

"I was in Hong Kong."

"I know! I know because *your secretary* told me."

Riley hesitated. "So . . . what are you getting at?"

Her face took on an incredulous expression. She lifted her arms and then dropped them to her sides. "I'm saying that this is the nuttiest friendship I've ever heard of—if that's what it is. Because I've got to tell you, Riley, friends don't kiss friends the way you kissed me in my kitchen."

"I know. I tried to apologize—"

His words were like dumping gas on a fire. "And turning tail and running wasn't exactly friendly, either. What am I supposed to think? That you hated kissing me? That you liked it but were disappointed that it was me you liked?"

"I liked it," he assured her. "I liked it too much."

A strangled scream erupted from her. "Oh, thanks! It's all clear now."

He shook his head. "Kellie, I'm sorry. I thought you would be glad that I put some distance between us."

She crossed her arms. "Oh, sure. So glad I've been calling your office until Doreen wanted to tell me to take a hike. So glad that I've been running around doing things that I never would have dreamed of doing before I knew you. I'm beginning to make my sister look sane."

"What do you want me to say?"

"I don't know." She shook her head and sighed. "I guess all I'm looking for is a sign that we really are friends. Or that you really want something more. Not the kiss-and-skedaddle treatment." She tilted her head up at him curiously. "How can you like kissing someone *too much?* What does that mean?"

He'd thought she would know. He had mentioned that his wife had died; he had hoped Kellie would have been able to guess that he just didn't have room in his life for this, that he couldn't possibly start over again so soon.

"I'm sure this is exactly what you want when you get off a plane from Hong Kong, right?" She shook her head. "Look, Riley. Don't say anything now. Go home and get some sleep. I'm sorry for being a pain in the butt, but I really do need to get this delivery made."

He nodded. Maybe she was right. He wasn't being fair. She had a busy, stressful life. No time in it for him to be adding confusion into the mix. "I wish I could do something for you."

"You did," she said. "The piano, remember?"

"Something more . . ."

"Don't do anything more," she said. "What I need

in my life is stability—and wondering about you and your gifts is definitely not helping my *compos mentis*."

He laughed.

When he was back in his car, however, the laughter faded to wonder. Had she really been thinking about him that much? It sounded almost as if she *wanted* a relationship. Which, a few weeks ago, was what she said she didn't want. But maybe that was what was causing all the friction between them. She was ready; he wasn't.

He didn't go home. He went to his office and tried to catch up. By the time he stumbled home that night, he was dead tired ... and completely unprepared for the sight of Jay on his doorstep, looking sweaty and worried. He was wearing a filthy T-shirt and an expression that said he'd lost his best friend.

"What happened to you?"

Jay looked down at himself and sighed. "I'm sorry, I should have showered before coming over."

"Where have you been?"

"Building a house for Habitat for Humanity." He paused, then sighed apologetically. "You're probably tired. I should go."

Riley pulled Jay off the top step and put his key in the door. The second the door opened, they were overwhelmed by a blast of opera.

Jay leapt back in surprise. "Good heavens! What's that?"

Riley pursed his lips. "Maria Callas. *Madame Butterfly*. Fayard and Nathaniel must be at it again."

His hunch was confirmed when Nathaniel appeared in the hallway with furry earmuffs clamped over his head. "It's been like this all day!" he exclaimed apologetically. "Ever since I told him that I wouldn't eat his frog legs *forestiere*. I really have to draw the line at amphibians."

Jay nodded understandingly, and Riley felt as if he might pass out. They were having frogs for dinner?

"Don't look so worried," Nathaniel told Riley. "The frog legs were *last* night." Just then, the diva hit a particularly brutal high note. "Maybe if you go into the den . . ."

Riley nodded. "Good idea." The wood paneling might help drown out Puccini.

When they were finally sitting down, Jay poured his heart out to Riley. "It didn't work out."

"What didn't?"

"Luanne."

"Who's Luanne?"

Jay looked exasperated. "I told you about her. She was in my reading group." His eyes widened as the music swelled again. "Are you sure Fayard is okay? I mean, he has access to all those sharp knives . . ."

Riley chuckled. "He's just temperamental."

"That's what I meant. Poor Nathaniel!"

Riley returned to Jay's problem. "So Luanne is history? I knew those reading groups were a bad idea."

"Well, I did meet Luanne."

"But you said it didn't work out with Luanne."

"But that wasn't Luanne's fault, really," Jay said generously. "I blame Joseph Campbell. That's who our group was reading. He advises people to follow their bliss."

"Well?"

"Well, that's what Luanne did. Only following her bliss meant running away with a beach bum."

"In Dallas? There are no beaches here."

"But there are in Australia."

Riley felt the beginning twinges of a headache. "What's Australia got to do with anything?"

"Because that's where Luanne and this guy have run off to. They're going to open a surf shop." This time, he let out the granddaddy of all sighs; he looked like a flaccid balloon when it was all over. "She's gone."

"It sounds like you're better off without her."

"Better off? How can you say that? Luanne was perfect

for me—except for the fact that she didn't seem to like me particularly.''

Poor Jay. He couldn't bring himself to think badly of anyone. He was generosity itself.

In fact, for the first time, Riley felt the need to unburden himself of his problem. Maybe Jay would have some ideas. ''Actually, I've got my own female troubles.''

Jay sat up straighter. *''You?''*

''Well . . . not quite like yours. You see, I know this woman. Maybe you remember her . . . the woman we saw at Wiggie's that day?''

His friend flinched. ''Oh, no! She was . . .'' He cast about in his mind for something kind to say about the woman who had screamed at them in the restaurant. ''Well, I hate to say it, but wasn't she a little *unpleasant?''*

''You didn't really see her at her best,'' Riley allowed. ''Anyway, I've taken a sort of interest in her.''

''Romantic interest?''

''No,'' Riley said carefully. One incredible, unforgettable kiss didn't make a romance, did it? ''You know I couldn't get involved with anyone right now.''

''Mm.'' If Jay had any arguments on that score, he was kind enough to keep them to himself. For once.

''But she's got a sort of tough life.''

Hearing about a hard-luck case perked Jay right up. ''What's wrong?''

Riley told Jay about Rick running out on Kellie, and how she'd worked nonstop for a year to pull herself up and start her business and raise her kids. He explained how he'd tried to help her (but not why; he couldn't bring himself to confess to that vision he'd had). ''So I sent Tina my piano, which was no sacrifice. But really it's the boy I'm worried about.''

''Trevor.'' Jay frowned, concentrating on this new problem.

"He's got some disciplinary problems, I think. He sort of gives Kellie a rough time because he misses his dad."

Jay lifted his finger and wagged it sagely. "There's the crux of your problem, friend."

"What?"

"You've run into a problem that can't be solved with money."

Usually Riley didn't think of himself as the type of person who threw money at problems in hopes that they would go away, but maybe that's what he had been doing. Most of the projects he took on—fund-raising for charity, building new libraries—*were* a matter of money when you came right down to it. Money made things happen, and he was glad to put his to a good cause, whether it was funding a public swimming pool or giving Kellie's daughter a piano.

But Jay was right. What Trevor needed couldn't be bought.

"Sounds like the boy needs a father," Jay said.

"Oh . . . I'm not so sure about that. The one he had ran out on him."

Jay shook his head. "Hopefully, next time round, his mother will choose someone more dependable."

"I don't think she's looking for a husband."

Jay shrugged. "Maybe she just hasn't met the right man yet." He smiled at Riley. "Unless you're willing to volunteer for the job?"

"You saw how we got along."

Jay chuckled. "It's true, she didn't seem so glad to see you. So why are you so interested in her?"

"I guess I just feel a little responsible for her. I wrecked her car . . ."

"Mm." Jay propped his chin against his knuckle, deep in thought. "Well, short of offering yourself on the altar of matrimony, all I can see for you to do is try to set this woman up with somebody."

Riley tensed at first. Kellie? With somebody else?

But why not? He wasn't ready. He couldn't keep some-one on hold until he felt the time was right to begin again. He was beginning to fear that time would never arrive anyway. Maybe some people weren't meant to fall in love more than once.

"But with whom?" Riley asked.

"Well, let's see . . ." Jay steepled his fingers. "She's hot-tempered, with two strong-willed kids, one of whom seems to have a personality that would try the patience of a saint. My guess is that you'd need to find someone extremely patient, tolerant, and steady. And marriage-minded. A real Mr. Nice Guy."

Riley nodded. The proverbial light bulb had gone off inside his own head minutes ago. He was just waiting for the obvious answer to occur to Jay.

"That's a tough order," Jay said.

"Uh-huh. But I think we'll figure it out." He smiled. "How about a drink. Bourbon?"

"Sure." Jay grinned. "This is sort of fun, isn't it? I've never played matchmaker before."

"Oh, I bet it won't take you long to get the hang of it," Riley assured him as he handed him a glass.

"How about lunch?" was all he'd said over the phone.

And, having nothing else on her agenda, she'd impul-sively agreed. He sounded as though he had something he wanted to tell her in person.

The prospect of seeing Riley again buoyed her more than it should have. She'd done her best yesterday to keep her feet grounded in reality. Even though she'd wanted to hop into his BMW the moment he asked her. Even though she felt like a jerk for taking him to task the way she had. But she had to try to keep her grip on reality, didn't she? Riley obviously didn't take her seriously or he wouldn't have done the hundred-yard dash out of her kitchen.

Only now, after speaking to Riley briefly, she felt an uptick in mood that had nothing to do with reality. She was beginning to wonder if she was losing her grip.

Alejandro came back from his break with a Big Gulp and a newspaper. "Look at this, Kellie. Your horoscope. 'A meeting today could change your life.' "

Her stomach did a little flip, which was just nuts. *Horoscopes?* She wasn't going to start believing in those! At the same time, she wondered if a lunch date could be considered a meeting.

By the time she arrived at the coffee shop they'd met at before, she was humming a jaunty tune to herself and feeling as if she were walking on a cloud. She hadn't been in this good a mood for years. Really, she felt ten years younger.

When she saw Riley beckoning her from a table, however, she took in his seatmate and felt something lurch inside her. They weren't going to be alone. She approached the table more cautiously and noted with interest the man sitting with Riley. He looked vaguely familiar. But it was hard to say where she'd seen him before, since he appeared frozen in the red vinyl booth, watching her approach like a deer caught in headlights.

Riley introduced them. "Kellie, I wanted you to meet my friend, Jay Howard."

Kellie smiled politely. But she knew, right at that moment, that this was a setup. And she wasn't quite sure why that should disappoint her so.

Chapter Eleven

Things were not going well.

Here they were, all reasonable adults, out for an enjoyable time at lunch, but no one was saying anything. Jay, who usually abhorred awkward silence, smiled nervously at his turkey sandwich and remained speechless. The only time he'd so much as glanced at Kellie, you'd have thought he feared she was a rabid rottweiler. Riley had tried to convince Jay that the lunatic he saw at the barbecue joint was really a very mild-mannered woman, but obviously he remained skeptical. And jittery. Across the table Kellie tensely snapped one of the packaged breadsticks that had come with her salad. The sound made Jay jump.

What was the matter with them? All Riley wanted was for these two people to hit it off, but you would think that he was asking two house cats to do pet tricks.

He was in the middle of a true altruistic binge, and he didn't like to be thwarted. He shot Jay an impatient glance, but Jay just stared back with the same dazed expression.

Riley looked over at Kellie, and she glared back at him. What was she so angry about? Ever since she'd walked in and saw Jay sitting with him, she'd appeared put out. He thought she'd welcome the company. And after all, wasn't this something friends did for friends? Introduce them to other friends?

Deciding it was time to resort to desperation tactics, he nudged Jay with his foot. Jay fastened his glazed stare on him, and Riley prodded him again.

Finally Jay popped to life. He fixed his eyes on Kellie as if she might explode at any second and asked tentatively, "How's your friend?"

Kellie's blinked in surprise. "Who?"

"The, um, woman we saw you with that time . . . that time . . ." *That time you went insane,* his look said. He swallowed. "At Wiggie's."

Her eyes narrowed. "My sister?"

"That was your sister?" Jay asked, disbelief as clear as bell in his tone. "She seemed so nice!"

Too late, he realized his blunder and whirled toward Riley with eyes bulging in panic. Riley could have clunked him on the head. What the heck was he bringing up Kellie's sister for anyway? Did he need to remind Jay that it was *Kellie* he was supposed to be interested in?

Fortunately, Kellie laughed off the possible slight. "She's fine."

"Is she single?" was the next question that popped out of Jay's mouth.

It was all Riley could do not to lower his forehead to the sticky tabletop and pound his head in frustration.

Kellie nodded. "Oh, yes."

Jay perked up quite a bit.

Riley saw his whole plan dissolving before his eyes. Even his blue-plate special of meatloaf, mashed potatoes, and gravy couldn't comfort him. He picked at it listlessly. "I thought Rita was practically engaged," he reminded Kellie.

"She is. Well, she thinks she is," Kellie said. "She's

been going out with the same guy for years now. Wendell. You could say they're a very definite indefinite item— but she's very determined to get him to the altar.''

Jay's shoulders hunched into a depressed slump. "Oh.''

This exchange was followed by another uncomfortable, protracted silence.

Riley cleared his throat, barely refraining from kicking his friend under the table. "You know, you two have a lot in common.'' They both looked at him questioningly. "Jay loves kids.''

"I do?'' Jay asked, as if this werc ncws to him.

"You volunteer with Big Brothers,'' Riley reminded him.

"Oh, right.'' Jay nodded. "Sometimes. The last kid I sponsored didn't work out so well, though.''

"What happened?'' Kellie asked.

"He beat me up after school one day.''

Riley let out a ragged sigh, which he tried to change into a laugh at the last second. Could Jay possibly make this more difficult? "Jay has a great sense of humor, doesn't he?''

Kellie smiled politely, if a little doubtfully.

"He's always telling jokes.'' He turned to Jay. "What was that joke you were telling me the other day?''

Jay blinked at him in panic. "Joke?''

"It was something about three guys ...'' Riley prompted him.

A light of recognition sparked in his friend's face, flickered briefly as he tried to concentrate, then finally was snuffed out in defeat. Jay shook his head miserably. "I can't remember.''

Riley bit back another sigh. He couldn't tell the joke for him. He couldn't do all the work here.

"My son told me a joke the other day.''

Riley and Jay looked up at Kellie, Riley with faint

leftover irritation and Jay with relief and expectation. Misplaced, Riley feared. His run-in with Trevor hadn't given him the impression that the boy possessed a rapier wit. He was more like a Moe Howard in the making.

But at least *someone* was trying to bail out their sinking conversational lifeboat.

She cleared her throat. "A bear walks into a bar and asks for a sandwich. When he's finished gulping it down, he takes out a gun and shoots up the mirror behind the bar. After the bear's gone, one guy at the bar turns to another and says, 'That sure was one mean panda,' and the other guy asks, 'How'd you know he was a panda?' and the first guy says, 'Because the dictionary says a panda eats shoots and leaves.' "

There was a doubtful hesitation in the air. Riley was so nervous about Kellie's joke going over well that he forgot to laugh himself. Then, after a moment of concentration, Jay broke up. When they all chuckled, it felt as though a huge crack had broken in the ice all around them.

"That's a pretty good one," Jay said. "How old's your son?"

"Almost eleven."

"He must be quite a character."

"Oh, he's a character, all right," she agreed. "Sometimes he makes me feel like a character, too—like Jimmy Cagney's mother in *Public Enemy.*"

Jay chuckled. "It must be great having kids. I've always wanted some myself. But I'm not married. Never have been."

Kellie chewed a tomato wedge thoughtfully. Riley couldn't understand how she could eat a salad with all this good food around. "It's great most of the time, but I'd be a liar if I said there wasn't stuff I miss from being single, which I almost never was. I was practically one of those graduation-to-city-hall teenagers."

Jay nodded sympathetically. "Doesn't give you much opportunity to explore."

"Exactly," Kellie said. "Sometimes I wonder what it would be like to be one of those carefree people who can just pick up and go to a jazz concert."

She liked jazz? Riley hadn't known. *He* liked jazz.

As if hit by a thunderbolt, Jay's eyes widened and his shoulders unhunched. "You like jazz?" he asked Kellie.

"Well . . . I'm not an expert or anything, but I listen to it on the radio when the kids aren't around to squawk their displeasure."

"Well, shoot!" Jay exclaimed. "If it's jazz you want, then I'm your huckleberry. I've got tickets to see Wynton Marsalis tomorrow night. He's playing with the Dallas Symphony. Why don't you come with me?"

"Oh, but—"

Jay laughed. "C'mon, weren't you just saying you'd like to be one of those carefree people who just pick up and go to jazz concerts?"

"I'd *like* to be, but I'm not. Tomorrow's a Thursday, and I don't have anyone to stay with the kids." She frowned. "Unless my mom . . ."

"Yes!" Jay said excitedly. "Let's bribe your mom."

Kellie's face flushed with laughter. "That's not so easy."

"Sure it is—what does she like?"

"Oh, not much. She's widowed now, and she's always been so thrifty she won't go many places. She likes board games, and she and her friends go out to the movies for matinees once a month or so—"

"Bingo!" Jay reached into his jacket, pulled out a small, colorful book, and shoved it across the table to her. "Movie passes."

Kellie's face screwed up in confusion as she leafed through the booklet. "You always carry around books of movie passes?"

"Jay's family owns half the real estate in Dallas,'' Riley explained. "Including movie theaters.''

Her mouth formed a perfect, impressed O.

Jay shrugged modestly. "He's exaggerating. I wouldn't say we could own more than an eighth—and just commercial properties. I like to carry the movie passes around, though, and give 'em to people. You know—kids, guys at the gas station, my barber.''

Kellie laughed. "A Johnny Appleseed for the silver screen.''

Jay laughed a little too hard at her joke. "So go home and bribe your mother, and I'll pick you up tomorrow night at seven.''

For an instant it looked as if Kellie might refuse, but suddenly her eyes sparkled and she relented. "All right. It sounds like fun.''

As she tucked into her salad, Jay looked over at Riley, glowing with relief and happiness. Mission accomplished. Riley felt as if he'd just witnessed a cumbersome aircraft suddenly lift off. But though he made a point of smiling, inside he felt the disappointment of the man still left back on the ground. He hadn't expected that.

After lunch, when they had waved Kellie off in her Toyota, Jay was beside himself. "That worked out pretty well, didn't it?''

"Sure.''

"You didn't tell me how shy she was, though,'' Jay said.

"Shy?''

"Yeah, and nervous. Didn't you notice? She hardly said a word there during the first half of lunch. Had me a little worried, because you know if there's anything I like in a woman, it's a good conversationalist.'' He smiled. "I think I handled that pretty smoothly, though. Especially thinking of the concert.'' He did a little soft-shoe. "Fast on my feet—know what I mean?''

Riley forced a smile. "A real operator."

Jay crossed his arms and rocked back on his heels. "You know what I think I'm going to do? I think I'm going to get the old Cadillac off its blocks. Really show Kellie the kind of stuff I'm made of."

Riley frowned. "The Cadillac? Are you sure that doesn't carry too many bad memories?"

"Of what?" Suddenly understanding, Jay shook his head. "Don't be silly, Riley. Linda's boxer shorts could have shown up in any car. It's still my good-luck vehicle. Just the thing for a hot date."

Hot date? For a moment, Riley felt the need to lean against his car. He felt short of breath.

Jay frowned. "You okay, bud?"

He nodded. "Fine. I just feel like I'm having a heart attack."

"You really should cut down on the greasy foods. When my cholesterol spiked, my doctor told me I should eat more grapefruit and oatmeal."

Unfortunately, it wasn't the kind of heart attack that grapefruit and oatmeal could fix. *Get a grip, Riley,* he told himself. *This was what you wanted. This was what being a friend to a woman was all about.* This was the right thing to do.

Of course, he hadn't expected things to move along so quickly. He hadn't been prepared for the invitation Jay had popped out with. He doubted Kellie was, either. Poor thing. He hoped she wasn't regretting agreeing to go. After all, the symphony . . . it was one of those stuffy things she was always talking about as being part of his world, not hers. What had he gotten her into?

Kellie couldn't believe she was going out with a man that she'd only met that day. And that Riley had introduced them.

That part had stung. Was he so eager to get rid of her that he thought he had to push her into somebody else's arms? Maybe, after their kiss, he was afraid that she was going to start chasing him—which was just hopelessly screwed up. If anything, *he* had been the one doing the chasing. After all, she had never sent *him* a piano.

Still, she was going out for a real night on the town, which she hadn't done since her fifth wedding anniversary. And the symphony sounded a lot more glamorous than *Wayne's World* and a game of putt-putt

And Jay was nice. He really was. He laughed at her jokes and said things like *I'm your huckleberry*. So he wasn't Mr. America. She wasn't exactly Cindy Crawford herself. And besides, there was something intriguing about it all. Madame Mira had mentioned a rich guy in her future. Jay was rich. The horoscope had said that a meeting would change her life ... and right afterward she had met Jay.

Not that she believed any of that garbage.

The phone rang and she snatched it up immediately. "Mom said you're going on a *date?*" Rita blared in her ear without preamble.

"To the symphony." She dashed off the phrase, trying to sound as if this were something she did all the time. No big deal. She felt a little giddy.

"With Riley?"

"No, with a friend of Riley's," she answered. "Jay."

"Oh—multiple men!" Rita sounded impressed. "What's he like?"

"Well ..." She hesitated. "Actually, you saw him. That day I flipped out at Wiggie's."

"Don Knotts?"

"Oh, for heaven's sake, he doesn't look—" Kellie sighed in exasperation as she wound the phone cord around her hand. "Anyway, what difference does it make? He's a very nice man. Very nice. He's practically devoted his life to charity.''

Not to mention, he's the first man to ask me out since Rick.

She didn't add that last part, though. She had some pride.

"So he's a rich guy, too?" Rita asked.

"Yes, I guess so."

"Wow! It's just like Madame Mira foretold."

"Oh, Rita, you know I think that's all hogwash."

"Right. Hogwash you, the penniest pinching of the penny pinchers, paid forty dollars to hear,'' Rita quipped. Then she cut to the real heart of the matter. "So what are you going to wear?''

A stab of panic shot through Kellie like a hot flash from high school. "I'm not sure."

"Nothing you own is even close to nice enough," Rita warned.

"Thanks," Kellie answered dryly. "Just the comforting words I needed to hear. I do have dresses, you know."

Rita snorted. "You own knit sacks with belts, Kellie. That might be okay for a temp assignment, or even for a balcony seat up in nosebleed heaven, but if this guy is rich and has season tickets, you're going to be in the orchestra section with all the socialites in sequins."

Kellie's first instinct was to tell Rita that she didn't know what she was talking about. When had *she* ever been to the symphony? Unfortunately, their shared history proved she couldn't dismiss her sister's warnings out of hand. Rita had also been the one to warn Kellie back in ninth grade that she wasn't good enough to try out for the twirling team. God knew she'd been right about that instance of self-inflicted public humiliation.

Come to think of it, Rita had never liked Rick very much, either. Suddenly, her little sister sounded like the voice of wisdom.

Good God, what was she going to wear?

"I'd loan you something, but anything of mine would fall off you," Rita said helpfully. "Besides, I don't own any sequins, either."

"That's okay," Kellie said. "Thanks for turning my mild panic into a heart-pounding fashion terror."

Rita laughed. "Good luck!"

Five minutes later her room looked as if a textile avalanche had taken place there.

"Jeez, Mom, your room looks like mine," Trevor said, leaning in the doorway as he munched on a peanut-butter cookie.

It looked worse, and Kellie hadn't even dreamed that such a thing was possible. Clothes sprang out of half-opened drawers and smothered her bed and cascaded out of her closet. She hadn't realized she owned so much—and what for? She didn't own one single thing suitable for a society function. Of course, maybe her dearth of finery sprang from her complete lack of a whirlwind social life. The best thing hanging in her closet was the light-gray wool dress she'd bought at Marshall's before going in for her bank loan interview last winter. Holding it up, she tried to be practical and work up some enthusiasm for it. But the prospect of wearing her bank-loan suit tomorrow night—the only sensible thing to do—made her feel unspeakably bleak.

"Why's the phone ringing all the time?" Trevor complained.

Kellie looked up. She hadn't even noticed the phone was ringing. She ran toward the kitchen, dragging an ancient silk blouse that had tangled around her ankle. "Hello?"

"I'm kidnapping you tomorrow."

It was Riley. She sighed. Hadn't he already disposed of her tidily enough? "I have a date tomorrow, if you'll recall."

"You'll be back in plenty of time. Just block off noon till three for me."

"Are you crazy? I have to be at Copycat," she said stubbornly.

"Can't Alejandro or Lana cover for you?"

The high-handedness in his tone got her dander up. "This is a small business, Riley. I'm accountable for success or failure. I can't slough everything off on the next guy. There is no next guy."

He chuckled. "You sure don't make things easy, do you?"

Her first instinct was to bray that life wasn't easy. That it was a battle every single day to keep life and limb, and her children's lives and limbs, together. She had no business running around with people who could live off their interest and take her to high-toned social functions she didn't have the right clothes for. But all she actually got out were a few incoherent sputters. All that wasn't what had her upset with Riley, anyway. What bothered her was that he wanted her to go out with Jay. With anybody else but him.

And that was just crazy, because Riley had never made any bones about the fact that he couldn't have a relationship. And now he was just trying to be nice. Friendly.

"I can spare two hours," she said.

The line was silent for a moment. "Two hours is pushing it."

"Two and a half."

"You're on."

Trevor was inches away from her when she hung up the phone. "Who was that?"

"Riley."

Trevor's face fell. "What did *he* want?"

"Just to talk."

"But he's not who you're seeing tomorrow night?"

Poor Trevor. His brow was furrowed with worry. "No, that's Jay."

"I think it stinks that we're being dumped on Grandma while you go out and have fun," he said.

"You like Grandma."

"Well, yeah, I like *her*. But her house is so dull. All she has to eat are Fig Newtons. And we end up playing those boring games *forever*. Maybe I should convince Grandma to get a Sony Playstation. I wouldn't mind going over there then."

"Don't you even think about it," Kellie warned. For one thing, she didn't like to think what would happen if her mother became addicted to video games. "Then you *and* Mother would both turn into video zombies."

"But I feel like a zombie when I'm there anyway," Trevor said. "I'm not kidding. She makes us sit and play these games *for hours,* and she *always* wins."

Kellie nodded sympathetically. Linelle could turn a round of tiddlywinks into a long night of nail-biting angst and humiliation. She felt a pang of guilt for putting Trevor through it—but then a solution occurred to her. "Friday night we'll order a pizza, and you can rent any movie you want."

His face lit up. "Promise?"

"Any movie that's not rated R or NC17."

"Okay." Trevor smiled grudgingly at this small victory. "I guess you'll be glad to stay home after a night in that ugly gray dress of yours, huh?"

A hairdresser in a pink Neiman Marcus smock spun Kellie, who was draped from mid-neck down in a pink-and-black vinyl poncho, to view a royal-blue silk dress. It was being held up by a woman whose face tensed awaiting Kellie's thumbs up or down. The garment had colorful sequins going up the bodice in the shape of a peacock.

"I don't think . . ." Kellie said tentatively.

Nathaniel, whom Riley had introduced as his butler and fashion consultant, nixed the dress more forcefully. "Ab-so-lutely not!" He twitched his nose in distaste. "It's *frowzy*. Like something an NBC executive would design for the Queen Mother."

Riley frowned at the woman pulling out dresses for Kellie's inspection from a portable rack. Apparently this was his way of compensating for the thirty minutes he'd bargained away—he was paying someone to bring dresses to Kellie while she had her hair done. Kellie had never experienced anything like it. But then, she'd never met anybody who actually had a butler.

"I'm not wild for it, either," Riley admitted.

Clippings from her bangs rained down in front of her eyes and distracted Nathaniel from the dress dilemma. "We don't want her looking like Cleopatra," he told the stylist.

Kellie laughed. "That would be an improvement, surely."

She couldn't believe this was her—that she was sitting in an expensive salon having her hair and nails done and having clothes pulled off a rack for her. It was like being in a movie—but who was she kidding? She wasn't the glitz-and-glamour type. She was already suffering from Cinderella overload. "And I didn't mean no to a particular dress, I meant no to all of them." She swiveled from Nathaniel's flabbergasted expression to Riley's amused one. "I'm not going to let you do this."

He was obviously enjoying himself immensely and she hated to be a killjoy, but she had to set some limits, didn't she?

"It's no big deal," he said.

Nathaniel nodded vigorously. "Riley gives away

money all the time. Buckets of the stuff. Why, just a few weeks ago he said he was flitting off to buy a Lexus for someone as an *apology!*''

"Imagine that." She suppressed a grin as she turned back to Riley. "Look, I let you convince me that you were bringing me here for free because you'd won 'A Day of Beauty' at a charity raffle. But there's no way you can convince me that this store was giving away designer dresses in a raffle."

"I never said that."

"No, but you were trying to sneak it by me."

He sighed. "I just realized that I had gotten you into a situation that you might not have been prepared for."

"You mean you think I've got a skanky wardrobe." She took a sip of the red wine they'd pressed into her hand when she'd sat down in the chair—probably the best wine she'd ever drunk and they were just giving away vats of it at a hair salon.

Riley laughed. "Maybe I felt I ought to apologize for being so high-handed in setting you up with Jay. I know you felt pressured to accept his invitation . . ."

"No, I didn't," she answered truthfully. "If I didn't want to go, I wouldn't."

His grin froze in place. "So you like Jay?"

"Of course. What's not to like? He's incredibly nice." *And at least he was obvious about his intentions.*

"Sort of awkward, though, I realize."

"Everyone's a little awkward when you're meeting them for the first time."

Riley tapped his foot and turned and absently began to flip through hangers. He pulled out a slinky black dress. It was made from a shimmery material that draped like a ballgown from the Fred-and-Ginger days. It had a few sequins around the middle, but nothing too-too. Kellie instinctively lurched at it, but was stopped short by the hairdresser tugging on her scalp.

"You like this one?" Riley asked.

"No," she answered quickly. Too quickly.

Nathaniel grabbed it. "*I* do," he said, racing over to her. He held the dress up against himself and vogued for her. "A little black sexy number is always welcome anywhere. And it's classic Calvin Klein. You can't go wrong with this one, Kellie."

"It doesn't matter. I have a perfectly good dress hanging in my closet at home."

Brows launched. They knew she was lying. She probably had *after-Christmas sale gray suit* written all over her.

"Why are you sitting around here playing genie anyway?" she asked Riley. "I don't mean to sound ungrateful, but shouldn't you be at your office looking into your crystal ball or your stock ticker or whatever it is you do?"

The moment the words were out of her mouth, she regretted them. Her tone had come out more caustic than she'd intended. Riley looked crestfallen. Almost as woebegone as Nathaniel seemed at the prospect of her passing on the little black dress.

She knew why Riley was doing this. It was obvious. He wasn't ready for a relationship, so he was foisting her off on his friend. Which wasn't such a terrible thing. She believed Riley liked her. Just not enough to overcome the grief he felt for the family he had lost. Grief that he obviously couldn't even talk about. Now he was trying to do a good thing, and somehow that made her resisting his charity seem a little petty.

With effort, she cleared her throat and forced herself to swallow her pride. Trevor was right for once. An evening in that gray dress would be pretty dismal. "I wasn't being honest with you, Riley."

His eyes, which had been focused inward, suddenly made contact with her again. He looked hopeful.

"I *do* like that black dress," she told him.

They watched her carry her garment bag into Copycat. She waved to them before going inside and they waved back, grinning.

When she was finally out of sight, however, Nathaniel pivoted toward Riley, his face a sour mask of disapproval. "You're crazy," he declared flatly.

Uh-oh. Riley began to regret his decision to bring Nathaniel to Neiman's. He should have known he would have mixed feelings about Kellie. Nathaniel had been devoted to Joanne. "You didn't like her?"

He laughed. "Like her? She was great. Though naturally I was a little taken aback that she was so Calvin Klein-resistant at first."

"I think she enjoyed her afternoon, don't you?"

Nathaniel laughed. "Oh, sure. What woman wouldn't enjoy being passed from one guy to his friend like the baton in a relay race?"

Riley sighed. "I didn't pass her off. I just introduced her to Jay."

"That's where you're crazy," Nathaniel said. "What are you doing to yourself?"

"Myself?"

Nathaniel rolled his eyes dramatically. "It's as plain as the nose on your face that you like her. I haven't seen you this animated in years. Why are you setting her up with Jay?"

"You know," Riley grumbled. If he'd been animated this afternoon, he certainly wasn't now. He felt like a turtle sinking back into its shell. Why was Nathaniel, of all people, giving him a hard time?

"Oh, sure. I know," Nathaniel said. "I know it would be just *awful* if you started to have a little fun in your life. God forbid you should get involved with the people around you."

"I'm involved," Riley insisted. "For heaven's sake— isn't that what this is all about? I've set up two of the people I like best."

"That's not getting involved. That's playing puppeteer. And mark my words, it's going to backfire on you. Have you thought about how you would feel if Kellie and Jay actually got together? As in permanently?"

Riley shook his head. He *had* thought of that, briefly. But he dismissed it. After all, he hadn't felt any sparks between those two. "Don't be ridiculous. It's just an innocent little date."

"Uh-huh." Nathaniel tipped him an incredulous look. "Do you know how many innocent little dates end in hot, kinky sex?"

Riley winced. "That's not going to happen. Kellie's not . . ." He remembered their kiss. It had been hot, passionate. And all too brief. But that was because they'd been interrupted. What if they hadn't been?

For a moment, he felt conflicted. He wanted to change his mind, go inside. Maybe this *was* all a mistake. But the alternative was either admitting he had feelings for her himself or just not seeing her at all anymore.

He looked straight ahead and turned over the car's engine. "I'm doing the right thing," he said, more for his own benefit than Nathaniel's.

Chapter Twelve

He just happened to be driving by. That was what he told himself. Of course, that was what he'd told himself an hour earlier when he'd cruised by and seen that Kellie wasn't home yet. Her porch light was on, and a single light shone through the living room window so burglars wouldn't know there was no one at home.

Didn't burglars have this figured out by now?

Riley considered going in and turning on all the lights. If Kellie was going to stay out till all hours, she at least ought to have her house secure. Except he didn't have a key and might get arrested for burglary himself.

God, this was nuts. Maybe he was going crazy. He'd felt out of sorts all afternoon—ever since Nathaniel had mentioned kinky sex. Which was just ridiculous. Jay didn't have a kinky bone in his body. He was a straight arrow . . . so straight it was almost weird.

A fine line of sweat broke out on Riley's brow. Where *was* Kellie anyway?

He should have just gone to the concert himself; he had season tickets. But he hadn't wanted to intrude on Jay and Kellie's first outing. Which made it sound as if there would be others, and frankly he wasn't so sure about that. Kellie and Jay really weren't all that suitable, now that he thought about it. What would they do when he wasn't there to cue them to speak? They were both probably struggling to get through the whole experience, poor things.

And what about Tina and Trevor? Were they going to spend the entire night with Linelle or was Kellie going to pick them up? He looked at the empty house and thought about the implications of the kids being away at Grandma's. He recalled Kellie wheeling her basket through the grocery store the night her kids were away; he remembered her saying that she was all at loose ends.

She wouldn't be at loose ends tonight. . . .

He shook his head in disgust. The distressing thoughts going through his head—of his best friend and his newest friend involved in heavy mattress activity—were definitely not worthy of him. Besides, what Kellie did with her nights were none of his business. He needed to chill out, to get a grip.

He needed to get those kids back into that empty house.

He sped to the nearest convenience store for a phone booth and looked up Linelle's address. She lived in the suburb of Plano, but that was okay. He practically broke the sound barrier getting there, not giving himself much time to back out—or to wonder what the heck he was going to say to the woman when he knocked on her door at eleven at night. This was crazy. What would he say to Linelle when he got there? The whole house might even be asleep.

But no. As he pulled up to the cozy little ranch house nestled in an old subdivision, the place was lit up like a Christmas tree. Maybe Kellie was even here. No harm in finding out.

He rang the doorbell, and Linelle answered with a smile. But as soon as she realized who he was, her grin faded to a pale mask of worry. "Is something wrong? Was there an accident?" She yanked him across the threshold.

He simultaneously shook his head and looked around. Tina was asleep under a multicolored afghan on the couch. Trevor was awake but bleary eyed, weaving slightly in his chair in the small open dining room in front of a Scrabble game. The chandelier above his head sent out prisms of light that beamed all around him. His dazed expression under the light made him look like the victim of some elaborate form of suburban torture.

"No, there was no accident. I was just in the neighborhood and thought . . . Trevor, are you okay?"

"We're playing Scrabble," he said miserably.

Linelle fluttered her hands. "Trevor always loves to play board games when he comes to see me. We've already done Parcheesi and Sorry. But Scrabble isn't his best." She chuckled. "He just hasn't learned to clean up with those triple-letter scores yet. Would you like a root beer?"

"Oh, no, I can't stay," Riley said. Would he really be able to pry these kids away from their grandmother? Should he even try? He felt as if he were truly going off the deep end. Still, he made a beeline for the dining room table.

"Kellie's not here," Linelle informed him.

Riley forced himself to stop and turn, feigning astonishment. "She's not? Oh, dear. I thought maybe since she wasn't at home . . ."

Linelle was quick to put him at ease. "She's bound to come by any time now, though. She's supposed to pick up the children, though I wish she wouldn't. We're having so much fun! Aren't we, Trevor?"

Trevor grunted.

Poor guy. Riley caught his bleary gaze and suddenly felt like a prisoner-of-war camp inspector. If there was a Geneva Convention for grandmothers, Linelle wasn't in compliance.

He, however, was receiving the five-star treatment. Linelle fluttered around him as though he was pure gold. "Sure I can't get you anything, Mr. Lombard?"

"Riley, please. Just some water would be fine."

"In a jiffy!" Linelle trotted to the kitchen to get him some water.

Trevor eyed at him warily with his bleary gaze. "What're you doing here?"

Riley shrugged. That was a good question. He looked with interest at the board and the two red-plastic blocks that were for scorekeeping and propping up letter tiles. Trevor's score peg had barely budged.

"'Cause if you're looking for my mom, she's out. With that friend of yours." The look in his eye said *thanks a lot!*

"Jay? He's harmless," Riley said with more confidence than he felt.

"Yeah, I guess so. He's got a cool car, too." He squinted at Riley. "So what're you doing here?"

Riley sat. "I guess I came here to help you."

Trevor shuddered miserably. "I hate this game."

"You ought to be loving it right now. You're sitting on a Z and a Q."

"So? Those are dumb letters. You can't make any words with them."

Riley grinned. "Really? How do you do at school on spelling quizzes?"

"Oh, not very . . ." In a split second, Trevor's whole demeanor changed. He sat up, took a slug of root beer, and looked expectantly at the kitchen door.

Riley did some quick consulting—not cheating, exactly—and when Linelle came back out, she discovered a changed universe. Suddenly, her grandson was triple-letter scoring her into oblivion. With a few subtle verbal cues from Riley, he was slapping down *quiz* and *foxy* and *revamp*. As far as that little house in Plano went, it was probably the comeback story of the decade.

Trevor was triumphant. As the clock struck midnight, he shook his head. "Mom sure has been gone for a long time."

That was precisely what Riley was trying not to think about. Why wasn't Trevor more worried? He would have assumed that Trevor would have punctured Jay's tires or performed some sort of elaborate sabotage to make sure Kellie didn't get her night out. But he was calmly sucking down a root beer as if it were no big deal. Riley felt a little irritated. Where was the old potato-salad hurler when he needed him?

"Did Mom invite you to my birthday party?"

"Uh, no."

Trevor frowned. "Well, I'm inviting you then. I can do that, can't I? I mean, it's my party."

Riley nodded.

"It's gonna be great, 'cause you'll be able to meet Dad. He's a really great guy. He's getting me a real cool baseball glove, too. Mom hasn't seen him in a long time. I'll bet when she does things'll be just like they used to."

"Oh, well . . ."

Trevor leaned back, obviously weaving a perfect birthday reunion scenario in his head. "I saw a movie where that happened. These two people were divorced, but then they realized it was a mistake. I think that probably happens a lot, don't you?"

Linelle chuckled uncomfortably. "Riley, would you like a Fig Newton?"

Riley shook his head just as the phone rang. Linelle's brows drew together, as he suddenly realized it wasn't her phone ringing, it was his cell phone. He pulled it out of his jacket.

"Thank God you answered!" Jay shouted over the background of traffic noise. "I'm sorry to bother you at this hour."

Riley leaned forward. Had something happened? "What's the matter?"

"I need your help, buddy. Kellie and I are stuck!"

Jay was nothing if not apologetic. In fact, he was so apologetic that he looked like a candidate for a coronary. "I *can't believe* this happened. It's my good-luck car. I'm so sorry."

"It's okay, Jay. You've already said you were sorry." About a million times in the past hour, which more than anything else was getting on her nerves. But she didn't want to stress that too much, lest he start apologizing for apologizing.

She could understand why he was a mess. Having his car break down on a Central Expressway exit ramp probably wasn't the grand finale he'd been hoping for this evening. Heaven knew she just wanted to get home herself. And get the kids home. Trevor was probably having kittens by now. But AAA was taking its time bailing out Jay with a tow. He'd called another towing service that said they would be even longer.

On top of that, it was a hot, steamy evening, made even hotter by the car exhaust that assaulted them as cars inched by Jay's blue 1953 Cadillac Eldorado convertible. It wasn't just the fact that people were having to squeeze by that was holding up traffic, though. People were rubbernecking like mad, either admiring the retro behemoth or honking angrily at it as they swerved past. Still in his suit coat and tie, Jay hovered protectively (and sweatily) next to the bumper, looking as if he were going to have a nervous breakdown.

Kellie tried to force some humor into the situation. She

nudged him with her high-heeled black sandal. "You can't blame people for honking. We look like escapees from a nineteen-fifties melodrama."

Jay refused to be distracted from despair. "How terrible of me! I didn't even think how uncomfortable you must be in your nice new clothes. Why don't you go sit—"

His words were mercifully cut off by someone honking in back of them. As Jay turned, his face slackened in relief. "It's Riley!"

Kellie also felt glad as Riley got out of the car, shaking his head at the spectacle they made. She'd tried to keep Jay from calling Riley—she didn't mind waiting for AAA—but now that he was there, she had to admit that he was a sight for sore eyes. He slanted a smile her way, and she felt her legs go shaky on her. She leaned back against Jay's car.

"Thank God you got here!" Jay said.

Riley fixed a perplexed look on Jay's hair, which was plastered against his head. "What happened to your hair? Do you bring out your grandfather's pomade along with his car?"

Jay brushed his hand across his stiff, slicked back hair. "Oh, that." He shot Kellie an uncomfortable look. "Trevor was opening a Coke when I went to pick Kellie up, and there was a little accident." He tried to put a good face on what Kellie was certain was sabotage. "You know how those cans can spew."

Riley and Kellie exchanged glances. Was he remembering the potato salad, Kellie wondered . . . or the kiss that was the indirect result? She caught his gaze dipping to her lips and had her answer. "You shouldn't have come out all this way, Riley. I told Jay I could just wait or call a cab."

Jay shook his head worriedly. "Her mother's probably waiting up. The kids are over there."

A shadow seemed to cross Riley's expression. "It's no trouble."

Kellie turned to Jay. "But what about you? You're still stuck out here. It's not fair."

Jay put on a brave face. "I'll be fine. Triple-A will be here any second now. I'll probably be home before you are." Sending an uncomfortable look in Riley's direction, Jay ducked his head and pressed his lips to Kellie's cheek with lightning quickness. "Thanks for coming out with me tonight."

"Thanks for asking."

Riley took her arm and led her toward his car. But she had to admit, leaning against that old car, Jay actually did look sort of dapper. Even if it was Coke giving his hair that Cary Grant sheen. She felt a wave of affection toward him. "Give me a call to let me know you got home all right."

He nodded, then looked over at Riley. "Thanks a million, Riley. I owe you for this, bud. You're a real friend."

That shadow passed over Riley's face again. Or maybe she was just imagining it.

"Don't mention it." He shook his head and grinned at that old hulk of a car. "And the next time you set out to impress a woman, maybe you should consider using your natural wit and charm, not fifty-year-old automobiles."

Enclosed in the cocoon of Riley's car, Kellie wondered suddenly at how differently the night had turned out than she had anticipated. She'd worried that she and Jay would have nothing to talk about during their date. After all, he was a very loosely employed multimillionaire and she'd been sandwiched so firmly in the middle class all her life, you could have called her tuna salad. But multimillionaires, apparently, saw the same movies and read the same books as everybody else. And Jay was quite a reader. He seemed to be juggling several volumes at once, and he was the first man she'd met who was comfortable talking about the classics or Bertrice Small. They'd almost missed the concert because they'd gabbed so long at the restaurant.

She'd also been worried that she and Jay would have an awkward, blundering good-night moment at her front door. But now it wasn't Jay at all who would be dropping her off at her front door. That was even more worrisome.

Riley cleared his throat. "You don't think Trevor figured out how to sabotage a Cadillac, do you?"

She laughed. "Don't ever underestimate him. He had the motive and the means, but not the opportunity. I kept my eye on him, especially after the episode with the Coke can."

"Well, other than the disaster, how was your evening?" Riley asked her.

"Fine."

She kept her eyes on the road ahead of them and her dress primly over her knees. How could she possibly have started out on a date with Jay and ended up with Riley? Did all roads in her life simply lead to this man?

That idea smacked of fate, and she didn't want to go there. Her days of furtively checking horoscopes and dashing off to Madame Mira were behind her. Riley was simply a man in need of friendship. That was why he was helping her. That was why he cared. Nothing more.

And she was grateful to him. She cut her eyes over for a glance at him in his T-shirt and perfectly fitting jeans. The car smelled faintly of that cologne of his. That had been one of her first memories of him from when he'd pulled her out of her wrecked car. She remembered it from the day he'd kissed her in her kitchen, only then it had been mingled with Ivory soap and barbecue and—

Think of something else!

She'd had a good time with Jay. He was nice and easy to talk to. The concert was enjoyable if a little sedate.

Jazz at a symphony? It just seemed a little ... tame. Well-mannered. Like Jay. Whereas a normal guy might bring out a racy sports car to impress a date, he chose his grandfather's Cadillac. And now instead of kissing his date good night, he was stuck alone on a busy highway waiting for someone to come tow his antique hulk to a garage. Poor Jay.

She tried to think of something else.

"Trevor's probably fit to be tied," she said. "He hates being at my mom's."

"He's okay," Riley said.

She turned on him quickly—just in time to see him clamp his jaw shut as if he wished he'd never opened his mouth. "How would you know?"

"Oh ..." He maneuvered off the expressway. "Well, I have a confession to make. I dropped by your mother's house tonight."

She gaped at him. He'd just blurted it out, as if there was nothing in the world odd about his paying her mother a social call. "Why?"

He lifted his shoulders. "I was just in the neighborhood. ..."

Right. Plano wasn't exactly a magnet for millionaires. "When were you there?" And what had he been talking to Linelle about?

He cleared his throat. "Actually, I was there when Jay called."

Kellie grabbed the armrest as he turned onto her street, but Riley's driving was fine. It was this conversation that was making her feel as if they were careening out of control. "What were you doing at my mother's house, for heaven's sake?"

"Playing Scrabble."

That, at least, was believable. "Riley, this is peculiar."

"I know."

"You're not being very consistent. I don't know

whether to thank you or to go to a judge for a restraining order."

He laughed. "I was just at loose ends. You know what that's like . . . Friday night, no one around the house."

Kellie considered this explanation. The last time she'd had a Friday night alone—the night she'd bumped into Riley at the grocery store—she'd felt strangely bereft, too. But at least she'd known Trevor and Tina were coming back. Remembering that Riley had nothing but an empty house to go home to sobered her.

She needed to stop making such a big deal of things. Riley was just trying to be a friend. Unfortunately, she'd never really had male friends. In high school, she'd had girlfriends, and then she'd started going out with Rick. But Rick, urban sophisticate that he was, would have freaked with jealousy at the thought of her seeing other guys just as friends. He wouldn't have believed it was possible.

"How was Trevor?" she asked, curious.

"Fine, except for the Scrabble game. I helped him beat your mother."

She barked out a laugh. "You must be his hero now."

"I'm not Ken Griffey, but he did invite me to his birthday party."

She folded her arms and smiled to herself. There. Maybe having men friends was really a good thing. Good for her, good for Trevor.

Riley frowned when he pulled onto her street. "Do you want me to drive you by your mom's to pick up the kids?"

She shook her head. "No, here's fine. You've already covered enough territory tonight on my behalf."

As he stopped the car in front of her house, he looked over at her with those blue eyes of his and her insides did an uneasy flip. If he was just dropping her off, why did he turn off the ignition?

"Well . . ." He smiled, drawing her gaze directly to that dimple.

"Well!" She willed herself to turn, to pull the door handle, but she remained motionless. The car was a silent, private world enveloping them. She could hear her own heart beating—thundering, more like—and felt her mouth and throat dry up like the Gobi Desert. She couldn't even gather the spit to mindlessly chirp "Well!" again.

It was as if they'd been dipped in a solution and were now hopelessly magnetized to each other. Because no matter how much her mind screamed *wrong, wrong, wrong!* at her, drawing closer to him felt incredibly right, right, right.

Riley pulled her into his arms, almost roughly at first, but that could have been because he hadn't been expecting her to be moving at him with equal gusto. Their bodies collided lips first, then arms, then torsos straining to make contact. She scooted awkwardly across the seat; then he grabbed her hips and pulled her to him. Her ribs hit the steering wheel, and he jabbed the armrest up and out of their way. It took long moments of positioning to make kissing in the front seat of a BMW less awkward or even halfway comfortable. She was only just perched on his bucket seat. Half of her was spilling over into the void where the gearshift was. Her neck was twisted, her body was contorted abnormally, and a sequin was poking into her thigh.

She was in heaven.

She'd seen footage of skydivers after they'd leapt out of their planes and imagined this felt something like that. Pure sensation. She didn't know whether she and Riley were necking in that front seat for an hour or a mere minute. Time was irrelevant next to Riley's warm lips against hers. Their bodies seemed to find a way to twine together, to stoke the desire beneath the kiss. Everything about him seemed wonderful to her. The way his large hands cupped her arms, her back, her bottom. The way his slightly stubbly jaw felt bumping against her chin. The way he seemed to be able to sense exactly what she wanted him to do next, where she wanted him to touch her.

He cupped a hand around her breast, and she sucked in a halting breath. At that moment she knew. He would be the perfect lover. Perfect.

Seconds? Minutes? She couldn't say how long they kissed. All she knew was that when Riley pulled back suddenly, she fell back to earth in a heap.

She lay against the uncomfortable armrest for a second, trying to gather her wits, trying not to audibly pant. Her body was howling with disappointment. She didn't want to open her eyes, but she did. Riley was hovering over her, blue eyes full of unquenched desire . . . and regret.

She pushed herself back over the gearshift to the passenger seat. Then, gathering what little dignity about her that she could, she hiked up the strap of her dress, untwisted her legs, and pulled her skirt back down to mid-thigh.

"Kellie, I'm sorry," he said.

Her teeth ground together. "It serves me right. I should have known if I let you mastermind my social life—even buying me a dress—you would expect a little something in return."

His head was shaking. "It's not like that. It's just . . ."

In the quiet of the car, there was a silence that stretched so long that Kellie couldn't stand it any more. She had to look over at him. When she did, what she saw shocked the anger and confusion out of her. His skin, in the meager illumination thrown from the streetlights, was pale, almost waxy. He looked terrible. As if he were about to be sick.

"Riley, what is it?"

When he looked back up at her, his expression was

heartbreaking. His eyes were so full of emotion—in one glance they conveyed all she'd wanted him to say since they'd first met. She saw all his sorrows in that look.

And then came his words. A flood of words. Words she'd so yearned to hear and now she wished she could stop. But she couldn't stop him because she sensed that he needed, finally, to tell her.

"I had a wife and daughter, Kellie. They died. In a car accident. It was . . . well, it was horrible."

"Riley, you don't . . ."

He either didn't hear or didn't want to hear. "And the most terrible thing is, I saw it all before it happened. I saw the accident. I was sitting up in my office, and I saw it all. The split second of panic, the sound of the truck falling and the shriek of metal as it slid across asphalt. The smashing of metal and glass. I was beside myself. I went nuts. By the time I called Joanne's car phone, though, it was all over. They were gone."

His head was hanging and Kellie leaned toward him, wanting to say something. But how did you comfort a man who was living with a memory like that one? She couldn't bear to have him dwelling on the ugly end of their lives. "What were they like?"

His face pinched in concentration. "Joanne? We met in college. In a huge history seminar at UT. She sat next to me one day and started *talking*. I mean, gabbing during the lecture." He snorted. "I wanted to tell her to shut up, but she was so pretty—and so she kept talking at me until suddenly I heard myself asking her out, and it seemed from then on we were best friends. We ate together, traveled together, slept together, for eight years. I never wanted anybody else.

"And Abbie . . . She was incredible. The best moments of my life were when I would come back to the house after a day at work and find her waiting at the front door—her face would just light up the room, it seemed like. I used to keep those little miniature candy bars in my suit jacket for her, and so that would be the first thing out of her mouth after she kissed me hello. Milky Ways! For months after the accident I kept finding them in my pockets.''

He stopped, taking a breath. For a moment, as he'd said Abbie's name, it had seemed as if he just might lose his composure completely. His not losing it was even worse. She didn't have to call up the girl's image from the newspaper; she was there, in that car, in Riley's heartbroken eyes.

''I know that doesn't really tell you much. I just don't know how else to describe them except to say that our lives together were as close to ideal as a human family could be. We were happy. We loved each other. We had all the things we wanted.'' He swallowed. ''After Joanne and Abbie died, it was as though my world ended. I mean, I kept going, but the meaning of it all had ended. Nothing made sense. Money didn't matter. People didn't matter. I didn't worry about trying to start over or make my life better because I'd had the best. The best wife, the best daughter. What was the point in trying to replicate perfection?

''So I just got through things. Oh, I'd go to functions, and I'd hang out with Jay. I gave a good imitation of a man who was handling everything. But I was on autopilot.'' He looked over at her, and her heart thumped heavily in her chest. For a moment she felt she couldn't breathe.

''Then I bumped into you that day, and suddenly I remembered that people *did* matter. And it wasn't just because of that weird chemistry between us. It was because I liked the way you made me look at myself. I started to care what happened to you. And then to your kids. Do you know what it was like for me to walk into your house and see Tina? Christ, she's about the age Abbie would have been! But so different. Different enough that for a while I could forget my own loss and get involved in the lives of a little girl who wanted a piano, a boy who missed his father, a woman who couldn't understand anyone making a fuss over her.

"I keep thinking I'm ready to put the past behind me . . . but then I'll remember. I'll remember those people I loved, and be reminded that everything can be gone in an instant. It's terrifying."

She reached into her little purse and pulled out a tissue.

Oh, yes, Kellie had wanted to hear all of this—because in the part of her brain that was programmed by Hollywood movies she imagined Riley would tell her his problems and everything would be better. That his pouring his heart out to her would be an indication that they had moved closer. But just the opposite was the case. His confession just seemed to pour another layer of cement over the wall that stood between them.

She faced forward again, frustrated and hating herself for being so selfish. In her heart of hearts, she wanted him to say that the past was behind him and he looked forward to a bright, happy future with her. The reality was that he was still grieving. They had collided at the wrong time. All the physical attraction in the world wouldn't change that. Life never offered tidy happy endings. Her life didn't, at least. That was why she had to be sensible.

But she couldn't just turn her back on Riley. And she couldn't believe that a man's life could be over, just over, when he was only in his mid-thirties. "You can't stop hoping that things will get better," she told him.

"I don't stop hoping. But I just can't be sure." He looked at her. "Kellie, I'm so—"

She shook her head so violently that the movement effectively cut off his words. "Don't say anything more. I understand. And if I wanted apologies, I would've stayed back with Jay,'' she said, smiling at him. ''Thanks for bringing me home.''

She got out of the car and sped up the walkway, forgetting that there was no real need for her to go into her house. She had to jump in her car and go pick up her kids. But in the back of her mind—the place that harbored her Tina-like girlish fantasies—she had visions of Riley coming after her, telling her that on second thought she *was* the woman who could turn his life around.

But when she peeked out the curtain of the front window, Riley's car was pulling away.

Swallowing her disappointment, she snatched her car keys out of her purse and went out to her car.

Chapter Thirteen

"So what'd she say?"

Riley frowned into his telephone. He'd spent an entire morning staring mindlessly at second-quarter company reports. He was having a hard time focusing on them with thoughts of Kellie and the night before still swimming through his head. Of kissing her. Of the pain in her face later, when he'd spilled his guts to her. How could he have lost control like that? He shouldn't have unloaded on her. He should have had more restraint.

At his continued silence, Jay prodded, "You know . . . while ya'll were driving home. Surely my name came up. Didn't it?"

The reminder of their drive home was like being goosed. "Oh, sure."

"Well, so . . . ?" He could envision Jay's nervous grin. "How'd I do?"

"I guess you did pretty well," Riley lied. "She said she had a good time last night."

"Did she?" Jay asked eagerly. "Because I did, too. Well . . . before the car broke down."

Riley leapt at the opportunity to change the subject.

"What happened to the car? Nothing too pricey to repair, I hope."

"Nah, the mechanic said I just need a new transmission."

Only someone like Jay would see a new transmission as insignificant.

Unfortunately, for once in his life, Jay didn't feel like talking about his most treasured possession. "C'mon, Riley. What about Kellie?"

What could he say? *I'm losing my mind over her,* he might have said to a disinterested party. But he certainly couldn't be that honest with Jay.

"Do you think I should call her again?"

Riley felt his jaw clench, but he knew the possessiveness galloping in his blood was wrong.

"I think I'm gonna play it a little cooler this time around," Jay said. "I'm gonna wait till this afternoon to call."

"Twenty-four hours is playing it cool?"

There was a pause. "Actually, it'll be more like twelve hours. I called her last night when I got home. Or I tried to. I guess she wasn't back from picking up the kids yet."

Again, Riley cringed. Of course she wasn't back yet. She'd wasted a good half hour parked in the front seat of Riley's car.

"You were right about her, Riley," Jay said. "I guess that just goes to show that you can't judge from appearances."

Riley stiffened. "What's that mean?"

"Well, from that first encounter at Wiggie's, I thought her sister looked like the nicer one, but according to Kellie, Rita's a little bit of a flake. Have you met her?"

"Rita? Yeah, I've met her."

"And . . . ?"

"Kellie's right. She's a flake."

Jay laughed. "Kellie's funny, isn't she? You know

what she said when the car broke down? She said, 'You're supposed to have the car break down in a romantic, secluded spot, not Central Expressway.' Isn't that funny?''

Riley chuckled listlessly.

"She was joking, of course," Jay said. "You might not believe this, but I don't think she's the kiss-on-the-first-date type.''

Riley did *not* want to be having this conversation.

"You were right about her being easy to talk to, too. We had a great time at dinner.''

"So you're really going to call her again?''

"Oh, sure," Jay said. "I like her. I really, really like her.''

Great. One date and he was suddenly Sally Field. What had he been thinking when he set those two up together?

That it would be a nice thing to do, you big jerk, his conscience reminded him. This was what happened when you played Good Samaritan.

"So you think I'm doing the right thing?" Jay said.

"What?''

"Calling Kellie so soon?''

Riley was stunned by the conflicting answers that warred within him. If anyone had asked him before this very minute, he would have said that he was a good friend. Always tried to be, at least. But it wasn't until now that he realized all the low-down sneaky thoughts he harbored inside himself. What would be the harm in saying, for instance, *Wait a week. Two weeks. You don't want to look too eager, do you?* Jay always took his advice on dating matters, never seeming to realize that he himself had a lot more experience on the dating front than Riley, who had married when he was a mere twenty-four-year-old.

"If you were in my shoes, what would you do?" Jay asked.

Oh, Lord, Riley thought, sweating his answer. Now was the time to show what he was made of. Hero, or goat? Friend, or fiend?

> *Forgive me!*
> *(How about a cocktail party tomorrow at 6?)*

Alejandro inspected the flowers that had arrived with the note Kellie was reading and gave his stamp of approval. "Smooth."

The thought of Jay as even remotely smooth made her laugh. He was still apologizing for his grandfather's car breaking down. But the flowers—a tropical assortment of flaming red and yellow—were impressive.

"You must be playing your cards right," Alejandro said.

"I'm not doing anything." *Except bumbling along,* she thought. Throwing herself at a man with more baggage than Samsonite. Then being stung when he told her a history she already knew and should have considered before she vaulted the gearshift to kiss him.

Alejandro laughed disbelievingly.

"There's no strategy," she insisted. "Jay's just a nice man. He's invited me to a party."

"An office party?"

She frowned. "No . . . I don't think he has an office."

"What does he do?"

What *did* he do? "He volunteers a lot. And he's the vice president of his family foundation. I guess that would be considered a job."

"You mean you didn't ask him specifically what he does?"

She shrugged. "It never came up."

Actually, she *had* considered asking him, but worried that he would be sensitive to such a question. Her life was in an odd state when she had to fret over hurting the feelings of *Fortune* 500 members.

Just when Alejandro had to ring up a customer and Kellie thought she would be off the hook from his prying questions, Rita breezed through the door. Given her timing—the morning after Kellie's big date—she obviously was trolling for gossip.

"You look like you borrowed Tina's pajamas," Kellie joked as her sister approached wearing a scrub suit with Sesame Street characters all over it.

"I'm on my way to work. Pediatric ward," Rita answered. She must have been in a hurry, too, because she wasted no time launching into her inquisition. "So . . . how was it?"

"Fine."

The answer didn't go far in satisfying Rita. "*Fine?* Kellie, the last time you had a first date with some guy, radio stations were playing 'Love Shack.' *Fine* is all you're going to supply me with?"

"There's nothing to tell."

"That's not what I heard. Mom said Riley came by the house last night. Late."

"Where were you?"

"Working."

Kellie puzzled over this. "You worked a late shift last night and now you're already on your way to work again?"

Rita shrugged. "I'm trying to make more money. You know, pay Mom back . . . and build up a nest egg for Wendell and me."

Kellie crossed her arms so Rita wouldn't see the fist that wanted to pop Wendell in the nose. "What does Wendell think about your working all the time?"

"Oh, he thinks it's great!" Rita said. "He's very supportive, Kellie."

"I'll bet."

"But you didn't answer my question," Rita pressed. "How was last night? And don't say fine—that doesn't cut it."

"The concert was good, but then we had car trouble on the way home."

Rita hooted. "Car trouble! That's the oldest one in the book."

"So is his car. We were waiting on the world's slowest tow truck, so Riley came to the rescue and took me home."

Rita's grin collapsed. "*Riley* took you home?"

Kellie nodded, and Rita looked over at the huge floral display next to the cash register. "So these are from Riley?"

"No, Jay."

Rita pondered it all for a moment. "Kellie, your life has gotten weird."

"That's the conclusion I've reached, too. Jay just invited me to a cocktail party tomorrow night."

"Good!" Rita frowned. "I guess it's good. A cocktail party? I thought those just happened in glossy magazines. What are you going to wear?"

Kellie laughed. "I haven't decided if I'm even going yet."

"That's why you need to figure out what you can wear. So you can decide. You *can't* wear that dress you wore to the symphony again."

More wardrobe worry—a reminder of why hanging around rich folk wasn't practical. "But it's the best thing I have."

"Kellie, you can't. He just saw you in that dress."

Alejandro, free of his customer, gave Rita an up-and-down appraisal and butted in. "I wouldn't take fashion advice from a woman in an Elmo suit, Kellie."

Rita rolled her eyes. "This is for work. Kids like it."

Alejandro looked doubtful. "When I was a kid, I liked

my first-grade teacher, who wore high heels and skirts above her knee." He grinned in realization. "You sort of look like her, Rita."

Rita blushed, and for a moment Kellie felt as if she'd been hit by a bolt from the blue. Rita? Alejandro? Alejandro was Rita's type—cute and boyish. He even had that ponytail look that she went for. Although maybe nineteen was a little *too* boyish. Rita would be robbing the cradle. Then again, anything was better than Wendell.

And Rita was just Alejandro's type—female.

But once Kellie got her hopes up, she discovered that the playful moment between her sister and her employee had passed, and they were both staring at her expectantly.

"Oh, sorry, I missed the question. . . ."

"I said why don't we go shopping tomorrow?" Rita asked with an impatience that told Kellie this wasn't the first time the question had been asked.

"I can't. Trevor has a game." And she had no money to spare for cocktail dresses.

Rita sighed. "Well, all right. I was just trying to help you win over Riley."

"Jay."

"Right." She looked confused. "So you really prefer the skinny bug-eyed one to the hunky one?"

Kellie flashed back momentarily to that kiss in the BMW and experienced a squeezing pressure on her chest. "The hunky one isn't available."

"Oh. Well, if you want me to baby-sit tomorrow night, that's okay with me."

"Thanks, Rita. I'll pay you." Though it galled her to think she would be contributing to Wendell's nest egg.

Rita waved away the offer. "It's been a while since I've had one of Tina's music appreciation lessons. Besides, I'd like to get another glimpse of this Jay guy. Maybe he's got something I didn't pick up on at first glance." She grinned mischievously. "Is he a good kisser?"

For a moment it seemed as if every machine in the place had stopped just in time for Rita to ask that one embarrassing question. She and Alejandro leaned toward Kellie expectantly.

She tried to artfully dodge. It certainly wouldn't help Rita's Jay-Riley confusion to explain how she'd ended up kissing Riley good night after her date with Jay. "Don't go getting ideas. There's no chemistry between Jay and me."

Rita's brows rose with interest. "Listen to you! I thought you didn't believe in stuff like chemistry."

Kellie felt her cheeks redden. She hadn't believed in chemistry . . . until Riley had bumbled into her life like a mad scientist. "We're just good friends."

Rita fixed an interested stare on her. "That's what you said about Riley. But when he left your house after the barbecue, I noticed that your *friend* had lipstick smeared on his mouth."

Kellie was stunned—not so much by the fact that Riley had been walking around with lipstick on his face as the fact that Rita had managed to keep quiet about it till now. "Well, don't worry, I didn't smear any lipstick on Jay last night."

Rita looked surprised. "*None?* After the guy went to all the trouble to take you to see Wynton Marsalis. That's being sort of a prude, isn't it?"

"Would you rather I were a symphony slut?"

Rita laughed and looked at her watch. "I guess you're right. I've got to get to work. Thanks for giving me the poop." Her lips turned down in disappointment as she recalled the meager low-down she had received for her efforts. "Or the lack of it."

"I'll call you tonight."

"It's Wendell's laundry night," Rita warned.

"Oh." Didn't want to interrupt that. "Tomorrow then."

"Okay."

"Bye, Rita," Alejandro hollered after her. "Don't work too hard."

Rita sent him a trilly fingered wave. "Bye, Alejandro."

After her sister had gone, Kellie stared wonderingly at Alejandro again as he copied a document. *Rita? Alejandro?* It was so tempting to try to set up her sister with anybody as long as it pulled her out of the clutches of the wretched Wendell.

But would that solve anything? It could be a disaster, and Rita might end up with no one. After all, Alejandro already had his harem—a fact that poor Lana was only now beginning to understand.

Though, frankly, Kellie was just as glad the workplace was cooling off a little. There was less tension during the day. Besides, if Riley had managed a love merger between Alejandro and a temp Riley had sent over out of the blue, she would have had to think twice about his supposed penchant for matchmaking. Including his ideas about the two of them.

Kellie concluded that she needed to get a handle on her own wobbly love life before she tackled Rita's. She glanced over at her bouquet. Jay was a nice man, and he'd been kind enough to invite her out again.

Of course, she didn't want to lead him on, make him think there was something more between them than there was.

Then again, she didn't want to stay home Saturday night moping over Riley, either. Maybe her mother was right. Maybe it was time to move on.

She picked up the phone and gave Jay a call.

He always felt uncomfortable at these things. Everyone in their stiffest clothes, sipping mediocre champagne and making polite chitchat with people who mostly saw each

other only at formal gatherings like this one to benefit
the art museum. Fellow well-heeled folks who had little
in common outside of money and the accoutrements of
money. Sometimes he felt like a kid who'd ended up in
the wrong kindergarten. When had these people become
his peer group? When had he gotten so old and stuffy?

Joanne used to be a whiz at these formal bashes—she
lived for nights like this, in fact. She'd grown up wealthy
and so seemed to know exactly how to maneuver among
clumps of people who looked as if they were fresh from
the taxidermists. She could make the stuffed shirts standing around dully with plates in their hands laugh with
the right word or even just a wink—that secret language
Riley had never learned growing up as the son of a
plumber. But all he'd had to do was follow Joanne, and
he felt like the life of the party.

His heart felt as heavy as a stone in his chest. Why
was he thinking these thoughts now? He'd been going
to functions right along, forcing himself to socialize even
in those first months when the thought of facing people
was about as appealing as facing a firing squad. He'd
gritted his teeth and gone. He'd managed.

Now he felt he was on the verge of not managing.

A woman in a crisp maid's uniform came by, and he
was grateful for something to do. He skimmed away from
the caviar, grabbed two cheese puffs by their toothpick
skewers, and immediately popped one in his mouth.

Jay found him in mid-chew. ''Ah, tearing into the food
already, I see.''

He swallowed and felt immediately better. Maybe this
was why he'd felt so alone. He and Jay usually stood
around these functions together. But Jay wasn't looking
so hot. His clothes were more rumpled than usual, and
his snowy white shirt had a dull red stain down the front.

''What happened to you?'' Riley asked, startled.
''Were you in an accident?''

Jay glanced down at his shirt. "Sort of. A run-in with Trevor and a ketchup bottle."

"Trevor?"

"Kid's a real butterfingers," Jay explained, "but so was I when I was a kid."

Jay obviously hadn't figured some things out yet. "What were you doing with Trevor?"

"I was over at Kellie's house." Jay tilted his head toward Riley in a conspiratorial way. "Were you right about him! The kid just cries out for a father figure." He jabbed his thumb toward his stained shirt. "Next week, I'm going to the Little League game to root him on."

Riley felt frozen. "You're going to Trevor's game?"

"Of course." Jay puffed up. "Used to play a little b-ball myself, you know. Joltin' Jay, they used to call me."

"Are you sure that wasn't T-ball?"

Jay raised his hands as if to fend off the verbal hit. "Say, why are you in such a sour mood?"

"I don't know," Riley said apologetically. "I was just trying to figure that out when you walked up."

"Well, I'm obviously not doing much to cheer you up. Maybe Kellie can, though."

"Kellie?"

Of course. Now that his neurons were firing again, Riley realized Jay had been ambushed by Trevor when he'd picked Kellie up at her house to bring her here. They were on a date.

"Here she is now."

Riley's mouth went bone dry as he watched her sashay through the room a little carefully on her heels. She was wearing the black dress—the one he'd practically pulled off her in the front seat of his BMW. She shot a few curious glances at the clusters of people standing around. A waiter stopped her when she was halfway to them, and she took a fluted glass of champagne. Something she said to the waiter made him tilt back his head and laugh. It was the first time Riley had ever felt jealous of a waiter.

"Doesn't she look great?" Jay asked.

Riley nodded numbly and clenched his teeth against his gut reaction to her. There were flashier women in the place, to be sure. More expensively made-up women. Women who had peeled and tanned and waxed themselves to a high gloss. But next to them, Kellie was like a blast of fresh air. He reacted to the sight of her like a kid just hitting puberty ogling a *Cosmopolitan* cover at the grocery checkout.

She caught Jay's glance and grinned. Then she saw Riley standing next to him and wobbled. Catching herself before she pitched over completely, she made her way more slowly toward Riley and Jay. More cautiously. A hint of a blush shone in her cheeks as she walked up.

She kept her expression a guarded neutral as she greeted him. "I should have known I'd bump into you."

"Didn't I mention?" Jay asked. "Riley and I always hang around these things together. The lonely single guys."

She looked at Riley doubtfully. "Something tells me you usually don't stay lonely for long."

Jay laughed. "Hear that, Riley? She thinks we're fast operators! I wonder where she gets that idea from."

Riley choked on his champagne.

"Just a hunch," Kellie said.

Jay grinned at them. "I'm starving. Why don't I go find a waiter with a plate of food?"

"That sounds good," Riley said, never taking his eyes off Kellie. Jay sped off somewhere, leaving them alone.

Kellie immediately looked as if she wished he hadn't.

"Jay and I show up at a lot of the same functions," he explained to Kellie, lest she accuse him of following her again.

"You mean this isn't destiny?"

"Well, it might be if you continue hanging around Jay." His tone came out more disapproving than he'd intended.

"And why shouldn't I?" she asked. "You were the one who set us up, as I recall."

"It just didn't seem to me, Thursday night, that you were all that wild about him."

"Thursday night I got sidetracked, but it's very clear that won't happen again."

"I see." He popped his last cheese puff.

She sighed, then touched his arm in a soothing gesture—which had the exact opposite effect. "Look, I didn't mean it to come out that way. I never told you the other night how sorry I was ... about what happened to you. I understand, Riley, I really do. And I even understand what you mean about some people not getting over things. I feel that way about my divorce sometimes."

"I can't believe anything would keep you down for long. You're a pillar of strength, Kellie. Look how you've managed your work and your kids. I admire you."

Her dark eyes shone as she looked off into the crowd. "You understand, don't you? I can't snub Jay just because you're trying to avoid me. We can be adults about this, can't we?"

"Of course." He frowned. "I'm not trying to avoid you anyway."

"That's good. Because we'll have to see more of each other in the coming weeks."

Riley felt alarmed. Were she and Jay a permanent item already? "Why?"

She blinked up at him. "Trevor's birthday party, remember? You promised to go."

"Oh, yes."

"You're coming, aren't you?"

He smiled. "Sure."

"Good." She really did look relieved. "I can use all

the cheering section I can get. My ex-husband's going to be there.''

Riley nodded. ''I believe Trevor might have mentioned that about fifty times.''

She laughed, and he felt a wave of relief, as if all wasn't lost if they could laugh together. ''He's very anxious about it all,'' she said.

''He's hoping you'll get back together with your ex-husband.''

''I should talk to him. I've been so preoccupied lately.'' Kellie looked lost in thought for a moment, as if she were piecing things together. ''You know, it's strange. Tina's younger, but she seems to have a firmer grasp on the concept of divorce.''

''It's because she's a girl. More practical.''

''You think so? Most people, most men, would say it's the other way around.''

''Women are more practical when it comes to the things that matter,'' he said. ''They're more levelheaded.'' *They can kiss one man on Thursday night and go out with another on Saturday,* was what he was thinking. But he didn't say it, thank heavens. It wasn't fair of him to think that.

Kellie shook her head doubtfully. ''I'm afraid my sister blows your theory out of the water. She's had her head in the clouds over this boyfriend of hers for years and years, and it's just going nowhere.''

''Where should it be going?''

''Well . . .'' Kellie shrugged. ''Is marriage too old-fashioned an idea?''

''But it sounds like you don't like the guy. Why would you want her to marry him?''

She laughed. ''I don't think he's good enough for her, but I'm offended that he doesn't want to marry her. Does that make sense?''

''In a big-sister, irrational way, maybe.''

"I just don't think he's the one for her."

"They're not destined for each other, you mean?"

She rolled her eyes. "I never said crazy stuff like this before I met you! Now it's popping out of my mouth all the time. Your weirdness is wearing off on me."

Jay returned bearing hors d'oeuvres. "Well, you two seem to be getting along like a house afire. What's up?"

"Kellie was just telling me I was weird."

Jay laughed. "I figured that out my first semester of college." He hovered over Kellie. "Here, take a barbecued shrimp. They're delicious."

Riley looked at Jay feeding Kellie finger food and felt a quick jab of jealousy, one that he knew he needed to get over. "Maybe I'd better go circulate."

But of course he headed straight for the door. He was always uncomfortable at these parties, but never more so than today.

That night there was an explosion in the kitchen. Screaming and pans flying. Strangled sobs and slamming doors. It was enough to wake the dead, or at least Riley's neighbors. He was halfway to the kitchen when Nathaniel came flying out into the hallway, a wet tea towel on his head, presumably covering a cut. Riley had never seen his butler look so unglued before.

"That's it!" Nathaniel cried. "That's the end! I don't have to put up with his insults anymore!"

Riley nervously knotted the belt on his bathrobe. "What happened?"

"Fayard! I've had it with him. I'm not even going to speak to him anymore. This is the end."

The situation felt like high tragedy to Riley. His whole life was unraveling. His best friend was going out with the woman he was attracted to. His house seemed rattly and empty and haunted. And now his cook and his butler—maybe both—were about to bail on him. "What happened?" he repeated.

"Fayard threw a roast at me!"

Riley squinted at the tea towel. "He beaned you with a roast?"

Nathaniel rolled his eyes. "No, the cut came when I fell in my hurry to get to the sink and rinse the gravy off my shirt." He offered his shirt sleeve as testament to the altercation.

Riley shook his head. "Something has to be done."

"No kidding!" Nathaniel said acerbically. "Gravy on silk—that's *murder*."

Riley felt as if he were holding his breath. This was the moment he'd been dreading. He just didn't want any more change. "You're not leaving, are you?"

"And let that Julia Child on steroids in there declare himself the winner?" Nathaniel tutted loudly, as if Riley should have known better. "I'd send my custom suits to the Salvation Army first!"

"Well, then . . ."

"I simply refuse to talk to him anymore." He lifted his chin. "There's more dignity in the silent treatment than in throwing a tantrum and walking out. Besides, this is my home as much as his. And *I'm* certainly not going to reduce myself to tossing large cuts of meat around." He turned his head and sing-songed loudly in the general direction of the kitchen. "That's nothing but *churlish, childish behavior!*" He took a deep breath and looked back at Riley. "Sorry if we woke you up."

They might have woken up half of Dallas. "Do you need me to take you to the emergency room?"

Nathaniel's lip trembled bravely. "No, I'll be fine. Though someday, Riley, *I'm going to be outta here. I'll run away to Europe and find a man who'll really appreciate me!*"

"You couldn't do that," he said, only half attempting a tone of levity. "What would I do?"

Nathaniel shook his head. "You? You'd be better off with a stout, headstrong housekeeper who would give you a stern talking-to instead of a wreck like me."

"That's not true."

He sniffed. "It is! You live around me so that you can kid yourself that *you're* normal. That *your* life isn't chaos. Look at you—the prime of your life and you're in bed by eleven. If you had a militaristic German housefrau around instead of a neurotic butler, believe me, you'd be out trying to get yourself a life!"

"That sounds like a nightmare."

"No, it sounds like just what you need!"

As Riley watched Nathaniel stomp off to his room, he wanted to contradict him. But was there anyone on earth other than himself who would believe that a grieving man, a lovesick butler, and an insane cook banging around the kitchen made for a stable household?

Chapter Fourteen

"Kellie, you're a nervous wreck."

That was putting it mildly. As Kellie fluttered around the kitchen, she felt distinctly on edge. She'd been cleaning and scrubbing since dawn, and the house still managed to look as if there were people living in it. Any moment now, all sorts of people she'd be happier not dealing with at all were going to descend upon her. And not just Rick, though heaven knew the prospect of seeing her ex for the first time since he'd left was enough to make her reach for some Prozac. There would also be her old in-laws to deal with. And loud, wiry friends of Trevor. And Jay. And Riley, whom she hadn't seen since the cocktail party. She hadn't stopped thinking of him since then, either.

And to top it off, she had Rita planted at her kitchen table, moping profusely, though of course she wouldn't come out and say exactly what the problem was.

Kellie slapped some more icing on Trevor's cake and tried to take her angst out on the task at hand.

"If you think I'm bad, you should see Tina," she told

Rita. "Tina's so excited about seeing her father again that she's lying prone on her bed in her best dress because she's afraid of mussing herself if she comes in here."

"And where's the birthday boy?"

"In his backyard lair. He's all keyed up for Rick to be here. Too bad I'm not. I'm just a nervous wreck."

"I don't know what you have to be nervous about," Rita said, nursing her unspoken sorrows with a can of Coke. "Everything's coming up roses for you. You're self-employed, you've got a terrific new boyfriend ... and there's Riley, whatever he is."

That list alone made Kellie want to jump out of her skin. Nothing like being reminded of the financial and emotional powder kegs in her life to make a body feel snuggly and secure. "Sure, and Trevor's made it eleven years without landing us even in small claims court."

"See?" Rita said. "Your life is going great. *I'm* the one who's having real problems."

Finally—here came the neurotic unveiling. Kellie looked over anxiously. "What kind of problems?"

Rita sat with her mouth agape as if she thought Kellie had lost her mind. "Are you telling me you haven't noticed something missing here?"

Kellie looked around frantically and noted the empty punch bowl. "Oh, shoot! I haven't made the punch yet."

Rita's mouth dropped open. "I'm not talking about punch, Kellie! I'm talking about Wendell."

"What about Wendell?"

"He's not here."

Kellie strained to remember. "Was he supposed to be?"

"Of course!" Rita's voice ramped up to a screech. "He promised me he would come with me. For heaven's sake, Kellie—I *told* you that."

Kellie had long ago stopped expecting Wendell to show

up at anything, but when it came to that boyfriend of hers, Rita's hopes sprang inconceivably eternal.

Of course she couldn't say any of this to Rita in the state she was in. Her poor sister really did look as if she were going to snap.

Rita took out a tissue and blew her nose noisily. "This time he promised me!"

"I'm sure he had his reasons . . ." Kellie began.

"Oh, right, so now you're defending him—that jerk!" Rita howled into her Kleenex. "You're never on my side!"

Kellie heard screaming in the backyard, then an ominous *thump* against the back wall of the house. Apparently, the first of Trevor's friends had arrived. "I *am* on your side," she assured Rita, "always. I've never made any bones about the fact that I think Wendell doesn't treat you right. He doesn't even act like a boyfriend at all. That's not what you deserve."

Rita hiccuped and squeezed her tissue into her fist. "You don't know him like I do. You never liked him."

"So what do you want me to say, Rita? Whatever opinion I give, it's wrong."

"I just want you to be truthful with me."

But if Kellie dared to speak the truth—that Rita should say *sayonara* to Wendell—she knew she'd have more than explosion on her hands. She'd have Krakatoa. "Let's not argue about Wendell," she pleaded. "It upsets me that he upsets you."

Rita shot up to her feet. "Well, maybe he wouldn't upset me so much if everyone didn't expect us to conform to their preconceived ideas! Maybe we're not like every couple in the world. So what? Maybe Wendell's not showing up today was his way of asserting his individuality." She blew her nose again. "Besides, he says it's good for us to spend lots of time socializing by ourselves, and I think he's right." She took a few deep, ragged breaths before breaking into sobs. "Only I hate going out by myself!"

The doorbell rang and footsteps clomped down the hallway. "I'll get it!" Tina yelled in a jackhammer voice.

Meanwhile, Kellie watched in horror as Rita sank down again and flopped her head on the kitchen table, weeping. "Rita, for heaven's sake. What's wrong?"

"I feel so, so . . . vague!"

"What?"

"Vague! It's just like Madame Mira said! I'm twenty-eight years old, and I'm just a nobody whose life is going nowhere!"

"Rita—"

Just that moment, she heard a throat clearing in the doorway. Kellie turned. Jay was standing there, staring at Rita, his face etched with concern. In fact, he almost looked as if he was in pain. And Kellie could well understand why. Her sister didn't suffer in silence; instead, her misery manifested itself in loud, snorting wails and tear ducts that responded like Niagra Falls.

Jay shuffled his feet anxiously. "Am I interrupting?"

"Oh, well . . ."

Rita shot upright in her chair in a valiant attempt to pull herself together. Her face was red and puffy, her nose moist. "No, please, come in. Don't mind me, I'm just having a nervous breakdown."

Jay, who was holding a big box wrapped in Pokemon paper, put his package aside and sat down next to Rita. "I know what you need. A joke. Did you hear that NASA is sending cattle into space?"

Rita looked at him doubtfully. "No."

"They're calling it the herd shot round the world."

The punchline was received with a pair of groans.

Rita frowned. "That's not very funny."

Jay looked up at Kellie in amazement. "It's not?"

Kellie shook her head, then laughed.

"Where did you hear that?" Rita asked. "Did you make that up?"

He brightened. "Would you like to hear another one?"

"No!" Rita raised her hands in surrender. "Please. Life is hard enough to take already."

Jay nodded. "That's right—you said something about feeling like a nobody going nowhere."

Rita nodded. "Does that sound dumb?"

"No, it sounds like a Beatles song."

Rita laughed and looked up at Kellie. "See, I told you you were lucky."

It had been three weeks since Kellie had started seeing Jay. In all that time, he'd been taking her to dinner, putting up patiently with Trevor's efforts at sabotage, Tina's impromptu piano recitals, and Kellie's lack of enthusiasm for a romantic relationship. Dating-wise, he was the Little Engine That Could. Nothing seemed to faze him or discourage him. And now Kellie was finally beginning to think she *was* lucky. She could have spent all day trying to get Rita's mind off her problems, but Jay had managed to cheer her up—or at least distract her from Wendell—in a matter of seconds. She looked at him and for the first time since they'd started going out, she felt something in her heart flip irregularly. He really was the sweetest guy. A gem. She wished she liked him as much as—

The doorbell rang and Tina came careening out of her room again. "I'll get it!"

Kellie only wished she liked kissing Jay as much as . . . well, as much as some other men she'd kissed. She wouldn't allow herself to name names, even to herself.

The cake. She needed to finish the cake.

"Is this where the party is?"

Riley was standing in the doorway. Looking at him, her heart did a mammoth flip. In a red print shirt and perfectly fitting jeans, dimple scrubbed and polished, Riley cut a dashing figure. She hadn't seen him in weeks, and over that time he hadn't lost any of his physical appeal. *Damn it.* Suddenly her nerves kicked into high gear again, and she had to put down her icing knife because her hands were shaking. She didn't want to decapitate Trevor's cake . . . or let Riley see how much he could affect her just by standing in a doorway.

"Come in," she said, backing against the counter. Then she remembered this was the exact spot they had kissed the first time and she hopped away.

She silently chewed herself out for behaving like an idiot.

Riley didn't appear to be having the same difficulties with motor functions that she was having. "Where's the birthday boy?"

"I think he and his friends are out back plotting the destruction of the universe. Or they could just be playing touch football."

Riley crossed the kitchen. "I'll see if they need any help." He twinkled a smile at Kellie before heading out the back door. "Playing football, that is."

She felt a strange mix of feelings as she watched him join Trevor and the other boys—admiration and a little disappointment. She was glad he was paying special attention to Trevor, but . . .

He wasn't paying special attention to *her*.

Then again, she hadn't invited him to this shindig. Trevor had.

Besides, the man she should be craving special attention from was Jay. Nice, kind Jay who was attentive to her family and looked like Barney Fife. . . .

She crashed over to the refrigerator and was pulling out a two-liter bottle of ginger ale as the doorbell rang.

"I'll get it!" Tina called out.

Within moments, the tiny kitchen was flooded with people. Her mother, Rick's mother and father, a parent delivering another of Trevor's friends, plus Jay and Rita, who were still sitting at the table, deep in conversation. The whole room seemed charged, expectant. And then Riley came back in with Trevor and two other boys. Kellie wove through them all, offering iced tea and Cokes and trying to finish making Trevor's favorite birthday concoction, lime sherbet-ginger ale punch. The stuff was so cloyingly sweet, it practically made Kellie feel sticky just thinking about it. But Trevor was the birthday boy, and as such he could have the disgusting beverage of his choice.

Just when the crowd in the kitchen seemed to be reaching critical mass, the doorbell rang again and Tina shrieked and ran for the door again. "Daddy!"

"Hello, Teeny!"

At the familiar voice, Kellie tensed. Then she looked over at Trevor, who was about to explode with joy.

"Dad!" He snaked through the guests in the kitchen, only getting as far as the door when Rick appeared.

Rick looked just the same. He might even have been wearing the same jeans and faded T-shirt he'd had on the day he walked out a year ago. His hair was longer, though. And the sight of his gray-blue eyes no longer made Kellie feel much of anything except a wave of the old irritation she forgot she'd lived with day in and day out for years.

It was who Rick had with him that made her jaw drop and the chatter around the kitchen fall silent. Holding Rick's hand was a blond woman tanned to such a high crisp that she was a dazzling contrast of bleached hair and dark skin. For clothing, she had donned a shiny red skirt (could it possibly be *vinyl?*) and a blinding white sleeveless sweater that fell so short of covering what it should have that the woman needed no words at all to proclaim her status as a D cup to the world.

Trevor stopped in mid-stride, his face a study in confusion. He looked as if he'd run into a concrete wall.

"Hey there, sport!" Rick exclaimed to Trevor. "Happy birthday!"

Trevor, who seconds before had been launching himself at his dad for a big bear hug, now meekly stuck out his hand for a quick shake. He glanced suspiciously at the woman.

Rick grinned. "Guess what I brought you for your birthday?"

For a moment, Trevor allowed his interest to be piqued. "A baseball glove?"

His father's brows rose. "Something better, sport. Much better! Guess."

"I don't know," Trevor said stubbornly. "I *wanted* a baseball glove."

Rick ignored his son's churlish reaction and pulled the woman on his arm another step farther into the room. "I brought you a brand . . . new . . . *mom!*"

Though Rick had boomed out his news like Johnny Olsen on *The Price Is Right,* the announcement was not met with cheers and squeals of delight. The kitchen fell so silent that for a moment Kellie thought everyone was holding their collective breath. Trevor's face went red, as did Rick's companion's.

As for Kellie, she felt a cold wave of shock hit her. *Mom?*

Even Rick looked a little taken aback now, so that he announced more soberly, "Everybody, I want you to meet Starr Sumners. My new bride."

The party was held outside in a heat so sharp that they could have baked the cake out there as well as eaten it. Guests wilted as they crossed the threshold from air-conditioned house to convection oven. But no one looked droopier than Kellie. Riley's heart went out to her, almost as much as it went out to Trevor, who after his father arrived had first looked miserable, as if the world had collapsed around him; now, as the group gathered around an outside table to watch him open his presents, he was a study in breeziness. The new mom thing? Water off a duck's back. He didn't look happy, exactly, and he pointedly avoided eye contact with his father. He was playing it cool.

Though every once in a while he shot a menacing look at Starr, a look that Riley remembered well.

He started to make his way toward Kellie, who was standing above the birthday cake in preparation for lighting the candles. She obviously saw the need to move the proceeding along quickly, before party guests started succumbing to heatstroke. He passed Jay, who was standing in a tight circle with some of Kellie's family.

His friend leaned in to him. "She's pretty, isn't she?"

Riley frowned in confusion. "Kellie?" Of course she was pretty. If Jay didn't appreciate that by now . . .

"No, Starr."

Riley was appalled. "I guess . . ." It seemed disloyal somehow for him to be mentioning the woman at all. He could only imagine how Kellie felt being broadsided by this turn of events. But of course Jay was just trying to be nice when no one else seemed to have a good word for the woman. Even Rick's own parents seemed to be confounded by their new daughter-in-law. They just sat in another clump, eyeing her silently with overly polite smiles frozen on their faces.

"Ha!" Rita barked, overhearing Riley and Jay. She scowled resentfully. "She looks like an exotic dancer on her day off. But I guess that's every man's dream."

"Not mine," Jay and Riley declared in unison.

"Oh, no, hon," Linelle said in a stage whisper to Rita. "Men might *say* they like flashy women with big breasts and scanty clothing habits, but what they really want is a woman they can marry."

"But Rick *did* marry her, Mom," Rita pointed out.

Linelle looked flummoxed as she fanned herself with a paper napkin. "Oh, that's right." She threw a sympathetic, lingering gaze at Kellie. "My poor baby—she must be feeling like last week's pot roast!"

Riley sighed and kept shuffling toward Kellie. Near the table he almost tripped over Tina, who was standing with her arms crossed.

"Well, hey," he said to her. "What's going on?"

Her mouth twisted in a disgusted line. "I just got through talking to Starr."

Riley felt a frown. "What did you talk about?"

"Nothing much!" Tina huffed. "Can you believe she's never even heard of Chopin?"

"Oh, well. I'm sure she knows about a lot of other things."

"Yeah, but *Chopin*," Tina insisted in a too-loud voice. "That's pretty basic!"

Riley took her hand. "How about some cake? We need to jockey for a good position."

She balked, bobbing stubbornly on the heels of her Mary Janes. "No, thanks. They just give out itty-bitty pieces at parties anyway."

"Well, I'm going to get some. Don't you want to see what Trevor gets for his birthday?"

She shrugged. "I can see from here."

Having no luck with Tina, Riley finally worked his way around the long outside table toward Kellie. She had a box of matches next to her and was leaning over the cake, about ready to start. She saw Riley, though, and he could see her troubles in those brown eyes.

"I'm sorry, Kellie."

She didn't even have to ask what he meant. "I wish he hadn't sprung her on us all like this. The kids are . . ."

"They're okay," he assured her. "Except I saw Trevor

giving Starr the evil eye. You might make sure that he doesn't handle any large plates of food.''

Kellie chuckled and gazed down at the chocolate frosted cake with a gleam in her eye. ''Or maybe . . .'' She shook her head, but it didn't take a rocket scientist to know what evil seed had been planted in her brain. ''No, you're right. I'll make sure she's seated safely across the table from him.''

He helped her light the candles, and moments later, after the usual shuffling into position and singing, Trevor nearly blew the icing off the cake.

Everyone clapped, although you could tell they were already too hot to show much enthusiasm. ''Phew, Kellie,'' Rick said, flapping his T-shirt dramatically. ''Isn't it kind of hot for an outdoor shindig? Why not have the party inside?''

''We don't have a table big enough inside.''

''What about the dining room table?''

''You sold it.''

Rick did have the good grace to look abashed. He leaned in toward Starr and explained in a whisper, ''Part of the whole divorce thing. Got pretty messy.''

Kellie hacked a piece of cake and handed it to her left, then turned to Trevor and suggested he start opening presents.

He looked at the pile of colorful boxes next to him with enthusiasm. He had a method, of course—the same one Riley remembered from his own childhood. The clothes boxes from his grandparents he opened first, doing his best to show excitement over button down shirts that he wouldn't be caught dead wearing except on school picture day. The one surprise was that Riley had bought him a Texas Rangers jacket, which he declared *awesome* and immediately put on despite the heat wave. The clothes over with, he moved on to his friends' presents, strange figurines the significance of which the adults were all completely clueless about. But finally he got to the big boxes Jay and his dad had brought in. He opened Jay's first.

"Cool!" he shouted, tearing the wrapping off of a Sony Playstation II.

Trevor's buddies whistled in appreciation as Kellie let out a yelp.

Jay grinned proudly. "Isn't that the one you said you wanted?"

"Exactly! Thanks, Jay. It's awesome!"

Jay elbowed Riley. "Kid's been dropping hints to me for weeks."

Kellie looked pale. Maybe she hadn't expected Jay to be so extravagant. "Trevor . . ."

Her son dove quickly for his last present. The grand finale. It was a tall rectangular tower of a box that appeared to have been hastily wrapped. There were even holes in one side of the box. He looked over at Rick. "Okay, Dad, what's the deal with the trick wrapping?"

Rick frowned. "No trick, but be real careful."

"Ha!" Trevor yanked the paper off the top of the box with a flourish, then looked down in confusion. "What . . . ?"

He pulled the wrapping down more, revealing a cage full of white mice. With growing disappointment showing on his face, he tore the paper the rest of the way down, revealing several colorful Habitrails.

Tina shrieked and ran over. "Gross, Trevor!"

"They're just mice, dummy," he scowled at his sister.

Riley looked at the mice and thought that Tina was right. They were kind of gross. They were thumb-sized things, white with beady red eyes, at least twenty of them, all scurrying around the too small cage or piled on top of each other in a corner.

"*Just* mice?" Tina said scornfully. "I read a library book called *You Were There in the Middle Ages,* and it said that it was because of mice that everybody was dying of bubonic plague!''

Kellie put a hand on Tina's shoulder. "That was a long time ago, Tina."

Her daughter looked doubtful. "Yeah, but . . ."

Rick stood. "Sure it was a long time ago—not to mention, those were different kinds of mice. Now these are just little harmless white mice, see?"

"They look like rats to me," Tina said skeptically. She pushed her glasses up her nose. "Baby rats. And you can still get bubonic plague. I looked it up."

"Well, you can't get it from these mice," Rick insisted with frustration. "They're certified plague-free, or else people wouldn't be selling them." He turned to Trevor, who was staring listlessly at his gift. "Now, these are live animals, Trevor—big responsibility. You'll need to feed them every day and clean their cage regularly."

Trevor's face was don't-give-me-a-lecture red. "Sure, Dad. Thanks."

"Thank Starr, too," Rick told him. "It was her who thought of it. See, her father owns a pet store in Tucson and we stopped over on the way here."

"Thanks," Trevor said to her automatically.

She beamed her brightest smile at everyone. "Daddy doesn't really own it. He's just the manager. Gets an employee discount, though."

"Who wants more cake?" Kellie asked in an overly bright, Florence Henderson voice. "Trevor, why don't you sit down and have some?"

Trevor dropped into his chair and watched as everyone else devoured the birthday cake. Across the table, Starr went on about the pet store business. "Now at first I thought we should maybe get Trevor a hamster, but Dad said they tend to croak at the drop of a hat. He said these little guys are a lot tougher, really, on account of they're the kind of mice people buy to feed to their snakes."

"Eeeeeeeew!" Tina exclaimed. Her cry was accompanied by shouts of varying degrees of pre-adolescent enthusiasm or disgust from Trevor's friends.

Starr blinked at them in shock. "It's not the mice's fault that they're snake dinner."

"Eeeeeeeew!"

"Anybody want more punch?" Trevor asked.

As Trevor wielded the punch ladle, Kellie and Riley locked gazes. But no one took him up on his offer, so he shrugged and stood pouring punch into his own glass.

"When you think about it, it probably builds character," Starr said.

"What?"

"Being eaten by a snake." When her statement met with confounded stares, Starr added, "I mean, being bred to be eaten. It's what they call evolution, I think. Makes you tougher."

Tina frowned. "What? I don't see how—"

The party never heard Tina's disagreement because suddenly a tidal wave of lime green punch was gushing across the table toward Starr—an unstoppable tsunami of foamy ginger ale and half-melted blobs of sherbet. Starr shrieked in alarm, but it was too late to jump out of her seat. She tried to push back her chair, but the back legs were stubbed in the grass and all she did was tip herself over at the exact moment the punch cascaded off the table. The other guests watched in horror—or, in the case of Trevor and his friends, barely veiled delight.

Rick helped Starr untangle herself from the chair. When she resurfaced, her white barely-there sweater was mottled with green. Her red skirt, shiny before, now had a sugary film all over it. The poor woman looked as if she'd been slimed.

Kellie turned on Trevor, quaking with rage.

He lifted his hands preemptively. "It was an accident!"

"Apologize!"

254 Liz Ireland

Perhaps influenced by the over-the-top anger he saw in his mother's face, he pivoted. "Starr, I am *soooooo* sorry." He almost sounded sincere, too.

Starr was too busy moaning and flicking blobs of half-melted sherbet off her face to care what Trevor was saying to her. "Yuck! What *is* this stuff?"

"Lime sherbet punch," Tina answered calmly, shaking her head. "You'll be sticky for days, I bet."

A titter came from Trevor's cheering section, and Kellie turned to Trevor again. "You'd better go to your room."

He stuck his chin out stubbornly. "You can't do that to me—it's my birthday."

"And you're grounded. Forever," she added.

"But I *can't* be grounded. I'm going to Grandma and Grandpa's tonight to visit with Dad and Starr."

Kellie looked momentarily thwarted, especially when Rick, of all people, chimed in on Trevor's behalf. Or maybe it was just his own turf he was protecting. "Yeah, Kellie, don't tell me I drove all this way across the country to see my kids and you're not even gonna let them come visit!"

Riley scratched his head in wonder. The man's wife was dripping with punch and he was criticizing Kellie for trying to discipline Trevor?

Trevor pleaded with her. "See, you *can't* keep me at home now, Mom."

Kellie's hands balled into fists at her sides. She obviously didn't appreciate being painted as the ogre. "Trevor . . ."

Rick's mother clucked her tongue. "What a waste! And I went to all the trouble to prepare Trevor's favorite meal for dinner. Chicken spaghetti!"

Trevor looked meaningfully at Kellie. "C'mon, Mom. Don't you want me to go so Tina and I can get to know *our new mom* better?"

Kellie still stood as frozen as a statue, but Riley detected a smile tweaking her lips. "Well, darn it all," she said, finally giving in, "I guess I wouldn't want to stand between your bonding as a family." She turned to her ex-husband with a graceful sigh of acceptance. "Okay, Rick. He's all yours till Sunday." She bestowed an extra-gracious smile on Rick's new wife. "Starr, I hope you like chicken spaghetti, too."

Chapter Fifteen

The blessed moment finally came when Kellie could push the last person out the door. That person happened to be Tina, who was not thrilled at the prospect of spending the night at her grandparents' house with a new stepmother.

"Can't I visit some other time?" Tina said in a voice close to a whine.

Kellie shook her head. "Your father's not in town for long. You don't want to be rude, do you?"

"No, I guess not," she responded glumly, an unwilling slave to good manners. "I just don't see anything good about Dad marrying this woman, Mom."

Kellie pulled a braid over one shoulder. "Well . . . he's obviously happy. That's good, isn't it?"

"I guess so." She clutched her pink suitcase in the doorway and smiled as an idea came to her. "And I guess I could pretend I'm Cinderella, now that I've got a real stepmother."

"Right. And you've got the white mice."

Tina's reaction to this observation was incredulity mixed with disappointment. "The mice were just in the *movie,* Mom. That was a cartoon. If you'd read the *real* fairy tale, you would know it was the birds who helped Cinderella.''

"Oh, well . . ." She never knew what to say when Tina caught her up short this way. In lieu of risking a further display of her literary shortcomings, she bent down and kissed her daughter on the head. "Have a good time, Tina. Don't keep everyone awake by staying up too late reading.''

"Oh, Mom!'' Tina exclaimed in disgust, banging out of the house.

Kellie waved as Tina got into her grandparents' waiting sedan next to a scowling Trevor. Then Kellie ducked back inside and closed the door. Actually she nearly collapsed against it in relief. Alone at last!

Well, alone if you didn't count twenty-two white mice.

She dedicated a moment to simply savoring her solitude.

And found herself not enjoying it at all.

The trouble was, now that she was alone, she felt . . . lonesome. The minute she was finally rid of all the people she couldn't wait to give the heave-ho out the front door, she suddenly found herself wanting to spill her guts to someone. But whom did she know who would sympathize with how diminished she'd felt seeing Rick with his beautiful new wife? It was too ridiculous. It wasn't as if she coveted her ex-husband. She didn't love Rick anymore; heck, it had been a long time since she even liked him. So why hadn't she been able to be more adult about the whole thing? More gracious? Instead, she'd packed Trevor off to his grandmother's house, knowing full well it was the divorcée's equivalent of tossing a Molotov cocktail through her in-laws' window.

The strain of the whole day had obviously taken its toll. The party. Rita and all her never ending problems. Her son's wheedling Jay into buying him the verboten

Playstation. Having to look breezy and happy in front of her mother and her in-laws. And Riley's being there— and then leaving at the earliest possible moment as if he couldn't wait to get away. Who could blame him? She would love to have been the first guest out the door herself. It was all too much.

She was so distraught, she did what she had rarely done in her life: she sought solace in the bottle. Ostensibly she headed into the kitchen to clean up, but within seconds she was eyeing the shelf above the refrigerator where Rick's old bottle of Jack Daniels was stowed. She pushed aside the stray dishes littering the counter to clamber up and retrieve it. Strange that she'd thought it would be better to hide the liquor on a shelf that required the agility of an adolescent to reach. She was just teetering onto her feet to reach over to get the bottle when the doorbell blared from its speaker two feet from her ear, nearly scaring her out of her wits. She scrambled down from the counter and, in jumping to the floor, managed to slip on the linoleum. She tried to brace herself against the counter to break her fall, but ended up half standing and half leaning. Her ankle stung.

"Shit!" she hissed, wincing in pain.

The doorbell rang again. She considered not answering it, but of course the bell ringer probably was Tina, who was forever leaving the house forgetting something. Her panicked pleas had made even hard-hearted school-bus drivers turn their buses around.

Kellie limped through the hallway and opened the door, prepared to hop around finding the missing book or piece of music, but instead of looking down at her daughter, she found herself looking up at Riley. The sight of him leaning his elbow rakishly against the door made her heart beat in bongo-drum rhythms.

His lips twitched into a boyish smile. "Forgot my hat."

When she locked gazes with him, she remembered

another tension that had been nagging her all day. It returned full tilt. "Come in." She frowned, trying to remember him wearing a hat. "What kind of hat?"

"Baseball hat."

He bustled right past her, breezy and efficient. "Something the matter with your foot?" he asked casually as he saw her critching along behind him.

She didn't answer. What was he doing? Didn't he know what a crappy day she'd had? Didn't he even want to say something comradely like "Aren't you glad it's over?" She'd never felt so strongly that she needed a friend. Anyone would do. Even somebody she had the hots for. "You sure were in a hurry to leave this afternoon."

"You looked like you could use some solitude. I thought maybe if I left, others would follow."

"They did, eventually."

"Let's see . . ." He sped through the living room, distractedly looked through the kitchen, then proceeded out the back door. When he came back in seconds later, bringing with him a burst of hot humid air, he shrugged. "I don't know . . ." He caught sight of the Jack Daniels on the counter and looked at her curiously. "What were you going to do with that?"

"Chug it."

He clucked his tongue in gentle reprimand. Kellie was about to tell him she wouldn't stand for a lecture on the evils of drink right at this particular moment when he turned and opened the fridge. "You can do better than that," he said.

She crossed her arms. "I need something stronger than milk, which is about all you'll find in there."

"No, not milk," he muttered, ducking to inspect the contents of the fridge. Compartments banged open. "Eureka!" He reappeared from the depths of the frigid land of leftovers bearing three lemons. Then he grabbed the bag of ice out of the freezer. "Everything we need for whiskey sours."

She watched him in awe and gratitude as he suddenly went into bartender mode, efficiently squeezing lemons and chipping away at the ice with a pick. The transition was so smooth that it took a moment for her to remember what had been nagging at her since his abrupt entrance.

"Riley, you weren't wearing a hat," Kellie told him.

He stopped chipping and looked at her, surprised. "What?"

"You weren't wearing a hat," she repeated. "I've never seen you in a hat."

He picked up a hunk of ice, wrapped it in a tea towel and handed it to her. "Here, put this on your ankle," he said. "You're right. I made the hat up as an excuse to come over. I knew if I called, you'd just tell me that you were fine. I wanted to see how you were holding up."

And how had he found her? Limping around with a whiskey bottle. God, she wanted to hug the man. She didn't dare, though. She already felt quivery.

"Crappy day?" he asked.

She nodded mutely, fearing she was about to have a Rita-style crack-up, which would be too embarrassing. She bravely, stoically, remained mum on the subject of her ex-husband and his new wife.

Her brave stoicism lasted through all of two whiskey sours. Then the dam burst. Before you could say pathetic drunk divorcée, she was shamelessly dumping her problems in his lap.

"I mean, can you believe Rick?" she said with a voice decidedly more slurry than it had been before. "He doesn't even tell his own parents he's married before he blindsides us all with his bride! Did he think the kids were going to do handsprings over this woman?"

"Quite a bombshell," Riley said.

"Bombshell is just the word!" Kellie bristled. "No

wonder he was in such a hurry to get away from me when there were nubile leggy blonds out there waiting for him. I just don't get it! I mean, granted, *I* was married to the guy for eleven years, but how could Rick—who you might have noticed is *not* Mel Gibson by any stretch of the imagination—how can he find gorgeous young things to fall in love with him?''

Riley nodded sympathetically. "Ernest Borgnine has been married five times."

"Well, Rick will probably match him when all is said and done, because I certainly don't see how his union with Starr the sort-of waitress is going to last. Do you know she was complaining to me about him? Told me he had a gambling problem! Said he'd forgotten their one-week anniversary and was already flirting with the receptionist who worked for his construction company. What was I supposed to do, break into a chorus of 'Ah, Yes, I Remember It Well'?

"Meanwhile, he couldn't even remember to buy his son a baseball glove!" Kellie said angrily. "I mean, what could have been simpler? Did he not remember? Did he just not care? It was such a great gift! *I* would have bought it for him, but Trevor wanted his father to get it. I think he wanted to know that Rick cared that much."

"Maybe the mouse discount was just too good to pass up," Riley said.

Kellie clucked in disgust. She was beginning to feel a little woozy. "And then Trevor makes everything more difficult—dumping punch all over his new stepmother. I've *got* to cure him of that habit before he's twenty. But part of me was gleeful that he'd done it, too, so in a way I'm almost as bad as he is."

"You handled the situation as well as you could," Riley told her. "You even gave in when Rick wanted you to."

She moaned and sucked down the last bit of moisture

from the bottom of her glass. "Don't kid yourself! I gave in because I knew Trevor would go over there and give them hell. That kid may be the cross I have to bear, but he's also my secret weapon."

Riley laughed. "You've really been through the mill today."

"What really makes me mad is that after all of this, *I* feel like a loser."

He looked alarmed. "You? Why?"

"Because Rick's managed to get on with his life, and I haven't."

"But—"

She dismissed his words before they were even out of his mouth. "Oh, I know, I've got my business. That's what everyone says. What never occurs to them when they're trying to comfort me with that thought is that it's not comforting at all. It's pressure. I sit up nights now worrying about not making ends meet and losing everything and throwing Alejandro and Lana out of work, for heaven's sake." She shrugged, feeling as if she were steadily losing it. But with her tongue loosened, and with the luxury of looking into Riley's eyes, which seemed to ooze sympathy, how could she stop?

"The trouble is, the business isn't the half of it. It's looking at Rick and seeing that he's the type of person who can end one relationship and just pick up and start on another one the next day. While I just seem to float along, reacting." She laughed bitterly. "Come to think of it, maybe I'm the one who's vague."

"Vague?" Riley asked, confused.

She shook her head. "Never mind. The thing is, Rick actually looked pretty good today. You know, I think he's actually happier than I am. He's probably an A on the mental-health radar, while most days I feel like a struggling D. Or worse, an incomplete." She took in a ragged breath and admitted, "But I'm beginning to think

I've just been kidding myself. I *would* like to have someone."

"You do."

Her kids again. "Tina and Trevor are going to grow up and—"

"I wasn't talking about Tina and Trevor. I was talking about me."

She almost laughed. She almost tossed the old dishrag sitting in the sink at him. Then she looked into his eyes. Her heart did an uneasy skitter in her chest, and suddenly her mouth was so dry she couldn't swallow. There was nothing to say anyway. *Him?*

He stepped forward and pulled her easily into his arms. Easily, because she was too stunned, too limp with wanting, to put up much resistance. Her mind was fuzzed with alcohol and desire. "We've both been through the worst of it, Kellie."

She nodded, still mesmerized by those searing blue eyes. Some part of her brain did try to hang on to reason. "Yes, but . . ."

"Maybe we need each other right now."

She couldn't deny that—not when her pulse was galloping like a herd of buffalo. Her need seemed to shriek at her from every corpuscle in her body. Need made her gaze fasten on his lips, then tiptoe closer, just for a taste.

Oh, God, he was right. The moment their lips touched, she felt as if she was being transported away from all her problems. Her head felt light; her limbs seemed to have a life of their own. Pure heat pounded through her veins, and right away one thing was clear. She wasn't going to be bothering with the dishes tonight.

He pulled her closer to him, and at the feel of his muscled chest pressed against her, every shred of reason seemed to evaporate. Impulse won. Riley won. His lips pressed surely against hers, and his tongue plundered her mouth expertly until she felt dizzy. Meanwhile his hands explored as much of her as their clothes, and their closeness, would allow. She'd never been kissed so thoroughly, so extravagantly. She felt like a delicacy being tenderly devoured.

Once she realized that she was being swept away, that animal urges were winning out over tiresome prudence, it was glorious. She pressed against him, needing him to relieve the growing ache inside her. In those breathless, fiery moments, it seemed she wanted him more than she had ever wanted anything in her life.

They made their way to the bedroom in a swirl of arms and legs struggling to embrace, walk, and disrobe all at once. Riley stopped long enough to pull her shirt over her head, and while her arms were still raised, he bent down and kissed her breast over her bra. She sucked in her breath, shocked at the intimacy of it, the startling heat he could build in her so quickly. Of course the bra had to go next, and he dispatched the job with ease. Then they had to stop again for him to blaze a trail from the valley between her breasts to her navel. And then Kellie decided it was time for Riley's shirt to go.

They lumbered along this way, a few steps and articles of clothing at a time, until they reached the bedroom. Occasionally one of them would stumble, and maybe they would chuckle until they looked into each other's eyes again and felt desire burning away their laughter. It was exhausting, exhilarating. They left a trail of discarded clothing behind them, and by the time they collapsed against the bed together, there was nothing separating them but Riley's socks.

As he removed those, Kellie grasped one last time for reason. She sat up, clawing through a fog of whiskey and lust, and was shocked by her own nakedness. "This is crazy," she whispered. "This—"

Riley turned to her, eyes dark with desire for her. The way he looked at her—it was ravenous. It was irresistible.

It made her mouth dry and her face feel as if she were standing in front of a furnace. Her gaze darted down, and she got her first look at all of him. His skin was smooth, with an almost caramel tan. A light dusting of hair feathered his chest, accentuating his well-defined muscles and rippled stomach. He was glorious.

Whatever she'd intended to say disappeared in her sharp intake of breath as he reached out and touched the hollow at the base of her neck. "You're gorgeous, Kellie. So beautiful."

She gulped. Gorgeous? Her? He was Adonis.

His fingertips skimmed down to her breast, which tightened into a hard bud at his touch. It was crazy. Crazy the way his rough skin against hers could make her forget just about every good reason she had for not doing this. His past, her past. Yet how could she think of the past when right this moment he was doing such incredible things to her?

She ran her fingers through his hair, which felt deliciously soft and yet bristly short beneath her fingertips. She wanted him with a ferocity that shocked her.

But you're not an impulsive person, a voice inside her head lectured.

That voice was shouted down when Riley's tongue brushed her collarbone. He bent down and pressed his mouth against the sensitive flesh he'd been touching moments before. Kellie sucked her breath between her teeth and let out a shivery moan.

She didn't want to think about tomorrow or any point in the future beyond the next body part she wanted him to explore. And as if he were a mind reader, he gravitated exactly where she wanted him to. She leaned back, enjoying being completely, thoroughly made love to for the first time in her life. Unlike their initial mauling in the kitchen and their awkward striptease through the hallway would have led her to expect, Riley set an almost agonizingly slow pace, seeming intent on savoring and consuming every square inch of her.

He left her breasts and kissed his way down her stomach, which turned taut and quivery with tension under his endless ministrations. How could a man have such patience? He seemed to have the stamina of a Kenyan distance runner. Kellie rubbed his shoulders, massaging them as his tongue dipped lower, then skirted the core of her desire to tease her thighs.

She moaned. Not that she was complaining. But she was itching for something to do. "Riley . . ." His name came out as something between a pant and a gasp.

He lifted back up and nuzzled her ear, her cheek, her lips. "Let's take our time, Kellie. This one night . . ."

His words disappeared on a sharp intake of breath as she began to do some exploring of her own. Her hands closed over the obvious evidence of his desire.

He shut his eyes. "Kellie."

The needful rasp in his voice thrilled her as much as his touch had. She moved her hand against the hard length of his erection, delighting in the velvety feel of him. And the way he reacted to her. She bent down and kissed his mouth. He pulled her toward him so that the entire lengths of their bodies touched. Lying against him, flesh to flesh, was like a drug to her.

"Riley," she murmured, pulling far enough away so that she could see into his eyes. His searing gaze inflamed her even more. "Let's not."

"Not what?" His gaze widened as if he dreaded what she might say.

She smiled slowly. "Take our time."

He released a breath in relief. "And next time?" he said, turning over so that he covered her with his body.

The weight of him against her stoked the heat building inside her. She reached up and rubbed her hands over his arms, up his shoulders, to his nape. Then she rocked her hips up against him invitingly. "Next time," she promised in a whisper, "we'll take it as slow as Christmas."

First he smelled coffee brewing, which lured him halfway to waking. Even so, he stretched and turned over before fully embracing the idea. Then, ever so slowly, he allowed one eye to wink open. The world was still half dark, and he looked at the unfamiliar room around him in momentary confusion before sinking back against the pillows and letting the memories of last night flood through him.

God, he had missed sex. It was pointless trying to deny it now, even to himself. He'd needed last night for a long time, and now he felt like a dam with the floodgates opened. The release was immediate, forceful, unstoppable. An overwhelming affection for Kellie knocked him for a loop. She was a more giving, more exuberant lover than he ever could have imagined. For the first time in ages, years, he felt connected to someone. He felt as if he might start waking up looking forward instead of backward.

The sound of a cabinet door shutting reached him through the closed bedroom door. What was she doing out there? More important, why wasn't she still in bed, snuggling with him?

He got up to investigate. Clothes led a Hansel-and-Gretel trail back to the kitchen, and he picked up his jeans along the way, hop-stepping into them as he walked. By the time he reached the doorway to the kitchen, he had them on. Kellie, armed with a bottle of Windex, was rocketing around her kitchen in a green terrycloth bathrobe. When she caught sight of him, her eyes flew open and her cheeks bloomed with red.

"Oh! Are you up?"

As postcoital greetings went, it was a little on the impersonal side. He nodded cautiously.

"There's coffee."

He looked at the clock on the microwave. "Kellie, do you realize it's five-fifteen in the morning?"

She nodded as she spritzed the counter with cleaner. "Of course."

"It's still early," he drawled, stepping toward her with very definite intentions of unbelting that robe and cupping her beautiful breasts in his hands. But the moment he moved, she seemed to hop across the kitchen like a waterbug skittering across the water. All he got was a handful of air. "Is it really necessary to clean right now?"

"I should have done it last night."

He scratched his head. When had the woman he'd made love to all night turned into Joan Crawford?

He decided on a different tactic. Stealth. He strolled across the room as if making for the coffee pot, then turned at the last minute and pulled Kellie into his arms, spray bottle and all. But it didn't feel right. In fact, after last night, the way their bodies had fit together perfectly, this morning they clunked against each other like two objects thrown together willy-nilly.

He looked into her eyes and detected a flare of something, and then her jaw stiffened and he saw only resistance. He let her go, reluctantly.

For a moment, he watched her scrub in silence; then he couldn't stand it anymore. "Kellie, is something wrong?" he said half jokingly. There was something so wrong here, he wanted to scream.

"Tina and Trevor will be home tomorrow, and I don't want them to think—well, I don't want them to have to deal with any more personal turmoil."

He smiled. Okay, he could handle this. She had post-pleasure stress. The jitters. He could understand that. Last night had been unexpected. "It's been a long time for me, too, Kellie."

His words only seemed to make her feel worse. "Riley . . ."

"No, I want to make sure you know this," he insisted, crossing his arms to keep from reaching out to her, since that only seemed to make her more tense. "I didn't think I could want anyone again."

She stood stock still. "And now you do . . . what now?"

The question astounded him. "Now we can be together."

"Oh, so it's that simple."

He lifted his arms away from his side, then let them drop. "Why not?"

"Because I don't know if you've noticed, but you're not a simple person." She let out a tired, ragged sigh. "First you tell me that fate brought us together, but that we should fight it. Then weeks ago you wanted me to go out with Jay. Then you seemed upset that I was going out with Jay. But at the same time, you told me you were still grieving, and I believed you. You made a very convincing case for staying just friends."

He shook his head regretfully. "I know that I haven't exactly been consistent."

Her face was pure anguish. "Riley, I'm no psychologist, but I think you're still working through things."

"I'll admit it's a little confusing," he said, "but relationships *are* confusing. Love is confusing."

"Exactly," she said, and he felt he'd just handed her the hanging rope. "But frankly, confusion isn't what I need right now. It's not what my children need, either, and I have to take them into consideration."

"Do you think they wouldn't like me being around more?"

"Are you kidding? They'd probably love it! Tina would think that her prince had come, and Trevor might even stop terrorizing you after a while. After what happened yesterday with Rick, they're probably spoiling to find a new father figure. But I don't want them to lose another father, Riley. I don't want them to depend on you if you're going to decide next week or next month or next year that you're not ready for a real commitment.''

"How do you know I won't be?"

"I don't." She let out a ragged sigh. "That's where things get difficult, isn't it? Because it would be so easy to say to hell with that, I love you and damn the consequences. I did that once before. But I'm thirty-two now, not eighteen. I can't make a mistake like that. I don't want to wake up in ten years and realize I've been letting myself get jerked around because once I impulsively decided I was in love. I've already been down that road.''

He was getting a little steamed. "Wait. You think *I'm* going to jerk you around like Rick?"

"No, maybe not, but who knows? I just want to face this thing and decide now whether it's going to work or not. And if it's not, let's be adults and admit it before either of us gets hurt.''

He stared at her in disbelief. She didn't seem to realize that she was asking for the impossible. "Kellie, that's not a very organic approach to a relationship.''

"I know.''

"What you want is for us to be able to see into the future. We can't do that.''

One of her eyebrows slid up. "Can't you?"

He shook his head. "It doesn't work that way. I don't have that kind of power. Shoot, you never thought I had *any* kind of power. And think about it. Even if I did say, yes, we'll be happy forever and ever, wouldn't it still be a gamble?''

"Maybe.'' She tilted her head. "I guess that's part of the problem. I don't want to gamble. Last night you said we both needed each other *right now*. Did that mean we wouldn't need each other later? Do you see me as just a step toward recovery?"

Her words felt like a slap in the face. The whole conversation did.

He should have known better than to get out of bed at five in the morning. No good ever came of it. "Kellie, I'm not a dishonest person. I'm not trying to lead you on. I wouldn't do that."

"But at the same time, you're not willing to make a commitment, either. Are you?"

He faltered. "Isn't it a little early for that question?"

She crossed her arms. "After last night, I feel like it's a little too late. I was wrong to make love to you in the state I was in."

"You can't blame two whiskey sours for something that's been building between us for a month."

Her mouth flattened into a thin line. "I should have listened to my brain. All I could think about this morning was how hard I worked all year to build something stable for myself and Trevor and Tina. I can't toss that away."

He could feel the pulse pounding in his temples. He wasn't sure which was the stronger emotion inside him: shock or anger. "But you can toss me away."

"I'm not an on-again, off-again kind of person," she said. "I lived with inconsistency and worry for years, and I don't want that again."

"I'm not Rick."

"I know you're not. But the situation feels just as insecure."

"For God's sake, you're so pragmatic that you'd throw away everything we began last night because you don't trust a flimsy little emotion like love? But it's not so flimsy, Kellie. It can pull at you even when you try to turn it off and forget about it. I know that better than anyone."

She looked white, but her dark gaze didn't leave his face. "I know you do."

The unspoken meaning was clear: she thought he was still rebounding from grief. She didn't trust him. She couldn't. What would he be able to say that would convince her that he was sincere, that he wouldn't flake out on her?

For that matter, how did he know that he wouldn't? Last night he'd been operating on impulse. On feeling. On desire. Maybe those weren't the most stable things to start a relationship with. But what else was there?

For Pete's sake, she now had him as confused as she was.

He sighed again. "We're not getting anywhere with this discussion, Kellie. It's crazy. I don't know what I can say to you."

A impenetrable curtain descended over her expression. It was as if she'd given him a cue and he'd completely missed it. "I'm sorry, Riley."

"Me, too." Frustrated, he turned on his heel and headed back to the bedroom, snatching up clothes as he went. He whipped on his shirt and hopped into his socks and shoes. By the time he reached the bedroom, he realized that there was nothing to do but turn around and leave again. Strangely, he felt used. Kellie had just been using him last night to forget her problems.

Well, that was okay, he decided. To hell with it. He'd enjoyed it, too.

He stopped at the kitchen. Kellie hadn't moved. Hair clouded messily around her shoulders, he saw now. Her face was a little puffy, her lips pale. In the dull glare of the overhead kitchen light, she was bleached out. The brightest thing about her was that electric blue cleaning fluid in her hand. But *damn it,* he still felt drawn to her.

"I'm leaving," he said. "I think what you're trying to tell me is that we moved too fast."

She tilted her head and fixed him with that inscrutable gaze, giving him that feeling that he'd just screwed up his lines again.

He sighed. No sense arguing now. "Good-bye, Kellie."

He walked out, unsure whether he would be back in two hours or two weeks. Or ever.

Chapter Sixteen

With the exception of an emotional glitch or two, Kellie felt satisfied about her decision to put the brakes on whatever was happening between her and Riley. The biggest exception was that terrible moment when he'd said good-bye so stonily and then walked out. She'd felt as if her heart were shattering in a million pieces. And occasionally—well, every other minute or so—she would remember making love and feel like diving for the phone to apologize, to say to heck with reason, let's just have a wild fling and forget about tomorrow.

Yet once those waves of illogic passed and she thought rationally about what they had said to each other, she was surprised at how levelheaded she had managed to be. Especially in the wake of one of the most devastatingly passionate nights of her life. A less emotionally evolved woman—one who hadn't had an eleven-year tutorial in the disastrous mistakes passion can lead to—might have buckled. In fact, Riley might have completely and irreversibly seduced that poor creature.

That creature probably wouldn't have gotten out of bed for at least two solid days . . . until, say, fifteen minutes before the appointed time her children were supposed to walk through the door. And to be brutally honest, Kellie had considered it. Lying awake spooning with that gorgeous body in the wee small hours of the morning . . . It was so tempting to confuse one night with forever. To believe that rush of happiness and satisfaction could go on and on and on. She hadn't felt anything like it since . . .

Well, since the last time she'd been in love.

But that had been when she was a teenager. She was a different person now. A smarter person. She knew better than to trust the most fickle emotion on earth. So she'd had her dreamy night of love—surely all divorcées were allowed one or two of those—and now she could get on with her real life. She could forge ahead through the weekend, taking advantage of her children's absence by going over her half-year plan for Copycat, which really meant she doodled on a yellow legal pad for three hours and hummed Supremes songs. She could rent a Mel Gibson movie Saturday night and be only slightly distracted by how mortifying it would be if Riley could read *her* thoughts. And then she could don her highest-necked nightgown and toss and turn all night in a bed that still faintly smelled of his cologne.

More important, she could spend an entire Sunday morning glaring at the phone, willing it to ring.

She was flabbergasted. Was he really not going to call her?

She wasn't a wishy-washy woman who said one thing and meant another. But she'd never dreamed she would have been so persuasive. Riley had never listened to her before. And considering the situation from his end, they *had* made love Friday night. Didn't that at least rate a follow-up call these days? Riley was the destiny man. If he really believed they were meant to be, wouldn't he be a little more persistent?

Of course, maybe in retrospect, after their roll in the

hay, he'd decided that they weren't such a match made
in heaven. Doubts clouded her previously clear thoughts.
After all, what did she know? Rick had been the kind of
lover who timed sex around the TV schedule. Passion
for him was something you slipped in after the ten o'clock
news weather report and finished up with before Letter-
man did his top-ten list. That kind of dispatch didn't
exactly allow her to hone a sexual prowess that could
bring any man to his knees.

By eleven o'clock Sunday morning, she was laid out
on her back on the living room floor with the phone on
her stomach. No one could accuse her of waiting by the
phone. She was actually under it.

But *damn it,* her telephone was on Quaaludes. It would
not ring. Not only did she not hear from Riley, she didn't
even get the usual panicked call from Tina telling her
that she had a stomachache and needed to come home.
What was more, her mother knew she was alone at home
today. Didn't she even rate an invite for brunch and a
round of Parcheesi anymore?

And where was Rita? You'd think that after yesterday's
debacle she'd be dying to chew the fat. She would see
Rick's return with a new wife as a romantic humiliation
equal to Wendell's lack of get-up-and-go and thus would
savor the opportunity to remind Kellie that her own love
life was a shambles. Even more of a shambles than Rita
could even guess at.

Why had Riley found it so easy to walk out? A part
of her was so disappointed in him. It was a girlish fantasy,
she knew, but why couldn't Riley have swooped her into
his arms and declared his sure and fast love for her?
She'd waited for him to say to hell with all her doubts,
he was certain their love would stand the test of time.
Why couldn't he have told her that he'd put the past
firmly behind him and was ready to march into a bright
and happy future with her?

Because it was absurd, that was why. As absurd as a grown woman lying under her phone wishing for scenarios that only happened in black-and-white Hollywood movies.

She was so concentrated on wanting her phone to ring that when it actually rang, it nearly scared her out of her wits. She nervously snatched up the receiver before the first ring had even finished trilling.

"Oh, good, I was hoping I'd find you in."

"Jay," she said a little breathlessly.

"The one and only," he echoed back, laughing. Then he paused. "Were you expecting somebody else?"

"No," she said quickly. "Just at loose ends. It seemed strange that I hadn't heard from my mom, because she'll sometimes invite me over for brunch or something. . . ."

"Well, heck, if it's brunch you want, then I'm your lucky penny! Where do you want to go? Your wish is my command."

Her first instinct was to balk, but why? "That would be great."

"Terrific! How soon can you be ready?"

"How soon can you be here?

"In two seconds."

"No, really."

"No, really. I'm right outside your house."

She frowned, then got up and walked to the window. When she peeked out of the blind, the huge blue Cadillac was idling in front of her house and Jay had his cell phone to his ear. He spotted her and waved.

She laughed and waved back. "Give me a second. I'll be right out."

She ran to her bedroom and gave herself a thirty-second makeover. Then she shoved her feet into a pair of sandals, snatched up her purse, and headed out the door.

"So where do you want to go?" Jay asked her when she appeared faster than he'd obviously expected.

"I know just the place," she said.

Joe's Café did its best business on Sunday morning. The booths were overflowing with humanity. Little kids fidgety in church clothes lolled against the vinyl with their syrup-sticky hands. Bleary-eyed parents bowed over coffee cups. A long line of men who seemed to be nursing hangovers bellied up to the counter seats.

Jay looked uncomfortable with it all. "You really want to be here? I could take you over to the Mansion on Turtle Creek . . ."

"This is better," she declared seconds before a toddler at a table across the aisle from them dipped her fist into her orange juice glass and chucked a chip of ice at Jay. He flinched. The little girl banged her fist with delight and directed a gummy laugh at them.

A waitress came by, and Kellie ordered a waffle; Jay asked for a glass of grapefruit juice. "That's all you want?" Kellie asked him.

He tucked their jam-smudged menus back behind the napkin dispenser. "I'm not hungry. I took a vitamin pill this morning."

Though she tried not to, Kellie kept a close eye on the door. Was it beyond the realm of probability that she might happen to bump into Riley here? After all, their paths used to collide all the time. And he made it sound as if he practically lived at Joe's. Maybe if she could just see him again, she would be surer of her decision. . . .

Or maybe he would have changed his mind.

The cherub at the next table made another direct hit. "I just love kids," Jay declared with more determination than assurance as he wiped orange pulp off his cheek. To Kellie's skeptically raised brow, he responded, "I really do. I've had no end of people tell me what a great father I'd make."

She imagined he would, too, but she felt too distracted to pursue the topic. "What was Riley like as a father?"

Jay's eyes widened. "Oh, the best!" He laughed. "I couldn't believe it—my old buddy from the fraternity house waking up at all hours to help with feedings. Changing diapers. He told me he did, at any rate, and seeing him with Abbie, you couldn't help but believe him. He loved his little girl more than anything in the world. They were together so much. Joanne told me she kept asking him if he wanted to have another baby—I guess she was thinking that he might want a son—but as far as Riley was concerned, Abbie was it."

When she'd asked the question, she'd been expecting to have her belief confirmed that Riley would be a good father figure. Instead, Jay's words were a jolting reminder of Riley's loss.

She drooped a little against the booth's back. "It's just so awful. Such a waste. It would be so hard to start again. . . ."

Jay shook his head. "Riley wouldn't even try. He's told me as much himself. I tried to help him, but he wasn't interested. Lightning doesn't strike twice, he said."

He'd told her something similar once, too. It made sense to her. Most days she didn't even believe in it striking once. This was a good reality check for her. She wouldn't be waiting by the phone anymore.

Jay frowned in thought for a moment before his concerned gaze honed in on her. "Are you all right, Kellie?"

"Hm?"

"You seem sort of green."

She shook her head. "I'm fine."

"That's good, because I was hoping that if you weren't doing anything this afternoon we could catch a movie. Maybe we could swing by and pick up Rita and she could go with us."

"It's usually impossible to blast Rita out of her house

on weekends. She reserves her free time for waiting by the phone for Wendell to call.''

"That's terrible!'' Jay exclaimed. "A self-respecting woman shouldn't waste her life that way.''

Kellie ducked her head, remembering suddenly that she'd spent the morning examining her phone for signs of life. "No, she shouldn't.''

"Well, then how about just you and me hitting the town? It's a beautiful day.''

She looked into his green eyes, so wide and expectant, and felt herself wanting to laugh. Which, after a day of moping, was definitely a step in the right direction. She brightened. She didn't need to wait around her house, pining. There were other fish in the sea. In fact, Jay was a very good companion himself. She was lucky to have him volunteering to squire her around.

"I'd love to,'' she said.

"What's the matter with Nathaniel?'' Jay asked Riley. Riley looked up at him in surprise.

"What do you mean?''

"He's got a bruised lip.''

Riley frowned as he tossed a shirt into his suitcase. He was barely paying attention to what he was packing. "He *said* he walked into a door.''

The past week had been a blur to him. He just kept thinking about Kellie, thinking about calling Kellie. But how dumb could he be? She'd made her feelings pretty clear. She wanted forever or nothing.

How could he promise forever?

That was why it was good he'd arranged for this business trip. All he was doing here was thinking about Kellie. Pining after Kellie. Going slowly but surely insane.

Jay made a face as he sank down into a chair in the corner of the bedroom. He was fooling around with a nine iron he'd pulled out of Riley's golf bag. "Do you think there's some trouble with Fayard?"

"There's *always* trouble with Fayard," Riley said.

"Someday we might need to stage an intervention on Nathaniel's behalf," Jay suggested. "He deserves better than that lunatic. My nonfiction club's reading a book now that would do him a world of good."

"Are you still going to those book clubs?" Riley asked him. "I thought you would have given those up after Lurlene."

"Luanne," Jay corrected. "That's ancient history. But just because Luanne didn't work out doesn't mean that I shouldn't still be trying to improve my mind."

"What's this book you think Nathaniel should read?"

"It's called *The Decisions Women Don't Make*, and Riley, it's a revelation."

Riley stared at him, amazed. "My God, you're turning into Oprah."

"It's a good book," Jay said defensively. "Sure it's targeted to women, but you can use your imagination. It's all about people not making choices—people who just want their courses charted for them, when really to be successful in this life you have to make your own decisions and follow through."

"Uh-huh." Riley was staring at his sock drawer. *He* couldn't even decide how many pairs of socks to take on a business trip. He finally pulled out the entire drawer and emptied it into his suitcase.

"Whoa! How long are you going to be gone?"

Riley shrugged. "There's a merger in Korea I need to keep my eye on. One of the companies involved is one of the Lombard Group's most significant international holdings." He sighed. "Then at some point I have to fly to New York because one of our fund managers is quitting." Decisions had to be made, and he was feeling a little off his game. He should have gone to New York last week, but he hadn't been able to bring himself to leave Dallas.

Now, maybe, it was best if he left for a while. He certainly wasn't getting anything done here.

"Well good grief, you're going to miss the big fun," Jay said.

"What fun?"

"I'm taking Kellie and her kids to Six Flags."

At the mention of Kellie, Riley felt as though he'd been slugged. "You're taking Kellie?"

"Sure. Why not?"

Right. Why not? Riley felt small for the sudden pang of jealousy he felt. He couldn't dictate whom Kellie could see. But he couldn't help feeling a little stung. "Have you talked to her much lately?"

"Yeah, I took her to the movies last weekend."

"How was she?"

Jay shrugged. "Fine, I guess. We had a lot of laughs together."

Laughs? His own mood had been positively funereal last weekend. "She didn't seem to be . . . preoccupied?"

Jay's eyes narrowed. "Oh, maybe a little. I think her husband's sudden marriage kind of freaked her out. Could you believe that clown?"

Riley shook his head. "She *said* that was what was bothering her?"

"She talked about it some," Jay said, then frowned. "But I don't think I'd say she was upset, really. She just seemed like the same old Kellie to me."

Same old Kellie. And he was a mess.

Unbelievable.

Jay laughed. "Are you feelin' okay, bud? You look sort of unfocused. Maybe *you* should read my book on course charting."

Riley frowned. "No, I'm okay. I just need to finish this packing."

"Well, I'll get out of your hair, then. I just wanted to pop by before your trip."

"Glad you did." Riley said as he showed him out. They parted amicably, talking about having a beer when Riley got back.

So Jay was taking Kellie and her kids on a family outing. Well, that was fine. It was just the kind of stuff friends did together sometimes. It wasn't as if he had anything to worry about. It wasn't as if Jay and Kellie . . .

Well, Jay never had any luck with women.

"You know, I think I'm actually enjoying myself," Jay said.

Kellie laughed. "Me, too."

They were standing in the stingy shade of a live oak at Six Flags waiting for the log ride to bring back Trevor and Tina, who would be soaked and probably squabbling. The amusement park had been Jay's idea, and though Kellie had had her doubts—it was a hot, sticky Sunday and the place was jam-packed with teeming humanity— the man would not be dissuaded. And she was glad. This outing seemed to be just what Trevor needed to pull him out of the doldrums he'd been in since his birthday party.

Rick's remarriage had knocked a little of the stuffing out of Trevor. Enough that she hadn't had the heart to make him return Jay's Playstation. The surprising thing was that Trevor didn't abuse the twice-a-day-for-a-half-hour limit she'd set for him to play with it. He hadn't disobeyed her once since his birthday, in fact. He hadn't even talked back or picked a fight with Tina or dumped a single drink on Jay.

She was worried.

And she was all the more thankful to Jay for his taking a special interest in her kids now.

"I didn't like these places when I was a kid," Jay told

her, munching a piece of Tina's blue cotton candy, "but I think I'm doing better now."

"You're handling it like a veteran amusement-parker." She frowned at the spun sugar in his hands and added, "Only a veteran would be able to stomach that stuff."

"It's pretty nasty," he agreed. "So what have you been up to lately?"

"Oh, you know, business as usual." She couldn't explain how much grayer her world seemed now that Riley had flown the coop. Even thinking about that incredible, unforgettable night made her uncomfortable around Jay. Not that she had ever made any promises to Jay.

"You know what I've been doing?" Jay asked.

She shook her head.

"I've been thinking about my life."

"Join the club!"

Her words encouraged him. "Really?" he asked eagerly. "Because I've been pondering how empty it all seems sometimes. How . . . uncharted, you might say. You know, I might have been born with a James Bond bank account, but I just don't think I was made to be a swinging single."

"That's too bad."

He looked as if she'd said the wrong thing. "Why bad?"

"Well, I'm sure there are lots of men who would love to be in your shoes."

"But . . ."

"Many a man in your circumstances would be off in the Bahamas, or Europe, doing nothing except living like a maharajah."

"Yeah, but see, what I'm trying to get across, Kellie, is that I'm not the maharajah type."

As he said this, she noted the short-sleeved shirt tucked into his khaki shorts, and of course his unfortunate choice of footwear. "No, I guess not." It was difficult to imagine a maharajah wearing tube socks with sandals. Even very expensive-looking European comfort sandals.

"My grandfather always gave me two pieces of advice, and one half of it was, get married to a good woman."

She nodded. "What was the other half?"

"Don't spend your principal. I've managed that part pretty well."

"But you've never married."

"Well, no. But that's not my fault. I don't know if Riley told you this, but for years—years and years, actually—I've been searching for just the right woman."

Kellie frowned. "Isn't that what everyone's doing? Searching for just the right person?"

Jay sighed. "Well, yeah, maybe, but the thing is, I've decided that I've found her."

Kellie looked up at him, surprised. "Who?"

"You."

"Oh!" His words so startled her that she jumped, accidentally knocking the blue candy out of his hand. It stuck in a solid blob against his white shirt. "I'm so sorry!" she said, trying to yank the paper cone off his shoulder.

"You're sorry I've decided you're the one?"

"No, no, no," she said. "I just meant your shirt . . ."

He shook his head and tossed the blue candy into the nearby waste bin, where a swarm of flies and bees immediately moved in for a feast. "Never mind my shirt. I think we'd be good together, Kellie."

He was declaring his love for her in front of the log ride? Or . . . well, actually he hadn't said anything about love. And why should he? In all the time she'd known him, they hadn't shared more than a chaste kiss on the lips. A peck.

Her true passion she'd saved for his best friend. She writhed with guilt. She didn't even deserve Jay. "Oh,

Jay—I wish I could say I was sure, too. The truth is, though, that I'm a little mixed up right now."

He looked disappointed. "I knew you would be. Seeing Rick—that couldn't have been easy."

"Right." She wasn't sure how to deal with this. How many men could she piss off in just a few weeks? "I just can't believe that of all the women in the world, you would choose me. I've got all this baggage, Jay."

"That's okay! Who doesn't have a little baggage by the time they're as old as we are?"

He made it sound as if she were Angela Lansbury. Which wasn't exactly romantic. "Yeah, but . . ." A plastic flume came scudding down the water slide, drenching its screaming passengers. She heard Tina's squeals and knew there wasn't much time. "Don't you think we should get to know each other better? It's been just a little over a month since I met you."

"That's what I'm saying, though, Kellie. I want to get to know you better."

"Oh." She felt a little foolish now. She'd jumped to the conclusion that he meant something more serious. More immediate. She'd forgotten she wasn't the type of woman men were apt to sweep off their feet.

"I see."

"I knew the moment I met you that you were . . . special. I told Riley so."

She frowned. She'd bitten her tongue to keep herself from asking about Riley, but she couldn't stop herself this time. "Where is Riley? I haven't heard from him in weeks."

"Oh, he's off to Korea and New York and who knows where else. Looked like he was packing for a six-month voyage."

Korea? And then New York? As the words sank in, they were like little needles pricking her. He'd left the country for heaven knew how long and he hadn't called to tell her. But of course it wasn't the first time. She could feel the blood draining out of her face and didn't know what she was going to do. Jay was still smiling at her expectantly.

Luckily, the kids came running up, Trevor flapping his hands and getting everybody else wet. He looked at the sticky blue stain on Jay's shirt. "What happened?"

"It was an accident," Kellie said quickly. Words she might have taken directly out of the mouth of her food-saboteur son. She was trying hard to appear normal.

Tina rubbed her eyeglass lenses on her shirt and flicked her wet braid unhappily. She wore the expression of a cat that had just been given a bath. "Can we do something less messy this time?"

"Roller coasters!" Trevor suggested at the top of his lungs.

Kellie would have told him to turn down the volume, only it was the first time since his father had visited that she'd seen him look so joyful.

"You and Jay will have to do the scary ones together," Kellie said. "I'm not climbing on anything that involves moving upside down at fifty miles an hour." Although, to be honest, sometimes it seemed that her whole life had started spinning and moving that way.

"That's okay with me!" Trevor said. "C'mon, Jay."

Jay shrugged helplessly, and the two walked ahead of Kellie and Tina. Watching them, Kellie gaped in wonder. Was she mistaken, or was Trevor actually being friendly to Jay? For a moment, her heart leapt into her throat as a mental picture of Jay being shoved off the Shock Wave flashed through her brain. But she dismissed it. Maybe Trevor was just grateful to him for bringing them here.

"What do you think of Jay?" she asked Tina casually.

"Jay's great!" She hopped as she walked. "Do you know he offered to give me and Margaret tickets to *The*

Nutcracker next Christmas? He says he can get front-row tickets. Do you think he can?''

She nodded.

"He must be really important!" Tina exclaimed. "I bet he's the nicest man in the world. Next to Riley." Tina was still loyal to her piano man.

How would she be able to explain to Tina if Riley had gone for good? That would be a hard lesson in heartbreak for a little girl.

A hard lesson for a thirty-two-year-old, too.

"Don't *you* like Jay, Mom?" Tina asked.

"Of course," she said.

But he would never make her heart stand still the way Riley could.

Then again, maybe that was Jay's biggest appeal.

Korea was a nightmare. The tech company Lombard had invested heavily in there was merging with a company that wouldn't stay afloat with the financial equivalent of water wings. It was a disaster in the making. Not to mention, Riley picked up a bug somewhere along the way after eating a meal that he hoped was not actually something that might be considered a family pet elsewhere in the world. You would have thought his years of eating greasy comfort food would have Teflon-coated his insides, but no. He spent the long, long journey from Seoul to La Guardia sprinting from his business class seat to the cramped airline john.

In New York he collapsed in a Victorian-inspired room at the Plaza Hotel. As he huddled beneath the chintz comforter, the phone on the bedside table rang constantly. Riley couldn't make himself answer the calls, but he could imagine the additional work piling up that each loud *brinnng!* represented. The problems. He felt overwhelmed without Doreen keeping the messy world at bay.

The New York office was a political morass right now. Several different managers wanted to take the place of Simms, the man who'd just jumped ship. Everyone wanted Riley's ear. He finally dragged himself out of bed to appear at the office and go to business meetings at five-star restaurants whose food he was lucky to be able to hold down. At the end of the long workday, he went up to his tastefully upholstered room, ate the mint on his pillow, and collapsed.

And thought of Kellie. He'd hoped that distance would provide objectivity and wisdom, but it hadn't. If anything, her arguments for them not being together just seemed to grow dimmer in his mind. He was more frustrated than ever. Why did she confuse him with someone like Rick? Why couldn't they just go along together for a while and see how things developed? Why did it suddenly seem as if there was a black hole of longing yawning inside him?

His second week in New York, on a Thursday morning, he trudged out of his room for a late breakfast meeting with one of the eager job candidates. But his heart wasn't in it. He wasn't sick anymore, but he was disconnected from all the hustle and bustle. It was early and he was already sagging. He had tossed and turned all night. And now, as he surveyed the Palm Court looking for his co-worker, he felt immune to the luxury around him. He would have traded his comfy room and all this five-star service for his cold stone house and snippy Nathaniel in a heartbeat. And where was the edge in eating haute cuisine if it wasn't prepared for you by a maniac?

The maitre d' approached him. "Mr. Lombard?"

Riley nodded. "Yes?"

"You have a message. Your party couldn't make it."

Riley frowned and went to the lobby to use the phone. The receptionist at Lombard told him that the candidate's wife was having a baby. Riley felt a grin tug at his lips and instructed the woman to send flowers to the hospital—the biggest arrangement that would fit through the doors of a maternity ward.

She laughed. "Anything else?"

"No . . ." He cleared his throat. "Except, um, I'll be in meetings for the rest of this morning. Take messages, won't you?"

"Certainly."

Riley hung up the phone, his heart fluttering like a butterfly's wings and his face burning from the whopper he'd just told. He didn't have meetings; he just didn't want to go into work today and face all those go-getters. He looked furtively around the lobby to see if anyone noticed that a CEO was playing hooky. As fast as he could without drawing attention to himself, he dashed out of the Plaza and didn't stop until he'd crossed the street into Central Park.

Then he jumped for joy in the hot, sticky July air of Manhattan.

He felt free—as if he could finally flush his brain of price-to-earning ratios and six-month charts and bond yields. He bounced through a faded hopscotch grid on the walkway and practically ran, arms outstretched, toward the first landmark he saw—the zoo. He knew it wasn't PC, but he loved zoos. He paid his money and dashed toward the tropic zone, where most of the animals—sensible creatures—seemed to be napping. Then he headed for the Polar Circle and watched a polar bear do a few laps in his pool. The aquatic grace of the huge white beast was mesmerizing, but when a crowd came up, Riley finally moved on to the penguin house.

It was cool and dark inside—heavenly—and the penguins were having their first feed of the visiting day. From behind the glass they waddled and dove busily. Riley couldn't help smiling. For some reason, the sounds they made, amplified for the visitors, reminded him of W.C. Fields.

Near Riley a little girl with her parents stood as close as she could to the exhibit, her face pressed up against the glass, and squealed with joy each time a bird dove into the water. She had curly brown hair and was wearing a plush red Clifford the Dog backpack. "Look, Mommy!"

There was no telling how long the family had been there, but judging from the tension on the parents' faces, they wanted to push on. The woman glanced at her watch and gave her girl's hand a tug. "Let's go, Muriel."

The girl looked panicked. "But the penguins are still eating!"

"We can come back and watch them eat some other time."

"You always say that we'll come here, but we never do! I want to stay!"

The mother grew angry and seemed not even to notice Riley's presence behind her. "We brought you here, didn't we? Now *let's go.*"

"But, but—" Muriel's face twisted in misery, and hot tears spilled to her cheeks. "But I want you and me to stay here! I don't want you to leave me at that place!"

Riley sank down on the bench against the back circular wall. He suddenly felt weak again.

Let her stay! he wanted to yell at Muriel's parents. He didn't know what was going on or where they were headed. What was *that place?* Day care? The dentist?

But he did feel as if he could have enlightened the parents on a few facts of life. Namely, that time was all too short. And maybe that someday they wouldn't all be together anymore and they would look back on this day and wish like hell they'd watched penguins all day. Because wherever they were going wasn't worth what they could find in their bond as a family.

Life's too damn short, he wanted to say. *Tell her you would do anything in your power not to leave her. Grab every moment you can.*

But maybe they didn't need him to tell them that.

"Let's check out the sea lions for a minute," the father said, bending down to Muriel's eye level. "Would you like that?"

Slowly, pushing away moisture from her cheek with a balled fist, she nodded. In a maneuver so flawless, it could only have been perfected with much practice, he swung Muriel up to his shoulders where she beamed a smile for her mom, the penguins, and even Riley.

Riley gaped after them and felt his heart surge with envy. And yearning. *Life's too damn short,* he'd been about to preach to those people. But what was he doing with his own life? He leaned back against the wall, closed his eyes, and gulped in several breaths. He'd lost so goddamned much. And for fear of losing more, he had backed away from Kellie. He pictured her now, with her kids. Where did Jay say they were going? Six Flags? He wanted to be there with her. He wanted to be with them, not alone in a penguin house assuming he knew the best advice to give everyone.

What an arrogant ass he was. And how cowardly.

He knew now what cue he'd missed. She'd been waiting to see if he would commit to her. For him to say, *I love you. Forever. This can work. Let's grab every moment.* But just as she was afraid of making a mistake after what had happened in her marriage to Rick, he was afraid of losing someone again. And because of that, he'd nearly lost Kellie.

He stood, sure now what he should do. He needed to get back to work. On his life.

* * *

"I had a serious talk with Wendell last night," Rita said.

Kellie wasn't sure how to react to this news, but she knew better than to laugh. "What about?"

Rita sipped her Coke, taking her time. They were at Wiggie's, the first time Kellie had been in the place since seeing Riley here weeks and weeks ago, but of course he wasn't there now. If she'd ever believed in fate, she knew for sure now that it was a lot of bunk.

"I told Wendell that if he's serious about me, then he needs to be more involved in my life."

Kellie nodded. "Good for you."

"I've really put my foot down," Rita declared. "I'm telling him what *I* want for a change. I'm not going to be reactive anymore. I'm not going to just whine to everyone else when Wendell doesn't behave like I'd like him to. I'm wasting my life doing that."

Kellie sat up straighter, impressed. "My God, Rita. What's happened to you?"

"Well, to tell you the truth, it's Jay."

"Jay?"

"I was talking to him about Wendell at your house the other night . . . you know, when we were watching that scary movie?"

Kellie nodded.

"And Jay said that I shouldn't do laundry on Friday nights with Wendell. He suggested I join a book club instead. Something for *me*."

"A book club?"

Rita beamed excitedly. "Yes—and I did! It's really fun. And not only that, the first book we read was called *The Decisions Women Don't Make*. Jay gave me his copy."

Jay? "What was Jay doing with this book?"

"He used to belong to the book club," Rita explained. "Which is weird, because it's all women." She shrugged.

"But he said he doesn't want to go anymore. Says he doesn't need to now."

Kellie frowned thoughtfully and tapped her fingers against the table. Jay was always surprising her these days. She couldn't deny that he'd been a godsend in her life. He'd been keeping her mind off Riley for weeks now. The kids liked Jay. And now Jay was helping get Rita's life together.

The man might actually be a miracle worker.

"You know what I think, Kellie?" Rita asked.

Kellie looked at her little sister with new interest. "What?"

"I think you should marry Jay."

Kellie laughed. "We're not quite to that stage."

Rita shook her head. "I don't think *you're* quite to that stage, but I believe Jay definitely is. You should see the way he watches you—like you're the answer to all his prayers. I think he's the answer to yours."

"I haven't been praying for a husband," Kellie told her.

"Well, why not? I thought that's what had you so upset since Rick came for his visit. If the thought of him getting on with his life depresses you so much, maybe you should start over, too."

"It's not Rick that's messed me up."

"Well, what is it, then?"

She knew she should keep mum, but she simply had to tell someone. "Riley."

"Riley!" Rita exclaimed, surprising her by the displeasure in her voice. "Why? Has *he* been around lately?"

"No . . ."

Her sister's face screwed up in confusion. "Well?"

"The truth is," Kellie said, squirming, "Riley and I made love."

Rita crossed her arms and fixed her with a horrified glare. "You mean you *cheated* on *Jay?*"

"Jay and I aren't involved that way."

"Puh-lease!" Her sister rolled her eyes dramatically. "Kellie, are you insane? The man is in love with you. He comes over to your house and takes your kids on outings. Does Riley do that?"

"No . . ."

"What does Riley have to say about Jay hanging around you?"

"I don't know. I haven't talked to him for a while."

"Since when?"

"Since the morning after Trevor's birthday."

Rita expelled an impatient breath. "Kellie, what are you saying? That you had a one-night stand and now he hasn't spoken to you for nearly a month?"

"Just a little over three weeks. That's my fault. I told him I wanted a commitment."

"And?"

"He said he wasn't ready. Or he as good as said it." She felt so foolish. So pathetic. Almost like the old Rita.

The new Rita was looking at her with spunky determination—to straighten *her* out. It was a humbling experience.

"You can't lead Jay on, Kellie. He's too nice. You need to make a decision."

"Like your book says?" Kellie asked doubtfully.

"Well, actually, yes. If you don't chart a course for yourself, you'll end up with your sails huffing, or luffing. Something like that."

The nautical lingo sounded vaguely familiar. "I guess that makes sense."

"Kellie, Jay is one of the nicest men in the world. Who else could get Trevor out to build houses for poor people on a Saturday afternoon? And think about it—the man was at your house, distracted by a movie, and Trevor didn't even use the opportunity to pour the crockpot full of *queso* over his head."

"I considered that," Kellie allowed. "I'm amazed at how well Trevor likes Jay."

"It's because there's nothing not to like. He's the nicest guy in the world. You can't deny that he's great husband material."

Kellie shuddered. "That's kind of a crass way of thinking about it."

"Why?" Rita asked. "It's just being practical. Doesn't he meet all the criteria you used to tell me about? He's financially sound—something Rick was definitely not—a guy who's looking for one true love—Rick was definitely not—and a great father figure."

"Something Rick is definitely not," Kellie agreed.

"You said you want companionship the second time around, didn't you?"

"Yes . . ." she admitted.

"Well, then? Jay's perfect."

Kellie sighed. Then smiled. "Yeah, I'm afraid he is."

Rita leaned forward. "You have to get on with your life sometime."

Another twenty minutes with Rita, and Kellie might have agreed to marry Jay right then and there. "There's one problem, though. He's never asked me."

"He will. You're so lucky!"

Kellie crossed her arms. "You seem to have my course all charted. What about your own?"

"Oh, I'm working on that." Rita sucked down the last of her drink. "And frankly, I think Wendell and I will be sailing off into the sunset real soon."

Chapter Seventeen

The moment Riley came dragging back, late, from New York City was not the perfect time to drop a bombshell on him. But Nathaniel had never possessed the best timing.

They bumped suitcases in the doorway. Riley was hauling his on the way in; Nathaniel was marching out.

"I'm sorry, Riley," Nathaniel announced. "I'm leaving you."

Riley dropped his bags and collapsed against the wall in the foyer. He'd returned from his frantic, awful trip feeling like a weary traveler seeking a calm port in the storm. Apparently, this wasn't the port he was looking for.

"You're *what?*" He asked the question as if he were surprised, shocked, and appalled, but was he? He'd known for years that Nathaniel was going to leave . . . eventually. He had just hoped that eventually would never arrive.

"I'm sorry," Nathaniel said with tears in his eyes. His voice quavered. "I just can't take it anymore. I waited till you got back so I could tell you in person. But now I've called a cab, and I'm going."

Riley swallowed. Anyone watching them would think

they were witnessing the end of a love affair. "So suddenly? Nathaniel, you can't—"

"But I have to!" Nathaniel pulled a handkerchief from his pocket with a flourish. "It's wrong, what we've been doing. We're codependents. Jay made me understand that."

Riley dropped one of his bags in astonishment. "Jay?"

"Mm-hm. He came by while you were gone and told me about a book I should read."

"A book?"

"Yes, it was called *The Decisions Women Don't Make.*" To Riley's quizzical glance, he said, "Okay, I had to adapt it a little for my needs. But he was right, Riley. The book has changed my life!"

"But what will you do? Where are you going?"

Nathaniel lifted his chin. "First I'm going on an Adriatic cruise for a little emotional detox. Then I'm going to work for a man named Nigel Beetlebaum in London."

The name sounded vaguely familiar. "How did you find this Nigel person?"

"Through Jay. I told him how I felt trapped, and he said it was the simplest problem to remedy because he just happened to have a friend in England who needed a butler. So *voila!* I'm Nathaniel *internationale!*"

"But you can't just pick up and leave," Riley said. He felt so forlorn and confused. Living in the house without Nathaniel was almost unthinkable. How would anything get done? Who would communicate to Fayard?

"Don't worry," Nathaniel said, reading his mind as always. "I took the liberty of getting interim help for you." He shouted toward the general direction of the kitchen. *"A nice elderly lady!"* He turned back to Riley. "Someone even that big jerk wouldn't dare push around."

"Elderly lady," Riley repeated. He felt numb. "When will she be here?"

"She's here," Nathaniel said.

Well, that was an efficient changing of the guard, Riley had to admit. "What's her name?"

"Matilda Schlink. She seems very . . . efficient."

She sounded . . . well, a little German.

He turned and discovered a large, muscular, redheaded woman in her fifties staring down at him.

"Hello!" the woman boomed. "I am Matilda."

Riley muttered a greeting and whirled back to Nathaniel.

"See what I mean by not being pushed around?" Nathaniel asked.

No kidding. Riley felt as if he were going to be living with the Gestapo. He remembered suddenly that Nathaniel had warned him that if he had a real housekeeper around, he would feel the need to go out and get a life. But as he'd finished up his New York business, he'd reached that same stark conclusion all on his own. His life wasn't what he wanted it to be. He didn't want to live in the past. He needed to take a chance on his future. Somehow, he needed to try to assure Kellie that he was ready for another commitment. Given their last encounter, that was going to be no easy task.

"Nathaniel, please—"

"Oh!" Nathaniel said, dashing out into the drive. "Here's my cab. Toodle-oo! I'll send you a postcard where you can forward my last week's pay!"

He hustled toward the oncoming cab before Riley could run after him and beg him to name his price.

With a faint heart, Riley watched one of his strongest links to the past drive off into the sunset. It felt even fainter when he turned back to Matilda.

"Well!" she exclaimed. It came out as *vell*. Riley tried to keep an open mind, though. "We shall take your bags up now, and then you must talk to the cook."

"Fayard." How on earth was he going to deal with a

temperamental Dominican chef and his new Teutonic housekeeper?

"Fayard," the woman repeated. "*Ja.* When I tell him to make dinner, he starts weeping and talking in-co-herently!"

So Fayard was heartbroken? Well, why the hell couldn't he have acted nicer to Nathaniel? Why did he have to mess things up?

Suddenly, he realized he needed to dedicate this night to getting his house in some kind of working order. Tomorrow, he would see Kellie.

And at some point he needed to see Jay, too, so he could tell him to keep his self-help books to himself!

"Kellie, some lady wants to know whether we can do two-hundred copies of a twenty-eight-page book of poems, bound, by this afternoon."

Kellie looked at Alejandro, then at all the machines that were filled with what mostly looked like students making copies. Lana was busy preparing a special order calendar and the big machine in back already had a mas-sive order going through.

"Sure," she said, regardless. They wouldn't get more business by turning customers away.

Of course, they wouldn't get it by being late or sloppy on new orders, either.

The business was thriving better than she'd ever dared to hope. In fact, her whole life was swimming along as well as could be expected. Tina was happy. Trevor hadn't been in trouble in weeks, and with school due to start in a few weeks, she prayed that he could keep up this pattern of good behavior. Rita was right; Jay was a gem. Atten-tive. Kind. Surprisingly kid-friendly.

And most of all, he was *there*. His presence these past few weeks had almost taken the sting out of Riley's disappearance. She'd stopped berating herself for making a terrible mistake with Riley. Right now she was just doing what Rita advised: concentrating on the day-to-day.

The door opened, and a giant flowered horseshoe moved toward her. Several people in the store turned to watch, and who could blame them? The arrangement looked like something pilfered from the winner's circle—a dazzling multicolored mat of carnations swathed with a ribbon that read *Good Luck!* The display perched atop two spindly legs. When it finally came to a rest in front of the cash register, Jay peeked around it.

"What do you think?"

She couldn't help laughing. "It's incredible! But what does it mean?"

"It means good luck."

"For me?"

"Of course."

"Thanks. But why?"

Her employees had migrated out from the back now, and even several customers were standing to the side, watching Jay with interest. "Because you might be getting married."

She tossed her head back and laughed. "Really, when?"

"As soon as you'll agree to be my wife."

Her laughter petered out immediately, and she stared at his expectant face in shock. "Jay, are you—"

Before she could finish, Jay reached into his jacket pocket and pulled out a square velvet jeweler's box. He opened it to reveal a diamond the size of the Rock of Gibraltar. Lana gasped. Alejandro whistled. Kellie stood stunned.

"Will you marry me, Kellie?"

Was he crazy? She couldn't force her mouth to close. Her face felt as if it were on fire. And everyone in the room went so completely silent that there didn't seem to be any noise in the world except for her heart booming in her chest and the sounds of copying machines.

"Please say yes," he said, going down on one knee so that all she could see were his eyebrows and the top of his head. She had to bend over the counter so she wouldn't lose sight of him. "All my life I've wanted to get married, Kellie, and now, as far as I'm concerned, you're it."

She was it? It, as in wonderful? Or it, as in his last hope? The end of the line.

"I promise I'll do everything in my power to make you, Trevor, and Tina happy. Everything. If you want the moon and the stars, anything, I'll figure out a way to give them to you."

Kellie was stunned. She'd even thought about this, since her talk with Rita. But she never thought she'd have to make a decision so soon. Or in front of so many people.

On television she'd once seen a feature about a man who had proposed to a woman over the loudspeaker during a televised NFL game. The woman had said yes. But at the time Kellie had wondered, what if the woman had wanted to say no? She would have looked like a terrible spoilsport. All the world wants the woman to say yes. Everybody wants a happy ending.

But now she understood those public proposals from the other end too, because she wanted a happy ending as much as Jay did. She felt caught up in the romance, in her audience, in Jay and his hilariously extreme gesture. What a corny, romantic thing to do!

"Yes!" she burst out suddenly. "Of course!"

How could she refuse the nicest man in the world?

And it wasn't just that. Right after the "yes" left her mouth, she felt a strange sort of relief. She was getting married to the sweetest, most stable guy in the world.

Her life was falling back into some sort of reason. Reason—what a great word!

The copy shop was jubilant. There were cheers and clapping, and before she knew what was happening, an impromptu celebration was taking place, and she didn't even know anyone who was celebrating. A stranger handed her a cup of water from the cooler, and she and Jay clicked Dixie cups in a toast.

"To us!" Jay said.

"To us," she chimed.

He stood outside Copycat, taking a deep breath. The flowers cascaded out of his arms, the Tiffany's box was a reassuring lump in his pocket. This was what he wanted . . . what Kellie still wanted, too, he hoped.

But maybe he'd just feel her out first. Their last encounter hadn't gone so well. He didn't want to blow this by going in and blurting out his feelings all at once. Maybe he'd just hand her the flowers and see how glad she was to see him. Maybe he would take it slow.

Slow was difficult, though. His heart was beating as crazily as it had when he'd asked Letitia Cox to go with him in seventh grade.

He decided to go for broke and pushed through the glass door. Immediately, he was thrown off-kilter. People, customers it looked like, were standing around, talking and eating Oreos off a paper plate next to the cash register. Also on the counter was Kellie herself, sitting there as if she'd been lifted in jubilation. There was a huge "Good Luck" sign propped prominently in one corner—a ridiculous horseshoe of flowers. And leaning against the counter at Kellie's elbow was Jay.

Jay?

They were all grinning like idiots.

What the heck was going on here?

Even though the bell rang over his head when he walked in, it seemed to take forever for anyone to notice him. And when Jay and Kellie did finally look up, their faces were a study in contrasts. Jay beamed and gave him a little jivey thumbs-up that left Riley completely clueless, while Kellie's face went ghostly pale. She looked as though she needed paramedics.

He proceeded in despite his confusion.

But halfway to the counter something happened that made everything gel. At first he thought it was another vision. Some trick of the overhead lights sent a ray beaming from Kellie's left hand, where a huge diamond now resided. He counted quickly and put it all together. Third finger, left hand. Oreos on the counter. Jubilant Jay.

He wasn't sure his feet were even moving anymore. The relentless *shushing* of the copiers added to the blood pounding in his temples. *Could he just not get anything right?*

Jay held his hands out, almost as if he expected a hug. "You son of a gun! How did you know we were here?"

"Well . . ." If only he could rewind time. Back up. "Kellie works here."

Jay laughed. "How did you know to bring flowers?" He turned to Kellie. "I swear to you, I didn't tell him."

"I believe you."

Riley had forgotten about the flowers. They felt so heavy in his hands, he might have been holding a brick or a bowling ball. His feeble romantic gesture had arrived too late. Minutes too late, if appearances didn't lie. He held them out stiffly to Kellie, who took them mutely.

Her eyes. He looked into her eyes to see what she was thinking. But she still had that bloodless, stunned aspect about her. The bewildered bride-to-be.

Now that his brain seemed to be working again, he was beginning to feel a little bewildered himself. And a little angry. Had so much happened during one business trip? The last time he'd seen Kellie, they'd just made love. She was yammering about needing to be careful not to make mistakes. She was lecturing him about not wanting to make any decisions while he was on the rebound.

So had she already rebounded from *him?*

He pulled his hand back from Jay, who was shaking the life out of it. "Congratulations." His voice sounded as if he'd just swallowed a cactus.

"Thank you," Kellie said stiffly.

He tilted his head in curiosity at her and was unable to resist a barb. "Good to see you're not being too impulsive these days."

At least he got some color back into her. Two red patches appeared in her cheeks, and her chin lifted stubbornly. "I guess it's true what they say."

"What?"

"That you'll know when the right one comes along."

Jay laughed. "Ain't it the truth?"

Riley crossed his arms. "Actually, it sounds awfully touchy-feely coming from Kellie."

"What I still don't get," Jay said to Riley, "is how you knew to come here and congratulate us."

Kellie smiled for the first time since Riley's arrival as she leaned into Jay. "Didn't you know? He's a psychic."

Jay laughed and put his arm loosely around Kellie's waist. Kellie. Jay's fiancee. Riley felt as if he'd just been kicked.

"You're going to be my best man, of course."

Riley nodded. "Of course."

Kellie looked panicked and pivoted back to Jay. "Best man? But I thought we'd just do the city hall thing. You know, keep it small and intimate."

Jay looked crestfallen. "You mean you don't want a wedding? This is a big deal for me—I want to show you off. There are a ton of people for you to meet! My folks, for instance.''

Kellie looked as if she wanted to slink off the counter and hide. ''But weddings cost money.''

Jay laughed and poked his thumb at her as he looked at Riley. ''She worries about money.''

He smiled. ''Imagine.''

''Kellie, money is no object,'' Jay assured her. ''But if you want, we can have a sort of intimate ceremony at my house—just a hundred people or so.''

''A hundred!'' Kellie fluttered anxiously. ''But that means we'll have to send out invitations and buy a dress . . . it'll take months to put it all together.''

''Well, let's say a month,'' Jay said.

Looking at Kellie's misery at the mere thought of a public ceremony, Riley started getting into the spirit of the thing. What exactly was it that she dreaded? Standing in front of a crowd of witnesses in a white dress, or waiting? Was she afraid she was going to change her mind?

A slow grin tugged at his lips. ''As best man, I reserve the right to throw the rehearsal dinner party.''

''Why would we need to rehearse?'' Kellie asked.

Jay laughed. ''It's just an excuse for the wedding guests to get drunk before *and* after the ceremony.''

''Oh, but—''

''I can have it at my house.'' Riley felt his lips flatten into a tight, thin line. ''I was just looking at the place last night, thinking that it could use a little life in it. And Matilda looks like she'd be a whiz as a party planner.''

Jay's eyes bugged. ''Matilda?''

Kellie also seemed startled.

''She's the Gestapo woman who moved in last weekend when Nathaniel decided to take a powder.'' He gritted his teeth. ''When my best friend got him a job in London.''

First his butler, now his woman. Who would have thought Jay could be so dangerous?

Kellie shook her head. "We can't let you throw us a party, Riley. The expense—"

"It'll be worth every penny to give you and Jay a good send-off." Riley released a contemplative sigh. "Who would have thought, my best friend marrying my—"

"Well, thank you!" Kellie said, quickly interrupting him before he could describe exactly what they had been to each other. "I didn't mean to sound ungrateful."

"Gosh, no," Jay said, giving Kellie another squeeze. Riley had never seen a man look so happy. "We owe you, buddy."

It felt like a farce. A Stooges routine. Somebody should poke him in the eye or whack him on the head with a golf club. Everybody should be breaking up laughing.

But nobody was laughing, least of all him. Or Kellie. And Jay was still looking at him with all sincerity. "Don't think that we'll forget that you're the one responsible for bringing us together."

Riley forced as gracious a smile as he could manage. "Don't think I will, either."

"A month?" Rita asked. "A month is nothing!"

She had arrived at Kellie's door that evening with an armload of bridal magazines, a stack of Post-it notes, and a wedding planner. In the background, Tina was practicing the first bars of Mendelssohn's wedding march. "Here Comes the Bride" played over and over and over till Kellie thought it was some new form of torture.

Rita pored over the magazines at the kitchen table while Kellie made tea. She didn't even want tea, but the thought of looking at all those model brides turned her stomach.

"Buying a gown is the biggest decision of the marriage process. You have to decide what kind of dress you want before you go shopping or else you will just be swamped," Rita lectured. "You need to familiarize yourself with all the styles so that you'll know what you're looking for."

"How do you know all this?" Suddenly Rita was Vera Wang.

"I read an article in one of these magazines."

"But Rita, that's what magazines tell you so you'll buy more magazines."

Rita let out an annoyed sigh. "Kellie, why are you in such a downer mood? I thought you'd be happy—you're getting married! To the nicest guy on earth!"

Kellie's stomach felt way beyond butterflies. Since this morning, a flock of Canadian geese had taken up residence there. "It's a serious step. Jay and I haven't even known each other for that long."

"So?" Rita's eyes practically glittered with love for Kellie's fiance. "It's Jay! You've got to know that you're marrying the best, nicest guy in the world. Look at all that he's done for me. I'm a changed person!"

"Mm," Kellie replied.

Rita flipped the magazine page noisily, gasped at an off-the-shoulder wedding gown that Cameron Diaz *might* be able to pull off, and slammed a Post-it on the page to mark the spot. "It's not just you we have to shop for. If I'm going to be your maid of honor, I'll need something, too. Maybe I can lose some weight. But a month—that's no time at all."

"It's too much time. I was hoping we could get . . ." *Get it over with,* she'd almost said. ". . . Get married sooner."

"What, and sneak off to city hall like you did with Rick? That's no good!"

Kellie sighed. "I guess you're right."

Rita slapped her magazine shut, frowning. "Look, are you having second thoughts about this?"

"No," she lied. Actually, she was already on her thousandth-and-second thought.

"Because if you are, you should definitely say so. Jay is the nicest man in the whole world, and he deserves someone who's going to love him unquestioningly."

"I know that." She wished Rita would stop calling him *the nicest man in the world*. Even if he was, thinking of him that way made her head ache. "It's just this whole wedding thing. It's taking me by surprise. I'm just not the big white dress type, I'm afraid."

"Oh, you'll look great."

Kellie laughed skeptically. "Anyway, it's not how I'll look. It's how I'll feel. I hate being the center of attention. And doesn't it seem sort of silly for a mother of two to be flouncing around in a wedding dress?"

"Yes!"

This was from Trevor, who crossed to the refrigerator for a Coke. Both he and Tina had looked distressed by the news of her wedding, even though Jay had told them that they would be going to live in a big new house. With a pool. Even though she'd assured them that Jay wanted their happiness as much as hers. Only when she'd promised Tina that she could play the wedding march at the wedding had Tina brightened at the prospect.

She was still playing it. *Here comes the bride. Here comes the bride. . . .*

Wasn't there any other song to play at weddings?

"Nobody asked you," Rita told Trevor.

"Of course," Trevor sassed back. "Nobody ever asks me anything. What I think doesn't matter!"

Kellie sighed. Did she have the only eleven-year-old in the world who could pout at the top of his lungs?

She and Rita waited for Trevor to retreat to his room, where he'd been holed up all evening, but he remained stubbornly leaning against the counter.

"There's also the problem of people," Kellie finally

told Rita, Trevor or no Trevor. "Jay knows a million people, but I'll be lucky if I can scrounge up twenty guests."

Rita shrugged. "That's no big deal."

"Plus if there's a real ceremony, what'll I do? I don't have a dad to walk me down the aisle."

Rita frowned. Then she glanced over at Trevor and brightened again. "Trevor can do it!"

Kellie and Trevor locked gazes, both looking equally horrified.

"Oh, no!" Trevor rolled his eyes in dread. "That's sooooo retarded!"

His aunt clucked at him. "No it's not. It'll be cute."

Trevor let out a strangled moan.

"You're the man of the family, Trevor," Rita pointed out. "You have to do this. Don't worry—we'll stick you in a tux with a little bow tie. You'll look great."

"A tux!" Trevor shrieked.

Kellie shook her head doubtfully. "You don't have to do it if you don't want to."

"Sure," Rita bit out, "you can just let your mother walk down the aisle by herself. You can just let her look like a moron."

"Thanks, Rita."

Trevor's face contorted in misery. "Oh, man! This is gonna be more painful than I ever imagined!"

Kellie almost laughed, but Rita turned on him in a huff. "Trevor, for heaven's sake, can't you do this one little thing? Can't you be adult for once in your life?"

"How can I be adult when I'm eleven?"

"You're acting like you're two!" Rita turned back to her magazine and flipped the pages with a vengeance.

Trevor looked from the back of Rita's head up to Kellie, then made a spinning gesture around his ear. Kellie had to agree. Rita seemed to be going a little nuts about this wedding thing.

"Let's all take a deep breath," Kellie said in a yoga-instructor tone. "We don't have to decide anything tonight."

"Good!" Trevor squeezed his Coke can into an hourglass shape. "I'm gonna go outside for a while." He slammed out the back door, hurrying to catch the last hour of daylight.

Kellie eased down in a chair next to Rita. "Rita, is anything wrong?"

Rita turned a *Modern Bride* page purposefully and marked the wedding dress there with a Post-it note. "I just feel like I have a lot riding on this wedding, that's all."

"*You* do?"

Rita sniffed. "Yes, I do, so I'd appreciate it if you would get more into the spirit of the thing."

"What difference does my wedding make to you?"

Rita looked up at her as if she'd gone bug crazy. "Kellie, think about it. Weddings are contagious. If you get married, and I take Wendell to your wedding, then maybe . . ."

Kellie nodded understandingly. But secretly she wondered how long it would be before her poor sister wound up in the state hospital. "Now I see."

"Do you?" Rita brightened. "Because I have a favor to ask."

"What?"

"Can Wendell be an usher?"

"I don't know if we'll have ushers."

It was apparently the wrong thing to say at that particular moment.

"For heaven's sake, Kellie!" Rita shouted. "*Of course* you'll have ushers. Every wedding has them. Why are you dragging your feet over every little detail?"

Rather than watch her sister have a nervous breakdown right there in the kitchen, Kellie capitulated. "Of course, you're right. We'll have several," she said soothingly. "Wendell can be the head usher. Best usher, or whatever they call it."

Instantly mollified, Rita sank against the back of her chair. "Oh, good. Because I think if Wendell has a major part to play, he'll feel more included. I really want your wedding to work out for us."

Kellie nodded. This was terrific. She could certainly use some more pressure.

The doorbell rang and the Mendelssohn blessedly stopped. "I'll get it!" Tina yelled. Kellie and Rita listened to Tina's skipping steps, then she cried out, "Riley!"

Kellie sank a little further into her chair, and Rita looked alarmed. "Does Riley . . . ?"

Kellie nodded. "He's agreed to be best man."

Rita looked relieved. Kellie wished she could be, too. But after their encounter that afternoon at Copycat, she had hoped not to see Riley for a long time. He'd been insufferable—almost as insufferable as she had been.

And what had he been doing there in the first place? He'd brought her flowers, but she didn't really think he'd had another of his visions. He'd looked too dumbstruck when he'd spotted the rock on her finger.

She still wasn't used to the engagement ring, either. It was so much bigger than the one Rick had given her. So much more conspicuous. All the way home, she'd been self-conscious, nervous that she was going to be mugged in the Shop-Save parking lot. How did rich women stand wandering around with their jewels on all the time? It felt like having an entire year's salary wrapped around her ring finger.

She put her hand in her lap now.

Riley appeared in the doorway and immediately cast a distasteful glance at the magazines stacked on the table. "I see you're wasting no time."

Rita turned and beamed at him. "There's no time to waste. A month is nothing!"

Judging from the way Riley flinched, Rita's battle cry of the evening had the same unnerving effect on him that it did on Kellie. "No," he admitted.

Kellie stood and noticed that he was holding a box in his hand. A wedding present?

For the first time, she felt something like real doubt. Because right then and there, she wanted nothing more than to rush into Riley's arms and have him kiss the daylights out of her. She wanted him to crush her to him and ask her what the hell she thought she was doing marrying someone else when he was so madly, passionately in love with her.

But of course, he had never said that he was madly, passionately in love with her. He'd made love to her and then left her to her own devices for a month. He'd walked out at her request, of course, but then he hadn't come back. Hadn't even called.

But she didn't want him to think that she was marrying Jay to spite him, because she wasn't. She was marrying Jay for any number of reasons, none of which had a thing to do with Riley. She was marrying Jay because it was so right—so sensible. Jay would be great for her and her kids. He had promised her the moon, and who in her right mind would turn that down? True, there was no consuming passion between them—but there wasn't any passion clouding her judgment, either. She wasn't going to wake up in five years and wonder what she'd ever seen in Jay.

And what's more, Rita was right. He was the nicest . . . well, he was wonderful.

She looked into Riley's blue, blue eyes and felt her heart skip a beat. But the passion she saw there, the longing . . . that wasn't real. It couldn't be. It was just more of Riley's badly timed weirdness.

She glanced back at Rita, willing her to go, but her sister remained planted at the table in front of her magazines, heedless of any drama going on around her. And of course, there was no reason why she should leave. Riley was just a friend.

Kellie cleared her throat. "I'm sorry about this afternoon. I wasn't expecting you."

"So I gathered." Riley's mouth mashed into a bitter line. Then he sighed and smiled. Sort of smiled. "Do you think you'll be happy?"

"I hope so."

"How could she not be?" Rita chimed in. "She's marrying the nicest man in the world!"

Both Riley and Kellie stared at her blankly.

Kellie crossed to the teapot. "Would you like something to drink?"

He shook his head. "Actually, I came to see Trevor. Is he here?"

Kellie frowned. "He's out back. But why . . . ?"

Riley held up the box. "I hope you don't mind. I got him the glove. I thought maybe he could use a pick-me-up tonight."

Kellie's throat went dry, and tears of gratitude sprang to her eyes. It was such a thoughtful gesture. At just that moment she could have hugged the man. But of course that would have been a terrible mistake. Given their history, a simple hug could explode into something both of them would regret.

She gestured mutely toward the back door.

He nodded. "I won't be long."

After he'd left, Rita Post-it-noted another wedding dress. "That was nice of him." She bit her lip, concentrating on the dress. Reluctantly, she withdrew the yellow sticky she'd just put down and winced at Kellie apologetically. "I think we should stay away from lace, don't you?

You're too short for it. You don't want to walk down the aisle looking stubbier than you actually are.''

In the next room, Tina started up again. *Here comes the bride. Here comes the bride. . . .*

No, the way she felt, a month wasn't going to be a short time at all.

Trevor was thrilled with his new glove. Riley even tossed him a few fast balls—all of which Trevor caught. You'd think the new equipment had turned him into Ken Griffey.

"This is so wicked!" he told Riley. "Thanks!"

"You're welcome."

"At least one good thing happened today," Trevor said, kicking his toe into the dirt.

Riley remained silent, though he could easily have kicked his toe in the dirt, too.

"What's the matter with everybody?" Trevor spouted suddenly. "First my dad, now my mom . . ." He slapped his fist into the palm of his new glove, breaking it in and working out some frustrations, Riley guessed. "Why do we have to have all these big changes all the time?"

"I don't know," Riley said.

"Just when I get used to things being how they are, Dad leaves. Or comes back married. Or Mom up and announces she's marrying *Jay.*"

"Don't you like Jay?"

"Well, yeah, he's nice. I like it that my mom seems to smile a lot around him. But . . ." His words trailed off.

Riley nodded. "Yeah."

"I'm tired of not knowing what's gonna happen!" Trevor said in frustration.

Riley bit his lip, trying to will himself to have a flash. A vision. But of course it never worked that way. He hadn't had a vision since first meeting Kellie, when he'd envisioned the white dress, the ring. . . .

Well, there was a ring on her finger now, and a pile of white-dress pictures on her kitchen table. Everything he'd envisioned was coming to pass, wasn't it? Maybe all along, that was what he'd seen. He'd foreseen Kellie marrying his best friend, but assumed that he himself was the groom.

Maybe the world really was unpredictable, even when you thought you had it all figured out.

"I guess the root of the problem is that adults aren't as smart as we think we are," he told Trevor.

Trevor blinked at him. "Well, duh!"

Riley laughed. So much for spreading his wisdom. He crossed his arms and grinned down at Trevor. "You know, whatever happens, if you need a friend to talk to, I'll be around. Jay's my best buddy. I'll practically be your uncle."

The kid slapped his glove again, thinking this through. "Would an uncle be better than an aunt? My Aunt Rita's sort of bossy these days."

"I won't be bossy, I promise."

Trevor nodded and looked up at him, a smile cracking across his lips. "You know what?"

"What?"

"I'm *really* sorry I dumped that potato salad on your head."

Coming from Trevor, the words sounded like a heartfelt declaration of friendship.

Chapter Eighteen

Bernie Teller, another of Riley's old college buddies, gave him a slap on the back. "Can't believe old Jay finally hit the marriage jackpot!"

"Me, neither," he agreed. Even after weeks of feverish preparation, that fact still jarred him like a thunderbolt.

Bernie lifted his glass in drunken salute. "Great party, Riley."

Even though he wasn't enjoying it, this *was* an amazingly good party, if he did say so himself. Which was a feat all the more remarkable given the fact that his housekeeper and his cook still could barely communicate. But everyone had done one's best. Fayard had insisted on preparing everything from canapés to cakes, and his efforts had been a rousing success. Riley had hired a bartender and few extra people to help serve. Marshaled by Matilda, everything proceeded as smoothly as the Munich Olympics.

He'd also brought in a Western swing band. Everybody was full of food and drink and ready to dance. Everybody, that was, except the wedding party. Riley looked over at them across the crowded dance floor and couldn't help smiling to himself. Jay, Kellie, and Rita stood to one side of the room looking like glum wallflowers in their formal wear.

Host to the rescue. He hurried over to them.

"What's the matter?" he asked.

Jay shrugged, but his glance told Riley to tread cautiously. "Little problem with . . . well, one of the guests."

"It's Wendell!" Rita exclaimed with tears in her eyes. She looked trembly and fragile.

"He's disappeared," Kellie said.

Riley laughed. If only all problems were this easy to solve. "No, he hasn't—I just saw him."

Rita brightened. "You did?"

"Sure, he was in the kitchen getting first dibs on the food. Also I think he's discussing Bertrand Russell with Fayard."

"Oh!"

Jay grinned at his soon-to-be sister-in-law. "See? I told you there wasn't a problem."

Rita's smile slowly disappeared. "Well, no. Except that he's in the kitchen and I'm out here. Hard to dance when you're in two separate rooms."

Jay turned to her. "Well, I'm here. May I have this dance?"

Rita looked up at him with something like adulation in her eyes. "Sure, if Kellie doesn't mind."

Kellie laughed. "Of course not."

Jay took Rita's hand and they Tennessee-Waltzed out onto the dance floor.

Kellie shook her head, never taking her eyes off them. "He's just the greatest, isn't he?"

Riley nodded. "Mm." He couldn't peel his gaze away from Kellie. She was dressed in a rose-colored long formal that perfectly set off her complexion and her dark hair, which was swept back from her face. He wouldn't say that she had a radiant-bride expression, though. More like a nervous, guarded one.

"I'm completely ineffective when my sister gets in one of her panics," she said. "But Jay always knows exactly what to say to her."

"Maybe they were made for each other."

Kellie scowled at him. But he thought it seemed like a playful scowl, at least. "Don't you have something hosty to do?"

He let out a dramatic sigh. "I was hoping to dance at least one dance at my own party. . . ."

"Well, there must be some nice woman around for you to couple up with. I think I saw Mother around a few minutes ago. . . ."

But luckily, Linelle was out on the dance floor with a gentleman from Jay's church. She looked pretty in a blue dress and seemed to be enjoying herself—though of course she had clucked at Riley through dinner about all the expense he'd gone to. Riley didn't tell her that no expense seemed too great when you were in love with your best friend's fiancée.

"What about that blond over there?" Kellie said, pointing at a woman standing in a black dress. "I bet she'd like to dance."

Riley shook his head. "She's the bartender's assistant."

"Oh."

"Face it, if you don't dance with me, you'll be an ungrateful guest."

Her face blurred with panic. "I *am* grateful, Riley. This is the nicest party I've ever been to, but—"

"But nothing," he declared, taking her hand and leading her out with him. Prudence be damned. What harm could come of one little dance in front of forty-something witnesses?

He pulled her into his arms and immediately had a hint

of the harm. Not in anything Kellie did, of course. Kellie
kept her eyes chastely focused on his lapel pockets and
held herself so stiffly that her body was about as sinewy
and seductive as a chunk of granite. The trouble was with
him. His hands seemed to have a memory of their own, so
that when he touched her waist, he immediately recalled
another time, another place. Her bed with the soft, worn
flowery sheets. He could remember the taste of her.
Remember how every inch of her felt beneath those
clothes. He remembered the expression in her eyes when
she'd looked up at him during lovemaking. He might be
looking at her perfectly sprayed and tidy hair now, but
his memory recalled how had it looked spilled across a
pillowcase.

Best man? Slimiest man, maybe. In some countries Jay
would be justified in killing him for what he was thinking.

But that didn't stop him from thinking it.

For a few moments, he concentrated on the music to
distract him from the notion of ravishing Kellie, and when
that didn't work, he tried thinking about something else
entirely. The most horrible meals he'd ever had. Minty
salmon stew at a fund-raising dinner. Orange Jell-O salad
from his elementary school cafeteria. His Korean mystery
dinner. Nothing worked. He still wanted to pick Kellie
up and carry her up to his bedroom.

Even the sight of her two kids sitting on the staircase
in their party clothes and staring straight at them didn't
stop the direction of his thoughts.

Kellie trained her gaze on his lapels. "I'm glad we're
having the wedding in the morning, aren't you?"

He looked down at her, still speechless. Still thinking
about sex. He was beginning to feel panicky and breathless. *You can't,* he wanted to say. But he said nothing.

Not that he needed to. Kellie seemed perfectly capable
of having her own conversation—both sides. "I've

always hated evening weddings ... all that waiting around. Mornings are much better.''

"Gets it over with," Riley managed to put in.

She nodded. "Exactly."

"Kellie . . ." She was probably going to kill him if he said another word. He decided the risk was worth it. "Are you sure you're going to be happy?"

Was there a substance stiffer than granite? If there was, Kellie felt just like it. "I should be, shouldn't I?"

Should be.

The song ended, and Kellie stood back abruptly and smiled at him. She moved to clap her hands for the band, but he wouldn't let her hand go. "That was fun!" she said in a clipped voice full of fake party cheer. She gave her hand a tug. "Thank you!"

She'd said she *should be* happy. That was a far cry from *would be*. And was that doubt he'd detected in her voice? He'd asked her a question and she'd answered with a question. Uncertainty.

He looked into her brown eyes, trying to decide what to do.

Someone poked him on the shoulder and he looked over to see Jay grinning at him. "Mind if I have my wife back for a dance?"

"She's not your wife till tomorrow," Riley reminded him. He held fast to Kellie's hand.

Jay grinned. "Yeah, but . . ."

For a moment, Riley imagined it all so clearly. The host, making an announcement. *My friends, may I have your attention? There's been a little mistake in the bride's choice of groom. . . .* This would be followed by shocked gasps, maybe a few angry shouts as he gathered Kellie up in an over-the-threshold carry and marched away with her.

Kellie's voice broke through his devilish reverie. "Riley?"

He was still holding her hand. Could he really bust this wedding up? Could he really be that much of a jerk?

Jay blinked at him, and it was like an alarm going off in his head. His best friend. *The nicest guy in the world.*

Riley stepped back. "Take your wife, please," he joked, handing Kellie over to his buddy.

Jay laughed. "Thanks."

"Don't thank me," Riley said honestly.

Trevor punched his sister's arm.

"Ow!" she yelled.

"See, look at them all now."

Still rubbing her arm, Tina shoved her glasses up her nose with her free hand and squinted down at the dance floor. "So?"

"They're at a party but they look miserable."

"Maybe they're tired."

He scoffed at her. How could anyone be such a little goody-goody? Disaster was just hours away, and she didn't want to admit anything was wrong. "It's only nine-thirty, dufus. Even *you're* not tired."

Tina leaned forward, propping her elbows on her knees and looking dreamily down at the party. "I don't think I'll ever sleep tonight. This is the neatest place I've ever been. It's like the castle in *Beauty and the Beast.*"

Trevor expressed a sigh. "Great. *Neat.* I'm worrying about the future and you're thinking about dancing candlesticks!"

His sister tossed him an annoyed glance. "I'm talking about the real movie, not the cartoon."

"No movie is real, Tina."

"You know what I meant. The one that was in French."

The last thing he wanted to be reminded of was that endless afternoon when he'd sat through that awful old movie that wasn't even in color. It wasn't even in English!

Naturally Tina would think *that* was the best thing she'd ever seen. She was just too weird to be believed, but she was all he had to work with.

"Anyways," he said, trying to get her on his side, "so maybe this house *does* look a little bit like a castle . . ."

"I told you it did."

"Wouldn't you like to live here?"

Tina gasped. "Why? Do you think Riley would adopt us?"

Trevor rolled his eyes. "No, dum-dum, I'm thinking maybe Mom would like to marry Riley."

Tina's face screwed up in confusion. "But she's going to marry Jay. Jay's house is nice, too. I'm going to have my own room and a whole room to myself just to practice piano."

"You could have that here, too," Trevor argued.

"Yes, but . . ."

"Besides, how many rooms a house has really doesn't matter. Mom won't be happy with Jay."

"Sure she will. Even Aunt Rita likes him."

"What difference does that make?"

Tina shrugged.

"Look at Mom's face. When was the last time you saw her looking like that?"

Tina frowned down at the dance floor. It wasn't that their mom was weeping or anything like that. She hardly ever got all emotional in front of them. But that look in her eyes—it was sort of blank. With a little bit of panic behind it. Trevor imagined it was pretty much the look he had when his math teacher gave a test on long division that he'd forgotten about. He'd known he was *so* doomed. He'd tried to act all brave—no big deal, he could get through this. But there just wasn't a good way to fake your way through division.

"Mom hasn't looked like that for a long time," Tina admitted.

"Not since Dad left," he told her. "Remember how bad that was?"

Tina nodded, then looked over at Riley. "Riley looks sad, too."

Trevor crossed his arms.

"I guess Mom and Jay could get divorced just like Mom and Daddy did."

"People just can't go around getting divorced all the time," Trevor told her. "That's too weird. Unless they're movie stars."

"Well, what's Mom going to do?"

"She'll probably marry Jay tomorrow and be miserable ever after."

Tina gasped. "Oh, this is awful!"

"It's a disaster." He'd been trying to tell her this for weeks now. But no, Tina wouldn't listen. She was too caught up in practicing that stupid wedding march and buying a new dress and *packing*. She'd been packed for so long that she'd run out of clothes and had to start *un*packing every morning in order to have something to wear. For weeks she wouldn't listen to his warnings that maybe this marriage thing wasn't so great.

"What are we going to do?" she asked now, finally on alert.

Now, when it was practically too late. They had to go spend the night at their grandmother's house tonight because their mom was probably going to be out late. With Jay, he thought gloomily. Plus, they were staying at Grandma's during the honeymoon, so actually there wasn't any way to get home and be alone with their mom and try to tell her that she was making the biggest mistake she could possibly make.

Tina looked at him anxiously. "You can't do anything to Jay, Trevor. Mom would kill you."

"I know that." He didn't really dislike Jay anyway. He *had* given him the cool Playstation.

"So what can we do?" Tina's mouth popped open and her eyes grew so big, it looked as if she were staring at him through the bottom end of two Coke bottles.

Trevor sighed. "I dunno. That's what we're going to spend tonight figuring out." He threw himself back against a stair. "I wish Dad were here!"

Though he didn't, really. His dad just seemed to mess up everything even worse whenever he was around. But it made him feel better to think that he had a father to help him out instead of a father who showed up with some weird lady and the wrong birthday present.

Suddenly, he sat up a little straighter. "Yes!"

"What is it?" Tina asked.

He grinned. "I think I know how to stop this wedding."

This is ridiculous. Ridiculous!

But no matter how vehemently Kellie scolded herself, no matter how many times she told herself that she just needed to turn the car around and go home and get some sleep, her foot just kept pressing down on that accelerator.

Maybe she'd had too much to drink at the party. But of course she knew that wasn't true. Two glasses of champagne in four hours. Not enough, even, to sustain a buzz. Trouble was, she didn't need alcohol tonight to make her feel tipsy. All she needed was one look into Riley's eyes, one innocent dance, and suddenly her whole life felt as if it was reeling out of her control.

She stopped at a light and glanced frantically down unfamiliar streets. Where was it?

For God's sake, Kellie, the waning voice of reason scolded, *go home!*

"There!" she exclaimed triumphantly, spotting the street sign she'd been looking for. She accelerated and then pulled onto the street .

Madame Mira's house looked the same. Dilapidated.

Frowsy. Incapable of inspiring confidence. But Kellie still leapt out of the car with the excitement of a person just moments from getting answers to all her problems. She tripped fervently up the walkway and pressed the buzzer.

It got stuck, of course. On the dark stoop, Kellie began picking at the button frantically. She could hear the faint, insistent buzzing from inside, and seconds later she heard familiar curses and footsteps clunking down the stairwell. The door swung open, and several things happened at once. First Madame Mira appeared in a long blue nightshirt that read *Beam Me Up, Merlin!* in shiny silver lettering. She was wielding her mallet and yelling, "Don't you know it's two o'clock in the morning?" Several cats shot out from the bushes into the house, nearly scaring Kellie to death. She bleated in surprise as Madame Mira began pounding on the buzzer.

The fortune-teller glanced at her, squinting at her through eyes stuck together with sleepiness and old mascara. "Oh, Lord, it's you!" She pounded on the buzzer some more until the buzzing finally stopped. "I figured you'd be back!"

"You did?" Already, Kellie was feeling skeptical again.

Madame Mira led the way up the stairs. "Want your cards read this time, don't you?"

How did she know? "Um, if it wouldn't be too much trouble."

"No, no, no—wake me up at two in the morning anytime, hon. No trouble at all." She let out a wheezy laugh. In the house, she punched Kellie into a chair by the chrome dinette, then headed straight for a bottle of Jim Beam on an end table next to a glass partially filled with water—Kellie suspected it was actually melted ice. She splashed some whiskey into the glass and took a long swig. While she drank, Kellie looked around the place. It was still the same, with the same overflowing ashtrays. By the stereo several old Bobby Vinton albums spilled onto a rug.

Madame Mira must have been having some night.

"Okay, now I'm ready." She hustled over and pulled an oversized deck of cards off a bookshelf. As she laid four picture cards down, she glanced up at Kellie's formal wear. "Hanging out with the rich one, I see. Just like I figured."

Kellie looked down at her dress and shrugged. She didn't want to give anything away. "I was at a party."

"Mm-hm." Madame Mira was distracted by the three cards she'd spread across the table. Her eyes widened.

"What?" Kellie asked.

Before she could get more than a glimpse at her cards, Madame Mira swiped them off the table and slapped them back on top of the deck. "Never mind, hon. Go on home and don't worry about it."

"Worry about what?" Kellie asked, worried more now than she had been before.

"I think you know."

"No, I don't."

Madame Mira went for another swig of Jim Beam. "The terrible tragedy. It's all in the past."

Kellie froze. "What are you talking about?"

Madame Mira leveled an even gaze on her. "Aren't you getting married?"

"Yes."

"And the man's had a tragedy?"

"No!" She stopped, considering for a moment. Did Jay have some tragedy? "Unless you can call having too much money a tragedy."

Madame Mira pursed her lips and glanced from Kellie to the cards. "There's no other man?"

Of course she thought about Riley. Riley did have a tragedy in his past. But Riley wasn't the man she was going to marry tomorrow. "All I want to know is if my marriage will be a happy one."

"I told you that. Yes, now that the tragedy is behind you, you'll be happy."

Kellie huffed in frustration. "I think you made a mistake about that tragedy business."

"No, I didn't."

"You must have," she insisted, growing panicky. "And if you're mistaken about that, you could be mistaken about everything. I could get married tomorrow and be miserable even though I've thought it out so rationally!"

"But I'm telling you, you won't be unhappy."

"Look, can we just do this over?" Kellie asked impatiently.

Madame Mira shook her head. "Do-overs are a bad idea."

Oh, this was ridiculous, all right. Kellie felt completely foolish. What was she doing here at two in the morning listening to some half-drunk charleton? After all, how much could Madame Mira really know? The woman listened to Bobby Vinton, for heaven's sake!

She stood, but instead of marching out as she told herself she should, she abruptly reached into her thin velvet purse and pulled out fifty dollars. All the money she had. So much money, she was certain now that she was going insane.

"I want a do-over."

Madame Mira quickly pocketed the money and laid another three cards out on the table.

They meant nothing to Kellie. Just a few cards depicting devils and people with swords and sticks. Kellie pursed her lips. Obviously, she'd just wasted her money. "Another tragedy?"

"No! Disaster!"

Kellie rolled her eyes. "I thought you said that was behind me."

"No, the *tragedy* is behind you. The disaster is looming just ahead."

She felt a prick of unease. "What kind of disaster?"

"Big." Madame Mira tapped the card depicting people with sticks. "Life changing chaos and stress. Disaster."

Kellie's heart thudded. "But you said I would have a happy marriage!"

"That's what the cards said."

"Well, what good does that do me? Now they're predicting disaster!"

Madame Mira swiped them back onto the deck. "This is why I'm not a big fan of do-overs." She shook her head. "Too bad you gave me that fifty bucks."

Kellie sputtered in outrage. "No kidding! Before I was just annoyed. Now I'm a nervous wreck!"

"Yeah, I can see why." Madame Mira started pushing her toward the door.

"Wait," Kellie said, digging in her heels. She knew she should get out of there—this was getting to be like a sickness, like an addiction to roulette. But she was still reluctant to leave. "Can't we try just once more? Go for two out of three?"

"No!"

"But I won't be able to sleep tonight."

Madame Mira's eyes widened. "Oh, no, I wouldn't sleep if I were you!"

Not with disaster looming, was the silent implication.

When the door shut behind her, Kellie clumped down the stoop, forlorn. She could have kicked herself for being so stupid as to come roaring over here to get a reading from a half-asleep, hungover nutcase. It was crazy.

The woman was hopelessly confused, obviously. There was no tragedy in the past, unless she was marrying Riley tomorrow instead of Jay. But that was impossible. Wasn't it?

She certainly hoped so. Because if Madame Mira were by some crazy coincidence right about the tragedy . . . then what about the disaster?

Chapter Nineteen

Disaster!

Riley shot up in bed in a cold, sweaty terror. Once he was staring at his bedroom wall, he couldn't quite put his finger on what exactly it was that had awakened him. It was all he could do to concentrate on steadying his heartbeat, his breathing. His mind was left with a jumble of horrifying impressions, all disaster related. Earthquake. Fire. Shelley Winters swimming underwater. And Kellie, something about Kellie. What was going on? Had he had a nightmare, or a vision of the future?

He pivoted toward his alarm clock and choked in panic when he saw the red numbers glowing at him. Almost ten o'clock! Kellie and Jay's wedding was an hour from now. And he was best man.

The recollection made him moan. How could he go through the rituals of standing in front of the world, handing Jay the ring, and giving a little toast afterward? How could he simply watch his best friend marry the woman he loved?

Then again, what was the alternative?

He pushed himself out of bed and hurried to the bathroom. He shaved in the shower and toweled himself off in record time. Dressing, at least, was a no-brainer. He tossed on last night's tux, shoved his feet into his shoes, and did up his cufflinks quickly. Time was tick, tick, ticking away. And his mind was no clearer now than it had been fifteen minutes ago. If anything, he was more worried. Disaster. The day of Kellie's wedding. It could only mean one thing.

Kellie should not get married today.

But how could he tell Kellie that she shouldn't get married without sounding self-serving? Of course the whole notion probably *was* self-serving. His subconscious trying to justify his selfish desires. But was it really selfish to want to save his friends long-term heartache, even if the winningest beneficiary of the scheme would be himself?

He rushed out his bedroom door and nearly slammed into Matilda's ample chest. He jumped back, startled.

"Mr. Lombard!" she trumpeted at him. "Ve must fire your cook!"

"Ve must?" he repeated, then shook his head. "Fire Fayard? Good grief, why?"

"Because he ist gone," she declared. "How do you say . . . flown the coop?"

Oh, good lord. As if he had time to deal with that now. "I'm in a terrible hurry, Matilda," he said, scooting by her. "I'll be back this afternoon. If Fayard comes back, please *don't* fire him."

He pounded down the stairs and rushed out to his car. With any luck, he could make it to Jay's house in time to tell Kellie his reservations.

Reservations, ha! Who was he kidding? He sped toward the wedding, hoping there would be no wedding.

* * *

"I can't go on with the wedding! I feel sick!"

For a moment, Kellie was stunned. It was as if her sister had taken the words right out of her mouth. But unfortunately, Rita, who was lying prone on the bed in Jay's spare upstairs bedroom, actually *looked* very sick, while she . . . well, as she glimpsed herself in the mirror, she decided she just looked like a slightly demented bride. Her bone-colored dress draped on her as only Christian Dior could. Beneath a veil her hair, with a few touch-ups, was still holding strong from yesterday's hair appointment. Her makeup was firmly in place. It was only her insides that were churning like the innards of a soon-to-erupt volcano.

But Rita was another story. Poor Rita. Inside and out, she was a bona fide wreck. The Titanic of bridesmaids. Mascara drizzled down her pale face. Her hair was a bushy frazzle—she'd been running her hands through it till it was a tangled mess. A drink stain slashed across the front of her pale blue dress, apparently from when she'd spit up coffee on herself when she'd received the devastating news.

Kellie perched on the edge of the bed, trying to soothe her. She wished there were someone else here—their mother, for instance. But Linelle had been dealing with Rita all morning. She'd looked so relieved when she'd delivered Rita at the bedroom door and toddled off to the kitchen in search of mimosa ingredients that Kellie hadn't had the heart to beg her to stay.

Unfortunately, she hadn't had the presence of mind to ask her mother to send some of those mimosas she was concocting up to the dressing room, either. It was ten to eleven. The bride needed some courage, and she was willing to settle for the liquid variety.

But she also had to deal with her sister. "Rita, you've got to try to pull yourself together. Everything will be okay."

"No! It's all over! My world has crashed around my ears, don't you see?"

Kellie nodded. "I know it probably seems that way. But it could have been worse."

Kellie's lame assurances had the effect of throwing down the gauntlet. Rita shot up to sitting. *"How?* What could be worse than Wendell running away with Riley's chef?"

As Kellie struggled pointlessly to fabricate an answer, her sister collapsed against the mattress, one arm flung over her eyes. The dramatic gesture smudged mascara all over her forearm. "Never mind! I just want to die! I actually would kill myself, but I wouldn't want to ruin your wedding day."

"Rita, please don't say that. Maybe this is for the best . . ."

She popped back up again. *"For the best?"*

Kellie shrugged. "I mean in the long run."

"Easy for you to say! You're getting married . . ." Her chest heaved with sobs. ". . . To the nicest man in the world!"

"I know, but you have to admit you and Wendell had problems. . . ." Apparently more fundamental problems than any of them had ever imagined. "You might not believe this, but I know how you feel."

"You couldn't possibly know!" Rita bawled, apparently forgetting all about Kellie's ex-husband and the divorce. "You have Jay. All these weeks I've been so jealous of you because you lucked into such a great guy. I would do anything to have a man like Jay in love with me. But I consoled myself with the fact that I had Wendell. Now I don't have Wendell or anybody. It's just like that fortune-teller said—I'm doomed!"

Kellie crossed her arms, frowning. "That fortune-teller is a fake. Believe me. She couldn't predict an earthquake if it had happened last week."

"Well, she was right about me. I'm a complete toad."

"She never said you were a toad."

"Well, I am."

Kellie tossed up her hands in frustration as Rita fell to the bed crying again. She didn't know what to say or do. The wedding was minutes away. Obviously Rita wasn't going to be in it, which was okay with her, but how could she have a celebration with her sister in this state? That would be like sticking pins under Rita's toenails.

Briefly, an idea sparked in her head. The bride making an announcement. *"Due to the fact that the maid of honor's boyfriend has eloped with the best man's chef . . ."*

Maybe not.

But time was flying. She could hear guests arriving. The noise level from downstairs was rising. Any minute now it would be time to start. What was she going to do?

Just as she was frantically trying to puzzle it all through, the door slammed open and Riley vaulted into the room. Kellie jumped to her feet, shocked. What was he doing here?

"You can't go through with this, Kellie!"

He'd started yelling before he'd had time to figure out where in the room she was, so that for a moment he spun in confusion before finally spotting her by the bed. Then he focused on Rita, whose hair and mascara tracks made her look like the maid of honor from hell.

At the sight of him, Rita's face went purple with rage and she scrambled to her feet. "You!" she shouted. "I blame you for this."

"But I'm trying to stop this!"

"Different this," Kellie explained.

She was so shocked to see him there, standing in this unfamiliar room, that she suddenly could hardly breathe. Was he really trying to stop her marriage? She couldn't believe it. Why hadn't he said something last night, or better yet, a month ago?

"What's happened?" Riley asked Rita.

"Wendell ..." He and Kellie watched Rita huffing and faltering in an attempt to get the words out, until Kellie couldn't stand it anymore.

"Wendell has run off with Fayard," she said.

"Eloped!" Rita corrected, tormenting herself. "All those years I was trying to wrangle him into marriage . . . I wasn't even the right sex!"

"I don't believe it," Riley said. "Why would Fayard run off with *Wendell?*"

He said the name with such distaste that Rita was immediately insulted. "Why would Wendell run off with Fayard?" she shot back. "It's your fault."

"How?"

"They met at your house!"

"I never even saw Wendell before last night."

Rita's face seemed to crumble before their eyes. "Neither had Fayard!" She sank back onto the bed in a heap, howling at the indignity of it. "It must have been love at first sight!"

Riley was stunned into silence.

Kellie jumped in. "Riley, what are you doing here?"

He shook his head in confusion, almost as if he himself had forgotten what had made him come busting through the door seconds ago.

Then he remembered. She saw it in his face. He approached her cautiously. "I had a vision, Kellie. Of disaster."

"Not you, too!" Kellie said with a groan.

He frowned. "Has someone else seen it?"

"Nobody I trust." Of course, she didn't trust Riley and his wacky visions, either. She tilted her head. "What kind of vision was this?"

"Disaster."

She didn't know whether to laugh or to weep. Nostradamus of the jet set! She knew she should toss him out on his ear. Was the whole world conspiring to make this day more confusing than it already was? Then something occurred to her that made it all come out clear. "Maybe you *did* see a vision of disaster."

"What?" Riley looked shocked that she would believe him without an argument.

She pointed to Rita. "It's already happened. My sister is heartbroken!"

On cue, Rita blew her nose noisily.

Riley tilted his head dubiously. "I don't think that was it."

"What? One disaster's not enough for you? There have to be two?"

Tina came running in, her stiff pink taffeta dress rustling. "Mom, Mom, are you ready yet?"

"Not just yet, Tina."

"Well, when will you be ready?" Her face contorted with anxiety. "We need to know when to start the music!"

"Soon."

At Kellie's unsatisfactory answer, Tina sighed and left the room.

Riley stepped toward Kellie; Kellie stepped back.

She crossed her arms and tapped her heel impatiently. "Have you spoken to Jay about this vision of yours?"

"No, of course not."

"Well, why not? It concerns him, too."

Rita sniffed, interested. *"Visions?* Kellie, *what* is going on?"

Kellie didn't bother to explain to Rita at this late date. "Besides, you've had visions before that were patently wrong," she said to Riley. "Your last vision was obviously completely false because I am about to marry Jay."

"Oh, screw it." Riley crossed the distance between

them and put both hands on her arms. "I'm not only here because of the vision, Kellie."

She bit her lip. When he touched her, it was last night all over again. Just a simple dance had caused doubts to back up on her like a traffic jam. "Why else?"

He took a deep breath. "Because I love you. Because I was wrong to walk out on you that morning. I love you and I want you to be my wife."

She gasped.

Rita squeaked through tears. "You have *two* men who want to marry you?"

Kellie was too flabbergasted to believe it. She gaped at Riley, who was mooning hopefully at her with those blue eyes of his, and she didn't know what to say. This couldn't be happening. It couldn't be happening *now*. Today was supposed to be the day she turned back into her old sensible self, but the whole day was turning into a . . . disaster.

Tina rushed in again in high panic. "Mom, we've *got* to start. Everybody's waiting and Trevor's all ready."

"Trevor?" She assumed he would be the last person who would want to get the wedding under way.

"Yeah! We need to start *now*."

Kellie felt frozen. Riley was staring at her with those heartbreak-blue eyes of his, Rita was gaping at her through her scare mask, and Tina was blinking at her impatiently. She had to make a decision. Now.

What about Jay, though? Shouldn't he be here making this decision with her? It wasn't fair to shut him out.

It wasn't fair for her to be thinking what she was thinking anyway. She shouldn't be having these doubts. Riley and she had a strange history together. Okay, she loved him. They had incredible sex together. But what they felt wasn't the dependable, steadfast kind of affection that would last a lifetime, was it?

She'd known all this when she agreed to marry Jay.

Nothing had changed. She was just under more stress. Riley was taking advantage of that fact.

"All right," she told Tina, "start the music."

The room let out its collective breath and Tina, beaming, dashed out again. Rita jumped and began wiping her face with a damp cloth from the bureau. Riley stood in front of Kellie, shaking his head.

"You need to go down," Kellie reminded him. "You have to stand next to Jay."

He was still shaking his head in disappointment, but he took her hands. "I respect your decision, Kellie. I just want you to remember that it's not over till you say 'I do.' "

He squeezed her hands, turned, and marched out the door.

Kellie stood in shock for a moment before turning to her sister. Rita was doing quick damage control on her face. "Oh, Rita, you don't have to do this ceremony with me."

"Are you kidding?" Rita said. "I wouldn't miss this now for the world!"

"You think I'm making a mistake, don't you?"

"Far be it from me to butt in, Kellie," Rita said, applying lipstick with lightning speed and not the greatest accuracy. "But it seems to me that you love Riley. You always did go for the weird ones."

"But Jay is . . . well, he's the nicest man in the world."

"Sure, and what are you about to do? Ruin his life by treating him like a consolation prize!"

Kellie was staggered. "I thought you *wanted* me to marry Jay."

Rita whirled on her. "I did! That is, I did until . . . until . . ." Her words petered out into a frustrated huff. For a moment she looked as if she was about to fall apart again. "Oh, let's just get this over with!"

She stomped out the door.

Kellie followed her slowly, feeling more uneasy than ever. What had happened? She was a bride, but instead of everyone telling her this was going to be the happiest day of her life—not that she would have believed them anyway—she had crazy people screaming at her that she was making a terrible mistake. No last-minute bridal rituals here; no one was lying to her about looking beautiful, or doing a final hurried adjustment on her dress. Instead, her mother was tossing back alcohol. Her sister was having a nervous breakdown. And the best man was ranting about visions of disaster.

When she flicked a brief glance in the mirror, she didn't see a blushing bride reflected back at her but a woman wearing the pale, stunned expression befitting someone who'd just been mugged at a bus stop.

Trevor grabbed her arm as soon as she stepped out the door. "C'mon, Mom! What's the holdup?"

This was the capper. Trevor, the one person who'd been dragging his feet throughout the long month of wedding preparations, was now twitching with excitement. He hauled her along the landing toward the staircase, then cleared his throat loudly. That was Tina's cue to start the music.

Rita, who was standing on the top stair, waiting, turned to her with eyes brimming with tears. "Are you sure, Kellie?"

The music started. "Yes!" Kellie hissed stubbornly, but it was a lie. She glanced down at the people gathered in the hallway, craning their faces curiously up at the three of them, and felt her stomach churn.

Rita started down the stairs in that unnatural hesitation step expected of her, though Kellie could see her shoulders shaking with the effort it was taking to hold herself together. Meanwhile, Trevor was still raring to go. He kept yanking Kellie down too fast, so that they ended up bumping into Rita. He stepped on his aunt's heel and Rita yelped out a sharp cry.

"Slow down," Kellie ordered him through the corner of her mouth.

"I can't!" He was like a colt chomping at the bit.

Ritalin, Kellie thought as they reached the landing. Maybe she'd held out against it for too long.

At the bottom of the stairs they turned to face the crowd lining the long open hallway that led into Jay's den, where all the honored guests were gathered. Where Jay and Riley were standing next to a priest by the impressive oak fireplace mantel. She felt dizzy.

Then she heard Rita start sniffling. Trevor tugged Kellie forward.

"Aunt Rita!" he hissed. "Would you mind hurrying up?"

It was as if he'd goosed her. With a sob, Rita suddenly gave up all attempts at the hesitation step and instead marched—or perhaps galloped was a more appropriate word—on ahead of them. Relieved, Trevor speeded up too.

Until they reached halfway. Then he stopped completely. "Sorry, Mom," he whispered to Kellie. "My shoe's untied."

She rolled her eyes. "For heaven's sake."

He suddenly disappeared, practically leaning into the lap of a woman Kellie didn't know. Then again, she didn't know half the people here. That fact made her all the more nervous. Of course, if she was worried about how she appeared before all these strangers, she needn't have been, because no one was looking at her or even at Trevor. Instead, everyone was gaping at Rita, the hysterical bridesmaid. She'd already reached the makeshift altar and was in full hysteria again, tears streaming down her face. From the front row of folding chairs, Linelle was trying to ask, in a too-loud whisper, whether everything was all right. In answer Rita just swiped her bouquet through the air and let out a repetitive barking sob.

Trevor straightened up again. "Okay, now we can go."

Kellie walked ahead, but her son held her back, tossing her an annoyed look. "Jeez, Mom, slow down!"

At that moment she locked gazes with Riley. She felt as if her entire being was quaking. *It's not over till you say 'I do,'* he'd told her. *It's not over,* her mind echoed now. She could just turn around and go back upstairs and call the whole thing off. She wouldn't be the first bride in the world to get cold feet.

She glanced over at Jay, who was as pale as a ghost and bug-eyed with nerves. Of course. This was the day he'd been waiting for. His big day. And *she* was thinking about cold feet!

That settled it. She'd promised Jay. He was the nicest man in the world. She wasn't going to back out.

At long last, Trevor parked her at Jay's side. Maybe now she could shut out Rita's wails and Riley's warnings. Maybe she would hear the familiar words of the wedding ceremony and know that she was making the right, the sensible, decision.

When she looked up at the preacher, she felt further reassured. He had iron-gray hair and a kind, wrinkled face. Grandfatherly—just like a preacher out of Central Casting.

"Dearly beloved," he began, "we are gathered here together in the sight of—"

A shriek from the crowd drowned out his words. The entire wedding party turned in unison.

"Rats!"

Suddenly, all hell broke loose. Ladies screamed, and guests were hopping and springing up on folding chairs in their Manolo Blahnik and Fendi stiletto heels. Kellie caught sight of her own mother doing a strange twitchy dance away from her seat. One woman ran screaming from the room, sliding across the polished floors and nearly falling on her Versace-clad tail. Men in suits scurried around, bent over, swiping their hands at the floor. It was pandemonium.

"What's happening?" Kellie asked, stupefied. On one side of her Jay was frozen in shock, and on the other Trevor was bouncing nervously on the balls of his feet.

Then she saw a white mouse dash across the runner carpet, sending up another piercing screech in the crowd, and she knew. She spun toward her son, fury coursing through her. But he was completely unrepentant. She'd never witnessed such a look of glee on a boy's face. It was as if his favorite team had just won the World Series.

"Trevor, how many mice did you let loose in here?"

"All of 'em." He laughed giddily, going for broke. "All twenty-two. I had them hidden in my coat pocket and my pants leg. This is awesome!"

One of the mice chose that moment to dart up Jay's father's shirtsleeve, sending the poor man twirling and jittering toward the center aisle, flapping his arm as if it were on fire. He dislodged the mouse, which then was tossed onto Jay's great-aunt Louise's mile-high hairdo.

"Eeeeeeeeeww!" Tina shouted. She had posted herself on the piano bench to get a better view. And probably to stay out of mouse reach.

Kellie stood aghast, not knowing what to do. Obviously, they had to round up the mice, but the little white critters were fast, darting under chairs and scampering for the walls, and the guests were stumbling around clumsily, shouting at rodents and each other. It was hard to know how to begin to restore order.

Surprisingly, it was Jay who stopped the chaos. Not consciously, true. But the effect was the same. For a moment Kellie had forgotten all about him. Heck, she'd forgotten about Riley, Rita, everything. All she could think about were the mice and the inexpensive, Spartan, and geographically remote military academy she was going to start searching for to send her fiendish son.

But suddenly she was aware of tension next to her. She cut a glance over at Jay and gasped in surprise. His eyes were as big as dinner plates. His whole body was as taut as piano wire. Veins in his skinny neck bulged, and his face had turned an alarming shade of maroon. Finally, he exploded.

"I can't do it!" He pivoted toward her. *"Kellie, I cannot go through with this marriage!"*

Immediately, the room was as quiet as a tomb.

A wave of heat slapped Kellie in the face. Her jaw felt as if it were on her chest. "What's wrong?" she asked stupidly.

She had to give him credit for keeping a straight face. After all, if a groom were looking for bad omens, or even reasons to run screaming in terror from the altar, this would be the ideal setup. Hadn't she herself been considering bolting just seconds ago? But Kellie was still coasting on lingering everything-will-work-out fumes. "If it's the mice . . ."

"It's *not* the mice!" Jay replied quickly, then changed his mind. "I mean, it *is* the mice. But I probably could have handled that. I could have handled anything Trevor dished out, I was so ready to make a happy home till death do us part. And I would have, except that ten minutes before the wedding started, I got nervous and went into the kitchen and drank a mimosa with your mother."

Kellie felt her face screw up in confusion. The whole room, bedlam just moments before, was now so breathless that it sounded as if Jay's words were echoing around them. "What?"

"Your mother told me all about Rita's boyfriend running off with Riley's chef . . . and . . ." Jay swallowed.

"My God, Kellie, I'm sorry, I just can't marry you. I'm in love with your sister."

Kellie's mouth dropped open, but it was Rita who shrieked out a response. *"What?"*

A streak of blue shot in front of Kellie. Rita hurled herself at Jay. They stood together, embracing, as Kellie tried to shuffle out of their way. It was either that or be stampeded by the love fest.

Rita's mascara-streaked face wore an expression of pure exaltation. "What did you say?" she asked Jay. "I *have* to hear this again."

He pulled her closer. "I said I loved you. I've thought of you since that moment I first saw you at Wiggie's, but everyone said it was impossible. That you were out of my grasp because of that guy, Wendell. And every time I saw you, it was Wendell this and Wendell that . . ."

"Wendell, schmendell!" Rita proclaimed joyfully.

"But you had been together for so long," Jay explained, "and I didn't want to break that up. So I guess if I couldn't have you, I thought it would be comforting to be close to you, but it was torture."

"Oh, Jay—you should have told me!" Rita exclaimed.

Yes, Kellie thought. He should have. And while he was at it, *she* would have liked to know all this, too. *Torture?*

"I'm sorry," Jay said, "I should have known I couldn't settle for the next-best thing."

Kellie listened to herself being described as "the next-best thing" and could only wish she could sink through the floor. It was dawning on her that she was now, officially, a jilted bride. And she'd been about to treat Jay as her own consolation prize! She felt sick. Someone was finally giving her that swift boot in the rear end she so deserved. Unfortunately, the person doing the booting was the nicest man in the world. And he was doing it in front of eighty-three witnesses.

"Don't be sorry, Jay," Rita told him. "I loved you, too, but I thought I was terrible because you were my sister's fiancé!"

Jay beamed in relief. "Oh, Rita!"

"Jay!"

They flew at each other again in a heartfelt embrace.

As her sister passionately kissed her would-be husband, Kellie shuffled uncomfortably. What on earth had possessed her to put on a wedding dress this morning?

She didn't dare look at Riley. She couldn't bear to see a smug, I-told-you-so glance from him. It was a disaster . . . at least, it was for her. Truly, she was beginning to wonder if there wasn't something to all this psychic business.

If only she'd listened to him . . .

Then again, she wouldn't have had to listen to his predictions or Madame Mira or anyone, if only she'd listened to her own dumb heart. If she'd looked honestly inside herself, she would have been saved all this. Unfortunately, she'd been so dead set on not making a mistake that she'd managed to make the most monumental error in judgment of her whole lifetime. At least, she hoped it was. The thought of something worse lying in wait ahead of her made her tense in dread.

Trevor, uncharacteristically subdued, shot her a sidewise glance. "Gee, Mom," he whispered just loudly enough for everyone to hear, "this must be pretty embarrassing for you, huh?"

At least the refreshments didn't go to waste. That detail appealed to Kellie's sense of economy. And frankly, the cupid ice sculpture made a more fitting backdrop for the giddy happiness of Jay and Rita's engagement party than it would have for her and Jay's wedding reception. Seeing them together now, kissing like . . . well, like two people disgustingly in love . . . made her feel a little better about how the day had turned out.

It had been difficult at first, of course. It was hard to slink away unobtrusively when she was encased in that white dress and veil. But somehow she'd managed to crawl upstairs and change into the only other outfit she'd brought—her new pink going-away suit. Once she was out of her jilted bride costume, she found it a lot easier to be magnanimous.

Especially when beaming guests kept parading up to her telling her how *big* she was being. "So big of you to stay for the party!" Great-aunt Louise told her.

"Wow, it's so amazing of you to put your sister's happiness ahead of your own!" Lana proclaimed when Kellie stopped to thank her and Alejandro for bothering to come. Though of course now she dearly wished they hadn't.

"Honey, I'm so proud of you," her mother said to her early on, giving her a reassuring pat. "You're being so big about your sister humiliating you like this."

Kellie had laughed, remembering all those frustrating nights of tiddlywinks and Monopoly. "If there's anything you taught us, Mom, it was how to be good losers."

"That's right!" Linelle beamed proudly. "And you certainly are, sweetheart!"

But Kellie thought perhaps her most gracious moment came when she approached Jay and Rita in their receiving line with a suggestion. "Jay, why don't you take our honeymoon tickets and reservations in London and fly Rita off for a celebration?" she said. "I wouldn't mind."

Jay and Rita exchanged uncomfortable glances. "Oh, well . . ." Jay stammered.

"Actually," Rita admitted, "We've already discussed this."

"London was okay for *us,* Kellie," Jay explained, "but Rita and I decided we'd like to go somewhere more romantic. I just called my travel agent and got her to reserve a little bungalow on a beach in Thailand for us." He hugged Rita to him for another quick cuddle. "It'll be just the two of us, sweetie."

"Mmm . . ." Rita said, nuzzling his nose. "You're my honey."

"And you're my four-leaf clover."

Kellie backed off, suddenly feeling all her bigness shrinking to a walnut-sized chunk of self-pity. She snatched a sparkling glass off a passing butler's tray and retreated to the privacy of the shade of a potted palm, where she could nurse her drink and a few petty, grudging thoughts in private.

But her privacy didn't last long. While she was occupied with wondering why she wasn't the type of woman men wanted to rent isolated little bungalows for, the man she'd been not-so-subconsciously trying to avoid since her hour of humiliation peered around the tree's thin trunk.

"The mice are all rounded up now," Riley told her. "Well, all except one, and that we think might have made a dash for freedom through the sliding patio doors."

For a moment Kellie envied that mouse. She would have liked to make a mad dash just about now, too. "Thank you for helping Trevor and Tina."

"They're very sorry, by the way," Riley said. "They explained to me that they just wanted to stop you from making a mistake."

Everyone had tried to stop her. So why hadn't she stopped?

She retreated further behind the tree.

Riley poked a palm frond aside and gazed at her. "Are you going to hide from me all day long?"

She looked into his blue eyes and felt her heart skip.

The best ending for this day would be for her to fly into Riley's arms and tell him what a fool she'd been all along. But of course she couldn't. She'd look like the worst kind of opportunist. Conveniently coming around to the conclusion that she and Riley were meant to be after she'd stubbornly insisted on going ahead with her doomed marriage just an hour before. That would be hideous.

"I wasn't hiding from you," she insisted. "I've just been preoccupied with being big."

He laughed. *Laughed.* She couldn't imagine being able to laugh right now. Although she did smile, in spite of her misery. It was hard not to, looking at the mirth in his eyes. "Did you know about this?"

He glanced at her doubtfully. "About what?"

"About Rita and Jay. You're supposedly the great matchmaker. Is that how you knew it would all be a disaster?"

He shook his head. "Scout's honor, Kellie. Although, if I had stopped to think . . ."

She practically choked on her bubbly. "Oh, yes. I'm sure if I had stopped to wonder why Rita kept singing Jay's praises, I might have been able to put two and two together and come up with a very obvious four."

"Maybe it's all for the best."

She harumphed. "That's what I said to Rita this morning after Wendell went AWOL."

"And what did she do?"

"She looked like she wanted to strangle me."

"Do you want to strangle me?"

She looked up at his face and shook her head in wonder. Strangle him? She wanted to kiss him. God help her, she wasn't the least bit heartbroken over Jay. Just nursing her stinging pride. And the best balm in the world was standing right in front of her, looking as if he were ready and willing to sweep her off her feet.

But her feet were still stubbornly planted in the tiles of Jay's cavernous living room. "I guess it's pretty clear that we both should have said 'I don't' to this wedding," she admitted to Riley.

An ear-to-ear grin broke out over his face. "Now we're getting somewhere."

She regarded him nervously. Her marriage to Jay might be kaput, but that flock of geese was still flapping away in her stomach. "Getting where?"

"To the point where you finally have to admit that we're fated to be together."

"Riley . . ."

"After all, I saw you getting married. And today proves that you weren't marrying Jay." He took her arm and gently pulled her around toward him. "That leaves me."

"You or one of five billion other males on the planet," she pointed out.

"But I'm the only one of those five billion who is about to pop if you won't say you love me, Kellie." He looked at her, and his smile faded. He was dead serious. "I wasn't kidding this morning. I love you, Kellie. I wanted to tell you so weeks ago, but then you threw a wrench into the works by getting engaged."

She froze. "You mean, when you came into Copycat with the flowers?"

He shook his head. "The worst day of my life! I'd come to apologize for staying away. During my trip I realized how empty my future seemed if you weren't going to be in it. I wanted to tell you that I wanted us to be together, forever."

Her heart ached at the memory. It ached now looking at him. She loved him. But today, after all the turmoil that had already happened . . . "What are we going to do?"

He gazed at her, confused. "What do you mean?"

"I mean I love you, too!" she said, practically shouting. "But I don't trust love."

He pulled her toward him. "Then don't. Trust me. Because I know what it means to love someone so deeply, you want her by your side for the next fifty years or so, Kellie. I know because that's how I feel about you."

When she looked into his eyes, his beautiful blue eyes, she felt her heart melt. Like it or not, she was putty in his hands. How could she ever have doubted him?

"But the timing couldn't be worse!" she exclaimed.

He pulled her into his arms. "Are you kidding? Anytime you want to say you love me is okay by me!"

She shook her head. "But so much strangeness has happened today. My sister's boyfriend ran off with your cook. My fiancé jilted me for my sister."

Riley's eyes glinted at her sexily. "So now the best man makes off with the bride. It's perfect."

"But shouldn't we make sure we don't do anything rash? I mean, while emotions are so high and everyone—"

While she spoke, Riley rolled his eyes, took the glass out of her hand, and set it inside the palm planter. Then he proceeded to scoop her up into his arms. Kellie let out a cry of alarm. "Wait, Riley, what—?"

"I'm sweeping you off your feet, damn it. Your small, flat, solidly-on-the-ground feet."

He strode straight through the crowded room with her. She caught a look of bafflement from Rita and Jay, shock from her mother and about eighty-two others, and complete confusion from Trevor and Tina, who scampered after her.

"Mom, wait! What are you guys doing?" Trevor said as Riley quickly advanced toward the door.

She looked up at Riley. "What are we doing?"

"I'm kidnapping you," he declared with amazing matter-of-factness.

Amazing because the desire flaring in those blue eyes

told her clearly that this wasn't going to be a day-of-beauty kidnapping. It was going to be more like a make-love-to-the-point-of-exhaustion type kidnapping.

She glanced back at her Trevor and Tina. It was a good thing the kids were already parked at her mother's house. "Be good to your grandma," she admonished them. "And don't eat too many Fig Newtons."

Her children gaped at her, and she felt a hitch in her chest. *You can't do this,* the voice of reason gasped at her. The kids had been through so much. They'd be confused, and face it, they were already screwed up enough as it was. She needed to be sensible.

Then, to her astonishment, Trevor and Tina turned to each other and exchanged a high-five. *"Yes!"* they cheered triumphantly.

Riley grinned at her as they left the house. "Believe in destiny now?"

She laughed and rested her head against his shoulder. It did feel incredibly right there. "All right. I give in. Fate, destiny, kismet—as long as it means you and me together, I'm all for it."

ABOUT THE AUTHOR

Liz Ireland lives with her family in Oregon. She is currently working on her next contemporary romance, which will be published by Zebra Books in July 2002. Liz loves to hear from readers and you may write to her c/o Zebra Books. Please include a self-addressed stamped envelope if you wish a response.